MW00534424

THE
SKY
ON
FIRE

ALSO BY JENN LYONS

A CHORUS OF DRAGONS

The Ruin of Kings

The Name of All Things

The Memory of Souls

The House of Always

The Discord of Gods

THE
SKY
ON
FIRE

JENN
LYONS

TOR PUBLISHING GROUP
New York

This is a work of fiction. All of the characters, organizations, and events portrayed in this novel are either products of the author's imagination or are used fictitiously.

THE SKY ON FIRE

Copyright © 2024 by Jenn Lyons

All rights reserved.

Maps by Jenn Lyons

A Tor Book
Published by Tom Doherty Associates / Tor Publishing Group
120 Broadway
New York, NY 10271

www.torpublishinggroup.com

Tor® is a registered trademark of Macmillan Publishing Group, LLC.

The Library of Congress Cataloging-in-Publication Data
is available upon request.

ISBN 978-1-250-34200-3 (hardcover)
ISBN 978-1-250-34201-0 (ebook)

Our books may be purchased in bulk for promotional, educational, or business use. Please contact your local bookseller or the Macmillan Corporate and Premium Sales Department at 1-800-221-7945, extension 5442, or by email at MacmillanSpecialMarkets@macmillan.com.

First Edition: 2024

Printed in the United States of America

0 9 8 7 6 5 4 3 2

For Rekka.
I think you would've liked this one.

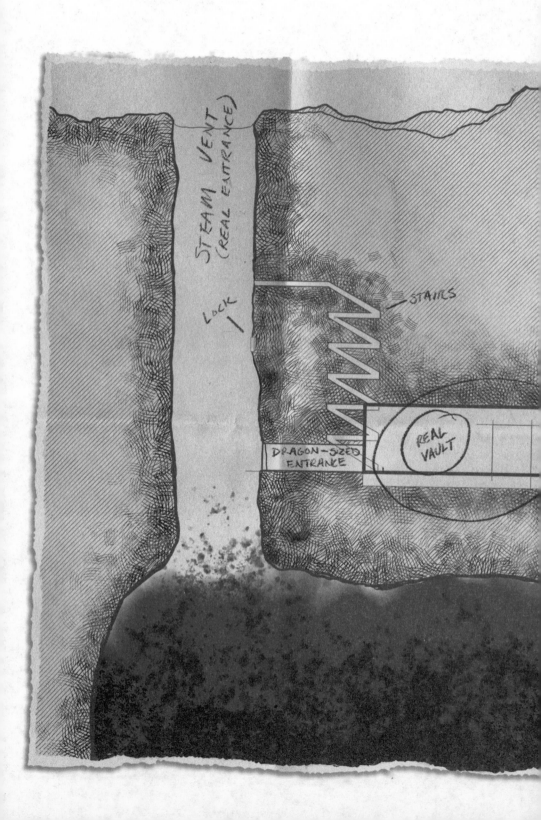

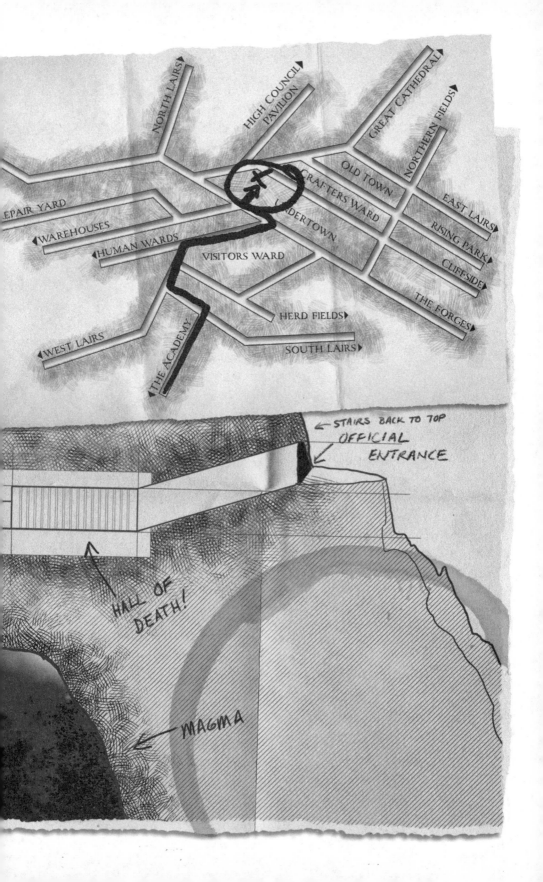

THE
SKY
ON
FIRE

PROLOGUE

The dragon's roar stopped all conversation.

A hundred people had been engrossed in feasting, drinking, and celebration, but at that sound, a hundred hearts stopped and a hundred heads tilted up. The banquet hall fell silent save for glasses and dinnerware rattling against each other.

A few seconds later, the stone building shuddered as if someone had dropped an enormous weight upon the highest ridge, an unwise architectural addition foreshadowing catastrophic collapse. More than one guest uttered a prayer to Eannis. Plaster dust drifted down onto uncovered dishes and into open mouths.

The mayor's wife kept enough presence of mind to check the building's warding plates. They appeared intact; this wasn't an enchantment failure. Inscriptions could only do so much against forces outside their tolerances—enormous dragons landing on the roof, for example.

"I thought Aldegon was nesting," the mayor whispered.

To which his wife replied, "She *is.*"

The mayor motioned for a city guardsman to investigate. A dragon's roar might be common enough in Crystalspire, but to land on a roof without warning or introduction was not.

That guard hadn't taken more than five steps when the front doors swung open with a thunderous boom. Chill night air swept in, making the candles gutter.

A dragonrider walked inside. He wore a blue-gray leather tunic over darker gray trousers tucked into long black boots. Silver clouds embossed his bracers, embroidered his mantle. A hematite-and-silver hair pin held back long black hair; a matching collar encircled his neck. He appeared young, although that meant little; a dragonrider's bond with their dragon caused changes few outsiders could even comprehend.

Silence again fell upon the hall. The dragonrider's lips curled in a smile as he took in everyone's shock.

"Now, now," he proclaimed, spreading his arms wide. "Why the long faces? Are we not having a party? This is a celebration!" He picked up a wide-eyed man's glass of wine as he passed a side table. The dragonrider sniffed it, wrinkled his nose, and set it back down again. "Only, what are we celebrating?"

The mayor stood and bowed. "My son's fifteenth birthday, Honored Rider. I am Mayor Aiden e'Doreyl. This is my wife, Belsaor Doreyl, and our only child, Gwydinion. Had we known to expect you—" E'Doreyl reconsidered his next words. "Please forgive our oversight, Honored Rider. You're welcome to share our table."

The boy, Gwydinion, appeared so much like a younger, rounder-cheeked version of his father that there could be no question of his paternity. He all but vibrated with excitement as he leaned forward across the table.

"What's the name of your dragon?" Gwydinion asked. "Are you here to take me to—" The boy's mother grabbed his arm in a clawlike grip and dragged him back down again.

"Silence," she hissed.

The boy's eyes widened in shock.

Mayor e'Doreyl's smile thinned, but he ignored his wife and son in favor of giving the dragonrider a second bow. "Please forgive my son's enthusiasm, Honored Rider. He is overeager to begin his training."

"Oh? He's a candidate?" The dragonrider's gaze turned calculating. "Congratulations on both your choosing and your birthday. Have you ever ridden a dragon, I wonder? I know a few."

Before the mayor's son could stammer out an answer, the dragonrider turned back to the boy's father. "I imagine he'll know a few himself soon enough." Something ugly flickered behind his eyes. "If he lives."

Before the mayor could respond, the rider swung out his arms again to encompass the hall and tilted his head. A bow, if observers felt generous. An insult, if not.

"I am Jaemeh Felayn, rider of the dragon Tiendremos of Yagra'hai." He pointed a finger toward the ceiling in case any might be obtuse enough to miss the importance of that second introduction. "Tiendremos would say hello himself, but this is meant as a friendly visit. For now."

For a few long seconds, the mayor found his mouth too dry for speech. Belsaor pinched his leg, hard, to snap him out of it.

"It is our pleasure to welcome you, Honored Rider," Aiden e'Doreyl said. "Although I admit to some confusion that you and Tiendremos should present yourselves here instead of at Aldegon's crèche. To what do we owe your visit?"

"Treason," Jaemeh said amiably.

The rough edges of the banquet guests' initial shock had hardly worn smooth by that point, but the crowd had been making an admirable effort. People whispered about the dragonrider—speculations on his origins, appraisals of his clothing, questions about his dragon. All that gossip stopped with that single word, replaced with stunned silence.

"Treason?" Mayor e'Doreyl's throat moved as he swallowed air.

Jaemeh flinched.

No reason for such a flinch made itself obvious. Then the dragonrider straightened and his eyes began glowing, as if lightning arced inside them.

Perhaps that was the truth, because electricity jumped around his bracers, played over his fingertips. An intangible presence descended upon the rider, taking up all the space in the room, smothering and terrible.

"Is it not treason," Tiendremos the dragon asked, using Jaemeh's mouth, **"to give aid and succor to those who have acted against your betters? Queen Neveranimas is sorely disappointed."**

"We would never—" someone in the crowd called out before a wiser soul silenced them. Agitated whispers rose once more.

"Quiet," Mayor e'Doreyl yelled at everyone but the dragonrider. "All of you. Clear the room, now. Guards, please escort everyone outside—"

"But the dragon!" It was unclear who'd shouted the protest.

The mayor's wife, Belsaor, slammed the table as she stood. "We have always served the dragons in exchange for their protection, and they have always provided. We will see justice done here." She put a hand on her husband's shoulder as she addressed the guests. "You have nothing to fear except insulting these honored guests. Now please go, with our apologies."

Aiden took her hand, kissed the knuckles. "You too, Bel. Take our son with you."

"Father—!"

"No," Mayor e'Doreyl said. "I promise I'll make it up to you later. Do as you're told."

The quick departures left the two men alone in the vast hall. Aiden e'Doreyl turned back to the rider. Lightning still arced over his body as he channeled his dragon's will. The mayor lowered his head to the table in submission. He then raised his chin enough to talk. "Your Eminence, I implore you to provide me with more information. Please tell me who in Seven Crests has been so brazen, so faithless, as to act against our guardians."

"You did," the dragon growled. **"Fifteen years ago. All you had to do was execute one insignificant human. Instead, you hid her. You protected her!"**

Mayor e'Doreyl's brows furled as he tried to recall some event—any event—that matched the dragon's claim.

He turned gray as an answer came to him.

"Am I to assume that you refer to Anahrod Amnead, Your Eminence?" His tone was both incredulous and horrified.

"**Yes!**" Tiendremos said. "**The rebel who swore herself to Zavad and plotted against the First Dragon. Did you think we would never discover the truth?**"

Aiden e'Doreyl stepped backward, nearly tripped. "Your Eminence, she was executed—"

"**She was *not*,**" the dragon growled. "**You betrayed your oaths by pardoning her life!**"

The mayor swallowed. "I would not dare disagree with one such as yourself, great dragon, but . . ." The man glanced up, saw the lightning eyes of the rider, and lowered his head again, shuddering.

"**I'm not interested in your excuses. Make this right or the First Dragon will assume you shelter the traitor here in Crystalspire. We'll see how much of your precious city is left when she's done with it.**" A second roar shook the building and made the cutlery dance across the tables.

One of the inscribed warding plates overhead cracked.

The dragonrider Jaemeh's eyes returned to their normal brown color. A shudder rolled over his body.

The mayor remembered to breathe. "Honored Rider, surely you realize—"

Jaemeh scrubbed the heel of his hand into an eye as he recovered from the possession. "Realize what, exactly? That you weren't even mayor fifteen years ago—?"

"Seventeen years," the mayor corrected automatically, and then flinched at his own gaffe.

Jaemeh squinted. "Yes. Right. Seventeen years. Whatever the number, you have inherited the sins of your predecessors. Fair or not, it's your problem now. My master's threat was serious. He's loyal to the First Dragon. He doesn't always behave rationally if she's under threat."

"The girl was fifteen. How much of a threat could she have been—"

Jaemeh scowled. "The question you should ask yourself is how much of a threat the dragon queen *will* be if you displease her."

Mayor e'Doreyl wiped his forehead with a napkin. "I've read my predecessor's files, Honored Rider. Anahrod Amnead was executed for high crimes, as ordered."

"And Lord Tiendremos has it on good authority that she survived." The dragonrider made for the exit, but he called back over his shoulder: "He's giving you one month to find her." He raised a finger. "Alive. Tiendremos doesn't intend to delegate her sentencing this time."

"He could give me a thousand years and it wouldn't be enough. She's dead!" Fear—genuine fear—shook loose any sense of diplomacy or tact.

The rider didn't take offense.

"Less dead than lost, it seems." The cruel humor returned to the rider's stare. "So, I'll give you a piece of advice. When I lose something, I always check the last place I remember seeing it. You may wish to do the same. One month. Make it count."

The rider walked through the doors, which slammed shut behind him.

Aiden e'Doreyl's hands shook as he lowered himself down to his seat. A few seconds later, the feast hall stonework creaked as the dragon launched upward. More dust floated down like snow flurries to mark the dragon's passing.

Then all was still.

He glanced at the warding plates, but no further damage manifested. Still, they'd have to be replaced. He shuddered to think how much Whitestone Division would charge for the task.

His wife placed a hand on his shoulder.

"I should have known better than to think you'd obey, Bel. You never have before." The mayor covered his face with his hands. "Did you hear everything?"

"Yes." His wife's voice was as ragged as a knife sharpened against granite, but when he glanced at her, her eyes were clear and cold. That didn't surprise him. Belsaor was the strongest woman he'd ever known. All the tears had been wrung from her long ago.

"And our son . . . ?"

"Already home," she said. "I sent him ahead."

"Good." He hesitated, and then grief and outrage shuddered over him. "I can't believe—" He shook his head. "To walk right into our hall like that—"

"I'll need to work quickly," Belsaor murmured. "The rumors will spread like a fire in the Deep. Our enemies will claim the dragon came here to accuse you personally."

Aiden blinked at his wife. "He *did*."

"No," she corrected. "The sins of your predecessors are Mayor Amnead's sins, not yours. I can slant this in a positive light. Make sure everyone realizes how noble you are for cleaning up her mistakes. This might even help us in the next—"

"The next elections can throw themselves off a cliff!" Aiden snapped. He grabbed his shocked wife's hand. "I'm not worried about the elections. I'm worried about you. This cannot be easy for you."

"What is hard about it?" Her voice carried a false lightness. Possibly Aiden e'Doreyl was one of the few people alive who could see through the lie. "Anahrod's been dead for almost twenty years. Neveranimas must be on the verge of going rampant if she thinks otherwise."

"Maybe so, but she's still the First Dragon—"

"Neveranimas"—the name was a snarl on his wife's lips—"has *never* been the First Dragon."

"A technicality, Bel. Ivarion will never wake and so she's a regent instead of a queen. Her word is still law, not just over her kingdom, but over all of Seven Crests as well." He closed his eyes, canted his head back against his wife's hip.

She stroked his hair, saying nothing.

He glanced up. "Do you think there is any chance, any chance at all, that she might have lived?"

His wife still said nothing, but this time it felt like she was marshaling her thoughts. "They threw her off a cloud cutter at fifty thousand feet, Aiden. There were witnesses to that effect." She scoffed. "Are we supposed to think that is not enough proof because no one risked the Deep to retrieve her shattered body?"

"But if she survived—"

Belsaor's eyes flashed. "She *didn't*."

The mayor exhaled. "As you say, then. She didn't. Which means we face an unpleasant fact: since we don't have her body"—he glanced significantly at his wife, but Belsaor remained silent—"we have no way to prove we executed her."

"Not 'we,'" his wife corrected. "Mayor Amnead. She—" Belsaor stopped, gathered herself. "*He* executed his own daughter."

Aiden heard the quiet revision and grimaced. He seemed about to make a correction of his own, but stopped, fingertips digging into the hard wooden tabletop. "It won't matter who held office," he said. "You know dragons can't tell us apart unless we're bonded to them."

Belsaor froze, then her eyes turned hard and cunning. "You make an excellent point."

The mayor shifted in his chair to meet his wife's gaze. "What mean you by that?"

"I mean exactly what you think."

"You cannot be suggesting we give the dragons some other girl in her place."

"Why not? Would this dragon know the difference if we presented him with any random woman and claimed *she* was Anahrod? And if she shouts and rants that she's innocent, that her name isn't Anahrod at all, who will believe her?"

"No one. No one would." Horror crossed the man's face. "I won't do it, Bel. I won't send an innocent person to their death like that."

A sad, sweet smile settled on Belsaor's face. "Ah, my love. I always knew you were too pure for this job." She touched his cheek and whispered, "The world is full of people who deserve nothing less than this. I would send a monster to her death in Anahrod Amnead's place in an instant and sleep well, knowing that for once, a guilty person had been condemned."

He took his wife's hands in his. "Then I suppose it's a good thing it's not your decision, isn't it?"

"Don't be a fool. You heard what he threatened!"

Aiden nodded. "Yes, I heard what he threatened. But I also remember when Neveranimas ordered Anahrod's execution the last time. A whole flight of dragons, including Aldegon, perched outside the city in broad daylight, with their magic carrying the sound of Aldegon's rider's voice to every nearby mountaintop. Every single person in Seven Crests knew what the accusations were."

"You think shouting accusations of treason in the middle of our son's birthday party was subtle?" Belsaor raised an eyebrow at her husband.

"For a dragon? Yes. If Tiendremos had any proof to back up this absurd claim, he would've shouted it from the mountaintops instead of invading our son's party."

Her eyes widened. "You think the dragon plays a game."

"He must. It's what we can do about it that concerns me."

They continued discussing their options, or lack thereof.

Neither of them heard their son sneak away.

PART ONE

THE
DEEP

HELL

Skylanders had another word for the Deep.

Hell.

A more appropriate brand, without question. The Deep was too bland a label, applied so vigorously to any land ranging from sea level to five thousand feet above it. Skylanders felt secure in the label's accuracy only because they measured from altitudes so much higher.

Whereas Hell, as a place of punishment hot enough to scorch, occupied by monsters and the damned, served as a far more accurate warning. Those people who made their homes in the Deep had their own feelings on the matter, but their opinions were never consulted.

If Skylanders considered the Deep a punishment, then it was also true that one could, by effort and necessity, learn to love Hell.

Anahrod had.

The Deep bore no resemblance to the indifferent mountaintops or the apathetic sky. The Deep demanded focus, insisted on attention. Anahrod might fear and hate her adopted home, but she couldn't deny that every part possessed a wild beauty, a riotous curve of unmolested nature too rebellious to be conquered, too perilous to be ignored. The suffocating, sticky air and the boiling heat were a mild irritation compared to the Deep's genuine threats: explosive oceans, howling storms, and giant, carnivorous animals.

In the Deep's jungles and savannas, its deserts and forests and violent, ever-shifting green waters, dwelt every monster unfriendly to humanity. The worst of which—Hell's true demons—would always be humanity itself.

A point Anahrod considered as she stared down the two Scarsea recruiters.

The Scarsea eschewed the green body paint worn by most jungle tribes in favor of shadow-valley violets. Ocean-green spikes thrust out in all directions from the shoulder plates strapped to their arms, lest one make the error of thinking them too friendly.

Anahrod had neither asked for nor been given introductions. She'd decided to call one man "Braids" because of his hair. Anahrod nicknamed the other one

"Scratch" since he kept picking at his paint, the cracked mud flaking away from one arm to reveal brown skin underneath.

"We won't make this offer again." Braids tightened his hand on his sword pommel.

As they "wouldn't make this offer again" on the last four occasions the Scarsea had found her, the threat's value had begun to wane. She allowed silence to be her answer. If they decided her consent was no longer necessary, Overbite waited, hidden behind a nearby hillock.

They didn't seem inclined to press the issue. Still, Scratch wore a sour expression, the look of a man trying to understand why Anahrod wasn't leaping at the opportunity offered.

"Your refusals have grown tiresome, but if you return with us now, His Majesty won't hold a grudge."

"Sicaryon, you mean?" She'd heard far too much of Sicaryon lately, none of it good. Not so long ago, he'd been "Chief" Sicaryon, after killing his uncle for the position. Then he was "warlord," gobbling up neighboring tribes with frightening speed.

Now he was "king."

Anahrod avoided Scarsea territory, but what did such matter when they sought her out instead?

"*King* Sicaryon," Braids corrected. He clearly expected her to be impressed.

She leaned forward as if to share a confidence. "I must know. Does he really have forty spouses that he keeps imprisoned by the sea?"

Scratch sputtered. "What? What rumors—"

"I know," Anahrod agreed. "The idea is ridiculous. Why would I think Sicaryon could handle forty husbands and wives when he couldn't even handle—"

Anahrod paused. She felt a spike of concern from Overbite, whose senses far surpassed Anahrod's own.

"—me?"

Sharp, high-pitched screams echoed from the jungle. Not human sounds, but she recognized them. Rock wyrms. Hunting.

A half second later, rock wyrms began calling to each other.

Anahrod drew her sword—but it was a pointless gesture.

Rock wyrms grew to over fifteen feet long, with tough hide and razor-sharp teeth. They used four of their legs for running and the remaining two limbs, which each ended in sharp, spiny points, to impale their prey. The females were solitary, but as there was no justice in the world, the males traveled in packs.

Anyone hunting rock wyrms used spears, arrows, pit traps, or best of all, sorcery. They didn't use *swords*. Swords weren't long enough to scratch a rock wyrm's hide before the monster was close enough to impale the wielder.

"You're the sorceress who can control animals!" Scratch snapped. "Can't you do something?"

Something ugly and bitter twisted her guts. So Sicaryon had told them what she was. "Yes. One at a time." Anahrod pointed into the jungle with her blade. "So, flee."

Scratch started to follow her order, which would've been hilarious in other circumstances. He caught himself, a stubborn look finding root on his face.

"I'm summoning my titan drake," Anahrod elaborated. "Run!"

Braids grabbed Scratch's arm. "Let her deal with them." He pulled the other man into the underbrush.

More baying sounded, but none in the direction the two men had fled. The two recruiters might yet escape.

[Overbite, sweetheart, I need you. We've work to do.]

Anahrod used a root vine to pull herself onto a branch. It was always easier if she kept herself tucked out of the way. Not safer (because rock wyrms climbed trees), but at least she wouldn't be underfoot.

Behind that hillock, the titan drake called Overbite pushed herself up on six thick legs. She was a massive specimen: twenty feet at the shoulder and fifty feet long. Striped scales camouflaged her in the dappled light of the jungle canopy. Despite her bulk, she moved with barely a rustle of foliage. A perfect hunter with teeth the size of swords, she could take down anything smaller than a grown dragon. In the Deep, that was everything, including most other titan drakes.

[Let's hunt.]

Overbite tossed her head in excitement. She was always eager for a hunt, even if she wouldn't technically be the one hunting.

Anahrod slumped back against the tree branch, body abandoned. Transferring her consciousness to an animal felt like swimming through an ocean of sap to gasp at clean air. Rising from the depths and taking in a deep breath of new reality. Her senses expanded as she settled into Overbite's mind. The world transformed into a tapestry of colors, odors, sounds. The nearby dama trees, the rock wyrms, the flowering coremfells—and the nasty stench of humans. Her hearing became hyperacute, distinguishing rock wyrms from birds, humans, and other predators.

Anahrod would've given Overbite her lead if the men had run farther, but they were too close. She had no faith in her pet's ability to control her hunting instincts. If it ran, Overbite would chase.

The rock wyrms loped into the clearing on four legs. They all stiffened and raised their heads, scenting a larger predator.

Anahrod stood to her full height, or rather, to Overbite's full height. She advanced on the pride, a lethal monster who had nothing to fear.

The rock wyrms turned to face her, heads down and growling.

Which wasn't the correct response. The wyrms should've gone after the weaker prey, fled before the stronger. They should've chased the Scarsea, allowing Anahrod to pick off the rock wyrms from behind.

She was committed now. Anahrod ran into the clearing, straight at one of the "little" monsters. She sank her teeth into a rock wyrm neck, snapped the spine. Hot blood flooded her mouth as the creature let out a pitiful yowl.

She smelled something new then, something familiar: Scratch's scent. That wouldn't have been so special, but the scent was on *this* rock wyrm. Along with many other human scents, none of which belonged. When would a Scarsea soldier have had contact . . . ?

She studied the wyrms a second time. Ropes. Scraps of leather. The clink of metal rings slapping against thick hide necks.

This wasn't a wild pride. These were . . .

These were trained animals.

She tossed the rock wyrm corpse to the ground as she searched for the warriors. She still smelled them, so where had they gone?

The pride was attacking. She roared, the sound vibrating through her borrowed body, barely audible to humans but a thunderclap to Deep animals. She bit a rock wyrm, gouging out a giant chunk of his flank.

The rock wyrms encircled her.

She heard metal clang against stone, followed by cursing.

When she turned, she saw the little Scarsea bastards hadn't fled. Instead, they'd circled around to the tree where Anahrod had hidden her body. Scratch carried Anahrod's unconscious form slung over a shoulder. Her sword had caused the warning sound as it slid free from its sheath and hit a rock on the jungle floor.

Anahrod growled. Sicaryon had told them *everything* she could do.

It felt like a betrayal.

Braids rushed back to retrieve the sword. "Go!" he screamed at Scratch. "The others are waiting!"

The others.

Her pulse thundered in her ears. This encounter had been a trap from the start. Sicaryon had no intention of suffering a fifth refusal. This wasn't a recruitment: it was a kidnapping.

A rock wyrm took advantage of her distraction to stab both spear arms into one of her—one of Overbite's—legs. She twirled, swept aside that attacker plus several pack mates who failed to dodge.

But the damage was done.

Anahrod felt the icy sting of blood flowing too fast. She kicked out with a middle leg, caught another wyrm in the ribs; she was rewarded with a satisfying snap of bone.

Another rock wyrm tried the same trick, stabbing at Overbite's front legs. She wasn't distracted this time, whereas he'd just wandered into the reach of her jaws. She savaged his neck and tossed the corpse to his pack mates.

Perhaps she could've fought them off, even outnumbered, but more humans approached. Likely the other Scarsea soldiers, coming to finish the job.

The implications made her gut clench: Sicaryon had learned to train rock wyrms. His great successes against so many tribes became easier to explain. Worse was the certainty that she knew where her sword-brother had come up with such an idea: *from her.*

The scent of fresh blood swelled in the air.

Human blood.

The smell confused both her and Overbite's lurking consciousness. No humans had been hurt. Yet the unmistakable, caustic scent of human blood flooded her senses.

Scratch stopped running. He, too, seemed confused.

He dropped Anahrod's body in an ungraceful heap. She winced: that would bruise. Anahrod still saw no sign of injury, even if Overbite's nose screamed otherwise.

Then Scratch made a choking sound. Blood poured from his eyes, his nose, his mouth—from every orifice.

Not a trickle, but a gushing exsanguination. His partner, Braids, shouted something at Scratch. His real name, perhaps. She had no idea why Scratch had died in such a way, but she could guess.

Sorcery.

That was when Anahrod scented the new arrivals. Not the second Scarsea group. These were something else. They smelled of perfumed lye soap and clean skin, weapon oil and writing ink, but it was the scent of spiced musk and hot metal that raised her frills. Overbite knew that scent too well, because it belonged to her only natural predators.

Dragons.

If a dragon lurked nearby, the situation had gone from the high surf straight into a tidefisher's nets.

"Now that is a lot of pissed-off lizards," a redheaded woman said in Haudan. She sounded delighted. "You grab the woman. We'll take care of the wyrms."

Anahrod bucked, kicking back while she roared to shake the ground. She brought a foot down hard, cracking a rock wyrm's back.

There were too many. She couldn't reach her own body.

Braids tried to retreat, but he'd decided too late.

A flash of metal sliced through Braids's neck, so fast and clean that his eyes were still moving as his head fell away from his body. The sword flew on its own. Something in the odd way it spun and changed course suggested a weapon fastened to the end of an invisible rope—a weapon somehow being directed.

Anahrod noticed the redhead again. She stood just past the tree line, spinning, moving her hands in a pantomime of a warrior controlling a chained weapon. Despite the Skylander garb, she had the bright hair and pale skin so many Deepers revealed when the skin paint came away.

Everything about the woman was a contradiction. She looked like a Deeper but dressed like a Skylander. She wore—or wielded—a sword but used it in a way that required either sophisticated magical inscription or sorcery. The latter seemed more likely given her Deeper ancestry, but the scent in the air suggested a different option: dragonrider.

How could a Deeper be a dragonrider?

Regardless, a dragonrider by necessity required a dragon, likely flying nearby. A dragon nearby meant Anahrod needed to be at least five miles anywhere else, immediately.

Anahrod's options narrowed to one: run.

The Scarsea still advanced. She could hear at least a dozen warriors moving in their direction, but she knew Sicaryon would have more waiting in reserve. Warriors who'd planned for this confrontation, who'd come prepared for a titan drake and a woman with the magical ability to control animals.

She cursed Sicaryon. He knew Anahrod too well: he'd witnessed her discovery of every spell. If she fled, it would be straight into a trap he'd designed for her.

Anahrod stood stuck between the cliffs and the tide.

Enough rock wyrms had died by this point to allow her some breathing room. The Skylanders proved more interested in killing wyrms than taking on the single enormous titan drake. Which Anahrod appreciated even as she marked it as strange.

The Skylanders' odd behavior would change once they finished with the rock wyrms. Overbite was too dangerous to ignore. Anahrod needed to reason with them—which she couldn't do as long as she possessed the titan drake's body.

She also needed to run—in her own body.

Anahrod jumped backward. Away from her real body, away from the Sky-landers, toward that first downed rock wyrm. She turned Overbite's back to the Skylanders, lowered her head to the still steaming corpse.

[Eat, Overbite.]

No titan drake needed to be told to eat twice. The distraction might only last seconds given Overbite's tendency to gulp her food, but hopefully, that would be enough.

Anahrod returned to her body. The transition was a cold vulnerability, the repressed panic of waking in an unfamiliar place. Her skull throbbed from where Scratch had dropped her. She was soaked in his blood.

She'd never learned his real name.

Anahrod sat up and raised her hands in surrender.

"Don't hurt her," she called out in Haudan, fighting not to stumble over rarely used words. "The titan drake's mine. We're about to be overrun. I can get us away from here, but we need to leave now."

An overdressed, middle-aged man gave her an avuncular smile. If he wore a weapon, she couldn't see it. "Oh, lovely dryad, what delight in your unexpected lucidity, but our fair scene requires no fast exit."

Anahrod stared. Had he just misquoted Huala Lagareb's *The Valley of Green* at her? She couldn't recall many other Skylander plays that referred to "green-skinned" Deepers as "dryads." It beat the normal pejorative—

"Troll girl, what he means is that as cute as it might be to discover that you can speak like a civilized person, we're not the ones in danger."

Mocking laughter preceded the speaker as she stepped into view. One of the two women—not the redhead. This one was younger and her Skylander heri-tage was more obvious: dark skin and tight-curled hair. Vivid scars crisscrossed her face with an uncomfortable symmetry—their positioning too precise to be anything but deliberate.

She dressed like she was still twenty thousand feet up: fully covered in a dark gray coat dipped black at the hems, a silver-stitched shirt underneath, little pops of bright color peeking out from charms that hung from her collar, from her belt. A lot of daggers.

"Call me troll again and you'll find out otherwise."

Sometimes, the best course of action was to pick the inevitable fight early.

The scar-faced woman evidently agreed. "Is that so?" She spun a bloody dag-ger in each hand, the sort of aggressively showy nonsense that meant nothing in a proper fight.

What did mean something was that the woman had used *daggers to fight rock wyrms.* The woman had been using daggers, not at a distance like the redhead, but close up.

Somehow, she still lived.

Anahrod moved fighting her into a column marked "not without a damn good reason."

A second man sniffed the air. "No." He was heavyset but not out of breath, and like the other man, unarmed.

The scarred woman paused mid-knife-twirl. "No? What do you mean, no?"

"More rock wyrms on the way." An odd accent flavored the man's Haudan. He didn't seem to be a native speaker. "More hunters, too."

At this, the redhead called her blade back into her hand. The woman's garden rings glinted gold in the light as she gave Anahrod an appraising stare. "Looks like you have a talent for making friends."

The redhead appeared to be in her early twenties, prettier than any jungle flower. Prettier, but also more delicate, like some priceless portrait carved on a thin shell. She wore yellow-gold rings, though. Who in Eannis's name would be brazen enough to wear gold rings?

"Apparently," Anahrod snapped.

"I'm impressed." The woman shattered any lingering perception of fragility by wiping the rock wyrm blood from her sword on her trousers. The woman looked like a Deeper, but she couldn't be one—not dressed like that, not smelling like that, and not wearing those rings.

"We have to leave," Anahrod said.

As she turned back to Overbite, Anahrod noticed a problem: that wounded leg. The injury bled a river of dark red down the titan drake's front leg. *Could Overbite run?*

Did they have a choice?

Even as Anahrod inspected the wound with an icy fist clenched around her stomach, the bleeding stopped. All at once, with no sign of clotting or scabbing, no bandage or dressing.

The heavyset man lowered an unadorned hand. "We leave now," he agreed.

He'd kept a Deeper accent even if he'd learned to dress like a Skylander. This man wasn't trying hard to pass, though. He'd skipped the garden and social rings and didn't wear his hair in pinned braids. Was he a dragonrider, too? She would've assumed such, but it made no sense. Since when did dragons take Deepers as their thralls? If he wasn't a dragonrider, since when did dragons allow sorcerers to live?

They had no time to waste on solving mysteries.

Anahrod pulled herself onto Overbite's back using a halter line. Overbite made no protest; she was used to it. She wasn't so used to the next part, but Anahrod promised herself she'd make it up to her pet later.

"Climb up," she told the others. "We'll outrun them."

"Or we can fight them." The scarred woman cleaned her bloody daggers before sheathing them. "We can handle some rock wyrms." The scarred woman gestured around the battlefield to make her point. She wore silver Skylander rings.

"No." The fat man made that single word into an entire argument.

"You heard the man: no." The redhead rubbed her hands together. "That means we're going for a ride." She raised her voice. "Gwydinion, it's safe to come out now!"

A third man ran from the bushes.

No. Anahrod corrected herself. A *boy* ran out from the bushes. A Skylander boy no older than fifteen, too young for garden rings, too young for a division ring. Almost as pretty as the redhead, although his beauty was wide-eyed and dewy-cheeked, while hers whispered more worldly promises. He was no more visibly armed than the other men.

Anahrod felt a flash of anger. They'd brought a Skylander *child* to the Deep? What were these people thinking? Had they been thinking *at all?*

"Climb up," Anahrod repeated. "I won't tell you again."

The boy's eyes widened as he took in the carnage; his steps faltered. The way he stared around the battlefield suggested he'd never been closer to death in his whole life.

Also, that he wasn't prepared to deal with the experience.

His eyes widened again when they reached Anahrod, although in that case likely because he had also never seen a green-skinned woman wearing nothing but a few scraps of leather. A real live troll girl, in the flesh.

The boy blushed and stared at anyone else.

The redhead reached Anahrod first, ignoring the rope she'd lowered over Overbite's side in favor of sprinting up the titan drake's spine. The others used the rope assist and the impromptu landing created by Overbite's bent leg.

"Hook in," Anahrod ordered the redhead.

The woman was already reaching for her belt when she paused and laughed, bright as sunlight glistening on the sea. Because Skylanders rarely carried spring hooks on their belts under normal circumstances.

Dragonriders were never without them.

Without releasing Anahrod's gaze, without glancing away from Anahrod for so much as a second, the redhead pulled the spring hook from her belt and snapped it to Overbite's harness. Her stare was answer, taunt, and promise, all neatly presented by the greenest eyes that Anahrod had ever seen.

The answer: yes, she was a dragonrider. The taunt: what exactly did Anahrod think to do about it? The promise: that there had never been a single moment in this woman's entire life where she had been anything but trouble, and she wasn't about to stop on Anahrod's account.

Behind them both, the others grabbed on to leather harness straps.

Anahrod glanced back for long enough to determine that there were indeed four other people besides herself and her troublesome dragonrider on Overbite's back.

A rock wyrm screamed from nearby: the Scarsea were closing in. The telltale hum of a loosed arrow buzzed in the air as at least one of their pursuers made a last-gasp bid to spill enemy blood.

"Hold on," Anahrod told her passengers.

[Run!]

Overbite sprinted into the jungle.

ONE STEP AHEAD

Nothing on land runs faster than a titan drake. The reason was simple enough: titan drakes were fifty-foot-long, six-legged, twenty-ton mountains of pure muscle and appetite. When a titan drake wanted to run, few forces could stop them. Not trees, not other animals, and certainly not rock wyrms.

But this wasn't a normal situation. Overbite's injury forced her to return to a walk. If Anahrod didn't do something, Overbite soon wouldn't be capable of that much.

Her passengers had pulled their mantles from their shoulders and were using the woven squares as a shelter from both wind and insects. More sensible than she'd expected, honestly.

They should've have been miserable in the heat, but they weren't acting like it. Did they have inscriptions sewn into their clothes? That was the only explanation that made any sense, even if it was an expensive solution. Inscribers weren't cheap and the clothes would wear away to nothing in weeks or months. It was a smart move—and it suggested that this trip hadn't been an accident.

Overbite walked for an hour before she started making whining noises and slowed even further. Anahrod winced in sympathy for the titan drake's pain. She unfastened her own spring hook from the harness and jumped down to inspect the wound.

She wasn't surprised when a Skylander followed her, but hadn't expected it to be the boy, Gwydinion.

"That was lightning!" he said, far too loud. "What's its name? Can I pet it? Do you have to clean its teeth? How did you tame it . . . ?" His voice trailed off as he noticed the open wound. "Oh."

Oh, indeed. The injury was as ugly as it looked. That one man had stopped the bleeding, but he'd done nothing to close the gash, which had torn through skin and muscle. It was a miracle that Overbite had limped as far as she had. Even with five working legs, the jungle wasn't kind to those with such a disadvantage. If they were lucky, the wound wouldn't fester, but Anahrod had long since abandoned hoping for that sort of felicity. She needed to take the time to treat the wound properly, or Overbite would pay the price.

And yet that was exactly what they couldn't afford to do.

Overbite nudged Anahrod, a gentle bump that shoved the woman several feet to the side. The message was clear enough: fix it.

Oh, how she wished she could. She rubbed a hand across the drake's brow ridge, although she had to stretch a little to do it.

"Is it going to be all right?" Gwydinion whispered.

"No," Anahrod said. "I don't think so."

Everyone came climbing down the titan drake's side then. The redhead placed a hand on the boy's shoulder, but her attention remained focused on Anahrod. "Do we need to press on without the titan drake?"

For a moment, Anahrod thought the woman was suggesting she put Overbite out of her misery. She started to snap at the redhead to mind her own damn business.

Except the woman was right.

Not about killing Overbite. Anahrod didn't have the means. Maybe these Skylanders possessed the magical power necessary to take the giant monster down, but Anahrod didn't.

No, the woman was right about needing to leave Overbite behind.

The Scarsea were fantastic trackers. It wasn't a question of whether they'd find Overbite, only when. Anyone still with Overbite would be discovered, too.

Anahrod pursed her lips. She didn't know what these people were after, but she knew she didn't want to be involved.

"You should, yes," Anahrod said to the redhead. "I'll take her and travel west, toward the Bay of Bones." Anahrod pointed appropriately. "That will throw them off your scent; they'll follow me. Head north, northeast, you'll reach the highlands—"

"You can't do that!" Gwydinion said.

Anahrod stared at the boy.

He flushed and fidgeted. "I mean . . . aren't they mad at you, too?"

"Didn't kill two of their people," Anahrod told him. "Which, yes, they'll know, because they know what it looks like when I kill someone."

She didn't want to go back to Sicaryon; she hadn't forgotten that the damn tricky tidefisher had ordered his men to kidnap her.

That didn't equal trusting *these* people.

"Even so—" Gwydinion gave the redhead a pleading look.

The redhead in question rolled her shoulders, stretched an arm. "Gwydinion has a point. You may have noticed we're not exactly natives. A guide would be useful."

"Find a holler and hire one," Anahrod said. "Haven't heard a good reason it has to be me."

"What's a holler?" Gwydinion asked the redhead.

"Small communities in the valleys," she answered, "but I don't know enough about them to find one, and even we did"—she laughed—"we'd have to understand the language. I can't imagine many of the locals speak Haudan half as well as she does."

Anahrod's mouth twisted. The woman had a point.

"As for why you should agree, I can give you a reason. I can give you fifty good reasons." The redhead pulled a bag from her knapsack and tossed it to Anahrod.

Anahrod checked the contents: Seven Crests coins, the oh-so-humorously named "scales." Probably fifty, although she didn't stop to count. Fifty scales went a long, long way in the Deep.

The offer of payment set the younger woman off. "Oh, come on! Why are we acting like we're scared of our shadows? We can always just kill anyone who catches up to us. Keep things simple." The scarred woman pulled out the knife, spun it in her hand for emphasis, rolled it over, then caught the handle again before sheathing it.

Anahrod had a feeling she'd be seeing that trick a lot from this woman. It was meant to look dangerous, and it did, but by Anahrod's estimation, it also made the woman look *young*. Young and hotheaded, too eager to prove herself to everyone, too rash to understand why it wasn't always wise.

"No," the fat man said.

The girl rolled her eyes. "*Yes*. You know we'd win." She tilted her head in the redhead's direction. "What do you say, Ris? I'll pick them off one by one. You and Naeron can handle the stragglers. We'll finish in time for Kaibren to make dinner." She helpfully pointed to each: the potential dragonriders, Ris and Naeron; the aging poet, Kaibren.

Ris muttered something under her breath that sounded a lot like, "Please stop helping."

Anahrod threw the bag back to Ris. "Sounds like you don't need me."

Ris laughed, tossed back her hair. "Oh, storms and ashes—" She swung back around. "If this is your idea of haggling, I must say it's working. One hundred scales, then?"

"How about the truth," Anahrod countered. "What you're doing down here? Because I'm having a hard time believing a couple of dragonriders need my help."

Ris started to say something—a protest, a lie, something.

"Don't pretend you're not dragonriders. Overbite knows what a dragon smells like, and you lot stink of it."

Ris raised both eyebrows. "Is that so?" Anahrod knew she'd revealed too much when she saw the sparkle in the woman's eyes. "Just the one dragonrider. Me."

Anahrod turned her gaze to Naeron. "You're not a dragonrider? You don't look like a priest."

"No," Naeron agreed. "Sorcerer."

Anahrod snorted. She wanted to call the man a dirty liar, but truthfully, he really didn't seem like a Skylander at all. She was having a difficult time imagining what motivation he could have for admitting to heresy. "Where are you from?"

"East," he answered. He started to add a comment, paused, looked frustrated, then spoke to Ris in a rolling, fast stream of words Anahrod didn't understand.

"He's from the eastern plains," Ris explained. "One of the Ilhomi."

Anahrod tried to place the name, succeeded, and felt sick. "Didn't the dragons wipe out the Ilhomi?"

"No," Naeron corrected, narrow-eyed. "They *tried*."

"Wait," the boy protested. "What do you mean, the dragons 'wiped out the Ilhomi'? You can't mean the dragons from Yagra'hai."

"We'll talk about that later." Ris dismissed the concern, focused on Anahrod. "But you see? We're not exactly first in line to attend church services. If you're concerned about draconic attention, don't be. We prefer to avoid draconic attention ourselves."

"You're a *dragonrider*," Anahrod pointed out.

"Oh, she's a smart one, isn't she?" the younger woman said.

"I don't mean *my* dragon," Ris said. "*My* dragon is the most amazing and wonderful dragon to have ever existed. It's the rest of them that are all—" She made a face like she'd just eaten rotting fruit.

"Good to know," Anahrod commented, although she was inclined to believe *all* dragons fell into the "blegh" category. "Why can't your amazing and wonderful dragon come get you?"

Ris stared at the woman before gesturing at the jungle canopy. "He might not breathe fire, but he's still a *dragon*. He would destroy a huge section of the jungle reaching me. If he misjudged it, we could easily end up as accidental victims. Do you want that? I don't want that."

"That just leaves one question."

"Yes?" Ris smiled.

"Why are you here?"

The Skylanders (or Skylanders by association, in Naeron's case) gave each other looks ranging from uneasy to annoyed. Anahrod recognized the attitude: they either weren't going to tell her or were about to lie.

"It's my fault." Gwydinion stepped closer to Anahrod. "My father's in some trouble. Quite a lot of trouble. It's not his fault, though! He didn't do anything wrong!" His eyes were shining.

Anahrod gave the boy a moment to collect himself.

"Ris is a friend," Gwydinion explained after rubbing his eyes. "So, I asked her to help my father. What he needs is only found down here in the Deep. I just didn't expect it to all be so . . ." He made a vague gesture to the whole jungle.

"Yeah, funny how that works." Anahrod studied the boy. Weirdly, he seemed to be telling the truth—or he was a fantastic liar.

That a fifteen-year-old kid had asked a dragonrider for a favor and had not only received it but had used that favor to travel into the Deep was *ridiculous*. So much so that Anahrod couldn't imagine anyone expecting such a story to be believed.

Perhaps Gwydinion was telling the truth. He had left out a lot of details, after all. Liars usually provided too much information, thinking it made their story more believable.

"Did you find what you were looking for?"

He brightened noticeably. "Yeah. I think we did. Now we just need to escape alive." The boy didn't seem worried about it being an issue.

Anahrod examined the group. Weird, puzzling, and dangerous. What the girl with the knives was failing to consider was that the moment Sicaryon decided they were an actual threat, he'd send his sorcerers. This wasn't like the Skylands, where everyone who could cast a spell either ended up a dragonrider, a priest, or dead. Sorcery wasn't something practiced under *every* tree in the Deep, but close enough.

No, the real problem was that these people were cocky. That was an attitude for which the Deep had little tolerance.

Anahrod mentally sighed. She just knew she was going to regret this. Not least of all because she would have to send Overbite off in the opposite direction. That meant she'd lose her. Even if the Scarsea captured Overbite instead of killing her, it's not like Sicaryon would just give the titan drake back. Better to leave Overbite with Sicaryon than the alternative, though, which was the titan drake slowly dying of a poisoned wound until some other predator finally took advantage of her misfortune.

Anahrod pointed to each person. "So, you're Ris . . . Naeron . . . Gwydinion. You must be Kaibren." The older man inclined his head politely in her direction.

That left one person without a name to match their face. "And you are?" She asked the hotheaded young woman with the knives.

"Yeah, like I'm going to tell you—"

"The lovely woman with the terrible personality is Claw," Ris volunteered.

"Claw?" Anahrod scoffed. "Let me guess: she picked that name out all by herself."

"Fuck off. What's your name then, troll?" Claw growled.

"Jhyanglae," Anahrod answered, which had the advantage of betraying who among them spoke Sumulye. Kaibren accepted her answer without comment, while Naeron's eyes darted to her in shock. Ris covered her mouth to stop herself from laughing. Claw didn't understand, but she was sensitive enough to the mood to realize that Anahrod had just made a joke at her expense.

Claw snarled and jerked her hand away. "What did she just say?"

"It was less of a name than an instruction," Ris said.

"Oh yeah? Let's see how funny you think it is when—"

Kaibren put a hand on the woman's arm. "Only the fool cuts his own rope while he's still scaling the cliff."

Claw quieted. As she nodded to the older man, a distant, rhythmic sound echoed. Drumbeats.

"Music?" Gwydinion cocked his head.

"No," Naeron murmured. "Message."

"Oh joy," Claw muttered. "Do the damn trolls use drums to signal each other or something? Oh, they do, don't they?"

It wasn't a good sign. The Scarsea didn't need to catch up to them if they could signal ahead. She had no idea how far Sicaryon's reach extended these days. She suspected a very long way, indeed. Anahrod had no confidence in these people to outpace their pursuers, and if Ris was telling the truth, they had no clue how to approach any of the locals.

"Where exactly do you need to go?" Anahrod asked Ris, squinting.

"The highlands," she answered immediately. "Somewhere open enough for my dragon to land."

That was easy enough. Bonus: they'd have to travel away from Scarsea lands. That part fit in with Anahrod's plans nicely.

"Fine." Anahrod held out her hand to Ris. "Give me the pouch. You've bought yourself a guide."

❯

As Anahrod finished tying donated clothing to Overbite's harness, she found Gwydinion standing next to Overbite's head, gently petting her nose.

What made Anahrod stop and stare was the fact that Overbite allowed this without protest. No growls, no snarls, no sign that Overbite was anything but pleased by the boy's attention.

"She likes you," Anahrod said.

"She's sunlight." Gwydinion's eyes were bright and too shiny. "I wish . . . I wish there was a different way."

Me too, Anahrod thought.

She scratched the edge of Overbite's jaw.

[I need you to do something for me, pretty girl,] Anahrod told her. [Just a little thing, and then you can sleep.]

Gwydinion took a step backward as Overbite moved her head, but he didn't flinch. The titan drake tilted toward Anahrod, who showed her what she needed. Anahrod overrode the enormous beast's protests and persuaded her to play nice to the next group of humans she saw. To lower her head and whine sweetly because these would be friends of Anahrod's.

It was almost true. She'd considered Sicaryon a friend, once. More than a friend. Now, Overbite's best chance for survival lay in the titan drake making her best impression of a tame vel hound begging for scraps.

[Go,] Anahrod ordered. [Don't stop until they find you. Don't go to them. Let them chase you. Then make friends.]

Overbite gave her one last nose shove and then limped off into the forest.

She exhaled slowly and ignored how dry and tight her throat felt. She turned to the Skylanders and gestured in the opposite direction.

"Let's go. Follow my lead. Don't lag behind. We need to be as far from here as possible before the Scarsea reach this position."

WHAT BURNS BRIGHT

They weren't moving fast enough to escape their pursuers.

Anahrod had to lead the group through any hazards and also swing back to cover their tracks. Ris and Naeron might have Deeper ancestry (Ris) or even come from the Deep (Naeron) but neither understood jungles.

If Anahrod had more time, she would've taught Claw, who had the right mindset, the right eye for detail. Unfortunately, expecting someone who'd lived her whole life at fifteen thousand feet or higher to learn all the skills necessary in minutes was a mountain too high.

Every time the Skylanders opened their mouths, Anahrod would snap at them to be quiet.

Something was wrong. Something was missing. Eventually she realized that the missing something was the drumbeat rhythm of Overbite's heart, the counterpoint tempo of her light footsteps on the jungle floor. Anahrod had grown so used to the noise that its absence left a painful wound.

But it wasn't only Overbite's absence that splintered fault-like through her perceptions.

Wind stirred through jungle canopy leaves overhead. Wild animals screeched, screamed, and vibrated the ground with their calls. The soft background roar of the distant ocean tide alternated between quiet and deafening. All around her lurked the scent of earth, greenery, flowers, and the faint, sharp smell of something oily and acid.

She stopped.

"What's wrong—" Claw said.

Anahrod held up a hand. "Quiet."

The Skylander was about to make a fuss, but Kaibren took the woman's arm. She fell silent.

Absently, Anahrod wondered who was minding who in that relationship.

Something approached. Either a herd or . . .

She touched the minds of rock wyrms.

They were close. Far too close. The Scarsea had either seen through Overbite's distraction or Sicaryon's sheer numbers made it irrelevant.

"What's going on?" Ris whispered.

"Is your dragon nearby?" Anahrod asked instead of answering the question.

"I don't see how it matters," Ris answered. "If there were gaps in the canopy large enough for him to fit through, he would've done it already."

"I don't want him to land. I want him to roar at my signal. A hunting dragon will scare rock wyrms. Some instincts will be too strong for a pride to ignore." Anahrod pointed to a tree with thick branches and plentiful foliage. "We're climbing this right now."

"We are?" Gwydinion asked, a weak and perfunctory protest.

Claw had already looped rope over a branch, using it as a guide to help the two older men.

The Skylander women helped Kaibren and Naeron up the tree with respectable speed before following themselves. Gwydinion scrambled up the rope as Anahrod made one last-ditch effort to hide their trail. Then she followed, yanking the rope up after her.

"What are we—?" Gwydinion whispered.

Anahrod clapped her hand over the boy's mouth as the rock wyrm pride loped into view.

The tree where they sheltered grew from a tangle of bushes. A normal clustering of jungle plants conducted the world's slowest botanical war as they made alliances, hoarded resources, and took advantage of every gap in the canopy. The rock wyrms didn't have enough room to stand underneath them. Which was good, because this pride all had riders, each wearing the violet body paint of the Scarsea.

Like Scratch and Braids, these wore little armor (because it was too hot for such nonsense without inscribers). However, the way they wore their belts, shoulder plates, and accessories showed a marked consistency. A uniform. Sicaryon's symbol, a blue wave on a violet background, was embroidered in multiple locations, including belt buckles and jewelry.

He really is trying to make himself a king. Anahrod swallowed a sour taste. *He'll likely succeed, too.*

The riders were heading in the wrong direction. If luck was on Anahrod's side, the riders would continue until they met up with the group tracking Overbite, at which point Anahrod would have the good fortune of never seeing them again.

If she was less lucky, these riders were performing sweeps.

Unfortunately, her luck proved even worse than that: the riders stopped around thirty feet away to rest. Close enough that the wrong snapped twig, the wrong glance at the wrong moment, would reveal their position.

She watched for any sign that this was anything other than a break to re-lieve themselves or feed their wyrms. It didn't seem to be; the men and women laughed and told each other jokes. Her suspicion about bodily functions was proven correct when one of the men wandered off to a tree nearby.

Something dropped from above and hit a rock on the jungle floor with a loud metallic clang. Whatever the source, it was man-made, and in the Deep, such sounds carried.

The Scarsea stopped all banter and joking as they searched the area. If they were competent—and there was no reason to assume otherwise—it wouldn't take long before they remembered to look up.

Anahrod grabbed Ris's hand. *Now*, she mouthed to the woman.

A flicker of confusion shone on Ris's face, gone so quickly it might have been a trick of light. Then she closed her eyes.

A dragon's roar echoed over the jungle treetops, loud as a roll of thunder.

If the Scarsea had come to attention at the small noise before, that was noth-ing compared to their reaction now. The rock wyrms panicked; two snapped their leads and started running. The soldiers shouted, trying to force their rides back under control. Those with mounts grabbed those without before they raced off into the jungle, chasing after fleeing wyrms.

[Need anything else, my dear?]

How many years had it been since she'd heard a dragon speak? Too many. And not nearly enough. This one was different, though.

She'd never heard a dragon be so solicitous.

Her thoughts were interrupted when Ris leaned back and shoved Claw off the tree branch.

"What was that for?" Claw rolled up again to her feet, cursing.

Ris jumped down as gracefully as though stepping off a stair riser. "Do you think I didn't see what you did?" Ris's voice was ice cold.

"My hand slipped," Claw protested.

Ris scooped something up off the ground as everyone else climbed down.

A knife. Specifically, one of Claw's knives.

Ris examined the blade with a critical eye. "Do you think I'm stupid?" Her voice was soft.

Claw's sullen expression disappeared, replaced by fear.

Anahrod glanced back at the others. Kaibren's face showed nothing but concern. He seemed about to jump between the two women, regardless of the personal peril. Naeron muttered under his breath as he tapped two fingers against a wrist, counting his pulse.

"I could've taken them," Claw said. "We were safe as hatchlings."

"It's not about your capabilities." Ris shifted the knife in her hand. "It's about your willingness to follow orders." She now held the knife in a grip suitable for throwing.

Claw stepped backward, shifted her hands toward her daggers. "Are we really going to do this? Here?"

Ris threw the knife.

Most people underestimated the difficulty of throwing a knife. Achieving anything other than bouncing a knife handle off one's target required precise control and timing. This knife, however, struck true.

It also didn't hit Claw. Ris had thrown it into the tree to Claw's left. The blade sank fully into the trunk, making it effectively impossible to recover.

Ris had either used magic, or she was far stronger than her delicate appearance suggested.

"No, we won't do this here," Ris agreed, "but disobey me again and I won't be so forgiving." She walked away.

Anahrod contemplated what she'd just seen. It's not like she'd have been brokenhearted if Ris had injured Claw. Anahrod was mad at the bloodthirsty little killer, too. As far as she could tell, Claw had tried to pick a fight just to sate her boredom.

If Anahrod had any doubts that Ris was a dragonrider, that little demonstration settled the matter. Dragonriders weren't in charge, but they acted as voices for the ones who were—dragons. That combination inevitably resulted in a group of people used to throwing their weight around.

"I'll be right back," Anahrod told the group, although only Naeron nodded at her to show he'd been paying attention.

She returned to the tree they'd just abandoned and started climbing. No one protested. She suspected they were too distracted by Ris and Claw's showdown to notice.

The jungle spread out in a confusing, dense welter of trees, vines, and choking plant life, too crowded and chaotic to provide useful information. Anahrod didn't dare stay up there for more than a few seconds, either. The tree branches were too thin, the predators too many. This close to open sky, blood crows waited for any opportunity.

She only needed a glimpse.

Anahrod found what she was seeking. An area where the trees changed in texture, turned dark-leafed and violet. The canopy was as dense as the foliage at her current location, but composed of fewer, larger trees.

She clambered back down. When she reached the bottom, she said, "If you two are finished, we're heading northwest."

"What's in that direction?" Gwydinion asked.

"A swamp."

"You're going to hide our tracks in a swamp?" Ris asked.

Anahrod shook her head. "No. Our tracks won't matter. The Scarsea won't follow us."

"Is that who's been chasing us?" Gwydinion asked. "The Scarsea?"

"Who cares?" Claw commented. "The real question is: Why wouldn't they chase us in there?"

Anahrod started walking, but she turned back to answer. "Because the Scarsea aren't suicidal."

CYCLE OF FIRE

One didn't need to be a native of the Deep to identify a targrove swamp as a place to avoid. If the jungles existed as places of exuberant, overabundant life, these swamps were their opposite. Little vegetation grew on the forest floor; what survived developed in ways both stunted and strange. Mushrooms and fungi had taken over spots left vacant by missing flora. Fumes filled the air, more than sufficient to make the eyes water and throat constrict, especially when combined with a second bitter, pungent aroma.

The trees themselves were offensively pretty: a violet dark enough to look black, the bark traced with a silvery sheen, the leaves a lighter violet-red. Their root systems were massive, intertwined monstrosities, often creating giant pits of rainbow-sheened water.

At the edge of the swamp, Naeron paused.

He wasn't the first person in the column, but Ris seemed attuned to his movements. Naeron stopped, so Ris stopped, so everyone else stopped.

"What is it?" Ris asked the man.

His brows and mouth both wrinkled in concentration. He focused his attention on Anahrod. "Targrove?"

"Yes," Anahrod said. There was no sense lying.

He nodded. "Thought so."

Naeron continued walking.

They made much better time once Anahrod wasn't trying to be in two places at once. Not that Anahrod found the experience pleasant, tainted as it was with acrid fumes, dark shadows, eerie silences. The whole swamp carried with it a strong sense of rejection, a spirit intolerant of outsiders and willing to make anyone's trespass their last.

"The air here isn't . . . poisonous . . . is it?" Gwydinion rubbed his watering eyes.

"We're fine if we don't linger," Anahrod told him.

"In all these words of comfort and security," Kaibren quoted, "lay not one stroke of truth-bound surety." He pursed his lips as he stared at her.

"He means you didn't say no," Claw translated.

"True," Anahrod agreed.

"Damn." Claw eyed her. "Anyone ever say that you talk too much?"

"Only in bed," she answered dryly, before adding, "Keep walking. This isn't a good place to stop."

"What place in the Deep ever is," Ris muttered.

"No goal is too far for rough dreams and the regrets of old men, but by dying light of life or day is made slave to the necessities of the coming dark," Kaibren commented.

Anahrod glanced sideways at him. He'd apparently found his voice, such as it was.

"He means it's going to be too dark to see soon," Claw translated. "What are we supposed to do then, light a torch?"

"No." Naeron's refusal was emphatic.

"No fires," Anahrod added. "Under *any* circumstances."

"Is that a cave?" Claw pointed to a dark shadow under a vine-covered rock face. "We could—"

"No caves." There wasn't a cave in the entire Deep that didn't have something living in it, but the rules changed in a targrove swamp. Here the risks involved fumes collecting in low spots until they starved out all the air and—in the case of this particular targrove swamp—a network of caves and tunnels crossing under the entire region, all leading to an underground river that fed straight to the Bay of Bones.

Unhelpful, as that led right back into Scarsea territory, never mind the ocean dangers, both beast and tidal. So Anahrod pointed to a tangle of knotted tree roots, barely visible in the gloaming light. "We'll stop here. Rest and eat. Then we'll continue. We can't camp here."

"Fine." Ris sounded tired.

They were all tired. The Scarsea had forced them to march through the hottest part of the day, breathing air thick enough to bottle and warm enough to boil. Anahrod was miserable; she found herself envious of the Skylanders and their magically inscribed clothing.

She would have been the first to suggest sleeping in a targrove swamp if she considered it safe.

Kaibren dumped out his knapsack, so stuffed with various supplies that she wondered if it was some new form of folding box. He paused, looking frustrated, then began stuffing items back into the bag. Kaibren whispered something to Claw.

She scowled. "No torches? Or no fires under any circumstances? Kaibren's good at shielding a flame."

Naeron threw a rock. "No!"

In response, Kaibren threw his arms up in the air. The "what the hell" gesture needed no translation.

Anahrod sighed. She should've anticipated this. "No fires of any kind. No heat. No sparks. Just—" She patted the ground. "Feel the soil."

Neither Ris nor Naeron bothered, but the others did.

"Why's it so oily?" Gwydinion smeared the dark grit of the sticky black soil between his fingers.

"Targrove," Naeron said, then more slowly, "*Tar.*"

"It is oily," Anahrod agreed. "And it's everywhere. The soil, the water, the very air. This is why the Scarsea won't follow us. In the Deep, fires burn hotter, but in a targrove swamp, the air itself can burn. There is no shielding a flame from that. One spark and this entire swamp goes up."

Several of them gaped at her in shock. Kaibren blanched and then began tossing more supplies back into his knapsack. Anahrod nodded. Good. They were taking the threat seriously.

"That doesn't make sense." Gwydinion glared at her, as though she'd just told him a lie.

Anahrod raised an eyebrow.

"There must have been fires before," the boy said. He spread out his arms. "If this all goes up every time there's the smallest fire, how has the swamp survived at all?"

She chuckled. "These trees use fire for germination. Everything here is either resistant to fire or good at recovering from it. The swamp will survive." She smiled. "But we won't. Unless your clothes are inscribed to protect against this level of heat?"

Ris gave her a long, narrow-eyed look. "Is this detour about keeping the Scarsea from following us? Or keeping my dragon away?"

Anahrod pulled a piece of chena out of her bag and bit into it. She looked the other woman straight in her pretty green eyes and said, "Why would it keep your dragon away? You said your dragon doesn't have a fire affinity."

Anahrod was being disingenuous. There were a dozen elemental affinities besides fire that might start fires in a targrove swamp.

Claw gave Anahrod a nasty stare as well. "If this swamp goes up in flames, you're here, too."

Anahrod shrugged. That had been the entire point. She appreciated they were finally getting it.

"Don't worry." Ris batted away the concern with a motion of her hand. "I've already warned him off." She pouted at Anahrod. "And anyway, *my* dragon doesn't breathe fire."

Anahrod waited a beat, but the woman showed no inclination to explain what her dragon breathed instead. Odd, in its way. Dragonriders were usually all over themselves to brag about whatever made their particular dragon so unique.

Anahrod turned to the boy. "The swamp has some virtues. Touch a root." Anahrod demonstrated, laying her splayed hand flat against the dark gray bark.

"Why—" Gwydinion did so, mimicking Anahrod's gesture. He blinked in surprise, snatched his hand back as if it had been scorched before he returned his palm to the surface a second time. "It's cold!"

"Lean against a tree and cool off," Anahrod said. "Eat something—" She paused as she heard a strange noise, off in the distance.

"What's wrong?" Ris asked.

"Shh." The noise was an odd, rippling kind of crackle. Faint, but growing louder.

She reached out to any animals she could sense. Animals lived in the tar-grove, despite appearances. Many animals, just of a different scale than the giant monsters elsewhere in the jungle. They were all very good at flying or running, or both.

Which they were all doing.

She felt a wave of emotion shudder through her. Fear and dread and a deep, bitter feeling of betrayal.

To think that Sicaryon would stoop so low . . .

No. It had to be a mistake, an accident. But did that really matter? The result was going to be the same.

Anahrod picked up her pack again. "Everyone up. Change of plans. It seems I misjudged the Scarsea response."

"Wait, you don't mean—" Gwydinion stared behind them in a panic. Not unjustified, to be fair.

"Yes," Anahrod said grimly. "Someone's started a fire."

INTO THE DARK

"Can Peralon—" Claw stared up at the dark purple leaf canopy.

"Not in time," Ris said.

Anahrod hadn't heard the name "Peralon" before. She filed it away as the most likely candidate for the name of Ris's dragon.

Because Ris was correct: they didn't have enough time.

"Could we hide under the roots?" Claw asked, which wouldn't have been a bad idea if only a fire wouldn't steal all the breathable air. Claw pointed at the possible cave entrance she'd called out earlier.

Anahrod studied the dark opening. What life Anahrod could sense ended early as wet soil gave way to stone. That was an actual cave, and not just an illusion caused by shadows from twining roots.

The girl had good instincts.

"Everyone into Claw's cave," Anahrod ordered. "Don't stop until you hit a wall."

They had one chance—slim, but better than trying to outrun the blaze. She'd seen targrove fires spread in the distance: no human ran fast enough. She'd seen fires where Overbite wouldn't have run fast enough.

Kaibren had been repacking his supplies.

"No time for that," Anahrod snapped. "Leave them."

The old man hesitated. Then Claw grabbed the knapsack in one hand, Kaibren's arm in the other, and said, "Sorry, but we're doing what the troll girl says this time."

Claw pushed Kaibren into the cave opening.

The rest followed.

The jungle heat shifted from miserable to scorching. The wind rose, summoning the scent of burning wood and bitter, acrid oil. The only real question was how deep the cave might reach. If it would be far enough underground to escape the fire's wrath.

Light bloomed up ahead. Magic from one of the Skylanders, rather than a true flame. The group ran. When they slowed, Anahrod shouted at them until they picked up the pace again.

As they moved farther in, farther down, the targrove's sharp fumes faded, replaced by the wet scent of water filtering through solid rock. They'd found an entrance to the cave system. If it was the same one she remembered, the caves joined at an underground river leading to the Bay of Bones.

Gwydinion stopped their flight by tripping and inelegantly face-planting into the cave floor. His cry echoed against the stone walls.

"Are you all right?" Anahrod pulled the boy to his feet.

"I'm just . . ." He bit his lip and scrunched up his face. He seemed to be about five seconds from a teary breakdown.

"I just banged myself. I'm fine." Gwydinion rubbed his chin, already bruising.

Ris turned to Anahrod. "Are we far enough from danger?"

"Should be. Air's cool."

The light came from a locket Ris held. No doubt an inscribed locket made by Kaibren.

Must be handy to have one's own personal inscriber.

"Can I borrow that?" Anahrod pointed to the necklace. "The tunnel opens up ahead. Might be a good camping spot."

Ris studied Anahrod for a long beat. Anahrod wanted to laugh: where, exactly, could she go if she stole the damn necklace? She answered herself immediately: nowhere.

But they didn't know that.

Ris stepped forward and motioned for Anahrod to open a hand. When she did, Ris hooked the locket chain around two of Anahrod's fingers. The locket swung crazily and everyone's shadows twisted on the tunnel walls. Ris closed Anahrod's painted fingers over the chain clasp. "I'm trusting you with this," she said.

Anahrod felt the touch of those fingers like a shiver moving through her body. She gently removed her hand. "I won't be gone long."

She wasn't. Anahrod scouted the cavern, then called for the others to join her. Ris reclaimed the necklace immediately.

This time, Anahrod made sure their fingers didn't touch.

The enormous cave floor slanted down to a precipitous drop. Ten feet, then ten feet again, before sloping downward to where a stream dutifully bored a channel into the rock.

"How beautiful," Ris breathed.

Anahrod looked again. Ris's light glittered against the rock, reflecting crystal facets against the uneven walls. Liquid dripped, dissolving the stone to create lances pointing down from the ceiling and rising up from the floor. Other sections of the cave stone had oozed out in gooey, thick fans before hardening again, resulting in a mineral mimicry of organic vegetation.

Anahrod suffered a vague guilt, a feeling of transgression for being too rushed to appreciate the view. Under different circumstances . . .

Perhaps if her entire world weren't falling apart.

A loud thump startled her. Anahrod glanced back to see that Kaibren had thrown down his visibly thinner knapsack. He angrily slapped the wall.

"How much of your food did you lose?" she asked him.

The man gave her a frustrated glare. "And humankind discovered the truth of Eannis's curse, for all food tasted of bile and ash, and provided no nourishment. There remained only one exception: humanity itself, and in the early days of hunger many died to fill the cookpots of their neighbors."

"No," Naeron scolded. "Not that bad."

"As bad as having to resort to cannibalism?" Ris began searching the contents of her own bag. "I should hope not. We all have a little. We'll pool our stores. I'm sure—" Her gaze halted on Anahrod, and stayed there.

Most Skylanders would've assumed that Anahrod would share her provisions. In the Deep, however, people didn't share food with outsiders.

"I'll double the price," Ris answered before Anahrod could comment. "Two hundred scales, if you include your food."

"Two hundred scales and you and your dragon forget you ever met me."

Ris's mouth quirked in a wry smile. "Are you sure that's what you want? We'd be happy to take you anywhere you like. No questions asked. Somewhere the Scarsea can't find you."

"You underestimate Sicaryon's tenacity."

"Sicaryon?" Gwydinion asked. "Who's Sicaryon? Is he the Scarsea's leader?"

"Yes. He's a local warlord," Anahrod explained, eyes still narrowed at the dragonrider. "One who thinks he's going to single-handedly re-create his very own Viridhaven down here in the Deep, but with himself in charge instead of ol' King Cynakris."

Ris and Naeron exchanged a look.

"Good luck with that." Ris's lip curled in something like amusement or contempt. Understandable, as legends of the destruction of Viridhaven went hand in hand with fables of Zavad. Those who worshiped the dark dragon came to an equally dark end, etc.

Anahrod shrugged. "Don't see anyone lining up to tell him he can't. He's the reason staying to fight would've been the wrong call. He's recruited every sorcerer he can find—and *you* killed two of his people."

"His reach only extends so far," Ris countered.

"Not into the Skylands, maybe, but I don't plan on traveling there." Anahrod gave Ris a thoughtful look. "Appreciate the offer, but I'll be content with the money and your silence."

The redhead sighed. "I suppose that will have to do."

While they haggled, the others started making camp. Kaibren, though, began drawing light inscriptions on cleared areas of wall, doing so with a speed and skill that made Anahrod blink.

Most inscriptionists needed to consult books, study blueprints and templates. Inscriptions were too complicated to be memorized.

Except, no one had told that to Kaibren.

"So are you going to pull some food out of that sack, Jungle, or am I going to go riffling through that myself?" Claw pointed Anahrod's bag.

"Good way to lose fingers," Anahrod said, but she also got the hint.

They could've made a fire there, if they'd had anything besides their own clothing to burn. Unfortunately, rock made for poor fuel, so they made do with cold rations. She added her own provisions to Kaibren's stores, and mentally wished, hardly for the first or last time, that the trip through the caves would be short.

Anahrod shivered and wrapped her arms around herself. She paused as her body's signals caught up with her.

She was cold.

How long had it been since the last time she was cold? She couldn't remember. Years and years. She wasn't equipped to deal with the cold. She didn't have any blankets or cloaks—no excess fabric of any kind. Even without inscriptions, the Skylander clothing was now exactly right for the environment.

Whereas she wore nothing but several well-placed leather triangles and body paint. People sometimes thought Deepers in the jungles wore body paint to protect them from the sun, but the whole reason Deepers were so pale was because the sun rarely reached them. No, the body paint protected against heat—and now made her vulnerable to the cold.

"Anyone have a shirt I could use?" she asked.

Silence answered her before Claw barked out a sarcastic laugh. "Sure, Jungle. Fifteen scales."

Anahrod raised an eyebrow. "And my fee just went up twenty scales. Care to continue?"

Claw made a rude gesture. "Where would a troll even spend Skylander scales down here? Do you have some local taverns I haven't heard of?"

"Hey!" Gwydinion shouted, and quickly silenced himself, swallowing his embarrassment as he gulped air. Gwydinion glanced sideways at Naeron. "Sorry. I didn't mean to shout."

The heavyset man appeared discomforted, but waved away the apology. He closed his eyes, then put the fingers of one hand to the opposite wrist and began tapping.

Gwydinion turned back to Anahrod and Claw and puffed up his chest in an adorable approximation of authority. "What I mean is that my father says that Seven Crests scales—which are minted in Crystalspire—are good anywhere for a thousand miles in any direction, up or down the mountains, because they're impossible to counterfeit. That makes them safe and reliable and is the reason that Crystalspire is the greatest city in Seven Crests and—"

"Breathe," Anahrod suggested.

He inhaled. Anahrod took advantage of the pause to ask: "Who's your father?"

Ris interposed herself. "Does it really matter?"

Claw transferred her irritation from Anahrod to Gwydinion. "It's cute that your daddy thinks anyone down here knows what Skylander coin looks like, but—"

"It's not cute," Gwydinion insisted. "It's sensible. Because there is trade between the trolls—" He gave Anahrod an apologetic glance. "I mean, between the Deep and the Skylands, with Seven Crests. We use a dye that can only be gotten from a jungle bug, and another dye made from rare seaweed. Important cooking ingredients can only be found here. We aren't—I mean, it's not like Skylanders come down here to harvest any of that ourselves, do we? That means trade, but I think you already know that. You're just saying otherwise because you're mean."

Anahrod bit her lip. She wouldn't smile. She would *not*.

Claw threw back her head and guffawed loudly. "I'm starting to like you. You've got more spine than I would've expected from a rich kid from Crystalspire." She then gave Anahrod a more serious expression. "I already gave you my extra shirt and you tied it to that titan drake. I don't have any spares."

"You can borrow one of mine," Gwydinion offered. "I brought extra." He retrieved said garment from his pack.

"Thank you." Anahrod slipped on the shirt, trying her hardest to ignore the hollow feeling as she noticed the smocked sleeves, the whitework trim. The sleeves were wider than she expected, likely to allow room for the pair of metal bracelets the boy wore, but otherwise the main hallmarks of Crystalspire fashion remained.

That single thin shirt made a startling difference in her comfort, but then: magic. Like everyone else's clothing, it was undoubtedly inscribed. If that shortened the garment's life to months instead of years, well, Skylanders could just buy another one, couldn't they?

Truly, the gulf between Skylanders and Deepers, who had no inscribers, was a span much greater than altitude. Deepers had sorcerers, but those magical talents were less useful for creature comforts than for fighting off actual creatures. The Skylands used its magic to live luxuriously, while the Deep used its magic to survive.

Dinner was eventful only in that it provided one more piece of unnecessary proof that Naeron was born a Deeper.

"That's chena?" Naeron asked Anahrod. He had a covetous look, desire warring with propriety and winning. His eyes were filled with a longing usually reserved for rediscovering the homemade treats of childhood—for that nostalgic reminder of hearth and home.

Anahrod tossed him a piece. "Yes."

He tore into it with unsubtle, enthusiastic vigor.

"What is that?" Gwydinion asked.

Anahrod shrugged. "Mushrooms fermented in loquari sap, dried, then coated in crushed honeyplum. Keeps forever. Good trail rations." Also delicious, but they'd figure that out on their own.

"My father—" That was as much as Naeron managed. Then he stood up, left the group, and sat down facing away from them. He put his arms over his head, rocking back and forth.

Ris inhaled sharply. "Everything's fine. He gets like this sometimes. I'll be right back."

She approached Naeron's position with the same delicacy as a heretic attempting to rob a church. She held out her hand, said something too soft for Anahrod to hear.

"Don't mind him," Claw said crisply. "Naeron just gets overwhelmed. He'll be fine once he has his heartbeat back under control." She glared at Anahrod as if daring the woman to pry further.

"I'll take your word for it." It wasn't any of Anahrod's business. Naeron had some odd mannerisms, but so did anyone, in the right circumstances. She did wonder, though, at a man who was perfectly calm while killing rock wyrms or people, but found himself overwhelmed to the point of collapse from remembering his father's cooking.

Sure enough, Naeron came back with Ris around a half hour later. Anahrod had put away the chena by then. Naeron didn't ask for another piece; she didn't offer one.

Sensibly, the Skylanders were using their mantles as bedding. Mantles were incredibly versatile garments that could be folded into bags or packs, or, yes, bedrolls. Not perhaps the most comfortable sleeping mats that had ever existed, but infinitely better than the damp rock floor.

Which was where Anahrod would be sleeping.

Ris cleared her throat. The woman eased herself over to the far side of the mantle she'd spread out on the ground. "It'll be a little cozy, but I'm willing to share."

Anahrod's instinct told her to refuse. It's not like the woman had been subtle in her flirting, but Anahrod had no idea if it had been serious. Ris might've been raised a Skylander, but as far as the dragonrider knew, Anahrod was not. By Skylander customs, it wasn't appropriate to flirt with Anahrod since she wasn't wearing any rings.

Ris had done it anyway.

But what were Anahrod's options, really? There wasn't room with Naeron, she wouldn't feel safe with Claw, and Kaibren would probably be fine, except she didn't know how his "bodyguard" would react. Sharing a mantle with Gwydinion seemed like a cruel thing to do to a boy in the middle of all the uncomfortable awakenings of his transition to adulthood.

So Ris it was.

Except what Anahrod said was: "I'll stain your mantle."

Ris stared her right in the eyes. "Only if we do it right."

Anahrod pinched the bridge of her nose. She walked right into that, hadn't she? Ris was enjoying herself. Teasing. Pushing.

Anahrod reminded herself that, no matter how beautiful this woman might be, she was a dragonrider. No one Anahrod could risk becoming involved with.

Not for a fling. Not for fun. Not ever.

That reminder did nothing to warm the chill lingering in her bones, so she walked over to the blanket and lay down in the space offered.

Ris behaved herself with impeccable propriety.

Anahrod told herself, repeatedly, that she wasn't disappointed.

THE RIVER THAT RUNS UNDER

Naeron woke Anahrod from her sleeping, nudging the woman's shoulder until she stirred.

"Your turn," he whispered. "Watch."

Ris remained asleep, even as the dragonrider held Anahrod close with an arm around her waist. So Anahrod had to disentangle herself from that, but eventually did so without waking the other woman. Sleeping next to Ris had been more comfortable than Anahrod would ever admit.

Naeron settled down on his own mantle, as Anahrod took her turn at watch. She found a rock outcropping overlooking the cave.

Was Naeron the one who'd made Scratch bleed out? Ris was guaranteed to possess magical abilities as a dragonrider, but controlling the sword would've taken up most of her attention. The simplest explanation was that Naeron was a Deeper sorcerer.

It's just that a dragonrider should've had no tolerance for Deeper sorcerers. It was the blackest of heresies to use the gifts of Eannis—magic—for anything but service to a dragon. Deepers saw it differently, partly because they didn't worship Eannis, but mostly because they needed sorcery to survive.

Ris didn't seem to mind Naeron, however. It was just one of the woman's many, many contradictions.

Anahrod felt a presence on the far side of the cave, recognized it as Gwydinion.

Who had wandered off all by himself, alone in the dark.

He wouldn't be the first teenager to search for privacy at the cost of untenable risk, but he wasn't alone.

Gwydinion had found an animal.

Curious, Anahrod picked her way through the forest of stalagmites, careful not to wake anyone. Also, careful to make enough noise for the boy to hear her coming.

He glanced up at her as her eyes adjusted to the light. The darkness wasn't as immediate or total as she'd first suspected: the light inscription Kaibren had carved into a wall reached just far enough to limn the edges of Gwydinion's expression. He was smiling at a small white serpent twined between his fingers.

"Isn't he cute?" Gwydinion held up the snake. "I think he's blind."

"What need would an animal have for sight down here?" Anahrod didn't recognize the species, but she knew it was too cold in the caves for the creature to actually be cold-blooded.

The snake was tiny and pale and—given the general trend of wildlife in the Deep—sublimely venomous. Fortunately, the creature was calm. Remarkably so.

Anahrod crouched down next to Gwydinion. "How'd you find him?"

"Oh, I . . ." The boy glanced at her like she'd caught him lying.

Anahrod hesitated. The boy had used magic. He just didn't want to admit it. "Eannis blessed you?"

It changed everything.

A dragonrider and her crew venturing into the Deep jungles at the behest of some random child from Crystalspire stretched the bounds of believability. Helping a dragonrider candidate, on the other hand . . .

If the boy was already touched with magical talent, then he would become a dragonrider. By law, those children belonged to the dragons.

They were told it was an honor.

"I guess so," he said.

"Your parents must be proud." She couldn't keep the bitterness from her voice. She didn't think he noticed.

"My dad, sure, but my mom?" Gwydinion shook his head. "She hates it. She doesn't want me to become a dragonrider at all. She says she doesn't want to lose me."

"Mothers can be protective." She swallowed back dark memories.

"I guess," he allowed, although his tone suggested he neither understood nor approved.

He gave her a furtive, quick glance. "Do you have any family?"

An innocent question. She didn't let him see the wound it opened. "I used to," she replied carefully.

"Do you miss them?"

She set her jaw hard against her neck, clenched her teeth. "No."

His eyes widened. "No?"

"Why would I?" she said in a flat voice. "They abandoned me, betrayed me when I needed them most." She shook her head. "I'll spare you the details. Trust me when I say if I never see them again, it'll be too soon."

"Oh." His voice sounded small.

"I'm sorry." She gave him an imitation of a pleasant smile. "You must miss your family a great deal."

Gwydinion swallowed. "I do, yes."

"You'll be home soon."

The boy held up the snake, which had become agitated. "No, no, little one. Don't be scared. We won't hurt you." That smile again, as he leaned toward Anahrod. "Truthfully, I'm pretty sure he thinks I'm a very weird rock."

She pressed her tongue against the back side of her teeth. At least that explained why Overbite had been so quick to take to the boy. "Is that just an expression or can you tell what the snake's thinking?"

"Oh, um." He scratched his neck. "This time, yes. I can't always. It's not reliable."

Anahrod stared back toward the small camp, toward people she hardly knew and definitely didn't trust.

Not everyone was sleeping.

Ris had woken. The dragonrider lay on her mantle, her head supported by one arm, watching them. Possibly listening, depending on how much magic she knew, and what kind.

Anahrod turned back to Gwydinion. "Release the snake and stop wandering off. In fact, go get some sleep."

Gwydinion seemed about to protest.

"Don't force the issue," Anahrod warned. "I tie a mean knot."

The boy let out a long-suffering sigh. He reached down to release the snake back into the wild.

Except he didn't. Gwydinion had pantomimed doing so, trusting that his own body blocked Anahrod's line of sight too much for her to notice what his hands were doing. He'd only moved the snake, not released it. The creature now curled up happily around one of the boy's wrists, hidden under his sleeve.

Anahrod should've made a fuss. He was a child, and the snake was undoubtedly dangerous. Revealing that she knew, however, risked Gwydinion asking unwanted questions about *how* she knew.

Anahrod had little desire to let Ris or any of her friends know the full extent of her abilities. She'd already said too much, and she didn't think Ris had missed her slip.

Trusting Sicaryon with that knowledge had proved a deadly mistake, hadn't it?

Anahrod dragged Gwydinion back to camp and sent him to bed. She sat on a rock for the rest of her shift and brooded about what she'd discovered.

It was none of her business. She barely knew the boy.

She knew, logically, that her feelings were a reaction to his blessing, the one that allowed him to control creatures and tell what they were thinking. It was the same as hers, and while that wasn't unknown, it was a weird coincidence.

Maybe it didn't matter. Maybe she'd have felt that way at the idea of sending any child to Yagra'hai as a dragonrider candidate. Her lips curled into a sneer as she stared out into the dark. "Candidate" made it sound like it was an honor, some kind of reward. It didn't begin to touch on what such children really were:

Sacrifices.

"What are we supposed to do now, huddle in the dark until the fire goes out?" Claw asked after breakfast the next morning.

"Wouldn't recommend it," Anahrod answered. "Fire will take a few weeks to die down."

"And if Sicaryon orders his people to put out the fire?" Ris asked.

"Then subtract a few days, but assume he'll have soldiers and sorcerers combing the swamp."

Claw made a rude gesture at Anahrod. "You could've just said going back up was a shit idea."

"Didn't want to discourage you from contributing," Anahrod said dryly.

Ris put a hand to her lips and choked back a laugh.

"With autumn a memory and winter at one's back, spring's only option is summer," Kaibren said.

Anahrod squinted at him.

"In other words: no place to go but forward," Claw translated.

Anahrod tugged the edge of Gwydinion's borrowed shirt over her knees. "Ris, you said you only need enough space for your dragon to land."

"Still true."

"Could he grab us as he flew past?"

Ris looked taken aback. "He'd still need an open area. A large one."

"Which he won't have," Claw pointed out.

"Would the ocean be open enough?" Anahrod asked. "There's an underground river," she explained. "Since it's the dry season—"

"*This* is the dry season?" Claw interrupted.

Anahrod ignored her. "—the river level should be low enough that water won't flood the tunnels. There'd be enough air to breathe. Assuming we survive the rapids and assuming . . ." She scowled. There was no sense being coy about it. "The river empties halfway up the cliffside of the Bay of Bones. If it's low tide, that's a one-hundred-foot fall to our deaths. If the tide's going out, we risk being dragged out into tidefisher nets. And if the tide's coming in . . ."

"If the tide's coming in," Ris said sourly, "we'll have the unique pleasure of finding out exactly why the Bay of Bones is called that as we watch a two-hundred-foot wall of water smash into us."

"Wow," Gwydinion said, eyes wide.

"You've been there?" Anahrod asked. Someone unfamiliar with the area might make the mistake of assuming Ris exaggerated the danger.

She didn't.

"Of course," Ris said sarcastically. "It's where I keep my summer home." Her mouth twisted. "If it's high tide, we'll exit the river underwater, but we can swim to the surface."

"This was a bad idea," Anahrod said. "Forget I mentioned it."

"When seas devoid of creatures flow, the bright fish becomes a curio," Kaibren said with a shrug.

"Nobody's had any better ideas—or any other ideas at all." Claw growled out the translation with obvious reluctance. "Do you even know how to swim, kid?" she asked Gwydinion.

"Do you?" he asked with such false innocence that Anahrod had to swallow a snicker. "I've been swimming the Illgwuel River since I was five."

Claw scratched her jaw. "I'm supposed to believe your mummy would let you anywhere near a river that dangerous?"

"You don't know my mother," Gwydinion pointed out. "I'm also licensed to pilot racing flyers and know how to use a wingsuit. If she could've paid someone to bring me down here and give me wilderness survival lessons, I'd know how to do that, too."

Claw laughed, the sound riding on the edge of hysterical. "Fuck me with razor blades. This'll be *great*."

"Do you know how to use a sword?" Anahrod asked the boy. It was mostly curiosity.

Nobody in the Skylands used swords. She glanced at Ris and corrected herself. Almost nobody. Dragonriders did, but that was status and boredom, not need. In the Deep, swords were necessary—at least until creatures like rock wyrms and titan drakes entered the fray. In the Skylands? Relics. Even the city guards used halberds and crossbows, not swords.

Gwydinion gave Anahrod and her own visible sword an embarrassed glance. "I do," he admitted, "but Ris said I shouldn't bring my sword with me."

Ris didn't deny it. "Someone might've expected you to use it."

That was the right call. Even if Gwydinion had been training since he was a baby, the Deepers down here attended a far tougher sort of school. They'd tear him apart in a serious fight.

"Can we get back to the part about dying by raging river, waterfall, tidal wave, or sea monster?" Claw asked sarcastically, although she settled down a little—a little—when Kaibren gave her a scolding look.

"No dying," Naeron said. "I know tides."

"What was that?" Anahrod focused on the man. He had contributed nothing to the conversation, but he'd been listening.

"I know tides," Naeron repeated. He started to say something else, grimaced, and then switched to Sumulye. That didn't seem to be his native tongue either, but he was more fluent in it than speaking Haudan. "Tides are like the body, like *blood*. They have patterns, rhythms, *beats*. Once the tide comes in, we have four hours of safety before the tide retreats. That's our window. Twice a day—once in sunlight, once at night."

"None of us want to do this at *night*," Anahrod confessed. "You can make sure we time it to hit the bay safely?"

He held up a hand and wiggled it. "Maybe. How far is it from here to the ocean? How fast is the river? Does that speed change?"

Gwydinion leaned over to Ris. "What are they saying?"

She responded, "I'll tell you when you're older."

Anahrod rubbed her chin as she stared out at the blank stone wall. "It's a day's walk from that targrove swamp to the beach," she told Naeron. "A day's walk for a human on foot. Not a day's walk for Overbite. Not sure how fast the river is. Won't know until we find it."

Naeron looked thoughtful.

"Would someone please tell us what the hell these two are saying?" Claw threw up her hands.

"We're saying that riding the river down to the bay might work," Anahrod said. "If it doesn't, at least our deaths will be quick."

"Garbage!" Claw spat. When Kaibren tried to quiet her, she turned on the man. "You cannot expect me to go along with a plan that *might* work, but will probably just kill us."

Kaibren nodded grimly and said, "In shadows deep, by hunger's mournful tune, our souls grow weak, as darkness claims its boon."

"Ugh!" The woman all but gnashed her teeth.

"It *is* a stupid plan," Anahrod said.

Claw's mouth fell open. "What was that?"

"You think I mind if you call it a stupid plan?" Anahrod shrugged. "It's a stupid plan. Risky. My preference is that we search for a tunnel leading to an exit outside the targrove swamp, sneak out past any Scarsea, and hike to the highlands—the original plan. But that will take days, if not weeks. Do we have enough food?"

Everyone turned to Kaibren, who shook his head.

"I don't see a better option," Ris said.

No one said a word, but then, no one needed to. Because Ris was right. They had no other options.

They were doing this.

BLACK WATER, WHITE WATER

Following the stream led them to a larger stream, which led to a brook, which opened up onto a still larger watercourse. Occasionally, the openings that the waterways flowed through were scarcely larger than the water, causing a struggle for the larger members of the group—Kaibren and Naeron.

Ris's sword, which had so skillfully decapitated a lot of rock wyrms and one Scarsea warrior, proved invaluable. She wedged it between rocks to provide steps or floated the blade so people could grab the hilt as a handhold—sometimes she used it as an anchor point for ropes.

This didn't mean the trip was enjoyable. The looming threat of a fatal slip and fall was ever-present. Anahrod came close to doing exactly that, when a foothold slid out from under her like a sheet of buttered glass as Ris and her sword were busy elsewhere. Naeron caught her arm, but not before Anahrod opened up a gash along her hip.

Naeron immediately stopped the bleeding, of course. Fortunate, but it still wasn't an experience she cared to repeat.

Anahrod was ill-equipped for this journey, wearing only a teenage boy's borrowed shirt and sandals never meant for rock climbing. She'd have thought Naeron would also be at a disadvantage, but the man's endurance proved extraordinary. He was stronger than she'd assumed.

Claw was the hero of the day. She had a talent for judging if a cliff face was stable, if a section of rock would slip, what would be the easiest and safest path.

When asked, she just grinned. "I'm from Blackglass."

"That can't be true," Gwydinion protested. "Everyone from Blackglass wears a veil."

"Oh yes," she agreed. "It's rude to show the scars." She grinned nastily to emphasize those features.

"I thought she was from Grayshroud?" Gwydinion looked at the others for an explanation.

Claw leaned over him. "I lived in Grayshroud, but I'm from Blackglass. It's traditional to give ourselves one scar for every person we've killed. You know, in duels and such. Then we wear a veil so as not to upset the rest of you delicate crystals with our bloodthirsty ways."

"Claw." The warning in Ris's voice was unmistakable.

The boy leaned away. Hardly a surprise. Even if one knew nothing at all about Claw (and Anahrod surely qualified) it was impossible to miss all the scars on her face.

Claw laughed as she straightened again. "What? Should I lie to the boy?"

"I hear the river," Anahrod interrupted. She heard something, anyway, a steady thrum of running water far greater than anything they'd encountered so far.

"Good," Ris said. "Let's go. I'm so eager to be done with this place. I can't even begin to tell you."

"You don't have to tell us," Claw said. "We all feel the same."

"No," Naeron said.

"I stand corrected," Claw said. "Let me guess: you find the quiet soothing?"

The mage nodded. "It's nice." His voice was wistful. "Reminds me of home." He gazed off into the distance.

"If you say so," Claw said. "Place gives me the creeps."

"Then why are you lingering?" Anahrod walked past the woman, down the passage that (hopefully) led to the main river tunnel. Everyone hurried to catch up, reminded of their time limit.

As if Anahrod could wander too far ahead. Ris still had the only light.

A short time later, the tunnel opened up onto a rock ledge, which jutted out over a large, hollow cylinder. One of those places where magma had once flowed. Now the liquid here was water instead of molten stone. The smell of wet rock hung thick in humid air.

The river had brought with it all manner of surface debris. Detritus, even runoff soil, which had gathered in the cracks and fissures to create a fertile environment for fungi and odd, lichen-like structures. Anahrod imagined this place as a sort of underground oasis. She felt the nearby animals hiding. Creatures who, like Gwydinion's pale snake, felt no need for sight or camouflage.

They'd caught a break. As Anahrod had hoped, the season meant the tunnels weren't flooded. That was their only luck, however. The river ran fast and deep. Nothing about it appeared the slightest bit "safe."

"No." Naeron turned around.

Claw caught his arm. "This was your idea. What were you planning to do instead? Bleed your way to safety?"

"Oh, this looks faster than the Illgwuel River." Gwydinion stared wide-eyed at the rushing white water.

THE SKY ON FIRE

Anahrod put her hand on the boy's shoulder. "Breathe slowly," she suggested. "Deep breath, then exhale. I won't let you drown." She studied Naeron. "How are we looking in terms of time? Can you make a guess?"

He sat down on a wet rock next to the river and stared at the water. He held up a hand. "One hour," he said. "Then we must go."

"Lovely," Ris said, cracking her neck. "Just enough time to really loathe the idea."

Anahrod leaned against the cave wall. "When we go in the water, don't swim. You won't be able to, anyway. Keep your arms by your side and your feet in front of you. Pretend you're sliding down a hill, feet first. Use your feet to kick away from rocks or obstacles. Every time your head is above water, take a breath."

"Great," Claw commented. "You know, Jungle, I don't think I've heard you string more than two sentences together unless you're talking about this damn river."

"I'm always loquacious when I'm about to die," Anahrod said. "Do any of you *not* know how to swim?"

Claw's smile wasn't enough to cover the pained look on her face. "How hard can it be?"

Next to her, Kaibren shook his head, and Anahrod was positive the man wasn't answering for Claw, but for himself.

Anahrod exhaled slowly and closed her eyes. This was going to be grim. If this was a brief ride—thirty seconds or so—it might have been reasonable to ask this of people who weren't strong swimmers. But they were riding this from here all the way to the coast. It would take *hours*. Even the best swimmers faced the very real danger of drowning. The idea of keeping everyone above water was so outrageous she might as well have been trying to teach them to fly . . .

Her eyes snapped open again and she turned to Ris. "Do you have sky amber on you?"

If it were *anyone* else . . .

Well, if it were anyone else, she wouldn't have asked, because the answer would've been no. With a dragonrider, though? Ris might carry sky amber as a matter of course, just in case her dragon should need it.

Ris looked excited for the barest of split seconds, and then bitter resignation settled around her. "Not in the quantities we'd need to keep us all above water."

Anahrod pointed at Kaibren. "You know Dralar's Inversion?"

He scoffed, as if to say, *Doesn't everyone?*

"Don't know the inscription myself," Anahrod clarified. "Only that the inscription exists. One of my mothers used it to—" She paused as a wave of grief threatened to overwhelm her. She wrestled herself back under control. "I've heard it can magnify the properties of another item, but at the cost of longevity. So if you had, oh, a tiny amount of meoren dye, you could stretch that into enough for an entire bolt of cloth, but it would shorten the material's lifespan drastically."

Ris gave her an arch look. "That's an oddly specific example."

"One of my mothers may have once—hypothetically—bribed a dyemaker's assistant to add that inscription to the fabric for an outfit being made for a rival just before a major soiree." Anahrod pursed her lips as she contemplated the memory. "His trousers didn't even make it to the fourth course before they disintegrated right off his body in front of a thousand people."

Gwydinion started laughing, so hard that Naeron had to grab the boy by the back of the mantle to keep him from slipping into the rushing water.

"Point is," Anahrod continued, looking at Kaibren, "can we do the same thing with the sky amber to make everyone's clothes *float?*"

Kaibren's eyes widened. "As the mountains soar into the sky—" He broke off and grimaced. "The oceans will beat death and dishonor onto a thousand shores before they wash away his pride!"

As one, everyone turned to Claw.

She swallowed. "I think he's saying it would work right up until the water washes away the inscription." Claw gave Kaibren a sympathetic look. "Sorry, old man. I didn't recognize that quote."

He scowled and waved a hand irritably at her before sullenly chewing on a nail.

"Nomad emblem, no. 3," Ris said softly, "using the northern cross correlation."

His head jerked up. Kaibren blinked at her several times, then grabbed his pack and began riffling for supplies as Ris added, "We don't have the time for embroidery. Paper maybe?"

"Screw paper," Claw said, with feeling. "If you can make it waterproof, put it on our *skin.*"

Ris sighed. "Do you remember when Anahrod said it would drastically decrease the lifespan of whatever it was used on? The word 'disintegration' may have come up at one point."

Claw opened her mouth, then closed it again. "Or we could use paper. Paper sounds great, too."

"Yes," Ris said. "That's what I thought."

After that, everyone helped grind up the ink and sky amber, combining both with water.

At one point, Claw said, "I thought sky amber was supposed to float innately."

"Not without help," Gwydinion explained. "Very proprietary. The Travelers

Guild zealously guards the process. Before that it's just"—he waved a hand at the tiny pieces of resin waiting to be ground down—"like this. The raw version is what the dragons burn as incense."

Gwydinion gave Kaibren a narrow-eyed look, like he might at any moment demand to see Kaibren's license to know the sky amber inscription formula. If so, he overcame the impulse.

They continued grinding as Kaibren began drawing out the inscriptions using sky amber–infused ink on paper. By the third sheet, Naeron had to start sitting on pages to keep them from floating away in the air. Before long, each of them had a page—all waterproof and trying to drag them airborne.

"Who's . . . who's first?" Gwydinion scanned the rolling waters below with ill-concealed dread.

"I'll light the way," Ris said.

Anahrod expected the dragonrider to say more, but Ris gave Anahrod a saucy wink and jumped. The water whisked her away so quickly all Anahrod could see was the reflection of Ris's amulet light on the walls.

"You next," Anahrod told Gwydinion. "I'll be right behind you."

Anahrod had to hand it to the boy. He didn't hesitate.

Neither did she, for practical reasons if nothing else: she preferred to stay as close to Ris's light as possible for as long as possible.

The water was warm, hinting at a volcanic origin or a long journey through the jungles before plunging underground.

Despite this advantage, the trip took on nightmarish qualities. Being impossible to sink did nothing to stop the violent white water from tossing her about. If she kicked too hard against a rock, she pulled herself sideways, an ugly position to be in if she wanted to avoid smashing her head. The light from Ris's locket reflected against the tunnel roof as they raced down the river, a one-color kaleidoscope fracturing its ambiance in all directions. Without the paper, it would have been nearly impossible for her to prevent herself from drowning.

While she was enduring all this, a stray thought occurred to her.

Ris had called her Anahrod.

She'd never told Ris—or anyone else in that group—her real name.

Whether it was the worst possible spot to panic or the best was debatable, but that was the moment that the river plunged into darkness.

───◆───

Anahrod had no way to know what had happened to Ris, or her light. Anahrod might have heard Gwydinion call out, but she couldn't be certain. The churning water drowned out all other noise.

She seethed in a world of roaring water and darkness.

The threat of braining herself against sharp rocks vanished, primarily because there were suddenly no rocks at all, sharp or otherwise. She couldn't think of an explanation for the sudden change in the river, but it distracted her enough that she didn't notice when the sound of the river shifted from whitewater noise to something more rhythmic.

A second later she plunged underwater, the world simultaneously muffled and roaring. The water pushed her violently forward before releasing her into a blue-green expanse, almost painfully bright when compared to the blackness of the river tunnel.

The river had emptied into the sea.

Naeron had been right, she thought. It was high tide in the Bay of Bones, and if she didn't swim up to the surface, she'd drown.

Fortunately for her, the inscribed paper knew which way was up, even if she was less certain. As she broke the water's surface and gasped for breath, something metallic flashed overhead. Gwydinion's voice called out for her.

Again, by name.

An arm wrapped around Anahrod before she could slip back under the water.

"Don't worry, beautiful," Ris whispered. "I've got you."

All the blood in her head rushed somewhere else. Not metaphorically, but literally.

Anahrod knew what flying sickness felt like, and this wasn't it. Something else was happening.

Naeron, she realized. Naeron and his power over blood.

Her last thought before unconsciousness overwhelmed all was that she should've gone with her first instinct.

Never trust a dragonrider.

PART TWO

THE
SKYLANDS

INVITATION TO AN EXECUTION

When Anahrod opened her eyes again, she was indoors. The moment she drew her first conscious breath, she also knew she was no longer in the Deep.

The air was too thin. Mountain thin. Dry and sharp and cold in a way no sea-level air could ever be. A weak, gelid broth compared to the Deep's warm honey syrup. Uncomfortable as she had often found breathing at sea level, to wake in this flat, wispy sky was like discovering that she had been a fish all this time, and could never breathe air at all.

She began coughing, daggers in her throat, each pulled breath scraping razors inside her lungs. Breathing was both too easy and too hard. She rolled over, holding her breath, fearful that the coughing would take on its own momentum, rattling through her until she heaved.

Interminable seconds later, she righted herself, inhaling in slow, shallow breaths to stave off another coughing fit. Everything was still and quiet in air too thin to carry sound the right way.

She'd sat up during her coughing bout, which meant they hadn't tied her up. She'd been sleeping—if that was the right word—in a comfortable Skylander bed, layers of quilted wool padding over a poured stone base.

Anahrod had questions.

How long had she been unconscious? Not that long: she wasn't weak from hunger or shaking from thirst. Her bladder wasn't full to bursting. Either they'd taken care of all her needs while she was unconscious, or she'd been asleep for less than a day.

Had Naeron attacked her? She'd leaped to that conclusion, but she'd been incapable of thinking clearly. If Ris's group had meant her harm, they'd had a hundred opportunities to kill her more conveniently along the way. But if they'd meant to kidnap her . . .

Ris and Gwydinion had both known her real name. So had Claw, she realized. They'd all known who she was.

She rubbed her brow. Just her luck to get rescued from one kidnapping by a second set of kidnappers.

Peralon must have arrived in time to save them. That flash of metal she'd seen—that must've been Ris's dragon. He'd pulled them all from the waters and brought Anahrod here.

But why?

A pang twisted in her chest as she pulled herself from the bed. Not hunger or issues with breathing, but the dull, flat resignation of knowing she'd been betrayed. Could she even go back? That would depend on whether Sicaryon's people had set the targrove fire intentionally. Since there was no way to find out that information without committing herself, it was safest to assume the answer was "yes."

So she couldn't return. She'd already lost Overbite. Now she'd lost . . . everything else. No matter what happened next, she would have to start over.

Assuming she survived whatever these people wanted from her. A question she admitted she had no ready answer to, given the state of her newfound prison—if that's what it was meant to be.

The bedroom was beautifully appointed, but the furnishings were too generic, too lacking in personality, to be someone's private chambers. Everything felt worn around the edges—the tattered dissipation of a room continually used by people with no emotional attachment or concern for its upkeep. Customers, not tenants. This wasn't a room where anyone lived, only stayed at for a short stretch before moving on again. A guest room, rented by the day.

She traced the motifs carved into the white polished walls, an endless geometric repeat of stars, while she tried to slow her runaway heartbeat, the spikes of panic drilling through her skin.

This wasn't *just* Seven Crests. The walls gave it away. There was only one city in Seven Crests that used that technique of carving polished clay over poured stone.

They'd known her name was Anahrod. They hadn't stumbled across her by accident. Somehow, they'd known who she was, and where she came from.

The sweet incense drifting in lazy curls was a choking fume as she lunged for the window. She couldn't escape that way: the window was capped with soapstone latticework, the star-shaped gaps large enough for fingers, but not an entire hand. She grabbed at the sharp edges of the stone screen as she gazed out at majestic mountain peaks and the violet-blue sky of early morning.

Anahrod knew that view. Seventeen years gone and she knew that view. Breathtaking in every horrible and ironic definition of the word.

This was Crystalspire.

She pushed down the panic, shoved it into a dark corner of her mind. Why bring her back to Crystalspire and put her in a very nice room? Why wasn't she in a jail cell?

Why wasn't she *already dead?*

She concentrated on her breathing, her heartbeat, the scent of halanwood incense, the clatter of traffic down on the street below.

She wasn't dead yet.

Anahrod calmed herself and focused on what she did best: surviving.

She started by searching the room. A flight of shallow stairs led to a plastered alcove that sheltered a deep bathing pool—more evidence that this was a guest-house room. Someone had filled the bath and heated it; steam rose from the water's surface. Either someone had made a good guess on when she'd awaken or the pool was inscribed to keep the water hot. The latter seemed more likely. The room was chilly enough to make that steam very enticing.

Looking around, Anahrod found a clever little hallway tucked behind the alcove. That's where they kept a squat toilet and a small, tiled fountain for washing one's hands.

Anahrod looked down at herself. She still wore what she'd been wearing previously: green body paint and Gwydinion's borrowed shirt, now filthy. The green paint was hardening in the dry Skyland air. Pieces were falling away in ragged sections. The bed was an embarrassing mess.

The only door locked from the outside.

There was an eerie quietness in the air, with no nearby noises to hint at the existence of other prisoners or any dubious behavior. No one laughed or gasped in pleasure, either. No music. No sound of dice, of bets, of drinking. If this was a ring house, it was a ring house that had taken a vow of silence. If it was a public house, then someone had rented out the entire space, leaving her as the establishment's only "patron."

Her search also uncovered fresh linens, towels for the bath, and a generous selection of bath soaps and oils, but the last two discoveries surprised her.

First was a wardrobe, and the clothing inside confirmed that the word in front of house was "ring" and not "guest." None of it was suitable for wearing in public. Or rather, almost none of it. By carefully matching parts of different outfits, Anahrod assembled an ensemble that wouldn't break public decency laws—but it wasn't easy.

Second were her belts and bags. The salty seawater had left its mark on both, causing the leather to twist and shrink. They hadn't been taken away, though, nor emptied. Both her sword and her knives were gone, however.

Using a chair to smash through the delicate soapstone window screen held a warm appeal. She could tie bedsheets together and climb down, like the heroine from *The Grey Fortress of Silence.* But the air was cold and she was still covered in green paint. She couldn't go anywhere looking like this.

Fortunately, that was a problem she could actually solve.

Anahrod took a bath.

⌄

Anahrod refilled the bath twice in the process of removing her green body paint. The water stayed hot the whole time and she gave silent thanks to whomever first discovered the inscriptions for hot water. Dragons, if one believed the Church's canon.

She stayed in the bath for longer than necessary. She wouldn't apologize for it. Nor did she suffer any guilt for the no-doubt terrifying plumbing repairs the body paint might cause.

Her hair needed help, however. The Scarsea shaved theirs off save for small strategic sections, but most Deepers took a different approach. No doubt a healthy part of the "troll" legend came from the tradition of matting hair into locks and weaving leaves and plants into the strands. Anahrod could testify from personal experience it worked splendidly as camouflage in the jungles of the Deep.

It would be the opposite of camouflage in Seven Crests.

Last she knew, local Crystalspire fashion preferred layers of neat braids pinned close to the scalp to form intricate patterns—that had certainly been true of Gwydinion's hair. Not something she could do herself.

Anahrod changed into her mismatched outfit, a combed doeynd ivory shirt with cloud violet–gray wool trousers and a lighter gray mantle woven with white and blue strands. The ivory shirt was nicer than she would've liked, decorated with Crystalspire's distinctive smocking. She twisted her hair out of the way until she could figure out what to do about it.

Anahrod had just finished dressing when a man entered the room.

She didn't recognize him. He was a handsome man in his early fifties, with dark brown skin and curly black hair streaked with silver. His tailored clothing lacked the ostentatious detailing Anahrod associated with the wealthiest citizens of Crystalspire, but the shimmering silk mantle he wore draped around his shoulders left little doubt he came from money. As did the two guards who hurried in after him, halberds in hand. Mid-level merchants rarely afforded or needed bodyguards.

The man came to an abrupt halt when he saw Anahrod, nostrils flaring and a look of unquenched fury in his eyes. There was recognition there, although of what she couldn't tell.

He spun on a heel and pointed to the door.

"I told you to wait outside," he said to the guards.

Anahrod stepped backward, putting a small, tiled table between them. The spin had shifted the man's mantle enough for her to see the chain of office around his neck. Actually, the movement had betrayed two things normally hidden under the man's mantle: it had also revealed a sword.

Anahrod wondered if he could use it.

The mayor's presence made her gut tighten: all her attempts to calm herself vanished under the weight of his appearance.

"Sir? But we—" Anahrod almost laughed at the scandalized look on the guard's face as he gestured toward her. Anahrod wasn't even tied up, after all.

A troll might do anything.

"Wait. Outside," the mayor repeated. "Don't make me say it again."

The two guards retreated, leaving Anahrod alone with the mayor. She inventoried any object in the room useful as a weapon. A shocking number of potential candidates were within easy reach: a hand mirror, the soap dish, an incense burner. Even one of the small side tables.

He wasn't the predator in the room; she was.

His jaw worked against his throat, the anger still sharp and cutting as he ground his teeth.

"Have they told you why you're here?" he asked like he already knew the answer.

"No, I imagine they didn't want to spoil the surprise."

He only scowled harder. Then he unbuckled his belt.

Anahrod reached for the soap dish.

But he wasn't removing his trousers; just the belt, or rather, just his sword. He wrapped the belt around the scabbard and tossed the result on the table in front of Anahrod.

She stared at the weapon. It wasn't a Skylander style, for all that such weapons hadn't been popular in the Skylands for decades. This was a gently curving blade, and very familiar.

Mostly because it was her sword.

"That's a well-made weapon," the man told her. "From the Fire Peaks?"

Her smile turned bittersweet. "The boy who gave it to me claimed it was from Viridhaven." A ridiculous notion. The sword was too new, too well made. Any weapons from the real Viridhaven would be, oh, copper or bronze or something, made in an age before they'd learned to use inscriptions to make fires hot enough to forge steel or titanium.

The mayor raised both eyebrows, as though he actually believed her. "Must have been expensive. It would be a shame if you lost it." He walked over to the window.

Anahrod picked up her scabbard. Now she had a weapon and he didn't, after sending his guards away. He was either very arrogant or very confident of his own abilities. Possibly both.

"Thank you?" She had no idea how to react.

The man turned his back to her as he felt around the edges of the window trim. "My wife taught me this trick," he muttered. "It's a safety precaution. In case of fire, you know."

"Mind explaining what's going on?"

A small, neat click sound came from the window. The whole stone grate swung open on a hidden hinge. The mayor nodded in satisfaction.

"Scales," he muttered. "You're going to need money . . ." He reached into his coat.

"Mayor," Anahrod said loudly. "What are you doing? And *why*?"

He glanced over then. He still looked angry, but there was a hint of something else in his furrowed brow.

"We have little time," he told her. "Not much at all. My people can only keep that dragonrider distracted for so long."

"Explain it anyway," she told him.

He swallowed, gave the tiniest shake of his head. "They're looking for Anahrod Amnead."

She held herself still. "I see." Suddenly she wished she hadn't taken the bath, hadn't cleaned off the mud. Accusing a green-skinned woman of being a Skylander was a far more ludicrous proposition than what was currently happening.

"That's why—"

"And who is that?" she asked.

The man's eyes widened. "You don't know who—?" His gaze flitted about the room, as if searching for the right person, who would no doubt pop up from behind a curtain any minute now. "But you—you have to—" He floundered.

"Who is this person?" she asked again, more sharply. "Some criminal?"

"Yes." His eyebrows drew together before he pulled himself up, stood straighter. He fell short of commanding, landing instead in the territory of confused. "She was from Crystalspire. My son . . ." He gritted his teeth, looked away. "Eannis help me, I thought I'd raised him better than this. My son wanted to help me by bringing her back."

Her stomach crumpled into something small and tight and painful. "Your son—" The answer was obvious enough. His son took after him, at least in appearance. "Gwydinion."

"Yes. I'm—Eannis. You don't even know who I am, do you? I'm Aiden e'Doreyl, and—"

Something ugly crawled along her spine. He looked so uncomfortable, and she recognized what that other emotion might be: guilt.

Her heartbeat quickened. She glanced down at the sword, then back at him. "What," she asked, "do you want from me?"

"Nothing. Truly. But you have to understand: a little over three weeks ago, a dragon interrupted my son's birthday party to tell us that Anahrod Amnead was still alive. That we'd all been part of some conspiracy to fake her death and we had a month to turn her over to the dragons or face their wrath."

Every muscle in Anahrod's body clenched. A giant wave of bitter anger washed over her; the world spun.

The boy she'd liked so much had played her for a fool more effectively than any of Ris's flirting. Not that Ris was absolved. It appeared that both were comfortable delivering a stranger to their execution.

The thought shouldn't have upset her as much as it did. She'd long since grown used to the idea that Skylanders were capable of the most vile perfidies. She knew they couldn't be trusted.

She'd let down her guard. Let down her guard, helped her kidnappers, survived the Deep—hell, she'd even confirmed her identity to them, hadn't she? That little anecdote about her second mother engineering a rival's embarrassment would have been as good as a confession to anyone familiar enough with Crystalspire politics—and the boy was the mayor's son. No wonder he'd thought it so funny.

The Crystalspire mayor was too busy grappling with his own issues to notice hers. "My son overheard my wife and I discussing our options and decided that the obvious solution was to travel to the Deep and bring back, well, *you*. I am . . . appalled. Truly, I know my apology means less than nothing, but you have it. A hundred times over, you have it."

In other circumstances, she might have laughed.

"So, what are you doing now? Helping me escape?" Anahrod's hand tightened on the sword hilt. She wasn't seriously considering drawing on the man, but it was a nervous habit. "Why would you do that? That's not in your best interests."

Aiden e'Doreyl pulled a large leather pouch from his coat and tossed it to the table. "I refuse to send an innocent person to their death just because the dragons waved a tail in this city's direction."

An innocent person. Anahrod blinked at the words. Was it possible that the man didn't think she was really Anahrod? She couldn't imagine him walking into that room and offering her a weapon along with enough money to book passage away from Seven Crests otherwise. No, he thought his son had dragged back a sacrificial yearling, someone guilty of nothing more than having the wrong name and bad luck.

Although, that last part was still true.

Zavad's dick, how had Crystalspire politics not eaten this man alive?

She glanced down at his silver rings. She didn't remember how to interpret the garden rings—she'd been too young to have any when she'd been tossed into the Deep—but the social rings were obvious enough: male, both by birth and inclination; in a committed, monogamous relationship; extroverted. No doubt he was a hugger and always offered to pay for lunch.

Anahrod buckled the scabbard around herself. She was used to carrying her sword across her back, because traveling through the Deep was easier that way, but at her waist would draw less attention in the Skylands.

"My son meant well, but—" The man shuddered. "I only see three options here. I can hand you over to the dragons, healthy and alive, and spend the rest of my life pretending my son didn't kidnap a woman just so I could send her to her death. I could hand them a corpse—woah!" He flinched as her sword blade appeared under his nose. "That was . . . fast. That was very fast." A thin sheen of sweat broke out along his hairline. "Not *your* corpse," he elaborated. "Someone else's—but even if I could find a dead body, there's no guarantee the dragons wouldn't have a way to tell if I was lying or if it's really yours. I mean, if it's really hers. Her body. Anahrod Amnead's body."

She lowered her sword but didn't put it away. "And the third option?"

"Oh, I'm so sorry, Lord Tiendremos," the man said in a mocking imitation of sincerity. "We found her, just like you ordered, but she was just so wicked and full of guile that she escaped immediately. But we did do what you asked."

"Don't recommend you try to win an argument with a dragon using soph- istry. You won't like their rebuttal." There was also the matter of how the mayor would be the very first person questioned by the dragons about the manner of her "escape." The man—what had he said his name was? Aiden?—was still sign- ing a different death warrant: his own.

He had to know the consequences.

"Let me take care of those details," he ordered. "You take care of making sure they don't catch you."

Anahrod grabbed her bags from the closet. As she did, the door opened a second time.

Ris walked into the room.

9

THE DRAGONRIDER

The red-haired woman wasn't dressed for jungle hikes this time, but then again, she hadn't been last time, either. She wore a scarlet wool coat, slim-fitting to emphasize a small waist. The coat flared out again at the hips. A darker red broadcloth shirt peeked out from underneath, worn over tight farul-skin leather pants and tall leather boots. Lace spilled from the sleeves. Her hair was pulled away from her face, fastened with a set of gold pins, and allowed to fall free behind her—a dragonrider hairstyle. Crystals in her ears chimed when she moved, matching a similar set of links around her hips, just visible through the gap in her coat.

Ris wasn't wearing her sword, but Anahrod wasn't naïve enough to think that meant she was unarmed.

Ris met her stare with a smile on lips redder than any of her clothing, shiny and freshly licked. Mocking delight shone from her green eyes.

It took all of Anahrod's will not to draw her sword.

"I see he told you." Ris wagged a finger at the mayor. "You and I will have words about this later, Mayor e'Doreyl. For now, take your men and leave."

The mayor turned to Anahrod like he was about to apologize.

"Please go," Anahrod said. "And tell your son—"

The words lodged in her throat, sharp and dry as the air. What would she say? That she was disappointed? That she hoped he burned in the Deep a thousand years?

She was only upset because she was on the receiving end of his betrayal. Would she have made a different decision in his place? She wasn't so naïve as to think she'd be anywhere near as noble as Aiden e'Doreyl in a similar situation.

She shook her head. "Just tell him to be careful out there."

"Of course." He threw Ris one last look of dread and then all but ran for the door.

He didn't close the door behind himself, but it clicked shut all the same, moving in time to a wave of Ris's hand. She hadn't taken her eyes off of Anahrod, not for one single second.

"I have no idea what the people of Crystalspire were thinking, electing an honest man to the position of mayor. Nothing but trouble." Ris walked over to a cabinet, pulled out a bottle of wine, and poured herself a glass. "If you're planning to attack me, reconsider. You're far too lovely to damage, but if you make me prove just how unwise violence would be, anything might happen."

"I'll keep that in mind," Anahrod said.

She was unlikely to have a better opportunity, however. Ris would expect Anahrod to listen to the other woman's explanation before trying something. That would be the rational thing to do.

So Anahrod did something else.

She never saw Ris's reaction; it happened that fast. The hard tiled floor slammed into Anahrod's back. Her feet were bound by—something. It felt like rope, but she suspected otherwise. Anahrod couldn't see her legs, though, because after throwing her to the floor, Ris followed. She drove all the air from Anahrod's lungs as she landed. Ris planted one knee on Anahrod's chest, painfully close to her neck, and the other knee on Anahrod's sword arm.

The ghost of her old teacher, Carvyx, would've been hurling mud clods at Anahrod in disappointment.

Ris smirked, then leaned over enough to scoop the wine bottle off the ground. "It didn't break! Lucky me."

Ris pulled out the cork with her teeth and took a big swallow. "What were we talking about? Oh yes. What you have to lose." Ris seemed more playful than angry. "Since I might be falling in love with you, I'll give you a serious answer."

Anahrod continued glaring, which amused Ris, who took another swig of wine. She didn't care that it was morning or that she'd spilled a drop of red wine to trace a path down her chin and neck.

Ris continued: "You have nothing to lose—assuming we were planning to kill you. But since we're not, well. Your health, your life, your freedom." She paused. "Your eventual freedom. So, in reality, you have a great deal to lose. One might argue: everything."

Anahrod couldn't trust her. She certainly couldn't believe her. She concentrated on breathing while she strained against whatever Ris had used to bind her legs.

"Eventual freedom," Anahrod said. "Do you deny that my choice means nothing? That you're going to force me to do—whatever it is you want from me—regardless of how I feel?" She still had one arm free, but throwing a punch just then felt less "unexpected" than "supremely foolish." She watched Ris take another drink.

Ris's grip on the wine bottle also gave Anahrod an excellent view of Ris's garden rings. It was the same jewelry the woman had worn in the Deep: finely made gold, delicate, expensive. Had no one ever explained that it was bad luck to wear gold jewelry? Zavad hoarded gold, and so to wear gold was to draw the evil dragon's attention.

Other than the obvious—flowers and leaves on her rings meant she preferred both feminine and masculine partners—Anahrod couldn't interpret specifics.

Ris noticed Anahrod staring and lowered the bottle partway. "Were you old enough to have picked out rings when they tossed you off that cutter?"

"Stop acting like you're helping me," Anahrod spat. The thin ribbon of wine had dried against Ris's skin, stark in contrast. Anahrod wondered how it would taste, and just as rapidly shoved that thought away.

"I *am* helping you." Ris wiggled her fingers. "I'm sure you had most of your social rings, but garden rings? You couldn't have been more than fifteen. That's too young. You couldn't have picked out your garden rings yet."

Anahrod didn't answer, which she knew Ris interpreted as "yes."

"We'll have to find you a set," Ris said. "Once you figure out your preferences. I'd be happy to go into what mine mean if you like. Maybe even give you a demonstration."

"Which ring means you like doing this?" Anahrod gestured—as much as she could, anyway—toward where Ris perched on top of her body.

Ris's smile turned, for just a second, into a guileless grin. "Why, none of them. This is work, not play." She bit her lower lip, a teasing pull of flesh through her teeth, recorked the wine bottle, and set it aside, out of Anahrod's reach.

Ris bent lower, until her face was mere inches from Anahrod's. "I wear jasmine. You're thinking of roses." She stayed there for an eternally long moment, too close, not nearly close enough.

Then the moment was over, and Ris straightened. She also stopped smiling. "Now, for this next bit, you're going to behave yourself. Because if you don't, I will break all your limbs and then let Claw work on her knife skills. Do we understand each other?"

Maybe Anahrod was taking the wrong approach. Anahrod didn't trust the dragonrider. She sure as hell wasn't about to play along with whatever game she was pushing.

But there was no reason to make that so obvious.

So what Anahrod said was: "You always say the nicest things."

Ris moved her leg, until the knee wasn't on Anahrod's chest anymore, but about to press into her throat. "Let me rephrase that." In a less friendly tone, she repeated, "Do we understand each other?" Her eyes had that same look she'd seen down in the Deep when Ris had confronted Claw—an endless ferocity, bordering on madness.

Anahrod inhaled. Flirting aside, Ris was a serious threat. She'd already proven that she'd win in a fair fight, with the definition of "fair fight" being that Ris was conscious. Ris hadn't even used her sword, and Anahrod had been *armed*.

"Yes," Anahrod said. "We understand each other."

"Good." Ris stood up, then offered Anahrod a hand. She seemed reluctant to let go of it afterward.

The two women both stood there, eyeing each other. The tension climbed higher, as though a second round of fighting were seconds from breaking out.

Ris had spoken one truth: if she'd wanted Anahrod dead, Ris had had plenty of opportunities to make that desire real. Her long-term motives were suspect, but for now, Ris wasn't interested in killing Anahrod.

Anahrod turned her back on the woman and settled into a chair by the now-open window, where she could enjoy the view. "But do you intend to feed me?"

Ris chuckled. "Of course. One moment." She stuck her head out the door and said something to whoever stood outside. When she returned, she said, "Naeron's bringing breakfast. Which Kaibren made himself, I should add, so there's no danger of some well-intentioned local who's watched too many plays about 'Anahrod the Wicked' getting any ideas."

Anahrod clenched her jaw. "Anahrod the Wicked?"

Ris threw herself into a chair sideways, putting her legs up over the arm. Given the fight (if it could even be called such) they'd just had, it struck Anahrod as mocking. A dare.

Ris waved a hand. "Sure. They've written plays. Some aren't even that bad."

Anahrod closed her eyes. Eannis. She'd always known that the gossips must have had a banner day with her. But the idea that the gossip had turned into stories, plays, that she was everyone's newest favorite cautionary tale? The news left a foul taste in her mouth.

"And why—" Anahrod stopped and stared out the window at the far-off mountains.

Ris patiently waited.

"You know who I am," Anahrod said.

"Haven't we established that?" Ris raised an eyebrow. "I couldn't have found you, otherwise, but the world? The world needs to think you're some poor, unfortunate woman from the Deep with the bad luck to share the same name as a very naughty criminal. You couldn't possibly be the real Anahrod. That would be silly. She died seventeen years ago."

Anahrod turned around to stare at Ris in disbelief.

"Let me—" She tried to calm her heartbeat and started over. "Am I really understanding this correctly? You kidnapped me and brought me here because you want me to *pretend that I'm pretending* to be Anahrod Amnead?"

Her grin was dazzling. "I knew you'd catch on."

Anahrod rubbed her forehead. "Why?"

"Real answer?"

"Sure. Why not? Let's be different for once." She banged her fist on the armrest. "Of course I want you to give me the real answer!"

Ris grinned amiably. "It's because the dragon Tiendremos needs to think you're Anahrod Amnead. The real Anahrod Amnead."

Anahrod lowered her fist. "Unfortunate, since that's something I'd never be fool enough to admit in front of one of the dragons *that wants to kill Anahrod Amnead.*"

"I understand why you might think that, but shockingly, Tiendremos doesn't want to kill you. I've convinced him you're too valuable."

Anahrod reined her temper back in with great effort. ". . . He's Neveranimas's right hand. Why would he possibly think that? And why . . ." She inhaled deeply. "Again, *why the deception?* Wouldn't it be simpler to just *say* I really *am* Anahrod Amnead?"

Ris pulled her legs around so that she was sitting right side up again and leaned her elbows against the table. "Simpler, yes. Better, no. I'm thinking long term here. What happens when people start hearing that Anahrod the Wicked is once again stalking the streets of Crystalspire? What happens when people start demanding that someone do something? On a good day, you'd be chased out of Seven Crests."

"On a good day, I had no intention of ever coming back."

"There's a difference between 'don't want to' and 'can't,'" Ris pointed out. "I would prefer to give you options. You deserve to have a choice."

That stopped her.

Did she really want to believe Ris was doing this to *help* her?

Yes, she wanted to believe. That didn't mean Anahrod did.

"How did you find me, anyway?"

"Oh, I had a little help from your warlord friend." Ris pulled a piece of folded-up paper from her coat and tossed it to Anahrod.

Anahrod unfolded the paper and cursed.

It was a reward poster, with a woodcut illustration stamped in the center. Sicaryon had put out a reward for her capture—alive—to the sum of five thousand scales.

Centered under the drawing was her name: Anahrod.

10

A FUNNY WAY OF SAYING YES

Naeron's arrival with food distracted Anahrod from the poster. The man gave Anahrod a small, apologetic smile, and backed away from the table hastily when she glared in response. He looked hurt.

That man had a lot of gall.

"Don't be like that," Ris said, after Naeron left. "He likes you."

"Clearly." That must have been why he'd knocked Anahrod unconscious in the Bay of Bones: feelings of camaraderie and friendship.

Anahrod thought about rejecting the offered food for approximately half a second before she pulled her chair back to the table. She'd spent too many years living on what she could catch, steal, or harvest to turn down free food.

Kaibren had put together a nice, if simple, spread. He'd made a thick soup of meat stock and root vegetables, served with a side of jaeld leaves, sliced thin and pickled in spicy vinegar. There was also a rich black bread, cultured butter, a soft white cheese rolled in ash, and a side of sweet golden plum jam with the raw fruit spread out around it decoratively.

Ris raised an eyebrow. "No demanding that I eat first? No worries that we might poison you?"

Anahrod poured a mug of tea. "If you wanted me dead, I'd be dead."

"How unexpectedly reasonable of you."

"Don't get used to it." Anahrod's fingers paused at the sliced golden plums before continuing on to the bread and cheese. The plums were raw—which meant they were inedible, both in terms of nutrition and taste.

Anahrod didn't talk while eating, while Ris seemed content to watch her instead of making conversation. It gave Anahrod a few valuable minutes to contemplate her situation.

Ris had mentioned Tiendremos. Anahrod knew that dragon, or at least, she knew of that dragon. One of Neveranimas's claw-licking peons. Powerful, big, but apparently not as loyal as Anahrod had always assumed. Because—if Ris was telling the truth—Tiendremos didn't want his boss knowing what he was up to.

She didn't trust it, and no matter what Ris said about her motives, Anahrod didn't trust her either.

Anahrod's skill with a sword wouldn't help her. As fast as she was on the draw, Ris was faster with magic.

But Anahrod knew magic, too.

While she ate, Anahrod reached out with her mind.

There had to be something bigger than a scrabber in a city as large as Crystalspire. Humans were social creatures who included animals in their web of loyalties. Anywhere one might find large gatherings of people, one also found large gatherings of animals. Placid pack animals. Small, adorable pets. Animals to move goods and people, and to provide milk, leather, and food.

Up above them on the mountain ice, a silver-ridged hunting drake roamed. They shared part of their name with Overbite's kin, but were much smaller. As the name implied, their speed and ferocity made them fantastic hunters—lightning fast, with razor-sharp talons capable of disemboweling a man.

That would do. She whispered a mental apology to the drake: it was unlikely to survive what happened next.

Anahrod glanced up. "What does Peralon hoard?"

"That's a very personal question."

"I'm just wondering what you're trying to accomplish here. What your dragon wants."

Ris cocked her head to the side. "Don't you mean what Tiendremos wants?"

"No. What he wants doesn't matter."

Ris straightened, interested. "Why would you say that?"

"Because of this." Anahrod tapped the wanted poster. "If Tiendremos had known about this, he'd have gone to the Deep and made his demands down there. At best, you're not sharing all your information with him. Just as likely, he doesn't know you and Peralon are involved in this at all. Either way, his opinion doesn't matter."

Ris grinned and clapped her hands together. "Oh, you're smart! Nobody told me you're smart!" She chuckled. "Wrong on a couple of points, but still—smart."

"Just tell me what the game is. What does Peralon want?"

She smiled fondly. "You have it backward. It's what I want."

Anahrod found that hard to believe. Dragons seldom indulged their riders' whims. "What do you want, then?"

Ris curled a lock of red hair around a finger. "Oh, you know. The usual."

Anahrod squinted at her. "Money?"

Ris threw her head back and laughed. For just a moment, something else peeked out from behind those exotic green eyes. That darker side of Ris who lurked behind all her cheerful masks.

"No." Ris let the smile fall from her face. "The oldest motive there is."

"Love" flashed into Anahrod's mind and was dismissed as quickly. Some instinct inside her whispered that the oldest motive in the world was far less sweet.

"Revenge," Anahrod said.

Surprise flicked across the woman's face. "People usually guess love."

"People are usually fools."

The two women stared at each other. Anahrod moved around the table, in Ris's direction. She raised a hand, as if to touch the woman's cheek. Ris leaned forward.

Ris said: "You already met the rest of the team, but tonight we'll—"

Anahrod channeled power from the silver-ridged hunting drake and struck.

This time, she caught Ris by surprise.

Anahrod pushed Ris against the wall with one hand, and with her other, set a handful of razor-sharp talons against her throat.

The talons weren't real. Rather, a golden outline of talons surrounded her hands like oversized gloves. Phantom as the energy seemed, however, the magical copies were every bit as sharp as the real thing. Just as capable of ripping someone's throat out.

"Don't scream," Anahrod ordered.

"Are you sure? I've been told my screams are lovely." Ris was still going for suggestive and flirty, but her heart wasn't in it.

Anahrod frowned. "If you try to cast a spell or call your sword, you'll be dead before you can finish."

Ris exhaled, and then nodded.

"Good girl." Anahrod watched the door and waited.

"I didn't know you could do that." Despite the claws at Ris's throat, she didn't look scared. No. Anahrod corrected herself. She wasn't scared. She was intrigued and excited, but not scared.

"We're all made of secrets." Anahrod continued looking toward the door. Continued waiting.

"You think someone's watching the room?" Ris wiggled a little under her touch, but nothing more. Yet. "Okay, yes. I was watching the room. No one else. Nobody's coming."

"Why not? Nothing's stopping you from telling your dragon exactly what's going on here." Anahrod's gaze slipped for a moment, down the length of Ris's body. She reminded herself to focus.

"Absolutely," Ris agreed. "If only he wasn't a two-hour flight from here."

Anahrod raised an eyebrow. If Ris claimed he was two hours away, he was probably five minutes away, and flying for speed to make it back in three.

Ris pulled her metaphorical feet back under her. "You're really running?"

"If my options are being executed for crimes I didn't commit or becoming a dragon's puppet, I pick 'neither.'"

"Neither works for me, too."

"So says a dragon's slave."

"Ouch." Ris grimaced. "Dragonriders aren't—" A spark of fire and frustration crossed her eyes. "We're not *slaves*."

"Lucky you. You chanced upon one of the 'good' dragons, the ones that take care of their little pets. Catch him on a bad day and disobey him. See where that takes you."

"We respect each other. Complement each—"

"Save it." Anahrod lifted Ris's chin with a claw. "Dragons don't see us as equals. We're slaves, we're pets, we're *things*. As far as they're concerned, our only purpose is to keep them from going rampant. What *we* want doesn't matter."

"It doesn't have to be that way," Ris whispered.

Anahrod felt sorry for her. She must have been new at this, still giddy at the idea she'd been chosen. She hadn't realized that any power she would ever have in that relationship was at the dragon's discretion—and they could reclaim that power at any time.

"Don't move," Anahrod told her, pressing the claw under Ris's chin to emphasize how she wasn't playing around.

She patted the woman down, feeling at her coat pockets and around her hips until she found the bag of scales—all two hundred—that she'd originally promised. They'd made a deal, after all. She tucked that into her belt and kept searching, lifting a dagger. No sword—or at least no sword that Anahrod found. There were limits to how thoroughly she could search a woman while keeping one hand clamped around her neck.

Anahrod suspected what the jasmine flowers on Ris's garden rings meant. Delicate, fragile—sweetest when bruised. It wasn't hard to imagine—far too easy, in fact—how tantalizing that creamy flesh would look, marked with purple and blue.

Even if Anahrod had never gained her own rings, she knew her preferences. Just stupid bad luck it was never meant to be.

Anahrod sighed. "I wish we'd met under different stars."

"Fair. I am very cute."

Anahrod didn't move her face closer, no matter how badly she wanted to. Ris struck her as a woman who was not above a good headbutt. "No. You aren't."

Ris threw her a hurt look.

"Not even the tiniest bit cute," Anahrod said as she leaned in close but to the side, so she was whispering in the other woman's ear. "What you are is the most exquisite person I have ever seen. And I believe you."

"You do?" Ris whispered. "Wait. You do?"

"Yes." Anahrod leaned back, again avoiding any obvious opportunities for a turnabout. She eyed the drapery pulls. Those might work. If only Ris wouldn't slice herself free in seconds. "I bet your screams are like music."

Ris shivered. It wasn't fear.

Anahrod could've knocked her unconscious, choked her, but she wasn't Naeron: there was no method Anahrod might use that didn't hold a chance of serious injury.

When she'd drawn her sword on Ris, she'd only been hoping to threaten her. Anahrod may have had her reservations about dragonriders, but she wasn't foolish enough to deliberately hurt one.

She'd seen what happened when someone broke a dragon's toys. But maybe violence wasn't the only solution.

"Strip," Anahrod said.

Ris gave her a surprised look.

"Take off your clothes," Anahrod elaborated. "And while I'm sure you could make it a wonderful show, I have places to be, so hurry."

Her eyes widened in faux innocence. "Why, Anahrod. You are full of surprises." She began unbuttoning her coat. Slowly.

"Remember that I warned you." Anahrod put her unchanneled hand around Ris's neck. The woman's eyes all but rolled back in her head.

"Don't move," Anahrod ordered, "or I'll hurt you."

"What—"

Anahrod hooked a claw under the woman's shirt and yanked. The smooth, dull front side of the drake's claw slid harmlessly against bare skin, while the sharp underside sliced through the fabric, lace, and leather like water. Four cuts. One down each arm, then one long pull down the center, sliding to the side, down first one leg, then the other. Her claws caught briefly on the crystal belt, but Anahrod yanked until the thin gold links snapped.

The result was Ris pressed up against the wall, wearing nothing but shreds of leather tucked into boots. Anahrod didn't look down again.

It was a view she didn't have permission to see.

"Roses," Anahrod said. "You said I was thinking of roses earlier?"

Ris nodded. She was leaning into Anahrod's hold on her throat, her eyes heavy-lidded with desire. "Yes. Eannis, yes."

Anahrod released the drake's claws. From a great distance, she felt their owner collapse in the snow. She might not have killed him immediately, but she'd left him too weak to fight off other predators. His fate was sealed. With her newly freed hand, she picked up the bag of scales the mayor had left her.

"If I had rings," Anahrod told Ris, "they'd be roses."

Ris closed her eyes for a moment, then blinked suddenly awake. "What? You can't just say that and walk away. Take some responsibility!"

"Here's to hoping you were telling the truth about not wanting to kill me. I'd prefer to remember you fondly."

The woman made a distressed sound. "That's so unfair!"

"Tell it to the mountains." Anahrod ran a finger across the edge of the woman's jaw. "Like I said: I wish we'd met under different stars."

Anahrod dove for the window.

MAGNITUDES OF RISK

Anahrod wrapped her hair up in her mantle as she headed to the docks. People would think it odd, but not nearly as much as her uncovered hair—cleaner and less green, but still knotted in vine braids.

The docks had changed little over the years. Crowded and loud, filled with people—a place to be invisible, hiding in the human herd. At any hour, people and cargo from the huge, winged merchant cutters were arriving or departing. Enterprising merchants set up small stands next to the boarding planks, offering discounts on merchandise they didn't want to haul back home. People from every city in Seven Crests went about their day, whether that was business or meeting friends—genuine or rented by the hour.

Anahrod barely glanced at the big, fat-winged ferry as she walked by it. A long line to board stretched into the street, all waiting to be taken to the next city in the mountain chain: Duskcloud. If they stayed on from there, they'd go to Grayshroud, then to Rosecliff, Windsong, Blackglass, and finally, Snowfell. There was no easier or faster way to leave Crystalspire in a hurry.

Or rather, there was no easier or faster way to leave Crystalspire if one didn't have the help of a dragon.

Since Ris had the help of a dragon, Anahrod wouldn't make it easy for her.

A dragon roared.

She paused, the old instincts kicking into focus. A very large dragon, near the edge of the city itself.

Anahrod turned to look. Everyone did.

Several people helpfully pointed farther up the mountainside, although given how far up Crystalspire was located, there wasn't much "farther up" that wasn't the dragon crèche itself.

Aldegon was a white dragon, with violet shading and amethyst eyes. This was someone new. Not Tiendremos—that beast of a dragon was a dark blue color.

This dragon was the color of molten gold.

"Speak of Zavad, and Zavad appears," Anahrod murmured.

This was Peralon—and Anahrod had been right to distrust Ris's assurance that her dragon was two hours away.

Eannis, he was beautiful, though.

An unlucky color, perhaps, but almost blinding in his glory, sunlight reflecting off his scales. The chattering crowd around her gossiped this dragon was new, although a few were quick to correct the tale. Yes, the dragon was new, but he'd visited earlier that morning, arriving in the hours before dawn.

Anahrod felt the old tension, the quickening of her heartbeat, the sense of awe. As a child, she'd been a lot like Gwydinion, wanting to be bonded to her own dragon. It had been her dream.

Well, no. It had been one of her mother's dreams, but Anahrod hadn't figured out the difference until it was almost too late.

The dragon let out another roar before launching himself airborne, flying up and out over the city on swift, sure wingbeats. As he soared overhead, Anahrod thought she saw a rider. She couldn't be sure: the dragon was too far away to make out details. Still, Anahrod assumed Ris had wasted no time changing clothes.

Anahrod whipped her head away from staring at the fading shape and instead took advantage of the distraction to slip through the crowd. She bought breakfast from a random cart, exchanging one of her scales into smaller Crystalspire coinage.

The second purchase she made—the most expensive purchase—was a set of rings. She might easily have exhausted the rest of her money had she gone to a proper metalsmith for platinum rings, but she needed nothing so fancy.

So instead, she found one of those shops where one might sell a precious item in return for quick money; where another might buy that same item for far less than its worth. It limited her options, but guaranteed nothing on her fingers would look new or expensive.

She barely remembered what social rings meant, let alone garden rings. She'd been Gwydinion's age—fifteen—when she'd gone to Yagra'hai, and while some of her classmates had been precociously interested in what rings they might one day wear, she had not.

Fortunately, since most young people eventually found themselves at a point in their development where they wanted garden rings but weren't sure which rings they needed (and would die of mortification if they had to ask their parents), guidebooks were easy to find. Little portable tracts one might consult to prevent embarrassing gaffes. She'd made up an elaborate story about buying one for a little brother before she realized no one cared.

The social rings were easy enough. Those were more limited in scope, the hardest part being the career ring. She ended up choosing a blood crow ring, both for the sake of irony and because "scavenger" allowed her the easiest excuse to explain why she wanted to switch to a different career.

The garden rings were trickier. She didn't expect to find her preferences for sale at a pawnshop, and in this she wasn't disappointed.

As she had no wish to claim a particular love of feet nor a true passion for mountains quite above and beyond what most people meant when they exclaimed, "I love mountains!" Anahrod settled on something inaccurate but plausible. Masculine partners only, monogamous, and in an exclusive relationship. Not much interested in sex at all. Common as gruel for breakfast, and wrong on every count. The hardest part was finding a set that wasn't silver tarnished to the point of blackness, but she settled on white gold and nickel steel.

After that, she could talk to people without concealing her hands. Anahrod then went shopping, this time with more vigor. She made quick purchases: a water canteen, basic provisions, cooking equipment, and a satchel to store them all in.

Clothing proved the greatest obstacle, since even in a city as large as Crystalspire few places existed where one might buy premade fashions. She could waste hours—if not days—sorting through castaways at a frippery stall.

So Anahrod cheated. She found a woman who was both her size and dressed appropriately and offered the woman five scales to exchange clothes with her. Anahrod claimed it was for a scavenger hunt, and dropped enough names from important banking divisions to lead the other woman to believe Anahrod might be some spoiled daughter of privilege, dressing up as one of the middle class because aren't rich people so eccentric? The young businesswoman haggled her way up to ten scales and then they ducked into a guesthouse to make the exchange.

There were two awkward parts.

The first came when the mantle Anahrod had wrapped around her head slipped, revealing her hair. The other woman had immediately commented on the style.

Anahrod ran a hand down one of the vine braids. "I just had them done. It's a surprise for the party next week. My mother's going to hate it." She grinned at the woman as if sharing a juicy secret.

The other woman pursed her lips. "I think it's a good look. I rather like it." She sounded surprised.

Anahrod nodded. "Mark my words: everyone's going to be wearing their hair this way in a year."

The second moment was when the woman had introduced herself as Jiedre, and then asked Anahrod's name. She'd at least given some thought to the matter, so she didn't hesitate to say, "Anah."

But she wasn't prepared for the woman's reaction.

"*Please* tell me your parents didn't name you Anahrod."

"Excuse me?"

She nodded emphatically. "I have a friend who has that name, and she had to petition to have it changed, because no one wanted to buy from an 'Anahrod.'" The woman shuddered. "Bad luck, you know?"

Anahrod forced a smile onto her face. "It's just Anah, praise Eannis."

The woman left after that, both convinced that she'd taken shameless advantage of Anahrod and possibly on her way to a beauty salon. Anahrod hoped so: it would be hilarious if vine braids became a fad just as Ris and/or Tiendremos were searching the city for a woman with that same hairstyle.

Not that Anahrod had any intention of remaining. She tried not to think about what that woman had said about her friend—that just having the name Anahrod was bad luck.

She had to know.

Anahrod ducked into a bookseller's shop and asked what books they might have concerning Anahrod the Wicked. The nearsighted old man didn't seem to think her request was odd; he just creaked to his feet and made his way into a back room, returning with five different clothbound books of middling quality. As the man spoke, she became motionless, her head tilted to one side, her breath caught in her chest, listening as he described how Anahrod Amnead had been a villainess of the first rank.

"Dead now, of course," he said, smiling gently.

"How . . ." She licked her lips. "How long ago was this?"

"Oh, I don't know," the man replied. "Twenty years? You'd have been a child." He squinted at her, trying to gauge her age. "Maybe not even born yet." He set a hand on top of the books. "You look old enough, anyway. They're garden books, you know. Not for children." He grinned. "Some of my best sellers, though."

"I'll take that one," she said, and pointed to one book at random, not because she wanted it, but so she wouldn't stand out.

Anahrod didn't open the book, afterward. She didn't want to see who'd written it, who'd published it, who'd profited from spreading titillating lies about her life.

Several blocks away, she tossed the book into a sewer.

As she'd done her shopping, she'd been amazed by how little had changed. The fashions, perhaps. The coats that had once flared out from the shoulders now fitted close to the torso. Some of the fabrics were unfamiliar to her, either made with techniques she'd never seen before or dyed in new, brighter colors. Her new mantle, for example, was a soft teal doeynd wool, interwoven with fibers of green and silver—all new dyes, either sourced from new trading partners or invented by some industrious chemist in Grayshroud.

But other things hadn't changed at all. Most skin colors were still Skylander dark, but Ris was hardly the only pale-hued person in the city. It mattered not, because regardless of one's skin tone, hair, or eye color, Crystalspire citizenship was recognized by a trait harder to counterfeit: arrogance. The pride and ostentation that Crystalspire was famous for demonstrated itself with every upturned nose and dismissive eye roll. Crystalspire's citizens were better, richer, and more successful than those of any other city in Seven Crests.

They knew it. They made sure everyone else knew it, too.

She told herself that she hadn't missed Crystalspire, didn't miss Crystalspire, wouldn't miss Crystalspire. This was the city that had betrayed her. Leaving it would be a pleasure.

She knew herself for a liar. She missed the noise and the crowds and the smell of honeyplum tea sold from food carts near the marketplace. She missed the water splashing on her as she sat at the edge of Oelvond Fountain. She missed sneaking up to the manor's roof in the early hours of the morning to watch the giant sky cutters fly into port and listen to Aldegon's suitors croon love songs from the cliff tops overlooking the city. She missed turning up a fur-lined collar against winter winds so cold they felt like sharpened glass against her skin. She missed her second mother's cooking.

She didn't miss the lies, or the sudden horror of realizing that her parents weren't coming for her. That they hadn't loved her, or at least, that they hadn't loved her half as much as they'd feared dragons.

If she'd had any illusions about her ability to stay, the people she'd spoken to had helpfully set her straight. Ris had been correct—she couldn't hope to remain in Crystalspire as Anahrod Amnead. That woman was a monster. Ask anyone.

At least Anahrod the Deeper was only a *troll*.

Fortunately for all involved, staying had never been part of the plan. She made her way to the docks to see about leaving town.

THE *CRIMSON SKIES*

Looking back, Anahrod's escape from the Deep sparked the idea. She'd been thinking of sky amber, since that had proved their salvation. Although one might argue sky amber was the salvation of all of Seven Crests.

Every dock in a Seven Crests city, from Crystalspire to Snowfell, invariably featured a statue of sky amber's patron saint, Laer Berosidge. She wasn't the one who'd discovered sky amber—the dragons had been using the stuff for meditation and ritual from the earliest days—but Berosidge had discovered how to use sky amber to make humans soar.

Anahrod rather doubted Berosidge had any idea how her discovery would change human society—or at least the human society that lived on the mountains, where the air was thin enough for human lungs. And she certainly couldn't have foreseen just how dangerous collecting sky amber would be, because the resin didn't come from a tree or fungus or mineral vein. Sky amber came from the only animal on the planet that lived their entire lives in the upper atmosphere, never landing at all.

Leviathans.

What Anahrod knew about sky amber harvesting was best summed up by its effect on trade: indispensable. Dragons would never degrade themselves by becoming mere cargo carriers or modes of transportation. Similarly, transporting goods on foot down a mountain, navigating the perils of the Deep, and ascending another nearby mountain to reach one of the other city-states of Seven Crests was prohibitively hazardous.

When sky amber became an option, it soon became the only option.

Unfortunately, since sky amber refused to cooperate by raining down on the cities, someone had to harvest it. Amber harvesting was the fastest way to die in the Skylands—and the fastest way to strike it rich. There seemed to be a never-ending supply of people willing to overlook the risk of the former in pursuit of the latter.

All of which meant that Anahrod stood an excellent chance of finding an amber cutter who was both hiring and uninterested in asking questions about her background.

The second cutter she checked, the *Crimson Skies*, had room for one more. The cutter planned to leave port with the evening wind.

A cutter was just a larger flyer, of course. They could've taken any shape—sky amber didn't care what it kept afloat—but Anahrod had never seen a flying craft not modeled on a living counterpart. Thus, most flyers looked like birds—blood crows or star kites. The larger cutters were modeled after the leviathans themselves.

The *Crimson Skies* was no exception: a large, sleek aerodynamic tube that flattened out to a rounded square in the front and narrowed to a point in the back. Giant sail-wings, pointed straight up while the cutter docked, could be moved in a circle around the whole vessel to catch the wind while flying. The cutter design was a matter of practicality: the only way to approach a leviathan was to make the giant creatures think the cutter was a stray calf.

The *Crimson Skies'* captain was named Bederigha, a plump, curly-haired man with only one hand who therefore wore his garden rings in his hair. He was late-sprouting, married, and preferred masculine partners. His garden rings included a cliff tulip, which Anahrod had wanted to find herself, as it meant "none of your damn business" in a less offensive way than not wearing any rings at all.

She liked him immediately.

He'd squinted at Anahrod, taking in the clothing, the sword, the knapsack, that blood crow career ring. "Ever gone harvesting sky amber before?"

There seemed little sense lying to the man. "No, Captain."

"You ever served on a cutter?"

"No, Captain."

"A flyer of any kind?"

"No, Captain."

He scratched his chin. "Ain't anyone told you that you're supposed to lie about that sort of thing? Make yourself seem valuable?"

Anahrod shrugged. "I don't start fights and I'm not afraid of work. Isn't that valuable?"

"You don't start fights?" His gaze slipped down to her sword. "While I am glad to hear that, if you're the sort that will finish them with that sword, we still have a problem."

Anahrod dropped her fingers to the pommel. "It's not like that. This is . . . it has sentimental value. I'm not fool enough to attack people with it."

"Can you use it?"

She shrugged. "Anyone who says there's no need for swords anymore hasn't tried walking the bad part of town after dark. It's damn useful in the right circumstances."

The captain made a face. She could see him weighing the risks.

Revealing her culinary skills would've guaranteed his acceptance (assuming he believed her), but it would also intensify doubts about her true motives. Trained cooks didn't hire on as regular crew. They didn't need to.

The captain finally snorted. "Fine, but the sword stays peace-bound and out of sight."

"Easily done. Thank you."

The captain squinted at her, waiting for her to say something else. Suspicion was creeping back into his expression.

Anahrod shifted on her feet, staring past the captain's shoulder toward the vessel.

Right. She was forgetting something.

Anahrod cleared her throat. "What does the job pay?"

Bederigha huffed, but also relaxed. Now they had returned to following the expected script. "This ain't paid by the hour. You're joining our division. You understand that, right? If we don't bring back anything, you get half a share of nothing. If we find some old grandpa out there, you get half a share of a fortune. You do fair by us, and we'll do fair by you."

He pointed up the gangplank to the cutter. "Go tell my first mate, Grexam, that you've joined up. He'll show you where to bunk. We leave in a few hours, so if you need to say goodbye to your husband, you best do it soon."

She almost protested that she didn't have a husband, but remembered her rings said otherwise. "It won't be a problem. Thank you, Captain."

He pursed his lips. "So, it's like that, huh? Well, you'd hardly be the first to fly from a bad marriage straight onto a leviathan's back. Now get yourself inside before we leave you on the dock." He waved her toward the cutter's boarding ramp.

The cutter was graceful for a hunting vessel. Beautiful, even, with no hard edges anywhere. Intricate painted designs ran all along the outside edges; it was impossible to tell which inscriptions were important and which were nothing more than elaborate facades meant to protect trade secrets.

The inside of the cutter wasn't as pretty. The fancy decorations gave way to weathered lumber and dull metal. Eventually, Anahrod tracked down Grexam, a hulking man twice the captain's size who climbed tall mountains with his bare hands and ate raw titan drake eggs for breakfast. His rings differed from Bederigha's only in that he wore a lower rank of career ring, wasn't late-sprouting, and was a lot more interested in sex—or at least watching other people have sex. His rings were also in the same style as Bederigha's, if not made by the same jeweler, suggesting the "mate" in his job title was more literal than usual.

When Anahrod tried to introduce himself, Grexam waved her back.

"I don't care what your name is," he growled. "I ain't gonna bother learning your name until your second trip out, understand? Until then, you're just Stupid, get it? When I call out 'Hey, Stupid,' I mean you. Survive this trip and prove that my name for you is wrong, well, then we'll give you a new one when we give you a new ring. Maybe even your real name if you're lucky. Understand, Stupid?"

Anahrod's mouth quirked. Not using her real name fit her own plans nicely. She could put up with being called "Stupid" if it meant the crew had no name to give pursuers.

"Yes, sir," she said.

He eyed her up and down as though he thought he'd find a tattoo on her somewhere confessing her incompetence. A dissecting, judging look. It didn't offend her. This was a dangerous job, and the crew needed to depend on each other.

"Fine then," he grumbled. "Stow your shit in the main cabin. Last bunk in the row. Find an empty chest for your stuff. No locks unless you brought your own. Stow the sword: you won't need it and you'd best not be tempted to use it."

Anahrod sucked on her teeth. She hadn't brought a lock. She hadn't even thought of it. Ah, well. She was wearing everything of value except for the sword, and if someone tried to steal that, she hoped they'd made peace with their loved ones first.

Anahrod shrugged and gave the man a bow. He gave her a huge stink eye in response, and she reminded herself to never do that again.

"And throw that damn blood crow ring over the side," he yelled after her. "You're a whaler now."

She went to store her meager possessions in the main cabin.

Anahrod removed the blood crow ring, but she didn't throw it away. She knew her stay on the *Crimson Skies* would be short-lived. Whaling cutters chased leviathans anywhere: leviathans held no respect for political boundaries. A chasing cutter would trespass anywhere they thought they could get away with. Which meant cutters often stopped off in other mountain cities—cities outside of Seven Crests—to resupply. That was all the opening Anahrod needed.

The first time the cutter stopped at such a city would be the last time they ever saw Anahrod.

—⌄—

Her plans had neglected to include an important variable. Her mistake was understandable: it depended on information she hadn't known and didn't discover until the cutter left Crystalspire.

By then, it was too late.

They'd put her to work immediately. Mostly tasks of the "carry this" and "pull on that" variety. Drudge work and heavy lifting. All easy enough. She'd spent too long in the Deep to find manual labor anything worth grumbling over.

The *Crimson Skies* had a few windows, small and high set—the captain probably had a lovely view, but such luxuries weren't for the crew. Anahrod thought nothing of it. The cutter felt oddly vacant because the experienced crew were busy manning the giant pinions that connected the wing sails, slotting them into position and then moving them again as the captain shouted down orders. The process involved a great deal of pulling, knotting, retying ropes, and swearing.

Around thirty minutes after leaving the city, someone pushed a bucket of water and a ladle into Anahrod's hands. "Go give the crew water."

So Anahrod did. Or at least, she tried.

As Anahrod carried the bucket, she glanced down through one of the pinion slits. The gap itself was only a foot in width—someone might trip or possibly jam a leg through the opening, but falling through it would've taken dedicated effort.

Anahrod stared down at an enormous drop of land sliding away from the mountain, white and gray toward Crystalspire before sinking down into the Deep's vivid greens and purples. She saw blood crows flying a few thousand feet lower, clouds weaving in and out underneath.

In between: twenty thousand feet of empty air.

Nothingness.

The next thing she knew, Anahrod hunched on the ground, her trousers wet from spilled water, her back pressed against the curved hull of the cutter. Her fingers scrabbled for purchase against the metal hull.

The world appeared and vanished in flashes. Anahrod picking up the water bucket. *Anahrod free-falling to her death.* She scratched at the wooden deck with her nails. *The wind slashed at her eyes and whipped back her hair.* Someone shouted at her. *She was all alone, tossed out like garbage by her own people.* Someone touched her shoulder. *She watched the earth reaching up for her.* More voices speaking to her. *Her ears popped as the air pressure changed far too quickly.* Someone spoke to her. *She couldn't save herself.*

Someone slapped her, hard.

The second time, she caught the wrist.

Grexam, the first mate, kneeled next to her, his expression more annoyed than angry. "What kind of fool signs up on a whaler who's scared of heights?"

Anahrod made a face, fighting off an outburst of laughter or tears. She couldn't tell.

Anahrod whispered: "The kind of fool who didn't know she was."

Grexam sighed. The sound was old and tired. "Kenerem, take her to the mess, would you? I don't have time for this shit right now." He stared down at Anahrod. "You, Stupid. Follow Kenerem. I'll find you in the mess when we're done adjusting the course, you hear me?"

Anahrod nodded and let Kenerem lead her away.

They didn't go far. The mess hall was empty since the crew was busy at their posts. Kenerem sat her down on a bench, giving her a pitying expression. The crewman looked like she'd been asked to care for a bird born without wings.

"You stay here, okay?" Kenerem didn't wait to hear Anahrod's answer. With Grexam's order accomplished, Kenerem retreated.

Anahrod pressed the heels of her hands against her eyes and sat there. She was numb. Scraped clean of all emotion but the dull, aching certainty that she was cursed.

All her plans, tentative though they'd been, had hinged on a false assumption. For a Skylander to fear heights wasn't impossible, but Skylanders who feared heights didn't sign up as crew on whaling cutters.

Or any flyer.

She thought about her life. All her life. All the years she spent in the Deep. She'd climbed trees. She'd even climbed cliffs. Nothing even close to the sort of height she'd experienced when the *Crimson Skies* had left Crystalspire. Nothing like the height in those awful memories, so awful they felt like a visceral fist clenched around her throat.

Blood crows screaming as they grabbed at her clothing. The snapping sound her bones made as she hit the tree branches.

The fear, the dismay, the desperate flailing attempt to grab hold of anything or anyone that might save her life.

Anahrod still didn't know how she'd controlled a flock of blood crows, all at once, but she must have. They'd slowed her fall enough to survive the impact. She'd broken both arms and legs, five ribs, and her collarbone, but she'd survived.

She raised her head and wiped her tears. Maybe it was just as well that she'd been unconscious when Ris and her dragon Peralon had carried her back to Crystalspire.

Regardless, now Anahrod faced a new problem.

Whaling divisions weren't known for indulging people trying to gain free passage. If Anahrod had come to Captain Bederigha from the start with an offer to pay a fare, he might have granted her permission. Maybe. But to suddenly announce that she couldn't perform the work she'd agreed to?

Anahrod eyed the door to the galley. She hadn't wanted to fall back on her cooking skills, but maybe this was the right time to make an exception.

She shakily rose to her feet and walked inside the galley, intent on having a chat with the cook.

This goal was complicated because there was no cook. The galley stood empty.

Anahrod frowned. The galley shouldn't have been empty. "Cook" was a vital position in any division, but triply so in a division that traveled. "Flyer cook" was a position just under quartermaster, equal to the crew doctor. Making sure any food served to the crew wouldn't make them sick was a full-time job.

The galley itself was clearly being used. It was clean and well maintained, possessed a large store of fermented ingredients and specially grown staple grains. The pantry was full to the brim with provisions.

The crew ate well.

Which meant that Anahrod had a decision to make.

If she guessed wrong, she might find herself tossed off a cutter for a second time.

13

THREE WHISTLES

"—I hope you have a good explanation for making a mess of my kitchen . . ." Captain Bederigha's voice trailed off as he walked into the galley. He stood there, blinking at her.

Anahrod set the pan down on the counter. "Consider it an apology?" Then what he said sank in. "Wait. *You're* the cook?"

"Always have been. I was the cook before I was the captain." He edged his way around an oven and frowned at the pan. "What is it?"

"A vegetable casserole." She carved a slice, laying it sideways on a plate so all the thin layers showed. She'd enjoyed cooking with something other than an earthen oven and a campfire. She took a bite out of the casserole (as was only polite), then handed the rest to him.

Bederigha threw the casserole a suspicious glare before taking a bite. He then stared down at the plate like it had bitten him back. "What."

"You don't like it?" She thought it was passable, but opinions varied.

"Don't ask foolish questions," he snapped. "Of course I liked it. Why didn't you volunteer you can cook like this?"

She started cutting the casserole into serving portions. "You're a cook, too. You know how it is. People aren't always willing to just let you walk away after." She glanced sideways at him. "How'd a cutter's cook end up as captain?"

"Oh, I wasn't the cutter's cook," he said. "I was the *assistant* cook. Then the old captain came down with food poisoning—never did figure out what caused it—and got so mad that he tossed my boss over the side."

Anahrod shuddered. "And then?"

"I led a mutiny," Bederigha said cheerfully. "Captains come and go, but good cooks are hard to find." He took one more bite and then threw down his plate. "Well, that's obnoxiously delicious. Can you follow someone else's recipes? Because if you don't want to stay here indefinitely, maybe don't tempt the crew with dishes only you know how to make."

"I can do that, yes." Anahrod didn't have a choice.

She thought he'd leave then. Or start making dinner—or ordering others around to do it for him.

He didn't.

Bederigha perched a hip against the main table. "You told me you wouldn't cause trouble."

"I said I don't start fights."

"My mistake. That's not the same thing at all, is it?"

She bit back on the urge to sigh. He wasn't finished.

"Grexam says you claimed you didn't know. Thinks you were telling the truth. Must have been a hard slap, realizing you're never going to look down again."

Anahrod didn't answer.

"Folks aren't born that scared of heights," he continued. "They get that way because something happened."

Anahrod started washing up. Water was more plentiful on the cutter than she'd expected, but that made sense when a refill was as close as the nearest cloud.

"Don't make me ask a third time."

"A third time? Were any of those statements questions?" Anahrod sighed at herself. Perhaps not the best way to go about convincing the captain to let her stay. "It's just what you're thinking. I fell."

"You fell, or you were pushed?"

Anahrod dropped the bowl with a clang of metal. She hung on to the wash-tub with both hands until her knuckles turned white against her skin.

"Pushed, then," Bederigha said. "That makes it worse. If you were just clumsy or a rope snapped, well. You'd tell yourself not to be clumsy. Check your ropes better next time. But pushed? Pushed is rough. That might happen again. Might happen anytime. You can't feel safe, even if you're roped off and wearing a harness. What if someone doesn't like you?"

Anahrod suddenly felt cold, the air in the galley making her hairs stand up. Or maybe it was the topic of conversation.

"Finish cleaning up," the captain instructed. "Then set up the tables for the crew. I'll bring out the evening meal."

"Right away, Captain," she said.

"We're not done talking about this. I don't care how good a cook you are. I won't stand for someone on my vessel who'll go to pieces the first time she wanders too close to a window."

Wonderful.

She spent the first week helping in the kitchen: cleaning dishes, hauling water, and preparing ingredients. In the evening, she sat by herself and picked out the knots in her hair. In return, she never stepped near the pinion slots.

Still, too many people had witnessed her breakdown. She could see how it must have looked. She came out of nowhere, the lowest of the hierarchy by cutter rules, and then lost her nerve. The captain had rewarded her for that cowardice with a kitchen assignment, lining her up for one of the highest-paying jobs on the cutter. All the gain and none of the risk.

It wasn't fair.

The inevitable result: pranks, whispered rude names, and attempts to provoke fights the crew would swear Anahrod started.

The only reason the rumors weren't worse was because Bederigha's and Grexam's rings were all leaves, and they only had eyes for each other. Still, every other motivation made the gossip rounds at least once, including a story in which she was the captain's long-lost daughter.

Grexam didn't care. He still called her Stupid.

She had nothing to prove to these people. Or rather, she had a lot more to lose by getting in trouble than she'd gain by causing it. So, no matter how much she wanted to throw fists, she didn't.

The only person besides the captain and first mate not offended by her presence was Bederigha's actual assistant cook, Kira. She was delighted—mostly because she dumped all the unpleasant tasks to Anahrod.

Kira didn't even mind it when Anahrod slept on the grain sacks instead of in her hammock. Which was good, because Anahrod was doing the entire crew a favor.

She'd started having nightmares.

They'd set in that first night. The crew's reaction had been to throw shoes at her until she woke, and then banish her from crew quarters. It only took two nights of that before sleeping in the kitchen pantry became preferable. It wasn't necessarily comfortable, but at least it was uninterrupted by anyone except herself.

On the sixth day, Anahrod woke to find the captain staring down at her.

He hadn't forgotten his promise.

"I can't stand gray vermin," the captain said.

Anahrod blinked at him. "What did you say?"

"Gray vermin. Scrabbers. Little scaly bastards. The way they sneak into a house, bold as sunlight, and nibble anything not locked up? Used to be I'd scream and be up on the furniture before anyone had a chance to so much as draw a knife. I've stared down dragons and once got pulled into a hurricane by a leviathan. But I was scared of rats."

Anahrod rubbed the sleep from her eyes as she stood up. "What did you do?"

"Found myself a nest of baby grays. Just a few days old. Raised 'em myself, by hand. Turns out even little scaled rat babies are cute. And by the time they weren't that cute, I was too fond of them to care. No more problems with gray vermin."

"Is there a point to this, Captain?"

He gave her a stern, paternal look. "You don't have to let your fears control you."

"No offense, but I think my situation is a little different from being frightened of scrabbers."

"You're wrong. It's exactly the same." He all but pushed her out of the pantry. "Starting small is the key. Little things. Fun things. Work your way up to the big stuff. Look fear straight in the eye and tell it to go fuck itself. You don't strike me as a person who'd let fear squeeze all the air from your throat."

Anahrod barked out a laugh. She thought of the Deep and Overbite and how for years she'd made what could only ironically be called a living. How she'd survived. "No, I'm not."

The captain nodded, satisfied. "That's what I thought. Come with me."

She did, but it was only when they reached the wingsuit lockers that she realized where they were going. Grexam was already there, already preparing ropes, harnesses, and leads.

"We're doing this now?" Anahrod protested.

"What? You're scared?" Grexam said.

"Yes. Or we wouldn't be here."

He just shrugged. "You're just lucky the captain's a soft touch. The old captain would've thrown you off the cutter five days ago."

Captain Bederigha's bright smile dimmed as the man glanced at his missing hand. "Not necessarily. He enjoyed fixing problems with an axe, too."

With that, the captain grabbed a rope line and clipped it to his belt. "I'll meet you topside." He gave them both a sharp nod and climbed the ladder, exiting the hatch at the end.

Grexam cursed under his breath.

"That what happened to his hand?" she asked. "The old captain?"

"Yeah," Grexam said. "Went after him with a hatchet." The scowl turned into something dark, malicious, and gleeful. "Course, the old captain found out the hard way a hook will do just as well as a knife for gutting a person." He threw down a wide leather belt. "Put that on."

The belt boasted an array of rings. One end of a rope hung from it by spring hook, while the rope's other end fastened to an iron ring fixed to the floor.

He opened the hatch.

The wind outside howled, while ropes slapped against the metal hull of the cutter.

"You're going to step outside," he told her. "I'll be here. I have your rope." He tugged on it for emphasis. "You can't fall."

Anahrod clenched and unclenched her fists. She could do this.

She stepped out into the bright sunlight on the top of the cutter. Land came into view on the left side of the cloud cutter, a soft gray-green fading away into mountain ranges. Clouds scuttled below the vessel.

"Nope." Anahrod turned around.

Grexam shoved her back outside.

She slid across the top of the cutter, coming to a halt far, far too close to where the slick metal surface slid away into nothing. She scrambled backward, overcome with the irrational fear that the cutter would tilt. She'd slide. The rope would snap . . .

Captain Bederigha chuckled. "Nice of you to join us. Put this on." He tossed a bundle of cloth to Anahrod, different from Grexam's belt.

Anahrod glanced around herself. A thirty-foot section of the cutter roof had been sectioned off and framed with railings. Assuming the cutter stayed reasonably level, it was as safe as any balcony—as long as she didn't look over the side.

Anahrod stood up with as much dignity as she could muster and inspected the bundle. If the fabric fastened the way she thought, it would leave large swaths of cloth connecting her arms and legs like sails . . .

She looked up at the captain with a stare she very much hoped conveyed the proper amount of "you must be joking."

Captain Bederigha was still not joking.

"You ever flown a paper kite before?" The captain waved a hand. "What am I saying? You're a Seven Crests girl. Of course you have. This is just like that. Except you're the kite."

A full-body shudder swept over Anahrod. Perhaps if she gave them all her remaining scales, they'd allow her to lock herself in a room and gibber until they reached a city again.

She clenched her teeth. That a woman who'd grown up in Seven Crests— who'd once wanted to be a dragonrider more than anything else—would now be afraid of heights was absurd.

No, it was worse than that. It was *humiliating*.

She refused.

"Is this how you learned?" she asked the captain.

"Me? Don't be ridiculous." The captain gestured at his generous waist. "I'd look like a damn balloon, wouldn't I? No, I don't harvest. That's your job. I just sit here, make soup, and look pretty."

Anahrod chuffed out a laugh.

"Fine. Let's get this over with." Before Anahrod changed her mind, came to her senses, or curled into a tight little ball and began screaming. That last one looked more appealing every second.

Anahrod reminded herself that she'd faced down titan drakes and killed vine creepers with her bare hands. She once swam through a tidefisher's stingers to pull a full-grown razorfin from the ocean—on a *dare*.

Air would not get the better of her.

"Stand over there." The captain pointed to the railing.

Anahrod swallowed, clenched her fists, and did so.

"Now hold out your arms and jump," the man said. "Doesn't need to be too high. Just enough for the wind to catch you. Maybe you haven't noticed, but there's a lot of that up here."

Anahrod couldn't move. She felt her breath quickening.

"Ready?" the captain asked.

"No," Anahrod admitted.

"Jump now!"

Eannis help her, she did.

She would've assumed a simple jump would be insufficient, but the driving wind flung her skyward and pulled her rope taut.

Anahrod screamed. She screamed a lot.

"Keep your arms and legs spread!" the captain yelled helpfully.

Anahrod would have yelled back all manner of foul curses regarding the man's nature and genealogy, but he could still have her thrown overboard. Also, she didn't think he could hear her.

She kept her arms and legs spread.

Thankfully, she couldn't see over the cutter's sides. She closed her eyes and focused on the most basic sensations. The wind lashing her face, the fabric pulled taut against her limbs, the chill temperature, the thin air. She spread her awareness out, concentrating on the world around herself to keep sane. Animals flew in the distance, too far up to be anything but different breeds of sky racers—small, large, and everything in between. Then she felt something so enormous she thought the height and her situation were playing tricks on her brain.

Her eyes snapped open. Only one animal could be that colossal: a leviathan.

Before she could consider what to do with that information, three sharp whistles sounded, loud enough to pierce the howling veil of wind.

Grexam pulled her back down.

Anahrod fell in an untidy heap the moment the wind proved too weak to keep her aloft. She had enough presence of mind to roll, but she wasn't used to doing so while tied to ropes, and nearly garroted herself.

She lay flat against the cutter, looking up at the blue sky, thinking: Isn't it funny that in the Deep they think I'm dangerous . . . ?

Grexam's giant shoulders eclipsed her field of vision. He held out a hand.

From somewhere to the side, Captain Bederigha said, "Lessons will have to wait. Three whistles mean the watch just spotted a leviathan. Now we earn our shares."

Anahrod took Grexam's hand and pulled herself up.

At least there was one mercy: she didn't have to debate whether she should tell them about the leviathan.

Make that two mercies: she could also go back inside.

14

THE OPPOSITE OF WEAKNESS

Chasing the leviathan meant heading into a storm. Thankfully, this storm wasn't one of the great hurricanes that battered the Deep, twisting trees and stampeding animals. This was a different kind, something born in the waters to the north, sweeping south with the wind and season. It was still dangerous—especially this close. The thought of flying into it wearing nothing but one of those winged suits made Anahrod's stomach churn. Fortunately, no one expected it from her after half a lesson.

When the captain gathered everyone together in the galley to explain matters, Anahrod wasn't the only one who thought this was ill-advised. The rest of the crew wasted no time making that opinion known.

The captain shut them all up with a sharp flip of his hand.

"You came here hoping to pull in a lifetime's worth of scales, yes? Well, you ain't getting any without some risk."

"But what happens when it starts fighting back?" someone called out.

"Zavad's balls!" The captain gave a hard stare to the newer recruits who, like Anahrod, counted this as their first voyage. "You lot don't think we mean to kill it, do you?"

The older crew laughed. The newer members gave each other embarrassed looks, because yes, they had.

"It ain't like that," Captain Bederigha said. "Dragons hunted leviathans almost to extinction. We don't do that. We leave them alive. It ain't in anyone's best interest to kill a leviathan—or even hurt one bad enough to make it panic."

"And no, we can't avoid the damn storm, so don't ask." Grexam scoffed. "They live in storms. We always try to herd them into clear skies, but sometimes they just won't. So what? You afraid of getting wet?"

Anahrod suspected they were afraid of being struck by lightning or blown off the cutter by howling winds. Or maybe falling to their deaths when it was too dark for the crew to notice. But what did she know?

Captain Bederigha ordered the harvesters into their suits and then gave Anahrod a contemplative look.

Anahrod's heartbeat hammered at her. "No."

Bederigha made a face. "No. Too soon. You get belowdecks and help any who need it. Stay away from the pinions. Don't look over the side. Try not to throw up if the cutter tilts."

She swallowed but nodded. That she could do. It was easier when she didn't have to look down. Her legs were still shaky from the entire ordeal. She felt heady and weak simultaneously.

She hated it, although what she really hated was her reaction. The brief kiting she'd done had honestly been fun. It was the sort of thing she would've enjoyed when she was younger, and the knowledge that she couldn't now because of this irrational fear, well . . .

It galled.

She wanted to look at a leviathan with her own eyes. She'd never seen one outside of paintings.

Instead, she headed to the galley.

She'd make sure everyone had something hot to drink when they returned. She didn't know how long harvesting sky amber took, but she suspected "a long time" was the right answer.

Several hours later, after she'd put a third batch of sour cider on the stove to simmer, Anahrod felt a flare of panic from the leviathan.

They'd been with the leviathan for too long for it to suddenly spook like this. This wasn't a reaction to pain or discomfort, but a prey animal's response to a predator. Except leviathans only had one natural predator: dragons.

She cursed. The captain had sent out at least a dozen crewmen in wing-suits and ropes to fly down to the leviathan's back. If a dragon panicked the leviathan—and it *would* panic—what followed would be a catastrophe.

The crew might make it back in time—if someone warned them.

If *Anahrod* warned them.

She sprinted up the stairs leading to the landing scaffold.

It took her a moment to acclimate as she exited the hatch. The rain drove down against the metal hull in wet, ringing splats. The wind screamed. Grexam stood on the platform, directing the harvesters. At first, she couldn't see those harvesters, but a second later, a lightning bolt lit up the sky.

Anahrod gasped.

The leviathan was six-limbed, as almost all animals were, but where a dragon had wings and four legs, a leviathan was nothing but wings. Three paired sets, diaphanous as veilfly's, but gigantic. The animal's head was blunt and wide-mouthed and covered with glowing mirrored beads. The crew members were tiny black specks on the creature's back.

The sky lit up as a second lightning bolt struck a wing directly. The thunder cracked in a deafening hammer stroke. An arc of electricity raced down the wing and across the beast's enormous body, racing across a network of glowing capillaries to arc and splash across all six wings, lighting up everything around them.

Anahrod felt a surge of satisfaction from the leviathan, muted as it was by the beast's growing distress.

"It's feeding," she murmured. "It feeds on lightning?"

She had no idea how the crew members on its back were still alive afterward, but they seemed unharmed. Maybe the flight suits provided protection.

Anahrod forced herself to remember why she was there.

"Grexam!" she shouted, leaning against the wind as she forced her way over to the first mate. "Grexam, something's wrong!"

He glanced toward her, then did a double take. "What're you doing out here, Stupid?"

"There's a dragon!" Anahrod screamed. "There's a dragon heading this way. The leviathan's going to bolt!"

"What are you on about? There's nothing out here—!"

Grexam stopped talking as another sound made itself heard above the din of rain, wind, and thunder.

A roar.

"That weren't no thunderclap," Grexam spat. "Sucking Zavad's dick! This is bad timing!"

Before Anahrod could utter another word, she felt the leviathan unleash a second, even more intense wave of fear.

And then it dove.

Countless rope lines connected the *Crimson Skies* to the leviathan. When the leviathan dove, it pulled the entire vessel with it.

Anahrod cried out as the cutter pitched nearly vertical. She would've fallen, except she smacked against the metal railing. She grabbed on to the bars and held on tight.

In her haste to reach Grexam, she hadn't tied herself off.

She didn't dare look down.

Screams rang out. Not just hers; at least a dozen people had been thrown from the leviathan's back. Momentum hurled them through the air. One poor bastard smashed against the *Crimson Skies* itself.

Grexam shouted something. She wasn't sure what.

Probably something important.

More cursing and hollering as the leviathan pulled up. Bederigha had done something clever to keep the entire cutter from smashing into the gargantuan creature from behind. The cutter managed a sharp turn with a screech of tearing metal that spoke of the cost: two cracked wings, twisted to uselessness by torque and stress.

The leviathan dove again, this time turning sharply.

Two giant hands yanked Anahrod away from the railing, snapping a spring hook and rope to her belt.

"Get inside," Grexam yelled at her.

She did, somehow making it to the hatch without being tossed over. The moment the hatch closed above her, she released the spring hook and ran for the observation deck.

[Stop fleeing. Calm down,] she shouted at the leviathan. She wasn't doing the creature any favors if the dragon really was hunting it, but a dozen people out there needed the chance to be hauled back to the cutter.

A dark shape flashed by so quickly it was only a blur passing between the cutter and the leviathan. The *Crimson Skies* lurched as the dragon's passage sheared all the ropes connecting the cutter to the leviathan.

Anahrod stared in horror. She had no idea if anyone had made it back in time or if the dragon had just severed a dozen lifelines.

The leviathan made a piteous cry and flew upward, away from them. The dragon didn't chase.

The dragon wasn't hunting the leviathan.

"No," Anahrod whispered.

A series of lightning flashes illuminated the dragon. He was enormous, the size of the cutter itself, dark blue and silver. The dragon's wings beat indolently as he turned to face his prize. Anahrod's breath caught in her throat.

She hadn't seen this dragon in years, not since she'd last been in Yagra'hai, but he was seared into her memory.

Tiendremos.

Somehow, he'd found her.

Of course the leviathan had panicked. Even if dragons left the harvesting of sky amber to humans these days, the leviathan's instincts remembered otherwise.

She needed to hide.

[Find her.]

Anahrod spun, wide-eyed, certain that she'd just heard Tiendremos's voice. She ran to the galley.

An oppressive silence settled over the cutter. She could only imagine how the crew felt—they'd found a leviathan! They were going to be rich!—only to have those dreams crushed by a creature they didn't dare rebuke.

Throwing herself from the cutter began to seem like a fine idea, never mind how much that thought transformed her into a screaming ball of fear.

That was what the sky had become to her. Fear.

For other Skylanders, every good thing came from the clouds. For her, the opposite was now her truth. The jungles might be full of blood-pumping danger, but at least she had solid ground beneath her feet. The Deep was a place where she knew the rules, where she was more likely to be hunter than prey. She'd seldom felt fear there, not since she'd discovered that the same ability she'd grown up using to tempt birds to her hand could instead keep the Deep's fiercest predators at her beck and call.

And if she had felt fear, it was the child of prudence and practicality. If she'd been forced to hide from a predator or enemy in the Deep, she didn't feel it like a wound. Like a hollowness inside herself.

Like cowardice.

Survival was not a synonym for either courage or fear. In the right circumstances, either response was a blessing. In the wrong circumstances, either was a curse. "Survival" was knowing which option fit the circumstances best.

Somehow, she'd forgotten that. Here in the Skylands, fear felt like failure, like weakness. Whereas fear was the foundation of common sense in the Deep.

Anahrod hid herself in the pantry. If they found her, she'd pretend that she'd been fixing the provisions tossed about during their ride.

The damage in the kitchen wasn't as bad as she feared: Bederigha kept the stores lashed down tight.

The captain banged the door open louder than normal as he entered the galley.

"—no, no," the captain was saying. "Cutters like this run on shares. We're a licensed division, registered with the Sky Amber Guild, not the Travelers Guild. We can't just be picking up everyone who wants a ride from one city to another on a whim. Crystalspire was a resupply stop, not a ferry run."

Anahrod felt warmth bloom in her chest. The captain was covering for her. She was unsure why exactly—perhaps Bederigha felt some orneriness, given how Tiendremos and his rider had made the *Crimson Skies* lose their hunt and cost lives.

Unfortunately, lying to a dragonrider was an excellent way to wind up dead.

"I see." A man's voice. Pleasant, throaty, genial.

"What did this person do that's so damn terrible that you had to mess with our harvest, anyway? Do you have any idea how much money we just lost?"

How had they found her?

Did they have some method of tracking her location? Ris had never explained how they found her last time. Wanted posters were a good excuse for how she'd drawn the dragonriders' attention in the first place, but not how they'd pinpointed her location.

Anahrod leaned back into the shadows behind a stack of shelves. A second later, the pantry door opened, and light flooded the small room.

"Is this really necessary?" the captain complained.

"As soon as we find her, you can be on your way." The rider sounded reasonable. "Nice kitchen. I bet your meals are amazing."

If the dragonrider was fishing for an invitation, the captain wasn't in the mood. "I'm not some fancy liner traveling from city to city. This is where I live, too."

The door closed; the room faded back into blackness.

Anahrod remembered to breathe and then pulled her sword out from behind a storage bin and buckled it around her waist.

She didn't remember the dragonrider's name. Maybe she'd never learned it. She thought Tiendremos might have had a different rider when she'd been at school, although she wasn't certain. She'd only seen the dragon from a distance and had never spoken to his rider.

The smart thing to do was to stay right where she was. They'd already searched the pantry, after all.

Just as she'd made this determination, a mental voice cut across her thoughts.

[You're a simpleton.]

She froze. As before, the dragon wasn't talking to her.

[Must I tell you how to do everything? The solution is obvious. Tell this captain that if he doesn't bring out Anahrod in the next five minutes, I will rip his flying vessel apart piece by piece until I find her myself.]

15

THE LONGEST FLIGHT

Anahrod shuddered. The dragon was serious. Tiendremos was widely known to be Neveranimas's favorite, the one she sent out to do the nastiest jobs, from wiping out villages in the Deep to hunting down heretics.

The dragon didn't stop talking. What followed was a continuous stream of abuse directed at Tiendremos's rider.

It was humiliating, and the dragon wasn't even talking to her.

This left Anahrod with only one option. She hadn't known these people for long—just a little over five days—but that didn't mean she was willing to watch them all die.

It wasn't a difficult equation. If she was going to die either way, she might as well not drag innocent people with her. Whereas if by some miracle Ris had been right and Tiendremos didn't intend to kill her, forcing him into a situation where he might do so by accident was hardly to her benefit.

She couldn't see the point of refusing in the long run. Hiding would only delay matters, not solve them.

Anahrod climbed back up the hatch stairs.

Grexam gave her such a relieved look that she knew the rider must have passed along Tiendremos's threats. Also, that the captain had continued to act ignorant.

Grexam plastered himself against the side wall so she could pass him. Anahrod walked out into the sunlight.

"Stop!" she yelled out. "Enough. I'm here. There's no need to involve these people. I'll come willingly."

In bright light, the dragonrider was an arrogant-looking man in clothing so dark a blue it would've looked black under other circumstances. He had deep brown eyes and straight black hair of the sort that had never once blown back into its owner's face. It wasn't doing so now, even though the wind blew the right way.

Anahrod looked into the man's eyes and saw a dance of fear and hate, a complicated twirl of emotions wrapped around a core of satisfaction and relief.

Absolutely nothing in that stare suggested mercy.

"Well, good," the dragonrider said. "Nice to see someone has some sense around here."

[Is that her? Have you found her?]

"Just leave the crew alone. I didn't even give them my real name."

[Bring her. We'll return to my lair.]

Anahrod froze.

Of course they were going to fly. She stepped backward when the rider reached for her.

He sighed. "I thought we'd established that you're smarter than this?"

"I am," she said. "But my cooperation is contingent on two conditions, non-negotiable. The first is that Tiendremos will repair this cutter and compensate the crew for loss."

The dragonrider laughed harshly. "Oh, you have a lot of nerve."

"The Sky Hunting Act of 1423," Anahrod spat. "Article 6, paragraph 5: Should any dragon cause willful damage of a vessel whose primary application is the harvesting and collecting of sky amber, the city of Yagra'hai agrees to pay for the full restoration of said vessel to insure a smooth and uninterrupted supply of sky amber to all involved trading parties." She might have messed up the quotation at least a little, but she'd have been surprised if the dragonrider had memorized the trade agreement.

He made an impatient gesture. "We were pursuing a fugitive—"

"The agreement doesn't care why you did it, only that the dragon is willfully responsible. Tiendremos qualifies." She leaned forward and lowered her voice. "I guarantee the captain here is familiar with the law. Do you want him limping back to Crystalspire to file suit? Making a huge stink about Tiendremos attacking his cutter unprovoked and pulling crew off his vessel?"

She saw his eyes narrow, saw the predatory gaze the rider gave the cutter. Knew that he was contemplating whether it would be worth it to wreck the cutter and kill everyone except Anahrod.

"Must I remind you that every sky amber cutter," she whispered, "comes stock with an inscribed plate the guild can use to track the location of a crashed vessel? In theory, it's so they can recover any harvested sky amber, but it also lets them find out exactly how the cutter was destroyed."

She was bluffing. She had no idea if the guilds could do such a thing, but it sounded plausible. Hopefully plausible enough to make the dragonrider think twice about eliminating witnesses.

It seemed to. He chewed on that piece of information for a moment, tongue working at the back of his teeth, before he said to Captain Bederigha, "We wouldn't want to jeopardize any treaty, would we? Bring your flyer to Yagra'hai and Tiendremos will ensure it's repaired."

Captain Bederigha's expression suggested he'd just witnessed his mortal enemy take a shit in his soup, but he nodded. "I'll do just that."

"And the second condition?" the dragonrider asked her.

"You're going to need to knock me out for the flight back." She turned to Bederigha. "Captain, do you have anything that can keep me under? Something for medical emergencies?"

"That ain't the way to get over your fears," he cautioned. "You can't make a habit of it."

"I know," she said. "But needs must. Please."

Bederigha signaled Grexam. "Go get the bottle of Alls-Night."

The man ceased his previous pastime of glaring holes into the dragonrider's backside and retreated down the hatchway.

"Why, exactly, do I need to keep you unconscious?" the dragonrider asked Anahrod.

Had she ever learned his name? She didn't think so.

Anahrod lifted her chin. "I'm scared of heights."

The dragonrider blinked at her. He had a slight smile on his face, the same one he'd worn from the start, but it looked especially brittle just then.

"Is that a joke?" he finally asked.

"I wish it were." It wasn't funny at all. Just how unfunny would become clear the moment they tried to lower her onto that dragon's back, and she began lashing out violently.

He swept an arm out, indicating the cutter, the question very clear. If she was afraid of heights, what in all of heaven was she doing here?

"She didn't realize until we were underway," the captain explained.

"That must have been quite the scene." He smiled brightly at Anahrod. "I'm Jaemeh, by the way."

"Pleasure."

"I rather doubt it."

[What's going on? What's the delay? Please tell me that even a fool such as yourself hasn't found a way to mess this up?]

Anahrod closed her eyes. Oh, Tiendremos was charming. Who wouldn't be swept off their feet by such sweet talk?

The dragonrider turned around, presumably responding to his dragon's demands. Anahrod suspected the rider was having to engage in some serious diplomacy to keep the dragon from doing something rash.

"Please tell him I've agreed to come quietly," Anahrod suggested. "We're just taking precautions to make sure I don't hurt myself when I panic."

"When you panic?" The fake smile slipped.

"When," she affirmed. Anahrod glanced back toward the hatch and wished Grexam would hurry.

"You aren't what I expected," Jaemeh said.

Anahrod didn't dignify that with the obvious response.

"I thought you'd be more . . . you know."

"Assume I don't know."

He gestured at her body. "Sexy hair and lots of skin. A wicked smile on your face while you convince people to sell you their souls."

"You're thinking of Ris."

He swallowed a laugh, giving a wary glance toward his dragon hovering off to the side. When he returned his attention to Anahrod, his gaze was dissecting, evaluating, appraising. It carried with it expectations for how useful she might be, what they might gain by keeping her alive.

"How did you survive?" He picked up a length of her hair and studied it before letting it fall from his fingers.

"Survive?" She ground her teeth.

"A fall from fifty thousand feet. How did you survive?"

She heard a short, quick inhale from Bederigha, and knew he'd put the pieces together. Not who she was, no, his expression didn't have the right level of disgust for that, but certainly what had happened.

Anahrod stared Jaemeh in the eyes. "I have no idea what you mean."

A flicker of confusion crossed Jaemeh's face. That confusion vanished just as quickly as it had appeared, replaced by panic. Jaemeh tried to grab her arm. She blocked him.

"I said I'd go back with you," Anahrod told him. "I didn't say you could touch me."

He lowered his voice. "You stupid bitch, I'm trying to save your life." His eyes darted to the side, to the captain still watching them, to his dragon.

He leaned forward. "Tell me you're Anahrod Amnead." He raised a hand and whispered fiercely, "I don't care one way or the other, but if you're *not* Anahrod Amnead, he'll swallow you whole. So, who are you?"

She scowled. "Anahrod Amnead. Or did you pick this cutter at random?"

Weirdly, that calmed him, although they continued to stare at each other in an unfriendly fashion until Grexam returned with a small dark violet bottle and a small glass.

Grexam poured a shot, which turned louche and silvery, then handed it to Anahrod.

"One drink's all you need," he said. "It'll work up quick, too, so this dragonrider here best be expecting to shoulder you back to his dragon."

"I think I can manage," Jaemeh demurred.

She hated this so very much. She didn't know or like this man. She knew nothing about Jaemeh except the color and name of the dragon he rode. Yet she was about to trust herself to his care for who knew how long.

She paused before drinking. "Just to make it clear. If you take advantage of me while I'm unconscious, I *will* kill you."

Jaemeh's expression shifted from consternation to anger. "How dare you imply I'd do something like that."

"Dragonriders dare a lot of things." With that, she tossed back the shot.

The liquor tasted like cloudberries.

For a good ten seconds, nothing happened. She was tempted to ask if anyone needed more than one shot, when—utterly without fanfare—night fell early.

❮

Sadly, she didn't remain unconscious for the entire trip. In hindsight, a cutter flying for over a week had traveled a distance that even a dragon couldn't match in a few hours.

She opened her eyes to stars. A whole sky full of stars, bright as flames or weak as ghost flies, but beautiful. It was Zavad's Hour, when the moon reached its darkest, letting the evening stars shimmer in a glittering procession.

Jaemeh had strapped Anahrod down to a leather-and-metal harness on Tiendremos's back. The dragon's muscles moved under her, flexing and relaxing with the pull and release of his wings. The space between his wings was wide enough for her to lie down sideways with room to spare—if she wasn't already tied down.

The harness itself bore no resemblance to a saddle. Dragons—full-grown dragons, anyway—were too huge. Instead, a harness gave humans a place to tie themselves, and a windbreak to duck behind. The nicer harnesses shielded the rider from inclement weather.

Tiendremos's harness wasn't fancy. It was barely better than "none at all"—an option some dragons preferred, even if it left their riders permanently grounded.

This harness was a wide lip of metal, around four feet tall. Enough to act as a windbreak, with just enough leather to hold it all together.

Mostly. The harness moved a great deal on a creature that already moved a great deal. It didn't feel stable.

Tiendremos made a wide, sweeping turn, banking on a wing. The entire harness lurched, and the leather straps holding her in place creaked. It was night and she couldn't see the ground, but suddenly she imagined it all too vividly.

She didn't want to think about where they were going. If it was Seven Crests or Yagra'hai. Either seemed like a different variation of a death sentence.

She closed her eyes and curled up on herself as much as the bindings would allow, shuddering. Eventually, exhaustion took over.

If she woke up again during the trip, she didn't remember it.

PART THREE

HOW TO
STEAL
FOR
REVENGE
AND
PROFIT

THE DRAGON IN HIS EYES

Anahrod was thoroughly tired of waking up in unfamiliar beds.

She wasn't in Crystalspire this time. The walls were unplastered brick layered in complicated designs. The floor was made from polished wood planks, covered by a thick rag rug. A brick fireplace warmed the room. There were no windows.

She recognized the style: Duskcloud. One of the prettier cities in Seven Crests, famous for its universities.

And for its blue dragons.

Tiendremos hadn't taken her back to Crystalspire *or* Yagra'hai.

Anahrod rolled out of bed. Someone had taken the liberty of changing her clothes while she was unconscious. She wasn't sure how to feel about that, since what she wore instead was a delicate lawn chemise under a long-sleeved shift of green mistberry silk worth its weight in sky amber.

Her own clothing lay neatly folded on a nearby chair, next to her daggers and sword. Either someone wanted to make very certain she didn't feel like a prisoner, or they didn't think a sword would make any difference.

Sadly, she suspected it was the latter.

[If you'd brought her to me first, this wouldn't have happened.] She recognized Tiendremos's unpleasant growl of mental "speech."

Anahrod didn't hear a response, so he was probably speaking to his rider, Jaemeh, rather than another dragon.

Tiendremos roared.

Someone must've said something he didn't like.

The sound shook the entire room; the stonework creaked ominously.

[Get her out here! I want to talk to this human that's been so much trouble!]

Anahrod contemplated her options. Easily done; she didn't have any. A sword was useless against a dragon, and she had nothing else to bargain with.

Almost nothing.

Anahrod grabbed a knife just as Jaemeh opened the door, holding it reverse-grip to hide the blade in her long silk sleeves.

"I'm sorry," he said, "but we need you outside. He wants to talk." Jaemeh didn't bother to explain who "he" was.

He didn't really have to.

She walked into the dragon's lair.

Anahrod exited one of several dozen rooms built around the periphery of a cave sized for dragons. Enchanted crystals hung from the ceiling on slender chains to provide light, but what they illuminated . . .

First, Tiendremos himself.

He might have been an asshole, but he was a breathtaking, enormous asshole, larger than most dragons. Tiendremos's blue color varied from a pale sky blue along his stomach to a dark indigo blue at the ends of his limbs—wings, arms, feet. Silver stripes ran down his length, except for places where the silver had spilled over in metallic blazes. The blue itself had an opalescent quality—shimmering with greens and purples—when the light hit it just so.

Behind Tiendremos, farther into the cavern, sat a collection of sculptures. They were all variations on a theme: a long pole with something affixed toward the top that spun. The materials and workmanship varied, and sometimes the sculptures were childish, but they were all meant for the same purpose.

That purpose became undeniably obvious when the dragon flapped his wings in frustration.

Weather vanes.

All dragons collected something, hoarded that something. It was instinctive, in the same way most people reacted to a baby crying. And in the old days, before dragons had cities and books and civilization, they often killed each other fighting over those hoards.

Now, though? No two dragons within Yagra'hai's territory could collect the same theme. This resulted in some interesting, even hilarious, hoards. Except a dragon could duel for the right to take over a different dragon's theme, so the more powerful dragons tended to have correspondingly impressive hoards. *Weather vanes?*

This wasn't the dragon's real hoard.

Her focus on the weather vanes distracted her from the dragon himself. Jaemeh's entire body convulsed, and his eyes glowed.

That was all the warning she had before Anahrod found herself pushed up against a brick wall.

"I'm not pleased to have been kept waiting," Tiendremos growled at her—using Jaemeh's mouth.

What could she say to that? Nothing that mattered. Her hair crackled and stuck to the wall as electrical sparks jumped from Jaemeh's body to hers, peppering her with an unpleasant tingling. Tiendremos-using-Jaemeh's-body shoved her hard, with one arm braced across her chest and the other one digging fingers into her waist hard enough to bruise.

Anahrod looked into those glowing eyes and knew that if she wanted to live to see a new day, she'd have to pander to the dragon's ego.

"I'm so sorry," she whispered, keeping her voice small. "I was scared. Please forgive me. I thought you were going to kill me, but your rider explained everything. I won't run again, I promise." She flipped the knife hilt in her lowered hand, while she splayed the fingers of her other hand across Jaemeh's/Tiendremos's chest.

How many times had she seen a dragon speak through their rider? More than she could count. And yet somehow, she'd always assumed the rider was a participant, that the sharing was mutual, consensual.

She found no sign of Jaemeh in those glowing eyes, no sign of him in that cold sneer. Would he even remember this conversation? Tiendremos was doing to Jaemeh what Anahrod did to Overbite.

Except she gave Overbite considerably more agency.

This was *Tiendremos* shoving himself up against her. Tiendremos grabbing her. Tiendremos staring at her with a look in his eyes that seemed equal parts fury, greed, and something that an ugly, dark whisper said could only be lust.

That last idea was ridiculous—and horrifying.

For Tiendremos to look at her with sexual attraction would be like a human experiencing sexual attraction to an ant. But she didn't know how else to interpret that stare. She wasn't imagining it.

Tiendremos's eyes narrowed. He removed his arm from her chest, but only to grab her throat with a hand clenched like claws. **"You had best not run again, or my anger will shake the skies. I own you, and you would do well to not forget it."**

Anahrod fought her instincts, which told her to spit in his face and bury her dagger in Jaemeh's groin. No one owned her. No man, no woman, no person, no *dragon* would *ever* own her. She'd kill herself first, assuming she couldn't kill them first.

"I won't forget," she whispered back. "But you're hurting me."

He frowned, a bemused expression stealing over his borrowed face. Tiendremos glanced down at the lack of space between them. His clothed form pressed against her, wearing only nightclothes. She must have looked vulnerable. Fragile.

He liked it. She could tell he liked it.

"Don't disappoint me, and my rewards will be beyond your imagining," the dragon promised.

His eyes stopped glowing. The cave echoed as the dragon returned to his body, claws scraping against the ground, scales sliding across each other. Tiendremos's agitation and frustration radiated with every shift of weight.

Anahrod didn't turn her head to look.

Her attention focused on Jaemeh, returned to his body only to find it in a more compromising, intimate position than when he'd started. He backed away, his face flushed with shame.

"I'm sorry," he said. "You have to believe me. He would never have done . . . he would never force himself . . ."

"You're right." Anahrod shifted the grip on her knife, so the metal caught the light.

He glanced down and stiffened as he noticed where her hand had been. Perhaps he noted the proximity to his groin, or how easy it would've been for her to open an artery in his thigh. Either way, the fight would've been over—at least for him—before he'd noticed the danger.

"I see . . ." he said. "The whole time?"

"The whole time."

The corner of his mouth quirked in a self-deprecating smile. "How humbling."

How much of that smile was a defense mechanism? Had Jaemeh learned to counter threats and abuse with humor and charm?

Probably.

"I wouldn't be offended if you were mad as hell," Anahrod said. "As long as you remember what 'no' means."

"Always." A smile returned to his face, brittle but still present, and he gestured to the side of the cave, to the tunnel leading back to the room where she'd woken. "In the meantime, when you're done changing, I'll bring you to the others—"

[Enough. This is pointless. I'll return later. Make sure she's cooperative this time, or you'll suffer for it.] The dragon turned on his hind leg, took several thunderous steps toward the cave opening, and launched himself into the air. Jaemeh watched him go, his face carefully blank.

"Interesting," Anahrod commented. "I never knew a dragon could flounce out of a room before."

Jaemeh made a shocked sound and shoved a knuckle into his mouth. His bite was so forceful that she winced in sympathy, wondering if he'd draw blood. When he finally pulled back his hand, white marks outlined the indents left by his teeth.

"Please," he murmured, breathing slow and shallow. "Don't be funny, I beg you."

Guilt stabbed at Anahrod as she realized why he'd fought so hard to stifle his laughter.

Because Tiendremos might feel his rider's amusement, and not think the joke funny at all.

SOMETHING LIKE A PLAN

When she finished dressing, Jaemeh led her into tunnels too small for a dragon to use—warren tunnels for human servants. She wondered how much of it was for convenience and how much was because it might well be a matter of life or death to stay out of sight from an angry dragon.

Tunnel systems aside, the room Jaemeh brought her to felt less like servants' quarters than the drawing room of a wealthy manor house. The inscribed lamps hanging from the ceiling were lucent and if Anahrod squinted, it was easy to mistake the painted landscapes on the walls for glimpses of the surrounding mountains through open windows. The air was sweet, which she assumed was also the work of inscriptions, but if so, the magic hadn't yet cleared the room of the aroma from lunch's leftovers. Her stomach grumbled.

As cages went, it was one of the nicest she'd ever seen.

Of course, more important than elegantly carved furniture or finely woven silk rugs were the familiar faces.

Claw glanced up from throwing a pair of dice and did a double take. "Who the fuck are you?"

Jaemeh laughed.

"Someone who needs tea." Anahrod made a flight line for the kettle, set over a candle flame to keep it hot.

"Wait. I know that voice. Jungle?" Claw sounded incredulous.

"What blinding brightness, to crest the mountain path, and see the sun," Kaibren murmured.

Claw rolled her eyes. "How the hell was I supposed to know? I never saw her without the green paint!"

Anahrod had no comment for that, but she couldn't help but smirk when Kaibren tapped on the table with the dice, distracting Claw with the fact that she'd just lost.

She poured her tea and focused her attention on Naeron and Ris, who'd both looked up from the paper they'd been studying but had yet to speak.

"Hi," Anahrod said, because she was always witty like that.

And yet Ris gave her a warm smile, as if she'd said something clever after all, and gestured for Anahrod to take a chair. "Welcome back."

Anahrod would've appreciated it if her memories of Ris had been flawed. If this reunion had revealed Ris to be less attractive and captivating than Anahrod's recollections of the dragonrider.

Alas, no.

Ris's hair was still a sultry mess of red curls spilling down her sides. She wore thin, tight green leather trousers tucked into tall black boots, and a white shirt barely darker than her pale skin. The shirt's fabric was so sheer that the only reason her nipples weren't on display was because of the green wool coat buckled on top. Bobbin lace shaped like leaves trimmed the coat's hem and sleeves, just to make sure no one missed the wicked green jungle symbolism.

It was probably just as well that she didn't see Gwydinion. Ris needed a "for adults only" warning sign.

Ris must have been the one who'd changed Anahrod's clothes: their outfits matched.

"Suppose this proves Tiendremos knows about you and Peralon," Anahrod commented as she sat down.

She contemplated kicking her feet up on the table, but she wasn't dressed for it.

Jaemeh gave Anahrod an odd look but didn't ask for clarification.

"I told you," Ris said.

"Yes, but you didn't lie, and that's the surprising part." Anahrod sipped her tea. "How did you find me?"

Ris waved a hand. "Inconsequential."

"I disagree."

"She's right: it doesn't matter," Jaemeh said, with a note of finality. "Just know that we can find you again, whenever we need to."

As if Anahrod could ever forget. "What do you want from me?" She saw no sense in wading in slowly.

"What I need you to understand is that—" Jaemeh began.

Claw leaned forward. "We're robbing a dragon's hoard."

Jaemeh glared at Claw. "Do you mind?"

"No," Naeron answered gravely, while Claw threw her head back and laughed.

When Claw recovered her composure, the young woman stage-whispered to Anahrod: "Seriously. Dragon's hoard. We are gonna be so rich."

Ris waved a hand lazily. "More specifically, since you're the only person who's ever successfully robbed a dragon's hoard before, you'll show us how you did it."

Had Anahrod been in a better position to do so, she'd have slammed her cup down on the table or made some other dramatic gesture. Ris had just made a comment so outlandish that it called for a grand, over-the-top reply.

"Fuck, no," she said instead, with feeling. "I'm not helping you."

Anahrod couldn't quite believe what she was hearing. A pair of dragons and their riders had both signed on for *this*? That made no sense at all. Unless . . .

"Which dragon?" Anahrod had a terrible suspicion.

There was an awkward pause.

"Neveranimas." Jaemeh watched her reaction closely.

Anahrod stood and started for the door.

"Anahrod, darling—" Ris called out to her. "Be reasonable. We're not asking you to do something you've never done before. We're not even asking you to steal from a different dragon than you have before."

Anahrod froze and slowly turned around.

She knew what the dragons had accused her of doing. It was difficult not to know when dragonriders had screamed it from the literal mountaintops seventeen years earlier. There was just one tiny problem.

She was innocent.

Anahrod should've seen this coming. The reason these people were so interested in a living Anahrod Amnead, instead of the easier-to-handle dead version, was suddenly all too clear.

Anahrod wanted to point out the many flaws with this plan, most obvious of which was ever believing Neveranimas's accusation. How ridiculous, how absurd, to think a girl no older than Gwydinion had broken into the most heavily defended vault in all Yagra'hai and stolen so much as a breath of air.

But she thought about what Jaemeh had said, back on the *Crimson Skies*. That the only reason Tiendremos wanted her alive was because he thought she was the "real" Anahrod Amnead. That had made little sense before.

Now, it did.

She didn't think admitting her ignorance of Neveranimas's security measures would be good for her continued longevity, however, so she replied: "You think she hasn't fixed the flaw in her security? It's been seventeen years."

"If she can," Ris said. "It's not necessarily easy to update security inscriptions."

"A grave may do fair work to keep a secret when a gag no longer binds," Kaibren said, which was a quote from a Dollagh Ser play.

"Sometimes killing the witnesses is easier than changing the locks," Claw translated unnecessarily. Kaibren gave the much younger woman a fond look.

Anahrod didn't have to fake the headache. It had come on with a vengeance.

"You expect me to believe that two dragons—dragons!—want to rob the queen of Yagra'hai? What could be worth that kind of risk?"

"Love," Ris said.

Anahrod gave her a look.

"Love," Ris repeated. "As in I would love to be rich. Wouldn't you?"

Jaemeh laughed. "My dragon's motive is less greed than ambition. Neveranimas has been a naughty girl, and this is going to allow Tiendremos to swoop in, reveal her corruption, and fly away with her job." He added, "Although for my part, I too would like to be exceedingly rich."

Anahrod abandoned tea and table in pursuit of fixing herself lunch. "Neveranimas, you said. And what, exactly, are we stealing?" She kept her voice steady.

She'd scream into a pillow later.

Jaemeh visibly relaxed. "Her hoard, obviously."

Anahrod paused in the middle of piling up a plate with food. "I take it she's finally changed her hoard?"

Even when Anahrod had been a candidate, Neveranimas's persistent apathy for upgrading her hoard had been a tiny scandal. Neveranimas had hoarded *books*. Yes, the dragon equivalent of books, but since dragons didn't think dragonstones were valuable, and humans weren't allowed to own them, they were interesting paperweights.

"Oh no," Ris said, "she hasn't changed her hoard. But you didn't steal from her hoard, only from her vault. She's cleverly hidden what she really hoards from everyone, because under no circumstances can she allow her fellow dragons to know that she's been hoarding diamonds for the last hundred years."

Anahrod nearly dropped her plate.

Everyone knew who hoarded diamonds in Yagra'hai, and it wasn't Neveranimas. The dragon king, the real, actual chosen Son of Eannis, the First Dragon, Ivarion: *he* hoarded diamonds.

Or he *had*. Since Ivarion was trapped in a cursed slumber, his hoard theme was off-limits: he wasn't dead but also couldn't be dueled.

As a result, *nobody* hoarded diamonds.

"Eannis," Anahrod whispered. "You're not stealing her hoard because it's not her hoard. She's stolen *Ivarion's hoard*?"

"See?" Ris nudged Jaemeh. "I told you she was smart."

"That's the beauty of this entire situation," Jaemeh said. "She can't say a word to anyone. Neveranimas can't tell people we've taken her diamonds because that would be a confession."

That was, simply put, rock wyrm shit. On so many levels.

Anahrod scoffed as she started to eat, angrily stabbing at her food with her knife. "Tell me you aren't so naïve as to think she needs to tell the truth to come after you. Because she doesn't." She rubbed her forehead. "And if you steal all the diamonds, how is your Tiendremos supposed to prove she committed any crimes? If you're going to lie to me, could you at least keep your story straight?"

Annoyance flickered over Jaemeh's features before he forced a smile. "We're not lying. Tiendremos doesn't need to recover *all* the diamonds. Just enough to prove she did, in fact, steal them. She gets kicked out; he takes over. We walk away with massive quantities of diamonds."

"So many diamonds," Claw said, "that we'll be able to hide places she'll never catch us."

Anahrod sighed to herself. These were educated people, or at least street-smart people. Surely someone had explained the scarcity principle to them. If they started throwing around an entire dragon hoard's worth of diamonds, an entire dragon hoard's worth of diamonds would soon prove worthless.

She looked up from her meal for just long enough to say, "So, what happens when Ivarion wakes up?"

"What are the odds of that?" Jaemeh laughed. "And if he woke up, he'd be rampant and the whole damn city would have to fly over to the Cauldron to put him down. He won't be trying to collect his diamonds."

Anahrod continued eating. The food was good enough. She wondered if they had a human kitchen hidden away somewhere in Tiendremos's lair or if they'd sent down to Duskcloud.

She felt everyone watching her eat, waiting for her to finish.

Anahrod paused. "So, what is this plan of yours?"

Ris caught her lower lip in her teeth and looked away, smiling.

"Plan?" Jaemeh spread his arms. "We couldn't plan before we found you. Now we can. You just need to"—he leaned back in his chair—"tell us how you did it last time."

Her pulse throbbed in her ears, turning the world silent and then loud in too-quick measures. She let her knife clatter down to the plate.

"No," Anahrod said.

"No?" Jaemeh gave an incredulous look.

"Did you forget what the word means so soon?" Anahrod said. "*No*. If the only reason *your* dragon hasn't murdered me is because of what I know, what motivation do I have to tell you?" She raised a hand to forestall the dragonrider's objection. "Right now, he could turn me in with no suspicion falling on him. If you want my help, I need reassurance my life isn't measured in how long I can keep a secret."

Ris started laughing.

"Damn it!" Jaemeh slammed the top of the table, tumbling a crystal scale Naeron had been spinning on its edge. The dragonrider turned on Ris. "This isn't funny!"

"Oh, but it is," Ris commented airily. "It's our fault. Aren't we the ones who insisted on summoning Anahrod the Wicked from the depths of Hell? Yet we're surprised when the daughter of Zavad has claws."

Kaibren raised a glass of wine. "Five times toll the bells for Zavad's sins, four times toll the bells for the southern winds."

Jaemeh gave the man an annoyed glance.

"She's not being unreasonable." Whether Claw was translating or commenting was unclear. "Just common sense to ask for more than our word that we won't cut her lines the moment we don't need her anymore."

"Easy enough for you to say," Jaemeh growled. "You're not the one who has to explain this to Tiendremos."

"Neither are you," Ris said, and in response to his incredulous look, added, "If she'd started to tell you, I'd have stopped her. You can't know the plan, Jaemeh."

"Excuse me?" He leaped from his chair, his face reddening.

Ris leaned on the table with both arms, smiling, but her green eyes had a lethal, sharp look to them. "Jaemeh, Jaemeh, Jaemeh. My team and I are going to take our share of the diamonds, leave Yagra'hai, and never be seen again, but you and Tiendremos? *You're staying.* That means when—not if, but when—Neveranimas questions Tiendremos, it is vitally important for the safety of both Tiendremos and yourself that he not know anything." She bopped him on the nose. "Which means *you* can't know anything."

Jaemeh paused, then exhaled and dropped back down into the chair. "Fuck." He waved a hand. "I'm sorry. You're right. Damn it. Of course you're right. We shouldn't know the details."

"Exactly. Please relay to Tiendremos that I have everything handled. Anahrod's smart. She'll help us." *Because her options would be grim if she didn't* went unsaid.

Jaemeh nodded. He gave Anahrod one last appraising look before he nodded and left the room.

No one said anything.

Then Kaibren exhaled in relief and Claw visibly slumped in her seat. "Fucking finally!" she said.

"Restrain your joy until we can guarantee he can't hear us," Ris murmured. "Kaibren, would you be so kind?"

The man grabbed his satchel from the back of his chair. He shut the door before pulling a roll of silk cloth from his bag and gluing the unrolled fabric to the door seam. Each fabric section had been painted with a complicated inscription of interlocking black lines, curving and crossing over each other in unpredictable ways.

Anahrod couldn't tell what spell was inscribed on the cloth, but she suspected it prevented eavesdropping. Given how he placed the fabric over the door seam, a ward against entry seemed likely, too.

When Kaibren finished—and he hadn't taken long—Ris turned to Anahrod with a broad, pleased smile on her face. "Beautifully done, my dear. I was a little worried when you were dropped into this without time to study, but what could I do? Neither Jaemeh nor Tiendremos would let you out of their sight. But you were perfect."

"I'm so glad you approve," Anahrod growled.

"If I didn't know better, I honestly would've thought that you *had* broken into Neveranimas's vault." Ris had a cheeky look in her eyes. She knew what kind of writhing tidefisher net she'd just dropped in Anahrod's lap.

Anahrod glared. "If you're already aware that I don't know how to rob Neveranimas, *why am I here?*"

Claw rolled her eyes and fished at her belt for a bag of coins, which she tossed at Naeron. He caught the bag without looking up.

Anahrod ground her teeth together. "You made a bet?"

Claw pointed at her using a small, pointed knife, too slender to be used for eating. "What of it, Jungle? I'm from Grayshroud. I'd make a bet against the sun rising if I could find the right odds."

"I'll remember that next time I'm low on funds."

Claw grinned. The scars pulled on the edges of her smile, warping it out of shape. "You do that and see where it gets you. Anyhow, we were betting on how you'd respond to Ris admitting she doesn't need you to get past the Five Locks. I thought you'd take longer to ask the important question, honestly."

Anahrod stared at the group warily. "Shall I repeat the question, then?"

Ris's grin could have lit up the night sky during the dark hour. "Not necessary. You, my lovely, are here for two reasons. First, as bait: Tiendremos only signed on to help us because we convinced him we had a way to locate you, and that only you know the secret to breaking into Neveranimas's vault. Second, as distraction: I don't expect Tiendremos to be as graceful about us keeping him in the dark as Jaemeh just was, but if Tiendremos thinks he already knows the answer, then he won't go nosing around."

Anahrod studied Ris. "The 'answer' being that I'm Anahrod the Wicked, who everyone knows already stole from Neveranimas once before?'"

"Exactly. If Tiendremos knew the entire story, he'd stop being cooperative, and I'm sad to say we need him." Ris shrugged, a "what can you do" gesture. "Just to be crystal clear here: we *are* still robbing Neveranimas. Diamonds are still happening."

Anahrod drank the rest of her tea. It was excellent tea, perfectly brewed. She worked her tongue against the back of her teeth.

"You realize Tiendremos will betray you at the earliest opportunity, right?" Anahrod swept her gaze over the entire group. "If he really wants to prove Neveranimas stole Ivarion's hoard, catching you in the act makes his case foolproof."

Ris waved a hand. "We know. It's already handled."

"Glad to hear it," Anahrod said. "Now, would somebody mind explaining one more time why you had to find *me*? Because you could've hired any actor off the street to pretend to be Anahrod Amnead and your marks wouldn't have known the difference." Ris still wasn't telling Anahrod everything. She could feel it.

"Read her in." Naeron had pulled a foreign coin from his newly gained bag of winnings and was now spinning that instead of the original Seven Crests scale.

"Naeron, it's a little early—"

"She's the fifth. She needs to know." Naeron stopped the coin spin by placing his hand palm down against the edge. He looked up.

Anahrod blinked. He was *angry*.

Ris seemed taken aback as well before her expression hardened into something more determined. She stared out at nothing for a moment.

No doubt rearranging her lies.

"Fine." Ris sighed.

And said nothing.

The whole table waited. Finally Claw said, "You want me to tell the story? Since you can't find the words for the first time in your whole damn life?"

Ris waved her off with an irritable flick of her wrist. "Have you ever heard of the Five Locks?" She directed the question at Anahrod.

"You mean besides Claw mentioning it one minute ago?" Anahrod said. "Yes. It's Neveranimas's vault."

"No," Naeron said. "Not a what. A who." His anger had ebbed, but still lurked behind his dark eyes.

Ris said, "The Five Locks was a human division, living in Yagra'hai, specializing in security systems for dragon hoards. No dragon would dream of hiring another dragon for such a job, so it's a human-only field of study."

Ris leaned back in her chair and, predictably, kicked her boots up onto the table. "This was around a hundred years ago. Ivarion had just gone rampant and fallen into a coma, leaving Neveranimas as regent. She decided to build a new vault for herself. So, she hired the entire division. All five families."

Given that the Five Locks Division no longer existed by the time Anahrod had been sent to Yagra'hai, she could already tell this story didn't have a happy ending.

"They did their job brilliantly," Ris explained. "It's probably the most heavily secured dragon hoard on the entire continent. They were paid . . . and then the families began having 'accidents.'"

"Fatal ones, I gather?"

"Oh, you've heard this story?" Ris was still smiling, but it seemed more feral than friendly. "Anyway, what was that saying, Kaibren? 'A grave will keep a secret when a gag no longer binds'?"

Kaibren didn't correct her, although it looked like a struggle.

Ris continued: "Neveranimas took it to heart. She wasn't content with just the men and women who'd worked on the project, either. She went after the whole division, down to the smallest child."

Anahrod closed her eyes.

"Those who could, ran and hid. Some fled to the Deep, others to the slums of various cities in Seven Crests. The Five Locks vanished as anything other than a misapplied nickname for the treasure vault of their murderer."

The story was tragic and horrible, but she could only think of one reason Ris was explaining it now. Anahrod opened her eyes again. "The Five Locks built a back way into the vault?"

Claw whistled.

Ris's eyes gleamed with pleasure. "Creating a security system like that—it was a huge job. Full of testing, modification, retesting. There came a point in the project where they could no longer safely enter the vault to perform those tests without Neveranimas personally disabling the security. But she didn't like all the interruptions. So yes, they made a key. In fact, they made five."

"One key," Naeron corrected. "Five parts."

"All right, yes. Five parts," Ris allowed.

Kaibren quoted: "Then sent I each part to a different quadrant, for I knew your word was as green as jungle and twice as fickle."

"Yeah, that's a good point," Claw said.

A pause followed.

Ris rolled her eyes. "Translation, please. If you must do this, don't be coy."

"Give the man a break. He's an artist." Claw pulled out several knives at this point and began cleaning them. "Anyway, he said that they must have been concerned that some too-greedy member of the division might try to swipe a copy of the key and come back later. So, they split the key up into five parts and gave each part to a different family. That way, they could only open the vault if everyone agreed."

Anahrod raised both eyebrows. "You got all that from what he just said?"

"Of course I did." Claw crossed her arms over her chest. "He quoted a line from *The Ice at the End of the World*, the closet play by Terren Podgra. And it's from the scene where a dying Meinwen tells Cledragh that he's split the treasure map into four pieces and hidden each piece in a different location because he always knew Cledragh would betray him. Given the context? Had to be about splitting the key to keep everyone honest."

Next to her, Kaibren nodded sagely.

Ris pinched the bridge of her nose. "Remind me why I keep you around again?"

"No choice," Naeron murmured. "Need her."

"Yes, thank you for reminding me."

"Yeah? Well, I hate you, too, water-for-brains. Go choke on Zavad's dick." Claw huffed and continued cleaning her knives.

Ris ignored her. "As I was saying, each family took one key. There are only two ways to open the vault—Neveranimas, or all five keys."

"Blood family," Naeron added.

Ris made a face. "Yes. That. Only blood descendants of the original five families can make the keys work. Another security precaution. And that"—she waved at Anahrod—"is why you're *really* here."

They couldn't be talking about her first mother's side of the family, because Anahrod wasn't a blood descendant of her first mother. Her second mother, with her ring-house ancestry and impoverished roots, had been the one to carry Anahrod to term. She was much more likely to be a descendant of survivors who had gone into hiding.

That side was just Anahrod and her mother, wherever she was.

Ris wasn't done talking. "Even that's not the only reason you're here. We *also* need the key. We have three of the swords and we know where the fourth is located, but we still need the fifth. Yours."

"Swords?" Anahrod choked out a laugh. "You said keys. When did we switch to talking about swords?"

Claw made a swiping gesture through the air with a knife, while Ris said, "The swords *are* the keys. They mimic Neveranimas's claws."

"Well, I don't have—" Anahrod glanced down at the sword at her waist.

"No, it's not *that* sword," Ris said. "I'd hoped that you'd still have the sword when we found you in the Deep, but I'll settle for knowing what happened to it."

Ris wore a strange expression, and Anahrod gazed at it for a long moment before recognizing it: anxiety. She was telling the truth about needing the swords. The plan fell apart—irretrievably, irrevocably broken—if Anahrod's answer was *The sword was melted down* or *It shattered and the pieces were thrown out to sea* or *I gave it away* . . .

Oh.

Anahrod slouched in her seat. Her stomach felt tight and heavy. "Why would you think that I'm the one who has it?"

"Because I've looked!" Ris said. "I've studied your whole family. Even your father, who's working as a damn sausage cart vendor right here in Duskcloud, by the way, just on the off chance that he somehow took the sword in the divorce. Your second parent used to have it—and the last anyone remembers seeing the blasted thing was just before you were dragged away to be executed. Are you telling me you *didn't* take it?"

Anahrod started laughing. Oh, Eannis . . .

The laughter became a wild and out-of-control thing. She laughed harder when she saw the furious, impatient look on Ris's face. Distantly, past the laughing and the tears and the hiccuping need for air, Anahrod noted that she'd finally touched on something Ris cared about. This was important to the dragonrider.

Ris had explained it, hadn't she? No matter what excuse Ris gave Jaemeh, her real motivation was simpler:

Revenge.

Four other people sat at the table; Naeron had called Anahrod the fifth. That meant that Ris, too, was descended from the families that Neveranimas had tried to destroy.

Exactly none of which changed just how screwed they were.

"Yes," Anahrod. "I had the damn sword."

She'd been running away. Anahrod hadn't thought Neveranimas wanted to kill her, just force her into a bond. Anahrod had snuck home to steal her second mother's folding box, the food in the pantry, and that damn antique sword on the wall. She'd never questioned the sword's provenance. It had been in her family—her second mother's side of the family—for generations.

The city watch never even searched her. She was thrown overboard with the folding box—and its sword—still tucked into her coat.

She was in danger of losing herself in laughter again, but the punchline was too good. Such a magnificent joke.

"Oh, Ris," she said, wiping her eyes. "I told you it was a mistake to kill two of Sicaryon's men, but who knew the consequences would bite your heels so soon?"

The redhead turned even paler. "What do you mean?"

Anahrod pushed her plate away from her. She was no longer hungry. "I mean that *Sicaryon* has your fifth sword, and I know that for a fact, because I'm the one who gave it to him."

18

A DRAGON, GOLD

That news ended the meeting.

Ris and Claw began arguing, which escalated into screaming, which drove Naeron from the room with his arms wrapped around his head. Anahrod slipped out after, bemused to realize that Kaibren had removed his inscriptions and escaped with no one noticing.

On the way to the main cavern, she passed human servants. They all seemed like skittish mice, wary of loud noises and cat bells.

By the time she reached the main cavern, Tiendremos hadn't returned. She walked through the weather vanes, spinning them as she went. Definitely not his real hoard. No dragon left their treasure out in the open like this.

This was a joke, a play on his elemental attunement to storms.

Now there was an uncomfortable thought: she hadn't known dragons could have a sense of humor.

It was also a perfect expression of everything she hated about dragons—so driven to hoard their obsessions that they divorced them from all function. What good was a weather vane left indoors?

She threaded her way to the cave entrance, curious to find out how difficult it would be to trek down to Duskcloud. There was no way in hell she was traveling down the mountainside on dragonback.

Anahrod received no warning. One moment she walked toward the sunny cave mouth, and the next a flaring light blinded her. She put a hand to block the glare, squinted.

Her vision returned in time to see a dragon duck into the cave. Not Tiendremos. This was a smaller dragon, with mirror-bright scales—what had reflected the sun into her eyes.

Peralon.

Although she'd thought he was a large dragon when she'd seen him from a distance, on closer observation, Peralon was small, even petite. But size wasn't always what made a dragon dangerous. What was his native element? Was he skilled at magic? She recognized most of the dragon attunements by sight, but she'd never heard of a gold dragon before. Dragons might sport gold accents on their scales, but never as the primary color.

His eyes were scintillating ruby red, his claws crystals. It was as though someone had carved a statue of a dragon—crafted it from gems and metals—and then magically transformed it into the real thing.

Anahrod had no idea how old he was, if he was younger than Tiendremos or older. She wondered what he hoarded, where he laired.

[Such a pleasure to finally meet you,] the dragon purred. [Ris won't stop talking about you.]

Anahrod stepped backward until the sharp end of a weather vane jabbed her back. She glanced around the cave, but they were alone.

The dragon was talking to her.

Not just talking to her. Moving toward her as well. His walk was graceful, elegant, hardly shaking the ground at all.

The dragon lowered his head farther still, until the tip of his nose was in front of Anahrod, until she felt his hot breath on her face. She didn't dare move.

[She says you tamed a titan drake. How did you manage it?]

Inside, Anahrod cursed. How had the dragon known she could understand him? How had he even suspected? She hadn't told anyone. She hadn't even hinted that she could understand *dragons*. Was he bluffing?

He might've been bluffing.

[I know you can hear me.] Peralon seemed less upset than amused, like he'd caught a small child lying on a test.

Ironically, her silence gave her away. A normal person—someone who wasn't trying to pretend they couldn't hear dragons—would've said something, bowed, gone to fetch Ris to be his translator.

They wouldn't have stood still, frozen in fear.

Anahrod's throat felt as dry as the air fifty thousand feet up. "You have to get to them young."

Peralon made a soft noise. The wind from his exhalation blew back her hair. Idly, she reminded herself that she needed to start braiding it again.

[No,] he corrected. [I must disagree.]

Anahrod wished running were an option. He blocked the exit, and there was no place to hide if the conversation took a turn for the worse.

"Excuse me?" she said.

[The trick of taming a creature,] Peralon elaborated, [is simply this: make them understand that they have no choices. That every good or bad thing that will ever happen in their lives comes from you. That their only option, their only path forward, is to make you happy, do whatever you ask of them, until they don't even realize that they're enslaved.] His jaws tightened in something like a smile. [It's easier with animals. Although I suppose you're right: it does help if you get to them young.]

Anahrod stared at him, wide-eyed.

They weren't talking about training titan drakes.

Ris's voice came from behind Anahrod: "Peralon, you're scaring her."

[Am I?] Peralon once again sounded amused. [I'd apologize, but I can't really be sorry for what I am, can I?] The dragon made a deep-throated chuffing sound—laughter. [I'm a dragon, after all. We're *terrifying*.]

"Yes, darling. You certainly are," Ris murmured lovingly as she lounged against the dragon's leg. She studied Anahrod with a thoughtful expression. "I admit, I expected you to be more excited."

Anahrod reluctantly pulled her eyes away from the dragon to face Ris. "About what, exactly?"

"You know"—Ris whirled a hand—"enough wealth to live comfortably for the rest of your days. Or should that fail to motivate, making Neveranimas pay."

"Ah." Anahrod felt acutely sensitive to the gold dragon's presence, to Tiendremos's impending arrival, but most of all, to how much she didn't want to talk about this. The giant cave felt claustrophobic and dangerous. "Easy mistake. If it makes you feel better, Sicaryon used to trip over the same root."

She'd have to walk past Peralon if she wanted to leave. The sense of danger itched across her skin, even though she logically knew she was in no danger because all parties involved needed her alive.

Ris scoffed. "Why wouldn't you want payback? How can you just let it go after the way she hurt you—"

Something inside Anahrod snapped. She could imagine Sicaryon's voice with such perfect clarity, asking the same questions in the same frustrated, angry tone. How many times had they had this same argument?

The next line was easy. She'd practiced it a thousand times. "And what would it fix?"

"What?"

Anahrod threw up her arms. "What would it fix?" she shouted. "Would revenge give me parents who give a damn? Parents who see me as something more than a political tool, who I'm good enough to please?" She paused for an inhale, and because she had more fuel to burn on the bonfire of her anger. "Would revenge change the fact that they've been writing plays and novels where I'm the definition of evil? Does anyone in Seven Crests dare name their children Anahrod these days? Don't bother telling me. I already know the answer."

Ris winced, and behind her, Peralon shifted as though the ground had grown white-hot.

Then, Peralon spoke: [No, but it will stop her from doing the same thing to someone else. You're not the first she targeted. You won't be the last. Not unless something is done.]

"It'll stop her," Anahrod agreed, "but it won't stop it from happening. Because *that* has nothing to do with Neveranimas. It won't change just because she's gone. The problem is not Neveranimas, the problem is that my people are not your equals. We're not your peers. *We're pets.* Eannis herself made us, remember? And when we grew too arrogant she cast us out of heaven to learn humility as your servants. How will revenge against one dragon fix that?"

Anahrod was screaming at a dragon. If there was anything riskier or more suicidal that she'd ever done in her life, she couldn't think of it.

She was a fool.

She wasn't even talking to Peralon or Ris, not really, but Sicaryon sure as hell had been on her mind recently, hadn't he? That wasn't a situation likely to change soon. Not until Ris recovered her damn sword.

She eyed the cave entrance. She'd never make it if the dragon felt like doing something.

Except Peralon didn't attack her, didn't roar, didn't seem offended at all.

[I see what you mean.] A comment directed at Ris, not Anahrod.

"I told you she was special." Ris approached her carefully. "You're right, of course. It won't fix any of that. But you're letting yourself be overwhelmed by the knowledge that you must chop down a whole forest, and you're forgetting that it always starts with one tree. But also: you're lying to yourself."

Anahrod felt a flare of indignation. "How dare you—"

"You don't want revenge? Liar." Ris's voice was gentle, but firm. "Yes, you do. Listen to yourself: you're furious. You have every right to be. Your whole life has been stolen, and I think you've spent the last seventeen years hiding in that jungle precisely so you won't have to think about how angry that makes you. How powerless you feel to do anything about it. What you're feeling is *justified.*"

Anahrod made a choking sound, eyes wide. She didn't—

She clenched and unclenched her fists, swallowed air that was still too damn thin. Ris stood there defiant and so fiercely beautiful Anahrod battled between continuing to fight or trying to kiss her.

But she couldn't—

Ris was a *dragonrider.*

"Maybe my anger is justified," she finally allowed, "but I've also seen what revenge demands a person give up: *everything*. And I refuse to be sacrificed on that altar ever again."

Ris started to say something. It would've been quick and cutting and oh, it would've bled. She paused. "No one's asking you to."

She looked the way Anahrod had felt while talking to Peralon—like she was experiencing that same slow, uncomfortable realization that the conversation had changed without warning.

[If the idea of riches or revenge isn't a sufficient motivator, perhaps this will be: when I speak of keeping this from happening to others, I'm not speaking in the abstract. You were not the first student Neveranimas has attempted to kill, nor are you likely to be the last. You are only exceptional in that you have survived.]

"I'm good at that," Anahrod said, and then her heart fluttered, panicked.

She thought of Gwydinion.

"Do you know why?" she asked him. "Why Neveranimas really wanted to kill me? It can't be what she claimed. I didn't do it. Is it—?" She ground her teeth. "Did she think I was *refusing* her?"

On dark nights when she felt unusually honest with herself, Anahrod could admit that more than revenge, what she really wanted was the truth. To just understand *why*.

She hadn't even refused Neveranimas. She'd asked for more time to make the decision. Anahrod didn't understand—she'd never understood—how that had somehow translated into rejection.

[She's never taken a rider,] Peralon answered, [so I see no reason to suspect her offer to you was sincere. Especially as you share the same blessing as her other victims.]

The cave suddenly felt even colder than normal. Her stomach rolled. There could be no confusion, though. She only had one blessing. "Talking to animals?"

[Yes.]

Anahrod felt like she might be sick. She knew another dragonrider candidate who could talk to animals, didn't she? Gwydinion . . .

"He knew you weren't going to be harmed, by the way," Ris quickly reassured her. Anahrod must've said his name out loud. "His father wasn't in on the plan, but Gwydinion always knew we weren't sending you to Yagra'hai. He never would've agreed to help us, otherwise. He's a good kid."

Anahrod swallowed with a raw throat. "Glad to hear it." She stared Ris in the eyes. "Just one question then, and I mean this sincerely. How does robbing Neveranimas's vault keep Gwydinion alive?"

It was the only question that mattered.

She didn't give a damn about diamonds or wealth or avenging great-grandparents she'd never known, but Gwydinion didn't deserve to go through what she had—not even a tenth of what she had.

Anahrod knew she was giving Ris all the leverage she'd ever need. She'd handed over what she cared about and linked it to her cooperation. All Ris had to do was tie it in a neat bow around Gwydinion's neck and Anahrod would do whatever she asked.

Ris quirked her mouth. "I've already cut a deal with his parents to smuggle him into a sanctuary city beyond Neveranimas's reach until this is all over. He's not going to be in any danger at Yagra'hai, because he'll never attend." She gave Anahrod an apologetic little shrug.

Anahrod could only stare.

Ris could've lied. No, Ris *should've* lied. Even if she never had a second's intention of letting anything happen to the boy, Ris needed Anahrod's cooperation, and this would've ensured it.

But this? This was . . .

This felt like trust. Anahrod didn't know what to do with that emotion except view it with suspicion, examine it for traps. Thankfully, they were in a dragon cave and there was a dragon *right there,* so that made it easier for Anahrod to push back the heady urge to kiss every part of Ris the woman would allow.

"So . . ." Anahrod took a deep breath. "You want me to go back into the Deep, don't you? Convince Sicaryon to give back his sword?"

He'd never do it, not in a thousand years, but she'd try. She had to.

[You have time to prepare. I must return home, but I'll be back in a few days.]

"What?" Ris seemed as surprised by the news as Anahrod. "Why are you leaving?"

[If Anahrod is to overcome her issue with heights, she'll need the proper tools.]

"Fly as quick as you can then," Ris ordered grudgingly. "I'd rather you were here when Tiendremos returns. He will not be happy with me."

Anahrod straightened. "When Tiendremos returns? That makes it sound like he's left Duskcloud entirely."

[He has. Tiendremos cannot leave Neveranimas's side for too long lest he rouse suspicions. He's flying back to Yagra'hai but will return when he can.]

Anahrod exhaled. Just the knowledge that he wouldn't be back soon made the whole cave brighter. "Hope he takes his time," she murmured.

Ris laughed softly. She rubbed Peralon's leg as if for luck and launched herself over to Anahrod. "Shall we go to Duskcloud, then? I don't know about you, but I'd feel more comfortable staying in town for some reason." She hooked a hand around Anahrod's arm. "We could visit your father while we're there."

Anahrod blinked. Ris had mentioned that before, hadn't she? And Anahrod had been too distracted to give it the proper attention.

"You mean my donor father?" Anahrod asked, wrinkling her nose. She had no idea who the man was, but if Ris had been researching her family, it made sense she would've tracked him down.

"Not at all," Ris said. "I mean the person who used to be your first mother. Turns out he was late-sprouting. Calls himself Dradigh now."

Anahrod stared at the woman. "Mayor Amnead? Here in Duskcloud?"

"Not the mayor anymore. And yes. As I said, he works a sausage cart."

Anahrod had been subjected to a barrage of emotions since waking, since leaving that meeting. Distantly, she wondered what Ris had thought to gain by telling her that information, what sort of reaction she'd expected to elicit.

Anahrod wondered about that, too. She felt burned away, her emotions withered to ash. She didn't have enough energy to be properly angry, or whatever emotion she should feel about the person she'd grown up thinking would always protect her. The person who'd instead ordered her thrown to her death.

She just blinked and stared out at nothing, until Ris put a hand on her shoulder, looking genuinely apologetic. "I shouldn't have mentioned this, should I? I'm sorry, I . . . I just assumed you'd want to know."

"I did," Anahrod answered. "I do." She realized there was another emotion banked in the embers of her feelings, even if it was nothing more than a tiny spark.

Curiosity.

She picked up Ris's hand from her shoulder so Anahrod could turn to face the dragonrider.

Anahrod said: "I want to see him."

19

STINGS OF MEMORIES PAST

"This is a bad idea," Ris said.

"No, it isn't," Claw corrected. "Walking out of the Black Ice Corner Club in Grayshroud without paying your tab? That's a bad idea. This is a fucking avalanche rolling downhill."

Anahrod ignored them both and continued watching her father work.

Leaving Tiendremos's cave had proved hilariously simple: Anahrod had walked. There was indeed even a path that Tiendremos's servants used, since they all preferred to live in Duskcloud.

She'd expected Ris to insist on accompanying her. Anahrod had been surprised, however, when Ris had grabbed Claw as well. Neither woman gave any indication that they'd been screaming at each other like surly laundrywomen not more than an hour earlier.

Claw had rummaged through her bag until she'd found a pair of black silk veils, the sort that started just below the eyes and covered the lower face: Blackglass veils.

"I thought you didn't practice any Blackglass customs," Anahrod said, less an accusation than a point of confusion.

"I do when it's useful," Claw said. "And right now, it's useful." Claw shoved a veil in Anahrod's hands. "Anyway, wear the damn veil. We can't have your own father recognizing you, now can we?"

Then it had only been a matter of tracking down the corner where he worked. If she were being entirely truthful, Anahrod had thought Ris was lying. That she must have been lying about this, because who could ever think her first mother—the mayor of Crystalspire!—would not only be late-sprouting but working as a street vendor?

But there he stood; head bent over steaming trays. She wasn't sure she'd have recognized him if she hadn't been explicitly told. He was taller and broader, and his face seemed harder. He needed to shave.

She assumed inscriptions were responsible somehow.

"What did you say his new name was? Dradigh?"

"Yes," Ris said. "You must realize that what happened was a tremendous scandal," Ris said as they continued to watch the man. To the uninitiated, the three women just looked like three students from the university sitting down next to a fountain to talk about philosophy or history or the latest inscription theories. People from all over Seven Crests came to Duskcloud to attend university, so it wasn't even odd to see someone with red hair or Blackglass veils.

Ris continued: "That scandal didn't reflect well on him. At best, his only child was a heretic and a traitor he'd sheltered until the dragons demanded justice.

"At worst, well. What kind of person sends his own child to death without question, without investigation? People wondered if perhaps he moved so quickly because he covered for his own sins. Everyone started paying attention. It wasn't too long before certain, well, let's just call them accounting irregularities, came to light. His wife divorced him. He didn't win the next election. His family disowned him. His division kicked him out. His whole life fell apart. No one wanted to work with him or hire him. Apparently, all the important patents had been owned by your birth mother, and she kept them. He was suddenly penniless . . ."

"So, he ended up in Duskcloud?"

"Exactly," Ris said. "And at some point, experienced an epiphany about his place in the universe, with the result you see now."

Anahrod stared at the food cart. Her father laughed at something a student said as he handed over a sausage roll. He wore an easy, friendly grin, one Anahrod rarely remembered seeing while growing up.

He looked happy.

Anahrod launched herself upright. "Anyone else hungry?"

Ris sat straighter. "That's not a good idea."

Anahrod pretended not to hear her. "I believe I'm in the mood for a sausage roll."

"Anahrod, no." Ris kept her voice down, glancing around herself to make sure no one else heard.

"I'll take one spicy," Claw said. "With pepper relish." She tilted her head in Ris's direction. "She likes hers with sweet pickles and cheese."

Ris gave the woman a betrayed glare. "You're not helping."

"Not trying to, boss."

"Great. Three sausage rolls coming right up." Anahrod half expected Ris to try to stop her, but the dragonrider merely glared her disapproval instead. Which meant her temper was largely performative; she'd seen Ris when the woman was genuinely angry.

Anahrod wiped her palms on her trousers as she reached the back of the line. His cart was popular. A long line of students waited their turn before it was time to return to classes. Anahrod watched as he laughed with the students. He knew a shocking number of them by name and favorite order.

The numbness was fading, pushed out by a tangle of emotions not so easy to identify. She'd balled her hands into fists by the time she reached the front of the line, to hide their shaking.

"What can I—" Dradigh Amnead looked up, and for just a moment, Anahrod thought he recognized her. "Oh, you're new here. Just starting classes?"

She hesitated. "Yes."

"You'll love it here, no worries about that," her father said, smiling. "Now what can I get you?"

She forced herself to answer. "Three rolls. One extra spicy with pepper relish, one with sweet pickles and cheese, and one—" She felt her throat closing on her. "One house special."

"All that food can't just be for you. Ordering for friends?" As he spoke, he never ceased working, his hands gracefully dancing over the ingredients.

She stared at his hands. Normally, that was rude, but watching him fix the food was the perfect excuse.

He wore a ring of sleep ivy. Exactly as one would expect of a late-sprouting man.

"Miss? Are you all right?" Her father's voice cut through her fugue. She focused on him, to see his brow creased with concern. He set the sausage rolls on the edge of the prep area. "You have any problems with those, you come back and see me, understood? I take care of all my kids. Ask anyone."

She had no idea if the sound she made was a laugh or a sob.

"I'm sorry." Anahrod set money down on the counter, some distant part of her aware she was overpaying. She grabbed the sausage rolls and retreated before he saw her crying. She couldn't stand it if he tried to comfort her.

It would be more than she could bear.

Dradigh shouted something, but she couldn't hear it over the blood rushing through her ears.

Her father wore other rings, too. He was a member of one of the local divisions, something associated with food. He was in an exclusive relationship circle, masculine only.

Somehow, she found her way back to the other two women. She shoved the sausage rolls into Claw's hands and continued walking.

Anahrod ducked into an alley. She didn't want to be anywhere out in the open when she broke down. She ended up in a tiny, dingy street sandwiched between two bookstores. It smelled of old food, piss, and, weirdly, leather.

She set her hands against the brick wall. Of course it was brick. Everything in Duskcloud was brick. She wanted to scream. Instead, she dug her fingers into the mortar so hard one of her nails bent backward. When her vision grew too blurry to see, she ripped the veil off her face and used it to sop up her tears.

"At least he's not your real father—"

Anahrod whipped her head up to glare at Claw, who stood at the mouth of the alley eating half a sausage roll.

"What is *wrong* with you?" Anahrod demanded.

How dare she. Of course he was her real parent. He was her real father. So what if he wasn't related by blood? She'd always known that. No inscription existed to allow two women—or a late-sprouting man and a woman—to conceive a child together. That had never been important, when he'd taught her math, law, rhetoric, and how to navigate Crystalspire's important treaties. He used to take her to fly kites at the park and had been the one to cave to her begging and gift her a vel hound puppy.

He was also the person who'd ordered her thrown to her death.

That's why it hurt so much.

"What's wrong with me?" Claw cackled. "We don't have that kind of time, Jungle."

"Fuck off," Anahrod spat.

Claw wrinkled her nose. "Nah. Ris was gonna come over, but the way she tells it, her old man never did a damn thing wrong his whole life and all the stars winked out of the skies in grief the night her parents died. She can't relate to this. She doesn't know what it's like."

Anahrod raised her head. "What it's like?"

"Yeah. You know. To love your daddy while also hating him so much you could put a sword through his gut." Claw set her back against the brick wall and continued eating. "Mine sold me to pay off his gambling debts when I was ten." She said it matter-of-factly, like she was describing the color of his favorite coat.

Anahrod stared in shock. "Slavery's not—"

"Not legal? Tell it to the mountains, Jungle." Claw traced a finger down her face. "Gave me my first scars, too, to make sure I was too ugly for ring-house work. He was fine handing over his little girl to murderers and thieves, but Eannis forbid she end up a whore." Claw shrugged. "Could've been worse. You don't want to know the shit Kaibren's daddy did to him. Gives me nightmares."

Anahrod's tongue felt thick enough to block all the air from her throat. "When the dragons came from Yagra'hai with their orders for my death, do you know what my mo—my father did?"

Claw talked around the last piece of roll. "Everything they asked?"

"Without question! Without a second's hesitation! He never even came to talk to me. Never asked whether I'd really done it. Neither of my mothers bothered to say goodbye." She glanced back toward the open courtyard where her father worked his stand. "He seems happy. I don't know how I feel about that."

"I'd be howling mad," Claw admitted. "Although I promise you this, Jungle: if he's happy, it's only cause nobody's around to remind him of his sins."

"I don't know. My first mother would've deemed working a food cart to be a humiliation worse than death," Anahrod murmured.

There was no shame in earning a wage by keeping people fed. Yet, her first mother wouldn't have seen it that way. She was a daughter of privilege, raised in one of the richest divisions in Crystalspire. That woman thought this work beneath her.

Which meant Anahrod didn't know *this* man at all.

"No," she whispered. "I think he might really be happy." She turned back to Claw. "He doesn't have to lie about who he is here. He doesn't have to pretend."

Anahrod felt an ugly wrenching sensation in her chest as she realized it was worse than sympathy; *she understood him.* Understood the appeal of living so the only demand the universe placed on a person was to be themselves. For her, that something had been surviving in the Deep; for him, selling lunch to college kids. In either case, it meant freedom from the expectations of people who had only ever made an endless series of demands.

She was so very much his daughter.

Silence spread out along the edges of the garbage and dirt of the alleyway.

"I'll still gut him for you, if you asked," Claw finally said. "As a professional courtesy."

"Kind of you, but no thanks." Anahrod swallowed back her grief. "We should return."

"Oh no. Wouldn't want Ris to fret." Claw's voice dripped sarcasm. "Don't let sweet cheeks fool you; she's worse than a thousand grandmas. Anyway, you go. Kaibren and I have tickets to a performance of *Sweet Mountain Snowfalls* over at the Players' House. In the morning we'll stop by bright and early to figure out what supplies we're gonna need for our next Deep expedition." She grimaced at the last part, clearly not looking forward to a return to sea level.

That made two of them.

PART FOUR

THE
RECOVERY
OF
PRECIOUS
THINGS

20

THE VERSATILITY OF INSCRIPTIONS

Anahrod would not, under threat of disembodiment by ravenous rock wyrms, admit that seeing her father had been good for her.

But it had.

As long as Ris never figured that out, it was fine.

For her part, Ris had apparently decided that their conversation regarding revenge, most especially the part about Gwydinion being a potential target, meant that Anahrod was "all in" and could therefore be treated as a full team member.

Ris wasn't wrong, but the swiftness with which Anahrod found herself on the group's "trusted" list still left her reeling.

The group spent the next several days preparing to return to the Deep. And also, at least in Anahrod's cause, shopping for clothes, braiding her hair, buying a more accurate set of rings, and studiously ignoring Ris's unsubtle flirtations.

Which she needed to do something about soon. Both Anahrod's and Ris's garden rings claimed their wearers were comfortable with casual sex, but Anahrod already knew that hers came with an unspoken caveat: *except for Ris.*

There would be nothing casual about intimacy with Ris.

Which could not be allowed because, as Anahrod was increasingly having trouble reminding herself, *Ris was a dragonrider.*

Anahrod tried her best to distract herself from walking off that cliff by working with Kaibren on what sorts of goods and commodities might entice Sicaryon to willingly part ways with Anahrod's family sword.

It was, she admitted, a bit like keeping her hand out of an oven by putting it in a lit fireplace. Luckily, any temptations in that regard were made easier to bear by distance and Claw's snarky comments. The young woman particularly enjoyed discussing the Scarsea king's forty spouses and her suspicions that he was overcompensating for a lack of bedroom skills.

He wasn't, but Anahrod didn't feel inclined to defend the man's honor.

They were still preparing by the end of the third day. The biggest holdup was that Kaibren could only make inscriptions so fast, and anyone they hired to help would almost certainly ask uncomfortable questions.

In moments of weakness, Anahrod found herself missing her second mother. Kaibren was an amazing inscriptionist in that he had an astonishing number of patterns memorized, but he wasn't an inventor. He didn't seem to have either interest or talent for innovation, whereas her second mother . . .

Well. It hadn't exactly surprised Anahrod when Ris had mentioned that her birth mother had owned all the family patents, that their division hadn't kicked *her* out along with the mayor. Her birth mother's genius had allowed her to work her way out of a ring-house division and into the biggest banking division in all of Crystalspire. Anahrod had absolutely no doubt that the woman could've scribbled out an inscription that would've made Sicaryon drool all over himself.

Dinner was an informal affair at the guesthouse where they were staying. The kitchen served whatever the cook felt like making that evening, although a stew always simmered in the pot for people who didn't want the main dish. That night it was roast fowl with dumplings.

Anahrod ate her own food, bought at the market. It's not that she didn't trust the cooks—

But yes, it was because she didn't trust the cooks.

Fortunately, the guesthouse allowed such behavior. She wasn't even the only one who made a habit of the practice. Ris ate her own food as well, likely prepared in advance by Kaibren.

They were both untrusting souls.

Anahrod noticed nothing wrong at first. Not until people fell around her like overly ripened fruit. A man sitting nearby gasped out, "Poison!" as he collapsed. He did not stand back up again.

Where was Ris? Anahrod didn't know. She hadn't seen Kaibren or Claw yet that evening, either.

Naeron . . . ?

Naeron was at one of the other tables, slumped in his chair, eyes closed, unconscious.

"Damn it," Anahrod cursed as darkness creeped in around the edges of her vision.

This wasn't poison.

People who said such things watched too many theater shows and knew nothing about poison. No one around her was vomiting, convulsing, or bleeding. Very few poisons led a person gently into darkness, soft as velvet wrapped around a throat.

And there were no poisons, not a single one, that affected all and sundry at the exact same time, regardless of size or dosage.

She'd eaten her own food, drunk her own wine. Yet everyone was sliding down to the floor, at best unconscious. Even one of the servers had passed out, and he'd just been carrying the plates . . .

Anahrod turned her plate upside down, ignoring the tiny stab of guilt she felt at wasting food.

Someone had drawn a complicated inscription array on the bottom. No sooner had she seen the inscription, however, than the world around her darkened.

The last thing she heard was the clattering of the plate as it slipped from her fingers.

Anahrod woke, stared up at an unfamiliar ceiling, and idly wondered if Claw would be open to making a wager on how many days it would be before Anahrod was kidnapped next.

At least she was still in Duskcloud, judging from the architectural style.

She raised her head. This was a study rather than a bedchamber, although someone used the room for the occasional nap. She knew that much because she'd woken on a lounging chair, with a pillow under her head and a silvertuff blanket tucked around her shoulders.

Anahrod's boots were missing, but she was neither bound nor gagged. She wondered what they'd done with her sword before she remembered that she'd left it in her room.

Her kidnappers continued to be considerate, at least.

"Hello, Anah," a man said.

She hadn't noticed him at first. He'd been sitting by a window, just outside the range of her peripheral vision.

He was certainly handsome, if a little pale, dressed in a style popular with Duskcloud students, all soft gathers and wide cuffs. His slim trousers were gray, tucked into darker gray leather boots. His shirt was a deep purple, which again made Anahrod wonder if Seven Crests had a new trading source. Last she knew, that color purple came from a shellfish found only in the same waters as tide-fishers, and was thus astronomically expensive. A matching purple ribbon tied his ash-brown hair back.

Anahrod rubbed the sleep from her eyes. Then some deep, soft part of her shoved aside years of separation and linked that voice, coming from a stranger, with the same voice, coming from a friend.

Anahrod wouldn't have recognized him if she'd passed him on the street. Not in this context.

She still knew his voice. She still knew his eyes, glittering and sharp, gray as the sword he'd once given her to seal their vows to each other.

"Sicaryon?"

Anahrod wondered if she might still be dreaming.

The moment she named him, his clothing became strangely indecent and provocative, even though logically this was more clothing than she'd ever seen him wear before.

What was even more concerning was how effortlessly Sicaryon wore the clothes. Like he was entirely used to such fashions, because naturally he lived in Duskcloud now. Didn't everyone who mattered?

She eyed his dark hair. A wig, she would wager. It wasn't the right texture, and Sicaryon was blond.

"Nothing to say?" Sicaryon crossed over to the desk and leaned against its edge. "Even for you, that's surprising."

At least he had an accent. Even so, his Haudan was excellent.

Of course it was, she thought bitterly, still in shock. He'd learned it from her.

"What are you doing here?" She looked around the room openly. No sign of weapons, or soldiers, or any sort of guard. No sign that Sicaryon wasn't alone.

She didn't trust it.

He raised an eyebrow. "Checking on my sword-sister."

"No, what are you—" She ground her teeth. "What are you doing in Seven Crests?" She glared at the clothes, the hair. She noticed his mantle draped over a chair, also gray and purple. A silver pin peeked out from under the fold, enameled with the Scarsea wave.

She laughed, despite herself, at the pin. The brazen bastard openly wore the Scarsea crest. Why not? It's not like any Skylander would recognize it. "Don't claim you came here for me."

His mouth quirked. "You might be surprised. Anyway, the plumbing."

She drew short. "Excuse me?"

Sicaryon's look was fond. "Remember your first year in the Deep? When you were still healing from all those broken bones?"

She shifted uncomfortably. "Obviously."

"You wouldn't shut up about bathtubs," Sicaryon said. "I decided to find out what all the fuss was about."

Anahrod blinked at him. He calmly stared back.

She couldn't tell whether he was joking.

"And?" she finally asked. "What's your verdict?"

"Amazing," Sicaryon admitted. "Wouldn't want to soak in anything that hot while in the Deep, but up here? Magical. This whole sewer idea is fantastic. Already stealing that."

Anahrod sucked on her teeth, tried to bottle the bubbling laughter threatening to spill out. "That's it? 'Spent some time in the Skylands. Love the sewer system'?"

He shrugged. "Food's better in the Deep. Just about everything else is better up here." His voice lost a little of its joking edge. "Your people have no idea how good they have it, do they?"

"No," Anahrod agreed softly. "Not a single clue."

"Anyway, around a month ago—maybe a little longer—I heard the oddest rumor. That the dragon queen's second-in-command had shown up in Crystal-spire and demanded they hand over Anahrod Amnead. I found that concerning. So much so that I sent people to invite you to come back to the capital, where you'd be safer." He gave her a wry look. "Apparently, that invitation was miscommunicated. Just slightly."

He wasn't holding a weapon. There was no sword slung across his back or resting on his hip. He wasn't armed at all as far as Anahrod could see.

He didn't want to scare her.

It was a little late for that. She felt the threat of him scrape along her skin, raising hairs as it passed.

"That was an accident," she said. "A group of Skylanders thought your men were kidnapping me with ill intent: rape or murder or both. Their intentions were good, just rash."

He huffed. "Hmm."

She put her feet under her and searched around until she found her shoes. "And yet, they didn't set a pride of rock wyrms on me. Or kidnap—" She bit her tongue. "All right, fine, they kidnapped me. Is it 'Kidnap Anahrod' season already?"

"Feels like it starts earlier every year." His gray eyes sparkled.

"I should fine people for kidnapping me without a license . . ." She glared then, in case he'd come to the entirely erroneous conclusion that she wasn't still furiously angry at him. "You're claiming this was all just a misunderstanding? You expect me to believe that your people were trying to help me by provoking Overbite into a fight so they could steal my body while I was distracted? And the five-thousand-scale reward for my capture was also 'trying to help'? What about lighting that targrove swamp on fire? How was that helpful? I'm dying to know."

"Huh." He chewed on a lip. "You know, when you say it like that, it doesn't sound like I had any good intentions at all, does it?"

She stamped her feet into her boots. "No. Weirdly, it really doesn't." Anahrod raised her head, noted his expression, and knew—just knew—that he was about to say something witty. Something to make her laugh and diffuse the anger the way he always did.

"And now this? You drugged—" She waved a hand to fend off his correction. "Enchanted, inscribed, whatever—and how do you have people who can inscribe, anyway? Nobody in the Deep knows how to make inscriptions!"

"Nobody in the Deep *knew* how to make inscriptions," Sicaryon gently corrected.

She stared at him. "What have you done?"

"No, no," Sicaryon said. "What have *you* done. Which was, by the way, teaching a Deeper troll how to pass himself off as Skylander. The university program here isn't that difficult if you're motivated. I even graduated a year early. You would've loved the graduation ceremony. Very solemn."

No, she was wrong. She had to be dreaming. This was a dream. Possibly a nightmare. "You, you—you what?"

Sicaryon shrugged. "You learned how to live in my world. Now it's my turn."

Anahrod could only stare and wonder if the feeling inside her was horror or respect. Maybe both. She pushed both feelings aside.

"That doesn't—that changes nothing. Even if you were trying to help the first time—" She inhaled sharply. "No! You were passing around posters offering five thousand scales for my capture. That was the whole reason that Ris even knew I was still alive. Don't play innocent."

He grinned. "Pretty sure we haven't been that since we were seventeen."

"Sicaryon!"

He pushed himself away from the table in her direction. "Who's Ris?"

"Not important."

"Huh. In other words, very important." She watched him mentally tuck away that information for later before returning to the immediate topic. "I may have mentioned that we might want to offer a reward for information on your whereabouts. Someone too eager to please interpreted that as a 'bounty for your capture.' By the time I found out, the posters were already out in the world."

She studied him. She still knew him well enough to spot the evasion. Not a lie, but not the whole truth, either.

The story itself was plausible. She knew better than most the nonsense that happened under the excuse of "bureaucracy." Sometimes that nonsense resulted from simple incompetence and sometimes it was the cloak drawn over malice and machinations.

She ran her tongue against the back side of her teeth, thought about normally sharp speech now gentled with "may have"s and "maybe"s.

Sicaryon wasn't that upset about losing two of his men. He should've been. Sicaryon was loyal to his people—assuming they were loyal to him first.

"So, who was *really* trying to kidnap me?"

He looked surprised for a moment, then started laughing.

"Sicaryon—"

"I'm uncertain," he finally said when he had control of himself again. "There are a lot of candidates."

"You *have* been busy, haven't you?"

He tipped his head in her direction. "Fair. Everything's changing quickly. There will always be people who hate that they don't have as much say in how that change happens as they think they deserve. At least they don't want to hurt you."

"That targrove fire suggests otherwise."

Sicaryon's smile faded.

She said: "Maybe they never planned for it to be a successful kidnapping—just something to make me mad enough to come after you."

"Maybe," Sicaryon allowed. He studied the wall, chewing on the edge of a thumbnail. "I'd lose no matter who won that fight."

He didn't seem to be aware he'd said that part out loud.

A gust of wind tossed rocks against the window, startling them both. A shadow fell over the area outside, a cloud rolling in front of the sun.

Except she knew something else was happening.

She'd had dinner in the evening. It was daylight now.

"How long was I out?"

He shrugged. "Since last night. It seemed like you needed the sleep."

She grabbed Sicaryon's mantle and threw it at him. "You need to leave. Right now."

He gave her a hurt expression. "But I thought—?"

She shook her head. This was her fault: she'd spent too long talking. "No, you don't understand. The dragons can track me."

The building shook.

This wasn't Crystalspire, whose buildings were designed to support a dragon landing on the roof. Duskcloud buildings were more fragile. If a dragon tried to land here, it would take the entire building down with it.

Tiendremos just wouldn't care.

"Run," Anahrod told Sicaryon.

He grabbed her hand. She immediately ripped it free.

"Damn it—"

"No! Run while you still can." She pushed him toward the door. "You *can't* rescue me, Sicaryon. Stop trying."

He stared at her for a split second, dumbfounded. Perhaps he even considered the idea. Running.

It would've been too late, anyway.

The sound of snapping, tearing wood and shattering brick filled the air. Slate tiles and freed nails fell about them. One wall groaned, mortally wounded, as it twisted away from its siblings, taking a window with it.

The gold dragon, Peralon, peeled back the roof like he was skinning a piece of fruit.

A NEW DEAL

[Are you injured?] Peralon's mental voice was thick with concern.

"You might've asked before you destroyed a building," Anahrod retorted. "I'm fine. I'm unharmed. But—"

[Cover your eyes.]

She shuddered as a gold claw grabbed her. Anahrod heard a scream—Sicaryon's.

"Don't you dare hurt him!"

The dragon laughed, like sunlight glinting off water flowing down a babbling brook. [I would sooner sit on a church than harm someone important to you. At least Ris would forgive me for destroying a church.]

Anahrod might've responded if all her attention hadn't been on covering her eyes and pretending what was happening was not, in fact, happening.

The wind whipped past her as she hid behind her hands like a child, somehow convinced that if she couldn't see the monsters, they couldn't see her either.

Some eternity later—a few seconds, perhaps—Peralon set her down. She fell, rolled, hit something, then stopped for long enough to push herself to her feet. They were back in Tiendremos's lair.

She'd hit a weather vane.

Peralon had also set Sicaryon on the ground, but directly in front of Claw, who now held a dagger to his throat. Ris and Kaibren both readied ranged weapons, hers a hovering sword and his a crossbow.

Sicaryon was unlikely to understand the threat Naeron represented, but he was there, too.

They might as well have been invisible for all that Sicaryon paid attention to them. His eyes only saw the dragon.

Given Sicaryon's claim of attending university in Duskcloud, he was guaranteed to have seen dragons before, but likely only from afar. Gauging a dragon's size was so hard when they were framed by nothing but the open sky. It was only when viewed up close that the terror had a real chance to grab on with claw and tooth.

Peralon kept his distance, although the dragon's threat loomed. Claw wasn't being so circumspect, and worse, the woman was three seconds from grabbing Sicaryon by the hair.

If she was right about him wearing a wig, then Claw accidentally removing it would be hilarious and embarrassing for both parties.

They'd never forgive each other.

So Anahrod intervened. She would've put her sword between them, but she hadn't been wearing it when Sicaryon had kidnapped her. Who wears a sword to dinner? She put her hand on Claw's arm, and hoped the woman remembered that Anahrod was an indispensable part of "the plan."

"Don't hurt him," Anahrod ordered. "That's Sicaryon. We need him, re-member?"

Ris gave her a surprised look. Anahrod ignored it in favor of the more imminent threat to peace: Claw and her eager knives.

"Sheath your claws, Claw." Ris studied the man. "Funny. I expected you to be—"

"More covered in mud." Claw pulled the knife away from Sicaryon's throat and backed away. "What's this world coming to when you can't even count on the monsters to look the part?"

Sicaryon put a hand to his collar and stretched his neck to the side. His gaze never left Peralon. "I'm not the monster in the room."

Her sword-brother dusted himself off. He straightened and pulled an invis-ible cloak of dignity back around his shoulders, as though he was the one who'd summoned them. He reverted to ruler, wearing no crown but the one that mat-tered: attitude.

Kaibren looked impressed, but the man was a huge fan of the stage.

Ris smiled her most charming smile. "I find myself more than a little curious what a Deeper king is doing above the cloud sea, let alone in Seven Crests."

Sicaryon turned to Ris for the first time then; his gaze turned appraising.

Anahrod could tell exactly what he was thinking, because it wasn't so far off from her own reaction upon first meeting Ris and realizing *what* she was: too bad *she's a dragonrider.*

Sicaryon turned back to Anahrod. "These are the people who 'rescued' you the last time? The ones who killed my men?"

"Shit," Claw muttered under her breath.

"Yes," Anahrod said. It was the truth, after all.

"We were rescuing her *this time*, too," Ris cut in, clearly unhappy about being dismissed from the conversation as inconsequential. "Because apparently *your* idea of helping your sword-sister looks a lot like kidnapping to anyone else."

The only sign Sicaryon gave that he'd heard Ris was a flaring of his nostrils. "Have I misunderstood the situation, Anah? You're happy in the lair of *a dragon?*" He glared at Peralon.

"I'm not sure I'd describe it as happy," Anahrod admitted, "but I'm convinced that it's necessary."

"Why?" Sicaryon demanded.

Ris started to say something; Anahrod answered first. "Because of Never-animas."

Sicaryon's expression turned judgmental. "So, you're interested in revenge then, after all."

She sucked in a breath.

The conversation always came back to this.

"No," she said. "That's not it."

"It's about money," Claw chimed in. "Huge, giant heaps of money." She gleefully ignored the "stop it" motions Ris was making.

Sicaryon glanced at Claw. "No, it's not."

Claw's eyebrows shot up. "Excuse you, troll boy? I just told you what our motive is."

"You told me what your motive is, yes," he agreed, "but Anahrod's not that shallow."

Claw put her hand to a knife hilt. "Ris, are you *sure* I can't kill him?"

Nobody else said a word. They all waited on Ris.

"Do you trust me?" Anahrod asked Sicaryon. It was an unfair question. She knew it was an unfair question. Once, the answer would've been obvious, but they'd been apart for too long.

Except the bastard didn't hesitate, not for one second. "Of course I do."

"Then please trust that I will explain everything to you later," Anahrod said. "I'm not in any danger. You know where I'm staying—clearly—so give us a way to contact you and we'll set up another meeting. Later. When everyone's calmer."

He narrowed his eyes. "No."

"You just said you trusted me—"

"I trust you," Sicaryon clarified. "Not them." He gave Ris a dark look. "Which means they don't have my cooperation until they cut me in."

"In men, greed oft surpasses valor's grace," Kaibren commented. He didn't seem upset, though. He mostly looked amused.

"No fucking kidding," Claw spat. "Wait. Cut you into what? What do you think is going on here?"

Sicaryon cast a contemptuous look at the young woman. "It involves Never-animas, her right hand Tiendremos is involved somehow, and it's an opportunity to get rich. You've told me everything I need to know." He raised an eyebrow at Anahrod. "Are we robbing Neveranimas's hoard, or someone else's?"

Everyone tensed. Not in an embarrassed way, but as a prelude to violence.

"We need him," Anahrod reminded the group.

They didn't know Sicaryon the way she did. He wouldn't go down without a fight. Anahrod glanced at Naeron.

Under normal circumstances, Sicaryon wouldn't go down without a fight.

Ris had that look in her eyes again, the one that said she was a woman who let nothing come between her and her plans. Her fingers tapped an impatient drumbeat against her thigh.

"Not important," Ris answered the man's question.

"I disagree," he told her.

Ris locked gazes with Sicaryon. "I don't care. It's cute that Anahrod's trying to save your life by making you seem important, but you're of vast insignificance. Count yourself grateful that I want to keep Anahrod's favor too much to just kill you out of hand."

Anahrod couldn't tell if Ris was serious or if this was a bargaining tactic.

She did know it was out of character for Ris to act like this—unless someone was jeopardizing her plans. Or she was frightened.

Maybe this was both.

In response, Sicaryon grinned rakishly at Anahrod. "I get it now," he told her.

Anahrod sighed.

Ris's green eyes turned cold. She motioned to the group. "Everyone, go back to what you were doing. We'll set up a meeting later. You—" She pointed a finger at Sicaryon. "We're talking in private. Now."

Anahrod tensed. "That's not a good idea."

"Oh no," Sicaryon disagreed, "this is a fantastic idea. Ris and I need to get to know one another. We have so many things to discuss."

Ris was practically baring her teeth. "I agree."

Claw grabbed Anahrod's arm. "Come on. I want to stay and watch the show as much as you do, but we should give these lovebirds their privacy."

Anahrod scowled. "They're going to kill each other."

"That's why I want to stay and watch." Claw tugged harder on her arm. She must have noticed that Anahrod didn't have a weapon. "Now come on. There's this fantastic puppet show they do over at the Southern Court Fountain. Want to join Kaibren and me? They're about to do *Daughter of Darkness*."

"No thank you, I—" Anahrod noticed Kaibren put his head in his hand, as though Claw had just said something embarrassing or rude.

Anahrod turned to Naeron. "What's *Daughter of Darkness* about?"

"You," he replied.

Of course it was.

Claw rolled her eyes. "Why do you have to spoil everything, Naeron? The look on her face would've been so worth it."

Anahrod just glared. "Go on ahead—"

"No," Naeron said. "We all leave." He wore a stubborn, unhappy expression.

Anahrod gave one last glance at Sicaryon and Ris. They were locked in an actual, honest-to-Eannis staring contest.

The swords would come out—literally as well as figuratively—the moment they were alone. Which was a problem, since Sicaryon wasn't armed.

[I won't allow it to come to violence,] Peralon told Anahrod. [Don't worry about your friend.]

In theory, she shouldn't have taken Peralon's word for that, either. He was biased.

She still felt reassured, and then annoyed at herself for feeling reassured.

"Fine," Anahrod said. "I'll find you both later."

⌄

Anahrod only left physically.

She had to at least pretend to leave, since Naeron, Kaibren, and Claw were escorting her back like she was under arrest, but she cast her awareness out at the first opportunity, looking for something small and easy to miss.

She found a scrabber, because scrabbers were everywhere.

Maneuvering the little rat proved the hardest part, but once it lurked in the right part of Tiendremos's cave, her eavesdropping opportunities were secured.

She knew it was rude, but there was no way she was allowing this conversation to happen out of her earshot.

Ris and Sicaryon had barely moved from the position where she'd seen them last, still glaring at each other. The staring contest had transformed into a battle of wills to see who would break the silence first.

"Fine," Ris eventually growled. "What's your price?"

Sicaryon's brows rose. "Price?"

"Yes. What do I have to pay you to make sure that you give me what I need and then we never see your pretty face again? Money? Inscriptions? *What is your price?*"

Sicaryon smiled wryly. "You really are jealous, aren't you?"

Ris's stare turned lethal. "Don't pretend that you're here for any reason other than indulging a puerile obsession. She means nothing to you, assuming she ever did."

Anahrod flinched and almost lost her hold on the scrabber.

Sicaryon stopped smiling. "You don't know that."

"I don't?" Ris tilted her head. "How many spouses do you have? Wasn't it something like forty? Not exactly a sign of true love, is it?"

He blinked. "What?"

"Don't pretend you didn't understand me. You speak Haudan just fine." She ran her finger along the edge of a rusted weather vane shaped like a castle, sending it spinning.

Sicaryon stepped toward her, then stopped as Peralon shifted his weight as a not-too-subtle reminder that there was a dragon still in the cave. Sicaryon gave the dragon a wary look before focusing once more on Ris. "I understood the words. That doesn't mean I have any idea what the hell you're talking about. I'm not married. I've never been married. Every time I go home, someone gives me grief about it."

Ris stared at the man. "You expect me to believe—"

"I don't care what you believe," Sicaryon told her. "I care what you drag Anahrod into. She's been through enough." He narrowed his eyes. "Oh. I see the problem. You think I don't know who you are."

Ris inhaled softly, took a step back. "I'm sure she mentioned my name."

He shook his head. "No. Not who Anahrod thinks you are. Who you *really* *are*. Not so many redheads who can make swords dance and ride a gold dragon in the world." He pointed a finger. "I grew up on stories about you."

Anahrod felt a jolt of shock, not just at Sicaryon's words, but at Ris's response.

Ris regrouped, stepped forward again—unquestionably a threat. "Then you know what happens to people who cross me."

"I do," he agreed, "which is also why I know this isn't about wealth, no matter what that girl with the knives said. You don't need money"—he glanced up at Peralon—"or power. And you don't want fame."

She crossed her arms. "Then what do I want?"

He pursed his lips, looked her over speculatively. "It's like you said: I know what happens to people who cross you. There are no more Valekings, are there?" He raised his hands. "Don't misunderstand. I'm a huge fan of your work. Positively inspirational."

Her nostrils flared with anger, and then Ris seemed to visibly shove all those emotions down into a deep pit. She smiled, more sarcastic than genuine, but still an effort. "Don't you have a kingdom to run?"

Sicaryon raised an eyebrow as if to say: *I see and accept your surrender.* "No, and I've worked very hard to keep it that way."

"Lucky you," she replied dryly.

"Like I said: you're an inspiration."

"And just what will it take to keep you from saying anything—"

"Hey! Wake up!"

Anahrod frowned as her attention jerked back to her own body, and her eyes focused on Claw. "Did you just slap me?" Anahrod prodded the side of her face. Tender.

"Given how good you are with a sword," Claw replied, "absolutely not." She gestured to a now familiar common area with its tables and sitting area by the fireplace. "But we're back at the guesthouse, so maybe you ran into a door?"

There was no use being mad, she told herself. Several times.

Naeron sat down by the fire and pulled out a thick ivory needle and yarn. He gave Anahrod an arch look. "Spying is rude."

Anahrod didn't bother trying to defend herself. She just gave him a nod and then hurried to her room, hoping she could reestablish the link in time to hear more of the conversation.

Ris and Sicaryon had already finished talking, leaving her with far more questions than answers.

At least Peralon hadn't let them kill each other.

MIDNIGHT VISITS

Someone knocked on the door to Anahrod's room as she was getting ready for bed.

She had a feeling about who it was before she opened it.

"Can I help you?" she asked Ris.

Her clothing hadn't changed, but she seemed different somehow. Smaller and more drained. Anahrod supposed even dragonriders grew tired.

Ris responded to the question with one of her own. "May I come in?"

That was a bad idea. Without question, a bad idea.

"Sure." Anahrod gave the woman enough room to squeeze past.

She did, and Anahrod closed the door behind her.

"I like the curtains in this room." Ris purposely glanced in every direction except at Anahrod. "Cute little ruffles."

Anahrod sat on the edge of the bed and watched her silently.

Ris wiped her hands down her coat and oriented back toward Anahrod. "I came to apologize."

Anahrod tilted her head. "Are you sure you're in the right room?"

"Who else would I—?" Ris stopped, and her expression grew irritated. "I am not apologizing to Sicaryon."

"How could you? You don't even know where he lives."

Ris barked out a laugh. "Yes, apparently not in the Deep, much to my surprise."

"On the bright side, we don't have to go back."

"Assuming he'll give us the sword."

"Ah, yes. I think that brings us back around to the apology part and the things we do for diplomacy." Anahrod studied Ris in the dim light of the bedroom. She should've pulled off some of the lamp covers, but Anahrod liked the way the other woman's eyes glittered in the shadows, like looking at a candle flame through an emerald. "I expected him to stampede over everyone. It's a cultural thing with his people. I wasn't prepared to see you do it, too. And I don't really understand why you did."

"He thinks he's so smart," Ris complained.

Anahrod raised both eyebrows. "That's because he is. Don't underestimate him. His uncle made that mistake."

She didn't think she needed to add that Sicaryon's uncle didn't live to regret it.

Ris drew in a deep breath and gazed up at the ceiling. The dimly lit room gave the impression that she was praying. "He's the reason you reacted so strongly to the idea of getting even with Neveranimas."

It wasn't a question.

Anahrod rubbed her forehead. There was really no sense in lying about this either—to either herself or Ris. "Yes."

"I'm not him."

"For many, many reasons," Anahrod agreed. "And I apologize for . . . for treating you like his twin. There was a time—" She sighed, lowered her arm. "Not making excuses. Just found it hard to watch him twist himself into knots trying to kill his uncle. Couldn't keep doing it. I'd seen how far he was willing to go, what his limits were—"

Ris didn't ask, but Anahrod heard the question anyway, just sitting there perched on red lips.

"He didn't have any," Anahrod said. "No limits at all. And I feared—" She swallowed thickly. "I feared that if we both kept going the same direction, I'd find out that I didn't have any either."

Ris didn't respond, a heavy, pregnant silence.

Then: "Huh."

Anahrod tilted her head back, gave the other woman a cool look. That had been singularly unhelpful. "What does that mean?"

Anahrod couldn't help but wonder what Ris was doing in her room, what her purpose was. Maybe she was just searching for more information on her newest enemy—Anahrod was a good source.

"It's just funny. He doesn't seem that bad," Ris finally said. "I mean, yes, he was an ass, but I can respect that. He wants to protect you."

"It was never my endangerment that was the problem."

Ris looked vaguely disgusted, but Anahrod didn't think the emotion was aimed at either herself or Sicaryon. "You need to know—" Ris swallowed, looked away. "I'm not like that," she said. "Or—no. I have been . . . like that. But I've been trying so hard to do this the right way, so only the guilty suffer. That must count for something."

Anahrod grimaced. "Don't take this the wrong way, but you sound like you're trying to convince me you can stop drinking any time you want."

Ris gave her a horrified yet also insulted look.

"Pretty sure you just took it the wrong way."

"Did I?" Ris snapped, but then she steadied herself, took long, slow breaths. "I'm trying to say I don't mind having limits. Even if I don't have them myself, if it's just that you're the one holding my leash. I wouldn't mind. I'd thank you for it."

Once again, Anahrod didn't think they were talking about the original subject anymore.

Or maybe . . . maybe they were.

In which case, she was in a lot of trouble, since she had rarely wanted anything more in her entire life. However, it was precisely that intense desire that made Anahrod hesitate. The higher the mountain one climbed, the farther one fell if they slipped.

Anahrod stood up, moved swiftly to stand before Ris. She picked up the other woman's hands. "Would you?" she asked, nothing in her manner flirtatious. "Ris, you barely know me."

The other woman's gaze was remarkably calm. "And yet. Maybe I just want to trust someone. Feel worthy of that trust." A smile darted across her face and vanished just as quickly. "Peralon doesn't count."

"I'll keep that in mind." She ran her thumb ever so lightly over Ris's jaw, then lower, tracing the path of a collar. "You might be jumping ahead in the race too early. Trust given too quickly is devalued from the start. I would rather your trust mean something."

She already knew the woman had secrets of a more exquisite flavor than the common variety. Anahrod didn't demand to inspect the interior of every closet. That was its own lack of trust—to a point.

Ris lifted her chin, bared more of her neck. It was almost—no. It was a dare. "What do you suggest, then?"

Anahrod cradled the back of Ris's neck with one hand. She drew the other woman closer until the smallest movement would brush their lips against each other. "We start small, for a start."

She closed the gap and felt fire alight along all the points of contact between them, but most especially their lips. Ris's were every bit as sweet as she'd imagined. Sweet and softer than rose petals.

"We have all night," Anahrod whispered.

Ris smiled—and then her eyes widened, and she cursed.

Anahrod felt dismay. "What—?"

Ris put her hands on Anahrod's arms, shook her head. "It's not you. I'm so sorry, but it's not you."

Anahrod's gut tightened unpleasantly.

"No," Ris repeated. "I mean it's really not. It's just that we don't have all night. I stopped by here to apologize, but also because Peralon wants us to meet up at Tiendremos's lair so he can hand over your gift. It's important."

Anahrod remembered to breathe. Oh.

Ris wrinkled her nose, looking thoroughly upset with herself. "We should've done the exchange earlier today, but I let myself be distracted by—you know—"

"The pretty Deeper king?"

"Pretty annoying," Ris sniffed.

"He's that, too," Anahrod agreed. "But the pretty part is hard to argue with. You should see him wearing nothing but body paint."

"That sounds like a crime against nature." Ris made it sound like something other than a compliment.

Anahrod picked up Ris's hands, kissed her fingers. She felt giddy and more than a little drunk, even though she was sober. "Are we sure this trip up to the lair can't wait until morning?"

Ris sighed and shook her head. "It really can't. We're expecting Tiendremos back in the morning."

Anahrod's focus sharpened. By extension, that meant Peralon didn't want Tiendremos to see whatever it was Peralon had brought back. "If we met somewhere else—"

She stopped herself. This wasn't Crystalspire. "Somewhere else" would have to be the top of one of the dragon towers. Did she really want to climb three hundred feet of spiral staircase, totally open to the elements, with who knows what sort of railing to stop a strong wind from knocking her over the side?

No, she did not.

She grabbed her mantle. "Tiendremos's cave it is, then. Let's hurry."

Which they did. There was just one minor problem.

Tiendremos didn't come back the next morning—he came back that night.

And he was very angry.

───◆───

In hindsight, Anahrod should've known something was wrong when the storm rolled in so quickly. Not all the Seven Crests mountains interacted with weather systems in quite the same way, however, and she wasn't familiar enough with Duskcloud's normal seasons to know the difference.

So, she and Ris had both been to the cave for shelter. They'd arrived laughing, shaking the rain off their mantles as even as they complained about the cold, too preoccupied with each other to notice the giant scaled mountain looming in the darkness.

Then Anahrod heard him.

[Where is she? Where is that red-hooded snake? I'll rip her out of her skin—] The dragon was fuming, ranting a litany of insults and complaints with no purpose except to vent his anger.

Anahrod turned to Ris, wide-eyed, but the dragonrider was still laughing. *She* couldn't hear Tiendremos.

Tiendremos was back early.

"Call Peralon," Anahrod said. "We need him back here right now."

"What's wrong? He's already on his way—"

Anahrod realized too late that she should've sent the message herself, so it would be silent, so Tiendremos wouldn't hear.

But he had heard. The gigantic dragon lunged, heart-stopping in his enormity, but instead of attacking them, came to rest against the cave mouth. Anahrod's confusion quickly turned to panic as she realized what he'd done.

Tiendremos had blocked the only exit.

Still, it limited his movement, and even the smallest dragon couldn't hope to follow them into the servants' tunnels. Ris must've had the same thought, because she grabbed Anahrod's hand. "Run!"

Just as they started walking, a whip of white-hot electricity tore through the darkness, blocking their path to safety. The lightning hadn't come from the dragon.

Or rather, it hadn't come from the dragon's body.

Ris staggered as another strike of the whip landed too close. The lightning bolts lit up the cave enough to see the source of the attacks.

Tiendremos-in-Jaemeh's-body was scowling as he advanced.

"Do you really think that I'm so naïve that I will tolerate you handing out orders like I'm a servant? Do you think that just because your pathetic excuse of a dragon allows you such liberties that I am as much a fool?" Electricity arced between his fingers.

Ris had said Tiendremos would be angry when he returned, but Anahrod had assumed . . .

She'd assumed he'd be reasonable. Rational.

Anahrod still didn't have her sword. She vowed she was going to carry the damn thing on her everywhere from now on, and to hell with the odd looks she received. She tugged at a weather vane, tried to pull it free from its stand.

Tiendremos-in-Jaemeh was not trying to have a conversation. He struck again, but this time Ris swept her hand up. The lightning flattened against some kind of invisible wall, deflected before it could reach her.

"Think, damn it," Ris spat. Her expression was more hateful than Anahrod had ever seen before on the woman. "I'm trying to protect you."

"Don't claim beneficence when your real motive is concealing how you intend to betray me." He did something then, a hand concealed behind his body.

The weather vane in Anahrod's hand vibrated and ripped free of its base. It jerked in her grip, too, racing toward Ris.

Every weather vane in the cave did the same thing. All of them were aimed at Ris.

Oh, Anahrod thought distantly. That was why Tiendremos kept the weather vanes around. They were a trap.

Faced with the coming onslaught of metal spikes and spears, Ris's expression wasn't fear or panic. She looked annoyed.

Then Ris's eyes changed color.

They turned gold, molten and glowing as Peralon took possession of his rider's body. He snapped his fingers, and the sound wasn't the expected pop but a deep, clear bell-like ring.

The weather vanes exploded.

The weather vanes were pushed back by an invisible wave of force, causing them to shatter into flying shards. Anahrod hissed as she felt the stings of shrapnel connect.

Peralon-in-Ris snarled, **"You forget yourself, hatchling."**

Tiendremos's unconscious draconic body was flung from the cave mouth, rolling across the floor. Since there were no longer any weather vanes to stop his momentum, he rolled all the way to the back.

Tiendremos-in-Jaemeh stared, mouth open, shocked.

Anahrod's mouth fell open, too, as Peralon—Peralon the dragon—swooped down into the now cleared cave opening. But Peralon—

She looked back at Ris, who stood triumphant and furious, then again at Peralon. Ris, whose eyes still glowed gold, who still channeled Peralon's voice. If Peralon was possessing Ris, then the only way the gold dragon could be conscious and mobile was if . . .

The gold dragon moved impossibly fast, little more than a blur before he—no, before *she*—had her teeth poised to rip out the larger dragon's throat.

The gold dragon's eyes were green. *They'd turned green.*

Anahrod had assumed the link was one-way, or that human riders didn't have the strength to deny their dragons, just as Overbite had never had the strength to deny her. When Tiendremos asserted control, the dragon pushed Jaemeh to the side, rendered him powerless within his own body.

But Peralon and Ris had *switched bodies.*

"You—you would dare? You would let your rider take your body—!" Tiendremos-in-Jaemeh seemed to have come to the same conclusion Anahrod had—that somehow Peralon and Ris's connection was two-way. Peralon had taken Ris's body, and Ris had taken Peralon's.

"Dare? She's my partner. For her, *anything* is permitted. Everything is allowed. As for you—" Peralon-in-Ris bared his fangs. **"You seem to think I am no threat to you. Would you care to reevaluate that belief?"**

Ris-in-Peralon made a noise, such as she could with fangs poised at Tiendremos's throat, the slow drip of saliva from Ris-in-Peralon's open mouth sparkling in the inscribed light of the cave. She'd laughed.

The giant cave fell silent, save for the sound of breathing and a few lingering buzzing noises from the electrical discharge. Anahrod's hair would've been standing on end if she didn't have it braided back.

"You need me," Tiendremos reminded Peralon, but his tone was uncertain.

Shocked, Anahrod thought, and had to bite her lip to keep from laughing hysterically at the awful pun.

"You should thank Eannis for that," Peralon replied. **"Because it's the only thing that saved your life tonight. I was old when your great-grandparents were nothing more than lumps of flesh hiding inside eggshells. If you had concerns, the appropriate response was to come to me. Not . . . this."**

Tiendremos was wide-eyed with fear, so much so that Anahrod wondered why he had stayed inside Jaemeh's body. But as she glanced back at that giant scaled form, she knew why. Tiendremos recognized that Ris, not Peralon, was the one who had her teeth gripping his throat. He was at the mercy of a *human.*

If the storm dragon could delay returning to his own body until Ris released him, Tiendremos could pretend it had never happened.

She understood Tiendremos's distress. It was fine for a dragon to love their rider, but for a dragon to love and trust their rider so much that they'd allow them to swap places? Who had ever heard of such a thing? Not even in the parables of Zavad and King Cynakris had Zavad granted such freedom to a human.

But it was worse than that. Out of the various reasons dragons might need a rider, the most urgent was the toxic effect of magic on themselves. Dragons were incredible wellsprings of power, capable of extraordinary acts, but every spell brought them that much closer to an unstoppable frenzy from which most dragons never recovered. For a dragon to go rampant was for them to lose themselves in such rage that everyone around them was in danger, including other dragons.

Humans were so much weaker—but immune to rampancy. An Eannis-blessed human might cast magic spells every minute of every day of their lives if they had power enough, and never lose control.

So, what did that mean for a dragonrider possessing a dragon? Ris had pushed aside Tiendremos's entire weight as though it were *nothing*. But Peralon had also used magic, tearing apart several tons of metal with a finger snap. Would Peralon pay the price for that later? *Would Ris?*

Anahrod was unprepared for the emotion that drowned her concern for Ris and Peralon. A burning wave of fire spread out over her, so intense she felt dizzy.

She was worried for the pair, yes. Concerned, definitely.

But mostly, she was jealous.

Her hypocrisy tasted like ash. She saw her sins reflected in the glint of Peralon's scales, in her awareness of an uncomfortable, gut-wrenching truth. Once again, she'd told herself that she hated something, but only to discover that what she really hated was how it wasn't hers.

Was she so different from a dragon? Were they simply more honest about their obsessions?

It took Anahrod a moment, blinking, to realize that the two dragons-in-human-skin had been talking.

"—panicked. **I know it's no excuse, but she's closed the ports, the docks, everything,**" Tiendremos-in-Jaemeh complained. "**They're checking papers for everyone who comes through. Humans need a work visa if they want to enter the city. She knows something.**" And now the dragon sounded scared.

So that was the real problem: Tiendremos's worry that his boss had discovered his plan to betray her. Naturally, the dragon had lashed out—at someone who had nothing to do with it.

[Look behind you.] It was Ris's voice.

Ris's voice? How could it be Ris's voice? That meant the ability to speak to each other like this was tied to the physical body, not the soul. Anahrod had no idea what that realization truly meant, only that it felt significant.

Shoving back her unease, she looked behind herself just in time to see a yellow sphere of crystal, roughly the size of a child's head, roll to a stop at her feet.

Peralon and Tiendremos were too busy talking to pay attention, and Jaemeh gave no sign of any awareness of his surroundings. Ris, though, watched Anahrod with a gleaming emerald eye as she kept her teeth fastened around Tiendremos's throat.

Anahrod's breath froze inside her for a second. The yellow sphere was a dragonstone.

[Is this . . . is this what Peralon left to bring back?] The tool he claimed would help Anahrod overcome her fear of heights.

[Yes,] Ris said. [Don't let Tiendremos see it.]

She could see the wisdom there. Not that Anahrod thought Tiendremos would turn her in (she was "important," after all) but because Tiendremos had, only minutes earlier, showed that he sometimes reacted in irrational ways.

And to think: he wasn't even rampant.

Anahrod quickly slid her mantle off her shoulders, tied off the ends to make a knapsack, and scooped the yellow crystal inside.

"Neveranimas does not know what we're doing," Peralon-in-Ris said with unshakable authority. **"If she did, she wouldn't heighten security. She'd destroy us."**

Tiendremos inhaled deeply and nodded. **"You're right. Of course you're right."**

It was almost funny how much Tiendremos reminded her of Jaemeh just then. She felt turbulent about it, her feelings conflicted on this reminder that Tiendremos and Jaemeh might share similar qualities.

"So go," Peralon said. **"Take a flight. Clear your head. Go hunt something. You'll feel better. We'll handle entering the city."** He paused. **"And I don't recommend it, but if you insist, we'll include Jaemeh in the planning and execution. If anything strikes him as suspicious, he'll tell you, and if anything goes wrong, you have an eye at the scene."**

Anahrod felt a moment's annoyance at rewarding the dragon's tantrum with exactly what he wanted, but she remembered the anger in Peralon's eyes, how furious he'd been. Too furious for her to believe that he'd so easily roll over for Tiendremos now.

So why had he?

It took her a second, but she saw it. They'd been concerned about Tiendremos betraying them to Neveranimas, but now Jaemeh would be deeply involved—or would think he was. Tiendremos wouldn't dare "catch them in the act" when his own rider would be one of the crew. If Peralon and Ris had insisted on this from the start, Tiendremos might have fought it, might have found a workaround.

But now Tiendremos thought this *was* the workaround.

His eye color shifted, returned to Ris's green, and behind them, Anahrod heard the shifting of scales as Tiendremos was released.

Tiendremos didn't say a word to Ris or acknowledge her. He returned to his dragon body, letting Jaemeh take over his own human body again. The dragonrider immediately slumped, limbs shaking and expression fighting between shame and resentment.

He looked awful. He was bruised, shivering, and needed a bath. Anahrod wondered when Jaemeh had last eaten—or slept.

Tiendremos left quickly. He had nothing to say to his rider.

Anahrod did, though, the moment Tiendremos was gone.

"Are you all right?" She offered him a hand.

Jaemeh knocked it away. "I'm fine!" He paused and shuddered. "Sorry. It's just—I'm sorry you had to see him when he gets like this. It's fine." He pointed to the tunnels. "Help yourself to anything you like. I'm going to—" He gestured vaguely. "I'm going to go."

Ris counted off her fingers. "Go eat some food first, and drink some water. Tea counts, booze doesn't. Then go to sleep. Take a bath in the morning when you're less likely to pass out and accidentally drown."

Jaemeh blinked at her, incredulous. "Who made you my keeper?"

"You might've missed it, but your dragon did. Welcome to the team. Now go."

When he, too, was gone, Anahrod remained, along with Ris, Peralon, and a small mountain of twisted metal.

Ris brushed herself off. "That was exciting."

"That's one way of describing it," Anahrod agreed. "Is he really part of the team?"

"No," Ris admitted, "but it'll be easier if they think he is."

"Understood." She shifted the knapsack on her shoulder. "So, what am I supposed to do with this thing?"

Peralon made a rumbling noise. [Let me show you.]

23

FAIR EXCHANGE

[You understand what a dragonstone is, yes?] Peralon asked, sitting back on his haunches.

"You understand they sentenced me to death for stealing one of these, right?" Anahrod raised an eyebrow at the dragon, then shared it with Ris, too, because had her dragon seriously just offered to explain *dragonstones* to her?

Ris sighed. "Peralon, love, I think we can skip the unnecessary exposition."

Peralon evidently disagreed. [But you've never used one, right?]

Anahrod waved a hand. "Still innocent of everything they accused me of doing, yes. I've never touched a dragonstone before tonight."

Honestly, she didn't understand why they were a big deal, why dragons guarded them more protectively than sky amber. She had a sneaking suspicion the dragons didn't know either, but by this point, it was just dogma.

She was tired. She always poured out an extra glass of cynicism when she was tired.

[Accessing the stone is akin to meditation,] the gold dragon told her. [Look deep into the depths of the stone and free your mind of worldly concerns. Think of not thinking. Let your mind float.]

He made a chuffing sound. [This will likely require some practice. I suggest we try it once here and then you can return to town and continue practicing in your spare time.]

Anahrod paused in the middle of removing the dragonstone, then shook herself and shrugged. Yes, it was illegal for her to possess one of these things, but she was already Anahrod the Wicked. Authorities wouldn't give her special treatment just because she confirmed their expectations.

"Let's try this," Anahrod agreed.

She settled down to meditate on the stone.

It took a while.

Eventually, the world vanished. The hard stone floor of Tiendremos's cave turned into blue skies and the vast emptiness of open space, but there was no feeling of falling.

She was flying.

Below her, wheat-gold savannas crept up to the foothill children of a fabulous mountain range that stretched from east to west. The world curving underneath her, the distorted atmosphere hazy in the air.

Anahrod wanted to panic, but she was incapable. It's not that she wouldn't have panicked under different circumstances, but the fear proved elusive, ephemeral. What she saw and felt had already happened. She observed with no power to make substantive changes, not even to her own emotional reactions.

She flapped her wings and understood.

Gold wings. If she peered down—if she'd had enough control to look down—she'd see Peralon's gold scales. She couldn't control this because these were memories—but not hers. Peralon was the one flying. She was merely an observer.

Naturally, she couldn't feel fear. Why would a dragon ever be afraid of flying?

She smelled the air's crispness and the wind's sharp edge. She heard wind shrikes crying, and farther away, a lovesick leviathan's lonely song. She felt— viscerally, emotionally—the power of flight. How free. How joyous.

She didn't know why Peralon had preserved *this* memory, why this was so special—a piece of knowledge that he'd immortalized forever.

Then another dragon joined him.

The newcomer was enormous, with scales the color of flame, deep red at the creature's head and then fading out to a hot orange at the claws. Anahrod couldn't tell the dragon's sex—to be fair, she'd never been able to judge that by sight—only that its presence made Peralon overjoyed, filled him with a quiet, glowing hum of contentment.

She knew the answer then, instinctively: this was Ivarion.

They flew together. Several times Peralon made playful loops around Ivarion to emphasize that the red dragon might be larger, but Peralon could still fly literal circles around him.

[You're showing off,] Ivarion chided fondly.

[Can't I just be happy to see you?]

[Of course,] the red dragon said. [But you might also show a little more decorum about the matter.]

[Decorum's for you youngsters,] Peralon said. [When you're my age, you'll stop caring about it.]

[I wish you'd change your mind. I want you to stay.] Ivarion sounded sad.

[I wish I could. It's just bad timing. Too much magic. I'm snapping at shadows, at children, at clouds. I'm the last dragon in the world you want to see go rampant. I won't be gone forever.]

The red dragon keened, confusion and question in one. [What will you do?]

[Take a nap.]

Ivarion chuffed out a laugh, stopped as Peralon didn't laugh with him. [You don't have to leave Yagra'hai to meditate.]

[I didn't say meditate, I said nap. I'll sleep for a century or two and wake as pure as a newborn.]

[A century!] Ivarion went so far as to stop flying for a moment, hovering in midair with giant wings buffeting the skies in broad, powerful beats. [Is there nothing else you can do?]

Peralon hovered, too, if only because it was rude to keep flying circles when his love was in such distress. He understood, he really did, but there was no other recourse. [No. If I had a rider—]

[Then take a rider!]

[I can't,] Peralon snapped.

[Can't or won't? I don't understand why someone who loves humans as much as you would push away their aid. Is it too late? The poison so bad that a rider wouldn't make a difference? Or is this just an excuse to be rid of me?] Ivarion's neck tendril thrashed in agitation. He began flying forward again, but it felt less like a leisurely soar and more like an attempt to leave.

He couldn't fly faster than Peralon, though. The gold dragon circled around in front of him. [Never believe that. Even in sleep I will dream of you, and miss you, and long to return to you.]

[You know you are welcome to sleep in my lair.] The offer was plaintive, anxious.

Ivarion was so young. He still thought this might be a rejection.

[I know, and I am thankful, but it would be unwise. I have too many enemies. I would never wake again.]

[I'm their leader, the chosen of Eannis. They wouldn't dare.] The dragon twisted in anger. What Peralon had just said could be taken as an insult, a slight on the red dragon's ability to keep him safe. Ivarion would not have stayed his claw if any other dragon had expressed the sentiment.

[You always see the shine on someone's scales and never the shadows underneath,] Peralon mused. [And you being named First Dragon does not make nearly the difference as you might think.] He wished it were not true, but he knew better. No one ruled by their own will alone. [I ruled them once, too. If they don't like the way you lead, you'll be removed just as I once was. You cannot force them to tolerate me just because we're friends.]

[But it's lies. It's all lies.]

[No.] Laughter from Peralon. [It's something much harder to kill than a lie. It's a story.]

Ivarion had nothing but silence in response, but it was a deliberate, sullen silence.

His poor dear Ivarion, who meant so well and had principles so high he would've long since scorched his wings on the sun if fire could burn him. Those same qualities were why Zyrsene had named Ivarion as heir in the first place—because she had thought having a genuinely *good* dragon on the throne would make a difference.

Peralon could've told Zyrsene not to waste her dying breaths.

[Don't be so upset. I'll be back soon enough. A century is not so long a time for our kind. It will give the younglings a chance to forget.]

Ivarion didn't respond. There was nothing to say that hadn't already been said.

[I've been thinking I might take a rider,] Ivarion shoved into the silence. He flipped over and then righted again, as if to get a better position to see Peralon's reaction.

[Ah.]

[You don't approve?] Ivarion sounded surprised—and disappointed.

[No, no. It's not for me to say what you should do. Take a rider—more dragons should—but be careful. Humans are weaker than you would expect and stronger than you can imagine.]

[You're not making sense.]

[When you find a rider, you'll understand.] Peralon tried not to think of his, and how much he still missed him. Missed him so much, even after all the years.

[Do you regret taking a rider, then?]

His neck frills ruffled, despite his intention to not let how the question affected him show. [Never,] Peralon said. [He was beautiful. He shone so brightly I could look at nothing else.]

[He shone? Humans do that?] Disbelief filtered through Ivarion's telepathic touch.

[Metaphorically, I mean. Some days I miss Senros so fiercely I would set the sky on fire if it meant bringing him back to me.]

[Then it's just as well you're not attuned to fire, isn't it?] Ivarion tried for humor and missed the mark. He twisted his head away. [I'm sorry,] the dragon finally said.

[Let's talk of something else. Anything else.]

A beat of silence. [How will I know when you wake?]

[I'll find you,] Peralon said. [I promise you that.]

With that, he rolled away from the other dragon, turned on his side, and spread his wings wide as he headed north. Behind him, Ivarion keened low and soft, which Peralon forced himself to ignore.

Ivarion turned back and returned to Yagra'hai. Peralon pretended not to watch him go.

Anahrod opened her eyes, and discovered she wasn't in the same place as when she'd closed them.

⌄

"At least I wasn't kidnapped this time," Anahrod murmured out loud.

She even recognized the room. Another bonus. They'd returned her to the guest room Ris had rented for her. Her sword lay on the table, her other clothes hung from inside the open wardrobe.

She lay on her bed, fully clothed. The dragonstone rested on the bedcovers next to her. A half-capped inscribed lantern glowed dimly from one side of the room, while moonlight from the briefly full moon filtered in from a window.

"You were not supposed to lose yourself like that so quickly." Ris's voice came from somewhere by the table. **"My sincerest apologies. I didn't expect you to be so sensitive to draconic magic."**

Something about Ris's voice seemed off, lacking in her trademark quicksilver sharpness. Anahrod glanced over at the woman and then sat straight upright as a shock raced through her.

This wasn't Ris.

Gold eyes stared back at Anahrod. This was Peralon, wearing Ris's body.

Anahrod felt paralyzed. Her mind was still overwhelmed by the memory of Ivarion. How accurate had it really been? After all, Peralon had not gone off to "take a nap" for a hundred years . . .

Or maybe he had. Maybe something had woken him. It had been a hundred years since Ivarion fell into rampancy, hadn't it? Maybe Peralon had "napped" for some of that.

But he'd also taken a rider, which he'd sworn he'd never do.

Maybe these things were not disconnected.

The dragon set a thin metal strip in the book's crease. **"More importantly, did it help?"**

"Where's Ris?" Anahrod asked. "Can she hear us?"

Peralon raised an eyebrow. **"Ris is busy."**

"Is she?"

The dragon closed the book and set it aside. **"Yes."**

"Busy doing what?"

"Flying," he said with perfect composure. **"She's fond of flying during the full moon. As I am fond of reading paper books."** He tapped on the cover as emphasis. **"Difficult to do when you have dragon-sized claws."**

"And she was willing to do that?"

"It was her suggestion."

"Did you teach her how to do that? How to . . . swap places with you?"

"Yes," he answered. **"Any dragon and rider can learn to do so."**

"Do the other dragons know that?" They must have some idea. Tiendremos hadn't been appalled by the idea that Ris could take possession of Peralon, but because Peralon had allowed it.

The dragons knew. They just weren't willing to share that kind of power.

He laughed, startled. **"Some, perhaps. The ones who pay attention. Probably not the ones who believe the lies."**

Anahrod's throat felt desperately, horribly dry. She sat up and poured herself a glass of water. "Lies?" she asked, finally, after. Her mouth still felt like the grim, dusty bottom of a neglected tomb.

"You know the ones. That humans were created to serve us. That therefore we must be superior. That Eannis created the universe. That she watches over us like a kind and attentive goddess, our mother in all ways." His expression might almost be fond, were it not so full of hate.

The dim light felt dangerous, precipitous. She felt unsteady and unsure of her balance in ways that had nothing to do with her body. "Those are all lies?"

"Every single one," Peralon assured her. **"If humanity was created, I know not by whom. You weren't cast from heaven to serve my race, or any other. My kind are not superior, which we will eventually figure out, although I fear we will learn the lesson in the most painful way possible. Eannis did not create the universe. She made us—dragons—but she also *left* us and *never came back*. Eannis was powerful enough to meet the definition of goddess, but I like to think a real goddess would've stayed around to watch over her children. Perhaps even answer the occasional prayer."**

"What about—" She swallowed. "What about Zavad?"

His gaze sharpened, and the smile there was ironic and knowing and far too aware. **"Zavad never existed,"** Peralon said. **"He's just a story. It's much easier to avoid taking responsibility for your mistakes when you have someone else to blame."**

She drank some more water while she unsuccessfully tried to think of nothing at all, unwilling to voice her terrible suspicions, as if saying the words out loud might give them life.

She also didn't need to say the words out loud. She didn't need to ask. She understood perfectly, didn't she?

She, too, was just a story. They'd written stage plays about Anahrod the Wicked. Stage plays and novels and who knew what else, all to tell an utterly false but no doubt engaging tale about a spoiled rich girl's descent into evil. She couldn't reclaim those stories, couldn't stuff cruel words back into mouths or pull libelous ink off pages. Anahrod the Wicked existed now, separate and independent of Anahrod Amnead the real person. In just seventeen years, that stain had set so deeply that it would never wash clean.

How much worse could it be, if the stories were old enough to become myth, to become *religion?* Old enough to change Eannis into the creator of all life, old enough to turn someone who'd disagreed with her into the source of all evil.

"I suppose dragons are like humans in that way," she finally said. "It's easier to believe the things that bring us comfort. Someone watching over us is . . . a comforting idea. As is, I suppose, the idea that our mistakes are not our fault." She pressed her lips tightly together. "Neveranimas. Does she know this is something *any* dragonrider can do?"

"Guaranteed," Peralon said. **"Although I suspect she'd rather cut off her left wing than contemplate such a notion. Tiendremos is her right hand, and has been for a century. And while he would never allow his rider such liberties, it's hardly a great stretch of intellect to theorize that a road that can be traveled in one direction can also be traveled the other. How embarrassing that Tiendremos does better than most dragons—at least *he* doesn't think he's too good to talk directly to humans."**

Anahrod's jaw worked against her throat. She'd never considered that angle, although she suspected Jaemeh might prefer his dragon to be a bit more snobbish. "Yet you have no trouble with it."

"I'm old," Peralon said. **"It gives one a certain perspective. And Ris is my other half. Why would I not trust her as she trusts me? How would that be fair?"**

Anahrod wondered if he was just telling her what she wanted to hear. He wouldn't have been the first dragon to whisper to her that humans should be dragons' equals rather than their slaves.

Neveranimas hadn't meant it, though.

Peralon seemed more genuine. Seemed. If only Anahrod could trust it. The true test of such a relationship would not be when facing a common threat, say, Tiendremos throwing a tantrum, but when dragon and rider disagreed. So far, Anahrod had yet to see Ris and Peralon do that.

Love turned flimsy and insubstantial when the whole world said only one side of an argument mattered.

Love. Her mind turned once more to the dragonstone.

"Ris said her motivation for doing this is revenge. What's yours?" The words were out of her mouth before she could stop herself.

The dragon stared at her, and somehow his stare wasn't less intimidating just because he wore a smaller body.

The silence stretched out between them until Anahrod thought it might snap, or at least sink between them into awkward tension.

"Hope." Peralon leaned back in the chair. "**All I can do is hope. Hope that what I need to cure Ivarion is buried somewhere in Neveranimas's hoard. That we can find it and act.**"

She could see the logic. Neveranimas had been the one with the most to gain by Ivarion's rampancy, and conversely, the one with the most to lose if he was cured. Even if she'd had nothing to do with the original sickness, she could easily imagine the violet dragon locking up anything that could heal Ivarion.

The moment Ivarion had gone rampant, he'd tried to take a "nap," hadn't he? He must've gotten the idea from Peralon, from the very conversation she'd witnessed. Unlike Peralon, Ivarion's slumber was one from which the dragon had never woken.

Church faithful whispered that Ivarion slumbered on the verge of Ascension. Every year, more pilgrims traveled to the Cauldron, the volcano where he slept, to pray and leave offerings.

No one thought Ivarion would wake.

"You and Ivarion—" She knew little of dragon relationships. What was allowed, what was taboo. Anahrod had always thought they didn't have romance as much as biological imperative—mating seasons and parents who might well never see each other again once the hatchlings were born. Stories rarely spoke of dragon couples.

Peralon picked up his book again. "**Yes. Me and Ivarion. Was there a question in that?**"

Only every question. How did they meet? How had they fallen in love? Had all the dragons known? None of them? Why or why not?

Why, why, was Varriguhl such a raging jerk if his dragon had been so wonderful?

If their ruler had been so great, why were the dragons like this? But Peralon had warned Ivarion, hadn't he? Warned him that being ruler wasn't enough. That he would know because—

Because he had once ruled, too.

Anahrod studied the dragon hiding inside Ris and wondered, again, just how old he really was.

"No," she said slowly. "I suppose there isn't a question there at all."

"**Introducing you to sleeping saints was not the object of this exercise,**"

Peralon reminded her. **"The point was the flight itself. The point was showing you it's nothing to fear."**

"Nothing to fear if you're a dragon," Anahrod amended.

Peralon smiled, nothing at all like Ris's smiles, which were coy and mischievous and full of baited promises. Peralon's smile was old and wise and a little sad.

"Your body won't make that distinction," Peralon said. **"You may tell yourself that it doesn't matter because you're not a dragon, but that's a logical argument. No more meaningful than you logically telling yourself that there's no reason to fear heights in the first place."**

He opened his book and began reading, pausing only long enough to raise his head and say, **"You should use that stone as often as time allows. No need to follow it to the bitter end, but let yourself enjoy flying. I promise, the experience will help."**

Anahrod wasn't feeling in the mood to do any such thing. She felt wrung out, both physically and emotionally. It was as he'd said: her body didn't know the difference between his memories and hers.

And Peralon had powerful emotions when it came to Ivarion.

Anahrod pulled her wandering thoughts back home. The dragon wearing Ris's body still regarded her, waiting for more questions. She couldn't decide whether he wanted to answer them or was merely resigned to.

Then Anahrod frowned. "How long do I have?"

His brow wrinkled. **"I don't understand the question."**

"How long do I have to go over the memory? Until morning? Tomorrow evening? When are you taking the dragonstone back?"

He laughed. **"I wasn't planning on ever taking it back. That's what a gift means."** Peralon stood up, book in hand. **"Don't let anyone catch you with it. I also wouldn't go through it so often you forget to sleep or eat or the like."** He paused on his way out. **"Speaking of sleep, you should do that. It's been a long day."**

She huffed. It had been at that.

But she couldn't stop thinking about the things he'd said to her. Even though she tried to sleep, her attempts were laughable. All she could think about was how desperately Ivarion had wanted to make things better, how his good intentions had meant nothing. How, at least according to Peralon, that had been cynically predictable. Because there was no mother comforting the cries of her children, no father waiting to punish the errant.

No gods at all.

They were, all of them, from the largest dragon to the smallest human, flung into the Deep, on their own. When the dragons couldn't have Eannis as a mother, they'd turned her memory into a goddess, an echo, and an excuse to enslave humanity.

There was no mandate from heaven keeping humans in chains. No hubris. They weren't thrown out of heaven to teach them humility.

It had made for a good story, though, hadn't it?

Sleep must have come to her at some point, but she only recalled tossing and turning, furious and lonely and desperately unhappy, before morning light rudely poked at her eyes through the window.

The next morning, Ris called for a meeting. Sicaryon must have given Ris a means of communication, since he was there, too.

"Do we have any idea why Neveranimas has increased security?" Anahrod asked the group.

"Who knows?" Jaemeh whispered, exhausted and resigned. "I gave up on trying to understand how Neveranimas thinks a long time ago, but she's"—he grimaced—"she's grown more paranoid of late. Tiendremos thinks she's risking rampancy if she doesn't take a rider soon. Which she won't. She never has before. Why start now?"

Anahrod sipped her tea. It was a fair point. She didn't know of any dragons who used spells as freely as Neveranimas did, and while the dragon's willpower was legendary, there were limits. Dragons liked to pretend they didn't need humans, but that clearly wasn't true.

"Don't change that we've got a real problem, does it?" Claw looked thoroughly disgusted. "Half of us don't have proper papers right *now*, let alone fancy magic-based identification. They're doing it through the divisions, you said?"

"I'm not sure—" Jaemeh paused, looked up and to his right.

Anahrod didn't hear his question, but she heard Tiendremos's sullen, angry answer.

"Yes," Jaemeh said. "Through the divisions. Each guild will oversee certifications, handed down to individual divisions. Just Yagra'hai, of course."

"No." Anahrod set her mug down on the table with a hard clink. "Not just Yagra'hai. She can say it's only for Yagra'hai until the moon spins itself to pieces, but she's forcing Seven Crests to come to *her* for these certifications. In a few years, someone will decide it's too much hassle to wait months for the approvals every time they send a new person to Yagra'hai and they'll start authorizing everyone who *might* ever need to travel there. Other divisions will fall in line rather than take a chance their competitors will gain an edge on them. Then the cities themselves will start doing that. And in a few years, it will *all* be running through Yagra'hai."

"This is just an excuse. She's consolidating power," Sicaryon murmured.

"Maybe so," Jaemeh agreed, "but right now, it's inconvenient. And by the way, who are you again?" The dragonrider gave Sicaryon a hard stare.

"Oh, I'm Cary." Sicaryon's smile was perfectly innocent. "Supply and logistics. Good thing, too, from the sound of it." He tapped his lips. "I have a question, though. Why did your dragon feel the need to trumpet his search for this woman"—he pointed at Anahrod like he'd just met her—"all over Crystalspire? That seemed a bit . . . no offense . . . unsubtle?"

Anahrod almost smiled. The best way to keep people from asking awkward questions was to ask one's own first.

Jaemeh visibly ground his teeth. Then he snatched a pastry from his plate and tore a chunk off it. With his mouth still full, he pointed at Ris. "Ask her why we did it this way. It was her plan."

Anahrod narrowed her eyes. "All right. Why make Tiendremos do something this flashy?"

Ris stared up at the unfinished beams of the ceiling. "It was necessary." She held up her hand when Anahrod protested. "That's all I'm going to say: it was necessary. The whys don't matter."

Anahrod didn't believe that for one second.

"Come up with a better explanation than that, given how upset Tiendremos is," Jaemeh pointed out. "He feels like he screwed this up because he listened to your advice, and he does not like failure."

"It's not failure," Ris said. "It's a complication."

"Kind of a big one, boss," Claw reminded her. "How are we supposed to do the job if we can't even get into the city? You'll be okay, Jaemeh will be okay. But Kaibren? Me? Naeron? Oh, let's not even get started on Anahrod . . ."

"My papers are in perfect order, in case you're wondering," Sicaryon offered.

"No one asked," Ris snapped.

Jaemeh raised an eyebrow at her. He said nothing, but Anahrod had little doubt he filed away that rather out-of-proportion response for later.

"Why change?" Naeron asked. "Cargo workers will still work."

"Because cargo workers won't have a reason to enter the city," Jaemeh answered, "so they won't be allowed to leave the docks. That cover no longer works. We need to think of something else." Jaemeh finished one of his pastries and frowned at the plate.

The other two pieces were missing. Naeron looked innocent.

"Anyway . . ." Jaemeh continued, "maybe we can bring you on with servant licenses? Tiendremos could approve them."

"Is Tiendremos going to be in charge of approvals moving forward?" Anahrod asked.

"Yes."

Claw rubbed her hands together. "Fantastic! That solves everything then."

Anahrod scowled. "No, it doesn't. Is Tiendremos personally overseeing approvals, or is he delegating that job?"

"Oh." Jaemeh frowned. "Delegating, I should think. It sounds like a lot of paperwork."

"Then that won't work," Sicaryon pointed out. "Because the person you're trying to hide this from is his boss, and if she's this paranoid, any change in routine will stand out like a full moon on third night. If he personally authorizes anything, the official reason he's doing so better be obvious and believable."

Silence fell again, this time frustrated and sullen.

Finally, Ris sighed and leaned back against her chair. "I know how to get us inside." She threw Anahrod a quick, apologetic look.

Anahrod didn't like that look at all.

"Great," Claw said. "Care to share it with the rest of us?"

Ris made a face. "Dragonrider candidates—"

"No." Anahrod stood up from the table. She felt flushed and brittle, and her pulse beat a furious tempo in her ears. "Absolutely not."

A number of the crew looked confused by her outburst, but not Naeron, and not Ris. "Anah, please understand—"

"You said you'd smuggle him out of Seven Crests," Anahrod hissed. "That no matter what happened, he wouldn't be sent to Yagra'hai. You *promised*."

Ris exhaled heavily. "I know that, but—"

"May I ask what you're talking about?" Sicaryon raised an eyebrow. "Or rather, who?"

Jaemeh scratched his cheek. "Is this about that kid back in Crystalspire?" Then his eyes widened, and he choked back a laugh. "Wait, isn't his father the mayor? The divisions are handling the paperwork, but it all goes through the mayor's office for each city. That's perfect!"

Damn it.

She'd hoped no one else would see the connection, but it was too obvious, never mind that Ris was probably sitting on a six-page essay justifying this obscenity. Gwydinion had been assigned to attend the dragonrider school, and he could bring his own handpicked staff, including guards. And the mayor of

Crystalspire would vet all those handpicked staff. Which meant that with the mayor's help, they'd soar effortlessly past all Neveranimas's extra security.

All they had to do was be comfortable delivering a fifteen-year-old boy directly to the dragon trying to kill him.

Anahrod clenched her fists. "It's not perfect. Neveranimas wants to murder him, the same way she's tried to murder every student whose blessing involves talking to animals. Neveranimas will pay attention to his coterie. This is a remarkably bad idea and *people will die.*"

"Be honest now. Do you have any strong opinions on this, Jungle?" Claw seemed less mocking than genuinely taken aback.

Sicaryon turned to Ris. "Is there any other way?"

She barely moved except for the smallest shake of her head. "No." Then she added: "I've already reached out to the family. They want to help."

Anahrod contemplated how long it had been since Tiendremos had informed them they'd need this level of documentation and ground her teeth.

Ris must have contacted the Doreyl family *immediately.*

Anahrod set her fists against the table and leaned across it, looming over a still-sitting Ris. "Do you remember when we talked about limits?"

A flicker of irritation shone in Ris's eyes. "Don't—"

"You just flew right past them."

Anahrod stormed out of the room.

⌄

There's a fine art to fleeing the scene of an argument.

It depends on one's goals, of course. If the point is to make the other person come find them, then one must be findable. If the dramatic gesture was the goal in and of itself, then what happened afterward was less important, and under those circumstances, Anahrod had always favored going for a ride. However, if the point was to get away from the argument itself, to go find someplace to think and brood, well, then hiding was the most important skill.

She had tried going for a walk, but she ended up encountering no fewer than three different stage or puppet shows that revolved around Anahrod the Wicked. It didn't take long before she suspected she would start a fight if she continued to surround herself with people, and so she ended up on a rooftop overlooking the university courtyard where her father sold sausages.

Sicaryon found her anyway.

She gave him a gimlet stare as he climbed up over the edge, using the very same collection of stacked crates she had. He had a basket tucked under one arm. She saw the neck of a wine bottle peeking out.

Anahrod sighed to herself. She supposed he probably had been waiting for an opportunity, and she'd certainly provided one, hadn't she?

"Do you have any idea how hard it was to find you?" he commented as he unpacked the basket.

"Not hard enough, it seems. If I told you to fuck off, would you?"

"Is that a thing you might be likely to do?" He set down a plate filled with cheeses, sour black bread, and—

"Where did you get chena?" she asked, incredulous.

"I know a local bakery," he confessed as he poured glasses of wine for them both. "They have a secret menu, if you know to ask."

She wondered just how many Deepers were secretly living in the Skylands. She didn't think Sicaryon would tell her, assuming he knew.

She had a feeling he did.

She took the glass of red wine when he offered it. "You didn't answer the question."

"I think you'll find I did, if you read between the lines." He took a sip of the wine, gave it a pleased appraisal, and drank a larger swallow. "I have no useful advice for you, but I thought you might like the company. Oh, and it's deeply unpleasant to watch someone else make all the same mistakes I made. I don't recommend it."

Anahrod paused in the process of taking a piece of aged cheese. "Am I the one making the mistakes, or is Ris?"

"Definitely Ris." He lowered his glass. "I'm sure you're also making mistakes. They're just not my mistakes. Her, though?" He chuckled wryly. "Oh yeah. I know all the lyrics to that song."

She scoffed and shook her head. What was she supposed to say? I told you so? She had, in fact, done that.

Anahrod drank a little more wine and watched the clouds. An occasional dragon flew by, too, but always at a distance. "Why are you here?"

"Because trying to rule a country is too much paperwork?"

She glared.

Sicaryon sighed and set his glass aside. "Because you were right," he said in a much more serious tone.

She'd have wondered if she was dreaming, but her luck had not been rolling that way of late. "Was I?"

"Yes," he said firmly. "I won't say that defending the family honor didn't improve some things, because it's never a bad day to decapitate a tyrant, but the cost?" His laughter was harsh, ragged. "It cost me everything. Everything that mattered, anyway."

She would've had to be a fool to miss the meaning there, considering the way he was looking at her. "You haven't changed," she said.

He was still a charming bastard.

"Now, now. There's no need for insults." Sicaryon's hurt expression was not entirely for show. He raised his hand. "Don't worry. I'm perfectly aware that I don't get to come marching back in with a blithe apology, a clean slate, and everything will revert to how it used to be. Some mistakes can't be fixed and the Deep doesn't give second chances."

"We're not in—" She stopped herself.

That wasn't a door she wanted to open. Logically, anyway. Emotionally and physically was something else. And with everything that had just happened with Ris, the timing was . . . unfortunate.

Sicaryon ate a piece of chena and then straightened. "I think I'm going to say something that you don't want to hear."

"Wonderful. It's what I've always wanted." She glanced at him sideways.

"Ready?" He waited.

"I have my sword with me today, you know," Anahrod pointed out.

"A good point," he said. "Okay, here it is: you don't get to decide for the Doreyls."

Anahrod's nostrils flared. "It would've been so nice if only you had the slightest clue what you're talking about."

"I told you that you wouldn't want to hear it," he reminded her. "But you need to hear it. I know you like to think that you are the only person licensed to go out and do heroic deeds, but as it happens, that is an individual choice. I asked around: he's fifteen. That's young, yes, but he's not an infant. If his parents are supporting the decision—"

"I'm sure they don't have all the facts," Anahrod snapped.

"What if they do?"

Anahrod's rebuttal died in her throat.

"By all accounts, the boy's mother is a terrifying spymaster and his father used to volunteer to fly into blizzards to rescue trapped travelers."

Anahrod made a face. "That does sound like the man."

"So, you should consider the possibility that Ris didn't need to deceive them, because they're brave, smart, and just maybe aren't thrilled about the idea of sending their only child into permanent exile."

She exhaled slowly. "I hate you so much."

Their eyes met.

The Sicaryon she'd left behind in the Deep would've tried to kiss her. Maybe she would've let him, too. This one did not.

Maybe the forty spouses were responsible.

He just smiled tenderly at her and said, "I hate you, too." Then he bounced a finger off the tip of her nose before she could dodge, and added, "Now we're both liars."

She shook her head, drank her wine, looked out over the city.

"As long as we're being so delightfully honest with each other, I—" She inhaled. "I don't know what to do."

"Fair," he allowed. "But I will repeat the words of a wise woman I knew when I was younger"—he gave her a significant look—"who said that just because you love someone doesn't mean you shouldn't confirm their sources."

Anahrod snickered. "Not my wise words. That was one of my second mother's favorite sayings."

"Fine. It's still a good idea. So do that: if you're curious whether Ris has fully explained the danger to the Doreyls, ask them."

Talking to the Doreyls proved more difficult than Anahrod had expected, primarily because she didn't have a good excuse to leave Duskcloud. Maybe Ris wouldn't mind, but Tiendremos sure as hell would if he returned to Duskcloud to discover her missing.

So, she hadn't asked them, and now they were back in Crystalspire, and she had very little time to fix that situation. Assuming she could.

Anahrod scratched her cheek through her veil, then resumed waiting along with the rest of the guards at the dock.

Sicaryon leaned his head in her direction. "Shouldn't they be here by now?"

Anahrod chewed on the inside of her cheek. "Maybe they changed their mind."

She doubted she would be so lucky.

She sighed and continued to wait. They were both dressed as guards, the mercenary sort employed by the rich. Ris had decided that since they both used swords, they'd draw less attention, ironically, if they worked together—like a matched set.

Anahrod suspected that this was also Ris's idea of an apology, although she had no proof. She just couldn't think of any other reason the woman would've put them in such proximity for the entire trip to Yagra'hai.

It was time for the dragonrider candidates to go to Yagra'hai.

Babies surrounded them. Not literal babies—none of the dragonrider candidates from Crystalspire were younger than fifteen. But fifteen was so young. Too young for what lay before them. Someone should've stopped them, warned them, said something.

No one would. Not even she.

Anahrod had an identity again. The irony was laughable. If she walked away that instant, she could start a new life as a Skylander. She had all the paperwork she needed to go anywhere in Seven Crests. Her name and background would stand up to any scrutiny short of personal interviews with friends or an interrogation under mirrorspell. She could join a division, settle down, live any life she wanted.

Admittedly, that life would be a violent one; her paperwork listed her as part of a mercenary division in Crystalspire, even if she was supposed to be—originally—from Blackglass.

Sicaryon's cover identity hailed from Snowfell. Ris must've done that on purpose, just as she'd dressed Sicaryon in a Snowfell-style shirt and breeches. People from that city rarely wore coats unless the weather dipped below freezing—their tolerance for cold was a point of pride.

Anahrod saw at least one benefit, namely that it put Sicaryon's breeches in full view. Perhaps that was the point: no one was looking at Anahrod when Sicaryon's tight leather pants were *right there*.

Sicaryon hated the cold, of course. Never let it be said that Ris couldn't be petty.

He inclined his head in her direction. "You do a good job of passing for someone from Blackglass, but you need to frown a little more. You can see it in the eyes, you know."

Anahrod glanced at the other bodyguards. Many of them *were* from Blackglass: bodyguard was a popular occupation for natives of that city traveling abroad. Mostly, people from Blackglass seemed to be everything Claw wasn't—taciturn, quiet, disinclined to engage in gossip, chitchat, or more than the barest minimum of casual conversation. They all wore veils.

Anahrod glared at Sicaryon, who grinned. "Yes," he said. "Just like that. Ah, this brings back memories, doesn't it?"

She stared at him. "When have we ever stood on a boarding causeway waiting for a fifteen-year-old boy to show up so we could escort him to school?"

"Never," he agreed easily. "But we're doing it together. Just like old times."

"Don't get used to it."

Finally, a carriage rolled up.

Anahrod snorted. She recognized the carriage: it was the same damn carriage she remembered from her own childhood. The mayor didn't own it; the mayor's *office* owned it, so it changed hands with each succeeding mayor. Each person to hold the office added a little more decoration to the carriage as well, transforming it over the years into a gaudy little beast: all silver filigree in the traditional Crystalspire angles, with purple enamel and inset crystals to catch the light.

Hideously expensive and simply hideous.

Anahrod doubted the excitable, overly enthusiastic Gwydinion had chosen to arrive last. The mayor could be expected to maintain appearances, which would include the idea that very important people could arrive last, to draw the maximum amount of attention.

Gwydinion jumped down before the carriage stopped rolling, while his father, Mayor Aiden e'Doreyl, waited for a more appropriately decorous exit.

A woman's hand appeared at the carriage window—Gwydinion's mother. Perhaps she didn't want to leave the coach's safety and suffer the unwelcome stares of the unwashed. The woman made an abortive motion, as though she'd been about to wave goodbye.

Gwydinion moved toward his father, then corrected and stepped back, head high.

Mayor e'Doreyl snorted and pulled his son into a hug, anyway.

Anahrod felt her lip curl.

It wasn't the hug that triggered her disgust. Just the opposite. She remembered a lifetime being forbidden from doing anything like that. Stand up straight. Be polite. Don't be too cheerful. Always hold yourself with dignity. Why are you smiling all the time? Do you want people to think you're a simpleton or a fool? Don't you know you're representing the most important city in Seven Crests?

She clenched her fists and looked away.

"Come along," Sicaryon whispered, snapping her out of it. He stepped forward to meet Gwydinion and his father.

Anahrod was unsure whether anyone had bothered telling Gwydinion she would be one of his guards. Someone must've, because when Anahrod approached, Gwydinion smiled even as he looked slightly embarrassed. The mayor, on the other hand, gave her a firm nod.

He didn't recognize her.

Gwydinion noticed Sicaryon, too, but his reaction was more confusion than shame. He'd probably expected the second person would be Claw.

"Mother said she wanted to speak with one of the guards." Gwydinion pointed at Anahrod.

Good. Because Anahrod sure as hell wanted to talk to Gwydinion's parents, and she didn't feel like having this conversation out in the open.

Why Gwydinion's mother wanted to speak with them, however, was a mystery. Probably the woman had questions about the level of security, in which case, she would not enjoy this conversation at all.

"Yes, that's fine," the mayor said brightly, and gestured to the carriage. "Please tell my wife to hurry, though: I believe the flyer's about to leave."

She bowed to the man and then hurried to the carriage. Sicaryon started to follow her, but Gwydinion blocked his way. "Just her, please."

Sicaryon shrugged and stepped aside.

Anahrod opened the door and hauled herself inside, sitting down on the empty padded bench before her eyes had finished adjusting to the dim light. The carriage had changed little: the velvet was dyed a brighter purple than she remembered, and several new inscriptions lined the sides.

Its occupant was familiar as well, such that when Anahrod's eyes finished adjusting, she couldn't breathe.

She felt dizzy, unmoored, and buffeted. For a second, Anahrod wasn't in her thirties, preparing to sneak into Yagra'hai as a criminal. She was fifteen again. Fifteen and being sent away from home for the first time.

Even though they all hailed from Crystalspire, Anahrod had never, not once, thought she knew Gwydinion's mother. She'd known no Doreyls growing up, and seventeen years was long enough for some ambitious newcomer to make the right friends. There'd been no reason to question the woman's identity. Why would she?

And yet, Anahrod did indeed know Gwydinion's mother.

She was Anahrod's birth mother, too.

PART FIVE

CONCERNING
TRAVEL
AND
EDUCATION

24

OBLIGATIONS OF BLOOD

Anahrod stared. She stared and felt three times a fool. Understanding came in an instant.

This was how Ris had tracked her down. *This* was why they'd brought Gwydinion with them into the jungles of the Deep. Naeron's sorcery centered around blood, didn't it? If he could track her location by blood left on a handkerchief, then perhaps he could also track her through a blood relative.

Like a half brother.

And now Belsaor had a new marriage, she was the first parent, and her spouse was *still* mayor of Crystalspire.

"Anahrod." Her mother said the name like a prayer answered.

She was older than Anahrod remembered—of course she was—but more dignified and elegant for the years, a beauty refined rather than diminished. She reached out a hand to Anahrod.

Toward the veil, Anahrod realized. She wanted to see her daughter's face.

Anahrod jerked away violently. "Don't touch me."

"Please," her mother said. "I must explain—"

Anahrod felt her teeth grind against each other. "I am so uninterested in your excuses. We are not doing this."

Belsaor lowered her hand. "I know you must be angry—"

"Angry?" Anahrod leaned forward and whispered, "Angry was when I found children throwing rocks at what I thought was an injured vel hound puppy for sport. Angry was the first time I saw a village turn out an old man because he wasn't their tribe and thus, they owed him neither food nor shelter. Angry was when I saw a flight of dragons burn down an entire holler for no other reason than because they'd discovered its location. How I feel about *you* goes beyond anger into an emotion for which I have no words." She drew back. "Oh, wait. No, I was wrong. I have the words. Three of them: *Go to Hell.*"

Her mother's sorrowful gaze was tossed aside like the mask it had always been. Her eyes blazed. "So, you're not even going to let me try to explain? I'm not giving you an excuse—"

"Good. Then we have nothing to say to one another." Anahrod stood up, as much as the carriage allowed it. She paused with her hand on the door handle. "But don't worry. Even though you're condemning a second child to that beast of a school, I'll make sure he comes back in one piece."

She was back outside again before her mother could respond. Anahrod intended to savor that moment—she'd never been allowed the last word as a child.

The mayor gave her a look of mild interest, but he still didn't seem to realize who she was. Gwydinion, though—*her brother*—looked so nervous that she knew. Sicaryon gave her one glance and went rigid, five seconds from jumping into the carriage to demand an explanation himself.

Anahrod had to pretend everything was fine.

She'd never been so glad for the veil.

Anahrod shook her head at Sicaryon as she fell in behind Gwydinion. Neither spoke as Gwydinion said his last goodbyes. Together, all three headed to the liner, waiting just for them. She wondered if her mother had planned that, too—Belsaor could've contacted Anahrod earlier, if she'd wanted a long and heartfelt conversation with her oldest child. This half-hearted attempt had absolved Belsaor of all responsibility, while freeing her from any ugly apologies. Even if Anahrod had wanted to talk, time wouldn't have permitted it.

"I'm sorry," Gwydinion murmured as they made their way toward their room assignment. The others had gone on ahead, likely already settling into their rooms. "This is so awkward. I'd understand if you didn't want to be around me . . ."

"What happened back there?" Sicaryon kept his voice low and casual, the cadence one of friendly chitchat.

"Nothing important," Anahrod lied.

"You could always swap with Claw," Gwydinion suggested. "I'm sure she'd be happy to wear weapons openly."

"Don't be a fool," Anahrod snapped. "Nobody could be around Claw for more than five seconds without noticing she's barely older than a child herself."

"I'm not a child—"

"Besides," Sicaryon interrupted, "I doubt Ris would've tasked Claw with monitoring me, whereas Anari is just the person to keep me from getting into too much trouble."

"Anari" was the name on her new papers. Close enough to Anah to justify if someone slipped up.

Gwydinion didn't question the name. Maybe he'd been told in advance. He did, however, take a moment to assess Sicaryon like a banker looking for counterfeit scales. "And who are you again?"

"I'm Cary. A childhood friend of Anari. I'm surprised she hasn't mentioned me."

Gwydinion squinted. "Don't tell me, then. I'll figure it out for myself."

Anahrod continued walking. No one said anything for several minutes.

It was a nice liner, although not as nice as the *Crimson Skies* in some regards. Larger wings, but fewer of them, slower to turn and adjust. Still, just a liner. Its most beautiful quality was how difficult it was to look over the side.

Gwydinion patted down his coat and retrieved a numbered key. "Our suite should be this way."

No sooner had they turned down the last hallway than another boy, running down the hallway in the opposite direction, slammed into Gwydinion, knocking them both down. Sicaryon put a hand to his sword, scanning the hallway for any danger, while Anahrod pulled the boy off Gwydinion.

"Hey!" the boy called out. "You hit me!" The accusation was levied at Gwydinion.

Anahrod corrected her first impression. Not a boy, but a girl. A quick glance at social rings confirmed that assessment. Admittedly, the girl *was* late-blooming, but still a girl. Behind the coltish newcomer, a burly man ran to catch up, out of breath and panting. He gave Sicaryon and his-all-but-drawn sword a look of stern disapproval. The man himself was armed with a truncheon and several daggers, all well-used.

"I didn't—I didn't do that—" Gwydinion protested.

"You did!" the girl accused. "You totally did."

A wave of protectiveness overcame her. Anahrod pulled Gwydinion behind her. "He didn't," Anahrod told the girl firmly. "Watch where you're going next time."

"Kimat!" the student's minder scolded.

"It wasn't me, Waja," the girl protested. "You have to do something. They tried to hurt me."

"Absurd," Sicaryon commented. "If we'd wanted to hurt you, we wouldn't have *tried*."

Anahrod sighed. That was perhaps less helpful than Sicaryon had intended.

The man's expression turned ugly. "What do you people think you're doing?"

"I know this game," she told the girl. "Don't."

"You're not going to reprimand your little troublemaker for hitting another candidate?" Waja didn't conceal his displeasure.

"I would if he had," Anahrod replied. "But I was watching him the entire time. He didn't. Whereas *your* little troublemaker thinks she's being clever." She stared at the girl, who was trying as hard as possible to force tears from her eyes. "Next you'll ask if I know who you are, or who your parents are."

Sicaryon laughed, while the girl blinked, bemused that Anahrod had guessed the next lines of the play.

"Let's just go," Gwydinion suggested. "I don't want trouble."

"Waja!" the girl whined.

By this time, the girl's bodyguard, Waja, had had a chance to give both Anahrod and Sicaryon a thorough examination. Waja was a big man—probably used to people being scared of him.

Neither Anahrod nor Sicaryon were scared of him.

His gaze fell to their swords and his expression turned thoughtful.

Anahrod flexed a hand. Underneath the veil, she smiled.

People who lived and died by violence became good at evaluating risk. A more foolish man might have studied Anahrod—not tall or bulky—and made foolish assumptions about her danger level. Even a foolish man, one who'd dismissed Anahrod as a threat, might still pause when faced with Sicaryon.

Waja wasn't a foolish man.

Waja clapped a hand on the girl's shoulder. "Let's get you settled in." He moved past them both, never releasing his charge.

The girl made a rude gesture as she passed.

Babies, Anahrod thought.

"I really didn't hit her," Gwydinion protested.

"A wasted opportunity," Sicaryon mused.

"She's going to cause trouble, isn't she?" Gwydinion was still giving Sicaryon the stink eye, still trying to gauge his role.

"Yes," Anahrod agreed, "without question."

"The best ones always do," Sicaryon added unhelpfully.

25

A BRIGHT AND SMILING TROUBLE

The *Silver Herald* was more lavish than even most Crystalspire liners (which was quite the statement). Gwydinion's room was splendor itself: large enough to house a full-size bed and just enough space to walk around it. The cabin also contained an en suite water closet and a smaller bedroom for a valet or personal assistant. The rest of Gwydinion's "staff" (i.e., Claw, Kaibren, and Naeron) were assigned a nearby cabin.

Sicaryon gave the second bed a quick glance. He didn't grin. He so purposefully didn't grin that Anahrod could feel it like an itch at the back of her neck.

"The other cabin sleeps four," she told Sicaryon as she dumped her knapsack on the bed. "There's an extra bed for you."

He gave her an unimpressed look. "And if there's a problem? I'm supposed to magically foresee danger and run over?"

"Are you under the impression that you're really here as a bodyguard?" She scowled as soon as the words left her mouth. She was being a massive bitch.

That she knew exactly why she was behaving so badly didn't excuse it.

Sicaryon ignored the question. "What happened back there in the carriage?" He raised a finger. "Don't tell me 'nothing important.' I don't believe you."

Anahrod ignored him in favor of studying the cabin. Several windows faced out from the main room, including a large glass door that opened out onto a small balcony. She closed the curtains over the windows and the door while averting her gaze, so she didn't accidentally see over the side. She unshuttered the inscribed lamps to keep the room from falling into a sullen darkness.

Gwydinion just stared at her unhappily.

"What are you doing?" Sicaryon still looked perplexed, but a different sort of perplexed.

"Reducing the odds of an incident." She knew it was no answer at all and she didn't care.

"Is it working?"

Gwydinion glared at Sicaryon. "But seriously: Who *are* you?"

"Gwydinion, I'd like you to meet 'His Royal Majesty,' King Sicaryon." Anahrod didn't bother to hide her disdain. "Sicaryon, meet my little brother, Gwydinion."

She almost laughed, watching their shock as they both realized each other's identity. Gwydinion never imagined Sicaryon would leave the Deep, and Sicaryon knew Anahrod was an only child.

"You? You can't be *Sicaryon*."

"Let me guess, you were expecting purple skin."

"No, but—but." Gwydinion jabbed a finger in the man's direction. "You set fire to that targrove swamp!"

"No. One of my soldiers did that and won't be doing it ever again."

"Okay, fine. But your people still tried to kidnap her! Anahrod, you expect me to believe—"

"Perhaps you shouldn't point fingers when it comes to kidnapping Anahrod," Sicaryon rebutted.

Gwydinion turned bright red and sputtered.

Anahrod sat down on the master bed and put her head in her hands. Gwydinion and Sicaryon both stopped yelling.

"One question, Gwydinion," Anahrod finally said. "Did you know the whole time? That you were my half brother?"

When she raised her head, the boy swallowed, and then nodded at her, once.

Sicaryon studied Gwydinion, then said to Anahrod, "You told me you have two mothers."

"It was true at the time," Anahrod said. "Although it turns out that one of my parents was late-sprouting. Gwydinion and I share the same birth mother."

Gwydinion looked uncomfortable. "I . . . well. That is to say—"

Anahrod gave him a questioning look. "How is that wrong? Belsaor's not your mother?"

"No, she is," Gwydinion reassured her. "She absolutely is. She's just, uh—" He seemed at a loss for words.

"What don't I understand?" Anahrod asked the boy.

"That I'm not your half brother." Gwydinion pulled a small box from his coat, roughly the size of a pack of playing cards.

She turned the sentence over in her mind until the answer to the riddle slotted into place. "Aiden e'Doreyl was my donor father?"

"I'm pretty sure, yes," Gwydinion said. "I mean, our mother wasn't cheating on her first spouse or anything. It wasn't like that."

"I'm aware," Anahrod said. The worst part about it was that she didn't think her first mother—her father now—had even wanted children. He just wanted to be mayor, and voters always elected parents. Parents were "less likely to make rash decisions."

She wondered if Mayor e'Doreyl had known who she really was when he'd tried to help her escape.

"Is that a baby cave wurm?" Sicaryon's voice, harsh with incredulity, broke her out of her stupor.

Anahrod's head snapped up. Gwydinion had placed that small box on the bed before unfolding it several times in exactly the way normal boxes didn't. After unfolding it to the size of a trunk, Gwydinion opened the lid and removed a small glass tank.

Gwydinion was unwinding a small, pale green snake from his wrist when Sicaryon had made the observation.

"Your snake survived?" Anahrod had assumed it must've drowned during the trip down the river.

Gwydinion gave her a broad smile. "It did, yes!" Then he leveled a much less pleasant expression at Sicaryon. "What's a cave wurm?"

"Incredibly dangerous." Sicaryon looked appalled. "I know how dangerous that venom is, and if I was back in the Deep, I'd have an antidote, but maybe you haven't noticed that we're not in the Deep?"

"Believe me," Anahrod said, "I've noticed."

He snorted. "And that is *not* a snake. Cave wurms are warm-blooded."

Anahrod nodded. "They'd have to be, wouldn't they?" She began unpacking her knapsack. She didn't have much, but the single object of value was extraordinarily so: Peralon's dragonstone.

"Also, I don't know how fast those creatures grow, but let's hope it takes a long, long time, because I've heard of cave wurms so large they can swallow a man whole. Are you just going to let him—" Sicaryon stopped short. "Oh."

Gwydinion also paused. "What does that mean?"

"You told me earlier, didn't you?" Sicaryon said to Anahrod. "He can speak with animals the same way you can."

Anahrod nodded, her throat tight.

"I've named him Legless." Gwydinion metaphorically ran right over Sicaryon's observation as he put the tank down on a side table, laying it on a thick matting of felted wool designed to cushion against air turbulence.

The announcement distracted Sicaryon. "Seriously?" He pointed a finger at the boy. "That does it. You're not allowed to name things."

"Feel free to roll your eyes at him like a proper teenager, Gwydinion. He doesn't get to tell you what to do."

"I already know *that*," the boy said, rolling his eyes at them both.

"Why did I ever think it was a good idea to leave the place where people treat me with respect?" Sicaryon asked the ceiling.

"I've wondered that myself," Anahrod admitted. "Aren't you supposed to be ruling something? I thought that job entailed more than just playing stud to your stable of forty spouses. You know, you should've stopped at thirty. That way, you could've had one for every day of the month. Fairer that way."

He squinted at her. "Why does everyone keep saying—? I'm not married!"

"That's not what I hear."

Sicaryon scowled. "And I hear you sacrificed at least three children to Zavad and seduced several priests, so maybe you shouldn't believe all the stories."

She paused, dragonstone still in her lap. "Fine, you're not married." Anahrod eyed the folding box. It might be the only place in the cabin where she could hide the dragonstone.

"Thank you."

"Oh, that's weird."

Anahrod turned her head. Gwydinion held aloft a piece of silver jewelry, examining it as though he'd never seen it before.

"Is it?" Sicaryon asked idly. He'd also started unpacking, much to Anahrod's consternation, because damn it, he was not sleeping there.

The jewelry was a mantle brooch, although the color—opal set in a silver knot—wasn't a Crystalspire style.

Gwydinion looked askance. "Yes? This was in my coat pocket—but it's not mine." All the playfulness vanished from his eyes. "That girl. She must have planted it on me." His expression turned amazed. "I didn't even see her do it."

A loud series of bangs shuddered the cabin door as someone slammed their fist against it repeatedly. "Open up! This is the *Silver Herald*'s security officer!"

All three of them looked down—first at the brooch in Gwydinion's hand, and second at the dragonstone sitting in Anahrod's lap.

Both items would get them into trouble, but only one would see them killed. She doubted "a dragon gave it to me" was an acceptable excuse.

Sicaryon grabbed the dragonstone and tossed it into the folding box.

"Give me that." Anahrod gestured to the mantle brooch, and Gwydinion threw it to her.

"One minute!" The boy grabbed the edge of the folding box, swiftly reversing his earlier actions to fold it back down to card size. He tucked the deck back into his jacket.

Sicaryon made a "gimmie" motion with his hands to Anahrod, so she tossed him the mantle brooch.

From the corner of her eye, she saw Sicaryon open the balcony door and toss the brooch outside.

"Open up now!" The voice didn't sound friendly.

"He said one minute!" Anahrod snapped as she opened the door.

These were not Seven Crests men. These people took orders from the dragons, from the school at best and Neveranimas at worst. They would neither respect nor care that Gwydinion was an important person who should be treated with ice-silk gloves.

They dressed like they meant business, too, each of them in dragon-embroidered uniforms and wearing the meaty, tough air of professional bullies. No swords, of course, because who wore swords anymore? But plenty of truncheons and daggers.

Perhaps they were the reason the dragonrider candidates traveled with their own bodyguards. They certainly hadn't when Anahrod had attended.

"May we help you?" she asked coldly.

The head guard moved to come inside. Anahrod raised an eyebrow and didn't budge. There was barely room for three people to stand, let alone visitors. She swung open the door enough for the guards to see that they were still unpacking.

"We've had reports of a robbery," the woman said.

Silence followed.

"That's terrible," Sicaryon said from over by the balcony door. "We'll let you know if we see anyone acting suspicious."

A guard in the back snickered and looked away.

The lead guard wasn't so amused. "What I mean is that one of the other passengers claimed your charge stole a piece of jewelry from her. We're here to search your room."

"Do you realize who this is?" Anahrod gave the other woman a frosty look.

It worked as well as she'd expected: not at all.

"I don't care who he is," the other woman snapped. "There are certain behaviors that aren't tolerated."

"That's true," Gwydinion agreed. "I heard about what happened to Dabra Hilras last year."

Anahrod glanced back at him. "What happened?"

"They sent him to the Church," Gwydinion said, "the moment they landed. Never set foot inside the school." He raised guileless brown eyes to the guards. "But I didn't take anything. A girl knocked me down when we were finding our suite, but if she dropped anything, I didn't see it. Is she the one who claimed I stole something?"

"I'm not at liberty—"

"I wonder who she was? She dressed like she was from Grayshroud," Gwydinion mused innocently.

Grayshroud had the worst reputation of all the Seven Crests cities. They were said to tolerate all the things that were illegal everywhere else. They put even the position of mayor up for auction every five years. Everyone knew Grayshroud was a city of criminals.

Not people who should be trusted.

Two of the guards glanced at each other uneasily. Unfortunately, the head guard never wavered.

"Where she might be from is unimportant," the woman said. "We're searching your room. And yourselves," she added as an afterthought.

"Of course!" Gwydinion agreed. "We're happy to help however we can."

The security officer gave him a suspicious, narrow-eyed stare.

Anahrod retreated, taking Sicaryon's place and "coincidentally" blocking the door leading out to the balcony. While the guards struggled to fit themselves into the space, Anahrod reached out to sense what living animals might be nearby.

Blood crows circled the flyer near the galley. Not unusual: blood crows trailed most flyers, quick to take advantage of discarded bones and skin and other delicious scraps.

She only needed one. Anahrod singled one out and directed it to pick up the brooch from where it had fallen. She sent the blood crow, with its shiny new prize, to some other balcony.

Now the guards would find the jewelry—just not in their cabin. That was one problem solved. Unfortunately, it wasn't the biggest problem.

"Who wants to be searched first?" a guard asked.

Sicaryon held up his arms. "I'm willing." He made it sound flirty without being an outright proposition. "As often as it takes."

Sicaryon made the expected jokes about courtships and marriage offers as the guard patted him down. The guard stoically ignored it.

Or not so stoically. At least one guard might have taken Sicaryon up on his flirting if their boss hadn't been watching.

They found nothing. Anahrod hadn't known if Sicaryon had any contraband on his person. If so, he'd hidden it well. Then came Anahrod's turn, with less flirting but a similar conclusion.

But they weren't the ones carrying the folding box.

"Where's your snake?" Anahrod asked Gwydinion.

"Snake?" A guard straightened. "What snake?"

"Oh, I—" Gwydinion glanced inside the tank and made a small, adorable gasp. "I'm so sorry. I forgot I was still wearing him."

"Wild animals aren't allowed—" The head security officer drew herself up in preparation for what would no doubt have been a thrilling recitation of whatever rules or laws governed behavior aboard a Yagra'hai cutter.

"It's a pet," Gwydinion, Anahrod, and Sicaryon all protested at the same time.

"Admittedly, a venomous pet," Sicaryon added. "Might I suggest you let the boy put it back in its tank?"

The head officer glared, then gestured for one of the others to step forward. "Search the tank first. Then once he's put the snake inside, search him."

Gwydinion seemed happy to let the guard do exactly that, but then, Anahrod suspected the folding box was still in his coat.

"Do you mind if we stand out in the hallway?" Not pausing for an answer, Sicaryon and Gwydinion simultaneously acted—Sicaryon moved while Gwydinion untangled the "snake" from his arm. Anahrod followed Sicaryon's lead, stepping in from behind.

The result as they moved around Gwydinion was predictable. Gwydinion tripped and Sicaryon reached out to save him. All eyes were on Legless, hanging from Gwydinion's fingers and about to be dropped on the floor, never to be seen again.

"Don't drop him!" someone called out.

While this was going on, Anahrod felt a brush against her coat. She didn't stop to check, but she would bet money (and was betting her life) that someone had just planted the folding box on her.

To an outsider, though, she seemed like the person who'd hung back, never making contact with the others.

"I've got him!" Gwydinion reassured everyone as he dropped the "snake" into its tank and shut the lid.

"Good," the head guard snapped. "Now, please step outside. And search that man again, in case the boy tried to slip him something."

As the guards went to work, a guard ran up, panting.

"They found the missing brooch, sir!" he said. "Two floors down. On a Windsong candidate's balcony."

The woman pinched the bridge of her nose. "Fine. Let's go talk to them."

"Can't do that," the guard offered cheerfully. "We haven't picked up the Windsong candidates yet."

"May I go back to my room?" Gwydinion asked plaintively.

Anahrod kept a neutral expression.

"Fine." The woman plastered an apologetic smile on her face. "Yes, you may. Sorry to have bothered you."

"No problem at all," Sicaryon told her.

Anahrod retreated to the suite as well. Sicaryon shut the door after Gwydinion was inside. The boy started to say something and Anahrod shushed him.

She waited at the door until she was certain she'd heard all the guards walk away.

Gwydinion beamed at them. "Did you see that? That was sunshine!" His smile faltered. "Except that was a setup, wasn't it?"

"Yes, it was," Sicaryon said.

Anahrod shrugged. "Don't think the guards were part of it. Just told information at the right time by that girl. If they'd really been involved, they would've tried to plant something themselves."

"Speaking of incriminating evidence, where did you get your hands on a dragonstone?" Sicaryon studied her carefully.

"Haven't you listened to the stories? Zavad gave it to me." Anahrod plucked the folding box from her coat and tossed it to Gwydinion.

"She's really something," Gwydinion mused. "The girl from Grayshroud, I mean. Kimat? I didn't even notice her sneak that brooch into my pocket. That's impressive!"

He didn't sound upset. Just the opposite.

"Stay away from her," Anahrod advised, although she suspected that advice would be ignored. "If you give her a chance, she'll try something again."

"Kimat." Gwydinion tried out the shape of the name. "You don't suppose they meant Kimat Kelnaor, do you? But Kimat Kelnaor is Magistrix Kelnaor's son—" He paused. "Oh. She must be late-blooming."

"Magistrix Kelnaor of Grayshroud, I assume?"

"Right. I met Kimat once when we were children, but her mother wasn't magistrix yet. Just, you know, involved in stuff that made Mother frown a lot."

Gwydinion threw up his arms, finally letting his frustration show. "Why do this? Why claim I hit her, then claim I stole something? Does she really think the dragons are going to kick me from the school?"

Anahrod sighed. "Perhaps she thinks it can't hurt to try." She paused. "The next few weeks will be dangerous for everyone. After that, most candidates should settle down and behave themselves, but from now until then . . ." She waved her hand back and forth. "Schemes and plots. People making the hilariously wrong assumption that the fewer candidates there are, the better their odds.

"The joke is that it doesn't work that way. A dragon picks whoever they like, and if they don't like someone, they don't pick. Nothing else matters. Some years only a single dragonrider is chosen, or none at all."

"Sunshine," Gwydinion grumbled, but he immediately straightened and pointed to the other two. "So, are you two . . . ?"

"No," Anahrod said at the exact moment Sicaryon said, "Yes."

"Yes and no," Sicaryon amended. "We used to be, but no longer." He regarded Anahrod fondly. "Although my door is always open."

"Yes, to half the world." She picked up his knapsack and threw it at him. "You are not sleeping here."

"He's not wrong, though," Gwydinion said.

Anahrod narrowed her eyes.

"He's not wrong," Gwydinion repeated. "There's at least two people on this liner—Kimat and Waja—who are actively trying to get me into trouble. I'd feel a lot safer if I had you both here."

Anahrod jerked a thumb in Sicaryon's direction. "Is he paying you?"

Across the room, Sicaryon started laughing.

QUIET MOMENTS

The bed dipped as Sicaryon sat down next to Anahrod. Neither said anything.

Gwydinion was still pulling clothing out of his folding box. He was also humming to himself.

Anahrod just shook her head. She'd asked for a folding box when she was sent to Yagra'hai. She'd begged for one, in fact.

Her mother—their mother—had told her they were too expensive.

Anahrod had gotten one in the end, of course, but only because she'd stolen it.

"Heights, is it?" Sicaryon's voice was just barely higher than a whisper, but he switched to speaking Sumulye.

Anahrod tore her eyes away from watching her brother. She cleared her throat. "Yes," she said. "Embarrassing."

"It explains a few things," Sicaryon said.

"That's why Peralon gave me the dragonstone," she said, gesturing to the evidence of that heresy. "I'll need to be over it by the time we—you know." She grimaced. "Been having nightmares, and I'd rather not wake everyone."

If he'd made some sort of puerile joke about offering to be her comfort blanket, she'd have hit him, but his survival instincts must've warned him in time.

"I'm used to sleeping lightly," was all he said, which could be read several ways. They'd slept with one eye open when traveling because there'd always been the possibility of an ambush at any hour. Perhaps the situation hadn't changed appreciably just because he wore a crown.

"You're not worried someone will stage a coup while you're gone?" Anahrod asked. A question that had nothing at all to do with sleeping patterns.

"They're welcome to try," Sicaryon replied. "But that's not the question I thought you'd ask."

"Oh?" She turned her head to look at him directly. "What was?"

"Who the Valekings were."

She couldn't remember the context for a second, and then did, and flushed with embarrassment. Her gaze snapped forward again. "You knew I was eavesdropping, didn't you?"

"It's not like I wouldn't have done the same if I had your powers."

"Ah." She wasn't sure how she should feel about the lack of judgment. Sicaryon wasn't exactly the first in line to be anyone's moral compass. "So . . . who were the Valekings?"

"Slavers," he answered. "Really nasty ones. Story goes they captured a beautiful girl with eyes like the jungle and hair the color of blood. She suffered countless indignities before she learned powerful sorcery. The story varies after that, but in most versions, she woke a sleeping dragon while trying to escape and *he* killed everybody."

She chewed on that. "Don't suppose it was a gold dragon?"

"In fact, it was. Stands out, especially since there aren't a lot of stories in the Deep where dragons are the heroes."

"No," she agreed. "There aren't." She didn't have to ask why he'd never told her the story, either. The last thing a teenage Anahrod had wanted to hear were positive stories about *dragons*. "You don't think it's just a folktale?"

He raised an eyebrow at her.

She sighed. "Fine. Neither do I." Too many details fit. Ris's age was no rebuttal, either: dragonriders often aged slower than normal humans.

"She is beautiful," he said.

"She is."

"Maybe a little baffling, though."

Anahrod snorted. "Like either of us is any better." She held out her left hand, pretending to admire the garden rings there. "Shame I couldn't find a ring that means 'I'm attracted to people who are vengeance-obsessed and prone to extreme violence.' Would've been perfect."

"Very niche."

"No, very niche is renic root, which apparently means 'I am sexually attracted to cloth dolls.'"

Sicaryon's bark of laughter was loud enough to startle Gwydinion, who gave them a faintly accusing and unintentionally adorable look.

Sicaryon laughed again, then kissed Anahrod on the temple and stood. "I'll go see if the quartermaster has anyone with a pair of singles who'd like to swap for one of our doubles." He retreated through the door, leaving her alone in the suite with Gwydinion.

"He seems nice," Gwydinion said, without an ounce of sincerity. "Nicer than I would've thought, considering," he added. "I expected him to be more, you know . . ."

"Covered in mud?" Anahrod rubbed a hand over her face.

"No. More 'evil king who doesn't understand what the word "no" means.' I was putting my money on Ris, but now I'm not so sure."

Thank Eannis Claw wasn't around to hear him. She'd immediately start a betting pool.

Anahrod sighed. Claw already had, hadn't she?

In any case . . . "She's a dragonrider."

Gwydinion grinned. "Is that such a bad thing?" The smile faltered. "I mean . . . I know you don't have any reason to like dragons, but they're not all terrible. Peralon seems pretty sunshine."

She resisted the urge to tell Gwydinion he was too young to understand. That wouldn't win her any approval, even if it was true. "Gwydinion, this isn't important." He started to protest, and she continued. "It's not. We are dealing with an evil dragon who keeps killing anyone who's sent to the school in Yagra'hai with the power to speak to animals, and that's *you*. That's both of us. You're going to be in danger from the moment we're within five miles of that damn mountain and I wasn't in the mood to forgive Ris for that even before I found out that you're my brother."

She shrugged. "It doesn't matter, anyway. I'm going to do this, then say my goodbyes."

Gwydinion squinted at her. "To do what? Go back to the jungle and pretend none of this ever happened?"

"I don't—" Anahrod's breath felt thick and heavy, despite the altitude.

What happened next?

"I can't come back," Anahrod said. "Even if we pull off the plan perfectly. If this—" She shook her head. This wasn't the right place to go into details. The suite wasn't secure, and she had every reason to think people were paying attention. "Ris hasn't told you what we're doing, has she?"

"Not intentionally," he admitted. "I've pieced together some clues, anyway. You'll finish with enough money for you to start over, yes? Maybe not in Seven Crests, but . . ."

"Maybe," she said. "Probably."

"You know Mom would do anything to have you back," Gwydinion said.

Anahrod didn't hide how ridiculous she found that idea.

"It's true," he protested.

She scoffed. He was a sweet kid. He really was. She could hardly blame him for wanting to have his happy family, the one that he must have decided could exist despite all evidence to the contrary.

"It's not." Anahrod frowned. "I'm sorry. That wasn't fair of me. But she hurt me. She hurt me a lot, and that wound's never healed."

He rocked back on his heels. "She never meant to. She's the whole reason I came after you."

Anahrod frowned, taken aback. "I thought the dragon—" She started over. "What do you mean?"

Gwydinion moved a curtain to the side, just enough for him to look out the window. "She was fine when I was younger, but she's so sad all the time now. Stoically, broodingly sad. Or she used to be. She's mostly angry these days, but honestly, that's an improvement."

"Sad?" Anahrod couldn't picture it. Belsaor? *Sad?*

"For the longest time I couldn't figure out why," Gwydinion said. "Then I realized it was me."

"Gwydinion—"

"I was reminding her of you. And she never got over being unable to save you."

Anger curled around her gut, stung her eyes. "She never tried."

"That's not true," Gwydinion said. "Or—" He sighed. "If it is true, she's compensating by being overprotective. I've told you about all the lessons, the training. I'm never, ever allowed to go anywhere without a wingsuit. I'm wearing one right now."

Anahrod raised an eyebrow. He wasn't.

"No," he reassured her. "I really am. She inscribed these." He held up his arms, with the bracelets he always wore. "I love her, but she *needs* to back off and let me be a stupid teenager. Father says it's an important part of my development."

Anahrod couldn't help herself; she laughed.

"So, you see," he continued, "that's why I need my sister back. You can defend me and complain when I'm allowed to get away with all the things that you weren't. What's the point of being the youngest child if I'm never treated like it?"

She exhaled. He was staring at her with wide eyes, enough to do any baby proud. "I appreciate what you're saying, kid, but . . ." Anahrod sighed. "No matter how this goes, I'm still a wanted criminal. Worse, I'm apparently evil incarnate. If I start hanging out with the Doreyl family, people will ask questions. Or have you not noticed how much I resemble our mother?"

He sighed. "No. I've noticed." He added, "So you're just going to leave?"

"I don't want to, but I don't have a choice." She hated the look on the boy's face, but she wouldn't lie to him.

She just didn't see any other options.

27

INTERROGATION UNDER SILVER

Neveranimas increased security. Again.

"Neveranimas is doing what?" Anahrod whispered.

The dining room was empty—all the new people on the liner had gathered outside on balconies to watch the final approach. Not to see the city—it was too early for that—but to watch the never-ceasing storm that perpetually encircled the top of the mountain.

Those more experienced stayed inside. The others would regret their enthusiasm soon enough.

"Inscribed mirrors," Naeron explained. "Reflection darkens if you lie."

"Mirrorspells." Claw said the word like it was a curse.

"How do we know this?" Sicaryon murmured. He didn't sound skeptical—this was a request for sources, not a denial.

"Bursar," Naeron said. "Worried about angry parents."

Anahrod knuckled the corner of her eye and bit back a groan. It's not like she hadn't known the threat was real. She stood up and paced.

"What choice now," Kaibren whispered, "with dawn approaching?" The old man was bent near double on the bench, with his hands on his head. She'd rarely seen a better depiction of abject despair.

Claw's eyes were wide as she stared at Kaibren. What he'd said had just penetrated; she let out a laugh just shy of hysterical. "What he just said."

Anahrod rubbed her hands over her upper arms and forced herself to stop pacing. The flyer shuddered as an echo of too-loud thunder rolled over the vessel. The liner had been flying at a slight tilt upward for hours now, but once they had flown over the storm, they'd begin their descent. That would be far more noticeable.

They didn't have much time.

Anahrod sat down next to Claw and lowered her voice, which made everyone bunch in to listen. "Remember: we have two dragonriders already in Yagra'hai who are likely finding out about the increased security right now. And remember, Jaemeh's dragon oversees this. We just need to buy them time."

"Buy them time?" Claw squinted. "How do we do that?"

"Literally." Sicaryon gave the ceiling a contemplative look. "You must have traveled before. There'll be a queue. There'll be someone who's in a hurry and doesn't want to wait, and they'll pay for that privilege. No one will question if you swap places to go later."

Claw snapped back, "And if we're already in the back?"

No one said anything for a moment. Long enough for Claw to realize she'd just asked for advice on how to find water while standing outside in the rain. "Yeah, yeah, laugh yourselves sick, assholes. That's the fucking plan? Delay and hope the dragonriders come to our rescue?"

"Delay and keep our eyes open," Anahrod murmured. "Don't panic. Answer their questions without lying. And yes, rescue is coming."

"And if it isn't?" Claw scowled.

"The Cauldron's rumble wasn't loud enough or early enough to escape the boiling," Kaibren murmured.

Anahrod winced. A quote from *The Lord of Fire* that referenced the fictional city of Viridhaven just moments before the Cauldron's explosion blew the top of the mountain apart (and took the city with it). She didn't need Claw to translate.

If the dragonriders didn't come to help them, they were screwed.

"Vanigh," a man yelled into the almost empty room. "Anari Vanigh."

"Good luck," Sicaryon murmured.

They had moved everyone into a warehouse on the docks while the interviewers worked through the passenger rolls. Anahrod and the others had forestalled the interviews for as long as possible, but they'd reached the end of their tethers. Everyone else had already been interviewed. There was no sign of Ris or Jaemeh.

"You too." His time would come soon enough. Anahrod stood, grabbed her bag, and headed to the indicated doorway.

The only reason Anahrod had stayed calm was because she'd realized an important fact:

The entire operation was as well planned and organized as stepping in drake shit.

The first problem was the guards who'd been commandeered to provide security, forcing them to abandon their "real" jobs. They were surly about it.

Then there were the mirrorspells, which could only be operated by people with magical talent. Since the idea of having priests fill security roles was seven layers of ridiculous, that left dragonriders as the only option. Dragonriders who knew the work was beneath them and weren't afraid to act like it.

Lastly, the entire process was new enough that no one seemed completely certain if they were even performing their jobs correctly.

Maybe it would work to Anahrod's advantage. Maybe it wouldn't.

She was about to find out.

Anahrod was led to a small, cramped room containing four items: a table, two chairs, and a large silver mirror. The mirror was set up to reflect the vacant chair.

The empty chair where Anahrod was supposed to sit.

Eannis. If this thing worked the way Naeron said, she wouldn't even get past "state your name" before the mirror gave away the game. She could try to coast by on a technicality—those legal identification papers—but she knew they were a ruse, and the mirror would check her belief, not facts.

She didn't recognize the dragonrider sitting across from her—an older woman, gray-haired, with a clipboard balanced on her lap and a cup of tea long since grown cold next to her. "Have a seat," the woman suggested in a way that wasn't a suggestion.

Anahrod tried to catch a glance at the woman's rings. She didn't like the idea of flirting her way through security, but she'd do it if she had to.

She noticed the rings and sighed internally. Leaves. So that wasn't even an option.

"Sit down and state your name, your city of birth, and your reason for visiting—"

She was going to have to stumble and break that damn mirror, wasn't she?

Anahrod made a move toward her seat. As she did, she hooked her foot around the chair leg in such a way that guaranteed that she'd stumble. She did, overcompensated, splayed out her hand for balance against the tabletop, then spilled to the side . . .

The door behind her opened as she began her ill-fated tumble toward the mirror.

"Whoa there!" A hand caught her by the elbow. "Careful. When was the last time you ate? You're shaky as a newborn calf."

Anahrod looked up with wide eyes.

Jaemeh stared back at her.

"Sorry I'm late, Glorigha," Jaemeh said amiably to the other dragonrider. "I think this one's about to collapse."

The other dragonrider, Glorigha, threw her clipboard onto the table. "She could decide to take a nap on the table if she wants, as long as you handle the paperwork." The woman wasted no time at all retreating from the interview room.

She didn't say even goodbye.

Jaemeh lowered Anahrod down into the chair. She didn't have to fake how shaky she felt, her muscles pulled so taut they all but vibrated in the hot, thin air.

"Have a seat," Jaemeh murmured. "When did you last eat?"

"It's been a while," she admitted. "No food allowed in the waiting room and that was—" She waved a hand. She was unsure how long it had been since they'd landed and first been called into the room. "Where's Gwydinion?"

"The boy?" He kept his voice down, a reminder that it would be wise for her to do so as well.

"Yes."

"He's fine." The dragonrider looked over his notes. "Passed his interview with flying colors." He grinned at Anahrod, a smile she did not return. "He's very excited to become a dragonrider, and you made sure he couldn't reveal what he didn't know. Good job there."

Anahrod stared blankly at the man.

She suspected Gwydinion had long since figured out what they were doing, but maybe he'd flown through on a technicality.

Jaemeh saw the look on her face, the question, and shook his head. "No, he was interviewed by someone else." Jaemeh shrugged, as if to both pass judgment and absolve guilt. "They never learn in time, do they?" He gave her the knowing look of one comrade to another, united by their mutual terrible experiences with dragons. If anything, he seemed a little jealous, but that made sense.

She'd escaped.

Anahrod ran a hand over her face. "Are we done?"

"Give it a few more minutes," Jaemeh cautioned. "That way it'll seem like I've asked you the right number of questions." He gestured for her to hand over her entry papers.

He stamped them with a thick, carved seal. "Welcome to Yagra'hai."

INVISIBLE WALLS

Normally, the *Silver Herald* would've docked at a private berth used by the college, but the change in entry procedures had complicated matters. The liner had been forced to dock at the main port. A carriage transported each candidate to the college separately as they were cleared for entry.

It rained the entire time, this being a day when the never-ending storm surrounding Mount Yagra spilled over its borders. The lightning made a stunning introduction to the city. The thunder echoed, often mixed with dragon roars.

Yagra'hai was "the City of Dragons," but it more realistically resembled a massive collection of palaces, towers, lairs, and warrens, each one stocked with its own draconic royalty. A thousand individual fiefs of various sizes, each ruled by its own dragon. The dragons themselves were ruled by a council of the oldest and wisest. Above them all, the First Dragon, a title handed down from one dragon to another since Eannis herself. Dragons often lived elsewhere—the crèches in each of the Seven Crests mountains, for example—but sooner or later, they all came back to Yagra'hai.

Unlike Seven Crests, whose cities nestled against mountainsides, Yagra'hai was built on top of the mountain itself, a gigantic, chaotic sculpture of ever-changing architectural elements and geographic features. There was no preparing a human for Yagra'hai—the scale of the place, the overwhelming clash of it.

And, of course, the dragons.

Dragons everywhere. You couldn't look up at the sky or across the city or at any building in sight without spotting a dragon. Some wore the decorated and jeweled harnesses of dragons with riders, but many did not. They were all colors and sizes, which was also true of their lairs. Dragons preferred those larger and higher, except for those occasions where a dragon insisted on living in a cave with no view at all. Anahrod never had figured out how dragon logic worked.

Yagra'hai, its architecture, and its dragons had always made Anahrod feel small and vulnerable.

Now it also made her feel hate.

"Eannis." Gwydinion watched the storm wall fade into the distance from the carriage window with wide eyes. "That takes my breath."

"That's not the view," Anahrod said. She was squeezed in between Sicaryon and the staff cook, whose name she'd never caught and who was guaranteed to be a spy for Belsaor. "It's the altitude. The air's thinner here than Seven Crests. We'll need a few weeks to acclimate." She glanced over at Sicaryon. "Maybe more."

The Scarsea king looked miserable.

"With feathered quilts upon the resting bed, soft whispers of the night's serene reprieve, take refuge here as weary souls are led to find in comfort's arms no will to leave," Kaibren said.

Claw crossed her arms over her chest petulantly. "I guess."

Kaibren gave her an annoyed look and shoved an elbow into her side.

"Oh, fuck off. Fine." She rolled her eyes and then said to Sicaryon, "He has an inscription that will help with that."

Sicaryon pressed his lips together in a tight, unhappy line. "This wasn't something you could've shared while we were still aboard the cutter?"

Kaibren patted Sicaryon's head like he was a young boy.

"Eannis!" Gwydinion gasped. "Is that Neveranimas?"

Anahrod pulled the boy away from the carriage window. She saw a dragon illuminated by lightning in the distance.

The dragon was violet, with bright silver slashes that reflected the lightning in quicksilver stripes down her back. Her violet wings faded to silver at the tips. Another lightning strike lit up the gemstones in her platinum jewelry; her eyes glowed a matching, vivid purple.

Anahrod ducked back quickly.

"Nobody look out the window again," Anahrod ordered.

Sicaryon said, "If you're worried about her seeing us, that's going to be a problem once we reach the school and have to exit the carriage."

"She's unlikely to approach school grounds," Anahrod said. "Unseemly. Dragons are always accusing each other of trying to snatch up candidates early. She wouldn't be immune."

"No," Naeron said.

"Is that a 'no, she wouldn't be immune' or a 'no, she can do whatever the hell she wants because she's rearranged all the security'?" Claw asked irritably.

"First one," Naeron elaborated.

"Some traditions are hard to shake," Anahrod explained. "School's sacred to Eannis, so it falls under the First Dragon's domain."

"But Neveranimas—" Gwydinion said.

"—is not the First Dragon," Anahrod sourly corrected. "Even if she were, she doesn't have a rider. The school is run by a rider named Varriguhl, who is"—she made a face—"retired."

"Dragonriders can retire?" Gwydinion asked.

"Yes, when their dragon is Ivarion. The school is technically part of Ivarion's dominion, and dragons don't invade each other's territory without permission."

"—which Ivarion can't give, because he's asleep," Gwydinion finished.

"And Varriguhl won't give because he's not a fool. Keep the curtains closed and you'll be fine. Dragon eyesight is weird, but they can't see through solid objects."

⌄

Ironically, there were benefits to Neveranimas's security measures, although this mountain would crumble to dust before Anahrod ever admitted that.

Her own first day at school had been a scene of unmitigated chaos. Nearly a riot, as students and entourages fought with each other, sometimes literally, under the mistaken impression that arrival order mattered. If any had taken the time to think the matter over, they'd have realized the idea was ridiculous. The school didn't hand out apartments on a first-come, first-served basis. They'd never risk a candidate with a single valet claiming a space meant for a dozen people.

This time, arrivals had been delayed, so by the time one group arrived, the one before was already settling into their new dwellings. Admittedly, it robbed the event of all its grandeur, but there were a lot fewer bruises and hurt feelings.

The greeting area was nothing but three wide banners hanging from the announcement poles. A sad-looking attendant had set up shop under an awning to protect himself from the inclement weather. Unfortunately, the windblown rain fell at such a steep angle that the poor man had retreated to the one small square kept dry by the awning. The table and chair with which he checked in students had been abandoned to the rain, along with a quill pen and an inkpot.

Gwydinion gave the man a cheerful wave and rushed over to the banners while Anahrod helped the others unload. Provisions made up the bulk of their cargo. The school fed its candidates, of course, but *only* its candidates—along with one personal chaperone. Any additional staff would be given shelter, but the school refused any responsibility for their feeding. The nature of Yagra'hai being what it was, human food was often at a premium.

Most groups brought their own.

Lifting a single barrel left her with a blooming headache and the sense that she shouldn't push herself. She was about to suggest leaving the lifting to the locals when Gwydinion tugged on her arm.

"Um, there's a . . . there's a problem." His voice hitched. Evidently, there was a big problem.

"What is it?" She pulled her mantle up to block out the rain.

"I better show you," he said.

Which he did. The problem was the assignment banners, which comprised a long list of names next to letters, each corresponding to apartments on a large map hanging from the center metal pole. The first thing Anahrod noticed was that Kimat was indeed Kimat Kelnaor on the official records. The second thing she noticed was an absence: the name "Gwydinion Doreyl."

She went back over the list three times, but no. His name wasn't listed.

Yes, a very big problem.

Anahrod stalked over to the attendant, who gave her sword an uneasy glance.

"Excuse me," she called out, "but Gwydinion Doreyl's quarter assignments aren't listed."

The man stared at her blankly. "What do you mean, it's not listed?"

"Exactly as I said. Look yourself and tell me if you see his name anywhere."

After searching the names on the banners, the man gave Anahrod an accusing look, as if she could be held personally accountable for this mess. He then huddled back as far under the awning as possible and retrieved an inconveniently large leather-bound book from under his mantle. He thumbed through the pages one-handed, balancing the large tome on his other forearm. He seemed ready to instantly close the book and conceal it under the mantle if needed.

"What did you say the name was again?"

"Gwydinion Doreyl."

He didn't seem to recognize the name. "Right. Gwydinion Doreyl, Gwydinion Doreyl—" He stopped, his expression now one of extreme agitation. "There must be a mistake."

"On this, you and I agree."

She couldn't help but wonder if whoever was ultimately behind Kimat's sabotage attempt had been so certain Gwydinion would be shipped directly to a monastery that they simply hadn't bothered to assign him quarters.

That only made sense if someone at the school itself was responsible, however.

The attendant looked stricken. He shut the book with a loud slapping sound, tucked the heavy volume under his mantle, and left the shelter of the awning to study the map. He evidently didn't care about keeping his own head dry as long as he kept the book safe.

Anahrod watched as he studied the map for a time. He started to point, evidently decided there was too much chance he'd drop his book, and instead said, "There's the problem. You see that space below assignment block G? That shouldn't be blank."

She raised an eyebrow at him. "Those are student apartments?"

"Not new ones, but—" He glanced over toward the buildings in question, although she doubted the offending dwellings were visible from this angle. They were located so far back that they had to be dug into the mountainside—but that wasn't a reason to leave them off the lists.

Of course, if the apartments were in need of repair, unfurnished, and unclean, they might've been left off for good reason. They might have been damaged in a rampant dragon attack, rendered structurally unsafe. And given their unfortunate location, if they had been made ready, they would never have been assigned to the child of a Seven Crests mayor. Yagra'hai was under no obligation to give the elites of Seven Crests any special privileges, but in the interest of diplomacy usually did anyway.

"An unfortunate oversight?" Anahrod suggested, less because she thought it true than to throw the man a rope.

He was quick to catch it. "Must've been, yes." He started to reach for the sopping-wet feather quill before common sense caught up to him. He audibly sighed. "I'm so sorry about this. I'm going to have to send the paperwork after you, but you're assigned to G8 and I will mark that down. I will also send word to housekeeping that they need to make the quarters ready for tonight."

Anahrod knew the man couldn't see her scowl, but her body posture had still conveyed the basic idea. "And if someone gives us trouble?" If someone caused a problem—a certain someone named Kimat, for example—she'd have nothing to prove they weren't interlopers.

"Tell them to talk to Administration. It's that building there"—he pointed— "and speak to Madinagh Brower."

Anahrod gave the man a terse nod. "Thank you."

"Of course. I am so sorry about the confusion."

As she turned to walk away, he suddenly yelled out, "Wait!"

She turned back. Everyone else raised their heads as well.

"I almost forgot!" The man shifted the book under his mantle in a nervous gesture. "Since everyone's arriving at different times and there's the whole dragon security thing, Headmaster Varriguhl has kindly agreed to move orientation until tomorrow."

"Wondered about that. Nice of him."

"Yes." He smiled as brightly as she'd seen yet, which was to say, neither widely nor sincerely. "So. Tomorrow morning, at five bells, in the main lecture hall on campus. Attendance is mandatory." He glanced past her, presumably toward everyone else. "Just the candidate and one guardian. Everyone else may sleep in."

"Gracious of him," Anahrod ground out. She'd forgotten the old bastard's love of making everyone wake at unreasonable hours. She suspected he thought it was character-building. "Thanks for the warning."

She rejoined the others and relayed instructions to have the hired local deliver their supplies. She wanted her people—

When had they become her people?

She shied from that thought. She wanted them out of the rain as soon as possible.

The last thing they needed was to delay the entire job because half the team had caught a damn cold.

29

A WELCOMING COMMITTEE OF ONE

"This is the worst!" Gwydinion's mouth dropped open as he rushed into the apartment. "They can't expect us to stay here, can they?"

Anahrod grimaced. Behind her, the staff weren't having a much better reaction.

As she'd suspected, the building was set so far back it merged with the cliff-side. It was advantageously placed next to nothing, with no view to speak of, and no noticeably redeeming features besides a roof and walls thick enough to keep out the weather. Animals had nested in the front room, spreading a corresponding amount of dust, debris, and droppings. The apartment's most redeeming feature was that it proved to actually be two apartments joined through a common door. So, they had twice the space—assuming theirs was the only such "error."

"Has this been cleaned?" Gwydinion continued. "Ever? In my lifetime?" He stopped in the middle of the main hall to glare at Anahrod, arms crossed over his chest.

Sicaryon grimaced. "It's dry, at least. Don't knock the comforts of being out of the rain." He sighed. "Not that I disagree with the complaint. I need to sit down."

"Don't let the garbage fool you. This place has hidden charms." Ris walked down the stairs from the upstairs bedrooms, smiling as if she'd just told a joke.

Ris was back in her red outfit, this time paired with a shirt of overlapping white lawn scales, trimmed with gold thread. Several strands of jewels wrapped around her neck, long enough to be lost in her cleavage. Her hair was a glory of cascading red curls.

The urge to go over and kiss the woman was so strong that Anahrod almost did so before she remembered she was still angry at Ris.

"Nice to see you again, Gwydinion. You've grown, haven't you? I'm certain you were at least an inch shorter when I saw you last." Ris's eyes turned to crescents as she smiled at the boy, who blushed nearly the same color as her coat in response.

"And I apologize for making such a dramatic entrance, but I'm technically banned from being on campus, so a stealthy approach seemed best."

"Banned?" Claw caught the edge of the conversation as she carried boxes inside. "What did you do, boss?" She squinted. "Or should that be: Who did you do?"

Ris stared at Claw flatly in response to the joke, which Anahrod fully supported, given the average age of the students. "*All* dragonriders are banned from being on campus without permission." She waved her wrist. "Yes, except Varriguhl, but he doesn't count. This is all Ivarion's territory."

"Does that mean *dragonriders* also jealously defend their territory?" Sicaryon was leaning against a wall and trying his hardest to look nonchalant, but he wasn't succeeding.

Ris examined him, frowning. "Not always, no. You look like hell."

"Thank you. I feel like it, too." He gave her a tight, unhappy smile. "I'd be in bed right now, but apparently we're going to need to clean the leaves out first." He raised a finger at Claw. "Do *not* make a joke about how I should be used to that."

Claw sighed.

"Completely different leaves," Anahrod said. "As you can see, we had a minor problem with the room assignments."

Ris scratched her cheek, not looking embarrassed as much as apologetic. "Sorry about that. The problem was me."

"You did this?" Anahrod gestured to the student-housing-turned-animal-den with a finger.

"If you mean did I dirty up the place, the answer is no. I hired professionals." Her gaze lingered on Sicaryon. "When will the sword arrive?"

"It'll be here by the time you need it." He moved debris out of the way to make room on the floor, then sat down and leaned against the wall.

Ris's lips thinned. "You don't trust me, do you?"

Sicaryon raised both eyebrows. "You're a dragonrider."

Ris pursed her lips. "A fair point. I don't trust most dragonriders either."

Sicaryon didn't seem to know what to think about that.

Ris then raised her voice and clapped her hands once, loudly. "All right, team. I need to show everyone the two most important parts of your new home." She waved a finger at the movers. "Not you. Just keep stacking boxes over there."

Naeron helped Sicaryon to his feet, who patted the other man on the arm. "You're a good man, Naeron. I'll think of you fondly when I rule the world."

Anahrod decided to assume Sicaryon was joking.

The entire group followed Ris, although only a short way, as she just walked to the wall by the side of the staircase. Ris pressed a plaster relief on the wall.

A grinding noise sounded from behind the wall; a section of the stonework slid away to reveal a dark tunnel.

"That's sunshine!" Gwydinion yelled.

"That is literally the opposite of sunshine," Sicaryon commented.

Gwydinion rolled his eyes.

"Nice," Claw said. "Does all the student housing come with secret passages?"

"Why no," Ris said brightly. "This is a special feature. There are other publicly available entrances to the tunnels. It's just that none of those are nearly this convenient." Her smile flickered for just a second, as she glanced at Anahrod, who instantly knew that Ris had left something out. Something important.

Anahrod followed the woman into the next room, frowning.

Said room was a very large study area, meant for students if the ruined tables and couches were anything to go by. At least the inscribed lamps still worked.

"Kaibren, if you'd be so kind?" Ris smiled at the inscriber, and everyone waited while the old man pasted up the fabric inscriptions to prevent eavesdropping.

Gwydinion offered to help, but Kaibren waved him away, mumbling something that might not have been a quotation.

When he finished, Ris said: "Welcome to our new headquarters." She sighed. "Admittedly, it needs some dusting. Since we have two apartment suites"—she ignored Gwydinion's cry of "Yes!"—"it saves the other study for its intended purpose and uses this one for ours."

"What was it you didn't want to say out there?" Anahrod asked.

Ris gave her a wary look. "That you should always use the tunnels, because there's a chance Neveranimas might recognize you."

Gwydinion, Claw, and Sicaryon all started yelling at once.

Naeron made a noise and sat down, wrapping his arms around his head.

"Can we please—?" Anahrod sighed.

Ris was standing on the other side of the room, looking deeply unhappy. Which was good, because Anahrod didn't think she could've handled it if Ris had treated this like a joke.

"Be quiet!" Anahrod screamed.

Everyone shut up.

Anahrod studied the leaf pattern on the floor for a second before raising her head to stare at Ris. "Mind explaining that?"

"I thought that was the whole point of wearing the fucking veils!" Claw complained.

"Quiet, you," Anahrod said. "Ris is answering a question."

"Dragons don't see the way that we do. They see—" She wrinkled her nose in frustration. Anahrod told herself it wasn't cute. "Dragons see the true nature of things. Or people. Which unfortunately means that disguises that would fool a human are meaningless against a dragon. People joke about how we look like ants to a dragon, but if a dragon knows someone well, they can pick that individual out of a crowd in seconds."

Sicaryon staggered forward. "You mean to say that you brought Anahrod here to Yagra'hai knowing that she can't be disguised and Neveranimas is going to recognize her on sight? You—" He abruptly sat down, holding his head. "I think I'm going to be sick."

Anahrod rushed to his side, but what could she do? She rubbed his back, while he shuddered and tried not to pass out.

"Too angry," Naeron chided gently. "Too much heartbeat, needs too much air. Slow breaths."

"Think I'll give you a knighthood," Sicaryon mumbled.

"Kaibren, could you please draw that inscription that helps with altitude sickness for the man?" Ris asked while chewing on the edge of a thumbnail.

The old man nodded and began clearing away an area of the floor.

Anahrod met Ris's eyes. "He has a point, though. Not feeling real trusting now."

She didn't ask Ris why she hadn't said something earlier. She knew why. Because Ris hadn't wanted to take the chance that Anahrod wouldn't come. Because Ris was still chasing after revenge.

Ris's face contorted into a scowl. "According to records, she only met with you three times. You didn't bond. It was seventeen years ago. There is no reason to think that Neveranimas still remembers what you look like. This is just being cautious."

Anahrod looked up at the ceiling, exhaling. "It wasn't three times. It was three times that anyone knew about. Not counting all the times I spoke to her at a distance to just talk about how my day had gone and what a jerk Varriguhl was being."

A slow look of horror came over her. "You're saying—?"

"Yes. Neveranimas knows I can talk to dragons—"

"You can talk to dragons?" Claw said. "Any dragon?"

Anahrod nodded and held up a hand to signal Claw to wait. "—and you would've known that if you'd explained this concern to me. Don't be so certain that she doesn't remember me."

Ris exhaled a shuddery breath. "Neveranimas can't come on school grounds or even near them. There are tunnels crisscrossing the entire campus. You don't need to ever see sunlight. She can't see through stone."

"As far as we know," Claw added sarcastically.

"Not helping," Ris spat.

"Not trying to, boss," Claw snapped back. She sounded unusually angry, even for her normal angry self. "We've gotten to the part where I'm honestly wondering what else you haven't told us."

Sicaryon raised an arm from where he was still hunched over, and punched it in Claw's direction, as if to say: *Yes, that!*

Ris examined all the faces in the room and sighed. She slumped in defeat at what she saw. "Fine. We'll—" She gestured vaguely. "Let's meet here tomorrow night after dinner and I'll explain everything."

"Two days," Naeron said, still studying Sicaryon. "At least."

Ris studied the Scarsea man. "Right. We can do it the day after tomorrow."

The air felt stifling and awkward. Ris gave Anahrod a smile so tentative it was more like a sketch. "I don't suppose it would help if I said I was sorry?"

"But you're not," Anahrod told her coldly. "You're only sorry I'm upset. That's not the same thing. Not even close."

"No," Ris said. "That's not what I—"

"You should go. We have a lot of cleaning to do, and Gwydinion and I need to be up early."

Ris didn't argue a second time. She left.

ORIENTATION

The main lecture pavilion was located in the center of a well-maintained garden, which dominated the expansive school terraces. Unlike the city, which often used narrow, cramped stairs and steep switchbacks to accommodate human needs, the school was a place of wide paths and gently sloping walkways.

Gwydinion and Anahrod arrived exactly on time.

She'd timed it carefully, so they'd end up seated toward the back, but couldn't be considered "late." Storm clouds blanketed the sky outside, but had they been absent, it would've still been dark. Five bells was an unholy hour to expect any-one to show up bright-eyed and ready to pay attention.

Although if she were a dragonrider whose dragon had gone rampant after being flown exactly once over a century earlier, she too might feel a perverse desire to torture the students who were hoping to gain everything she'd been denied. Or perhaps she was overthinking the matter.

The simpler explanation was that Varriguhl was just an ass.

No one ever guessed the school headmaster was over a hundred years old. His appearance gave proof to the belief that bonding with a dragon granted longevity, if not immortality. He seemed at most a decade older than Anahrod, with dark, tightly curled hair he wore knotted in a style long since out of fashion. His eyes had the stare of a man who'd seen too much.

Some might have found him handsome, but Anahrod was incapable of see-ing it. To her, he would forever be fixed as the hateful, horrid teacher who'd tormented her.

His most notable quality had nothing to do with his appearance: he sat in an inscribed chair set on wheels, the fabric of his trousers tucked up under legs that ended at his knees. The prevailing rumor had been that he'd lost his legs when Ivarion went rampant. Varriguhl himself had never seen fit to clarify the stories. He simply pointed out that a dragonrider had no need of legs when their dragon could fly.

No one had ever been brave enough to point out that was only true if one's dragon was willing—and awake.

The headmaster was saying something as she entered, but she couldn't hear it; the roar of her heartbeat deafened her. She closed and opened her fists, reminding herself she wasn't a student, that no one knew who she was, that she hadn't been fifteen years old for longer than these students had been alive.

A low murmuring filled the air as the candidates gathered, their guardians filling the back rows. That was the whole reason she'd arrived as late as possible: earlier students found themselves separated from their guardians. A plus or a minus, depending on how a student felt about the guardian in question.

"—to Yagra'hai." His voice hit as hard as the thunder outside. "I am Varriguhl, headmaster of this school, First Rider of the city. You are all here hoping you will be chosen for the highest and most holy calling that any human can hope to achieve: rider to a dragon.

"This is not, as some of you may believe, a matter of presenting yourselves all in a neat row before an equally neat row of dragon eggs until they hatch and the dragon inside is drawn to their soulmate. In reality, the dragons will be adults and you won't meet one until you have mastered the basic skills required for your roles. Reaching this point will not be easy. Many of you will never do so." A flash of lightning punctuated his statement with such perfect timing that he seemed to be commanding the storm itself.

Unlikely. Ivarion's attunement had been fire, not lightning.

Varriguhl scanned the students in the front row. "Not all of you have what it takes. And if you do, you still may not be picked. Let me be clear on one matter from the start, because every year this causes confusion: this is not a contest. I'm not saying this to be kind. I'm saying this because contests have rules. Contests are *fair*. Whereas nothing about this is fair. The person who scores highest on their tests is not guaranteed a dragon. You only have to pass—you are not required to surpass your fellow students. You gain nothing from sabotaging others, as you don't know what criteria a dragon will use to pick a candidate. I don't know what criteria a dragon will use. No one but each dragon knows that, they are under no obligation to explain themselves, and they rarely do.

"That said, if you fail your classes, if you cheat, if you misbehave, if you cause problems, you will be expelled from this school, after which you become the Church's problem. I will do this without hesitation.

"I do this not for my benefit, but for yours. This bond is for life. There is no breaking it, there is no changing your mind. Once done, it is done forever."

Anahrod's jaw ached. She realized she'd been clenching her teeth so tightly she was in danger of pulling a muscle. She exhaled slowly.

Meanwhile, the headmaster continued: "You are here for one reason. It may surprise you to learn that the reason is not bonding with a dragon. That is the means, not the goal. You are here for one reason, which is the sole reason that

Eannis put all humans on this earth: to keep dragons sane. That is your only purpose in life: to keep your dragon from going rampant. If you cannot handle that responsibility, leave now."

He paused, as if expecting some teenager might actually do it.

Anahrod was glad beyond words that Ris had insisted on the veil. She could only imagine the faces she'd been making during his speech. Varriguhl's orientation speech hadn't changed by so much as a word from when she'd been one of the excited babies sitting in the front row. He still spouted the same lines.

She'd missed a detail when she'd been younger and more eager to become a rider, however: Varriguhl hadn't lied. Not once.

He had laid out the truth with diamond-sharp precision. To become a dragonrider was to be all but a slave, perpetually locked in obedience to a single master, from whom one could never be parted.

Not in the human's lifetime, anyway.

Eannis, she wished she could just throw Gwydinion over a shoulder and leave. If only Anahrod could do it without bringing the wrath of the dragons down on Crystalspire. If only leaving the school didn't mean destroying the cover the team needed to justify their presence in the city.

But the moment the heist was done, she was taking Gwydinion and leaving. Let Tiendremos have his power-grab and Ris have her revenge; Anahrod would take her family and hide.

"Are there questions?" Varriguhl asked, one eyebrow arched as if daring someone to say yes.

A hand shot up immediately: the girl from the liner, Kimat.

Varriguhl threw the girl a withering stare. "Yes?"

"What if we've already met a dragon who's going to pick us? Can we skip ahead?"

Varriguhl did not look amused. "No."

"But—"

"No," he repeated, in the same sharp tone one might use against an errant vel hound. "Anyone else?"

Gwydinion raised his hand; Anahrod groaned internally.

"Yes?" Varriguhl frowned at the boy.

"Are we going to learn magic?"

Given the other students' murmuring, he'd asked a popular question.

An indecipherable look crossed the man's face. "Yes, you will."

The room exploded in noise.

"Silence," he snapped, waving an arm.

When the children quieted, he continued, "You will. A dragonrider serves their master in a magical capacity. We are not children of Eannis, and thus not cursed by Zavad to become rampant. Dragonriders are expected to cast spells for their dragons whenever possible."

"But what if we learn all this magic and don't get picked?" a boy in the crowd called out.

"Raise your hand first." Varriguhl deliberately ignored the boy. "Anyone else?"

Gwydinion raised his hand again. Anahrod pinched the back of his arm, but he ignored her.

"Yes?"

"What if we learn all this magic and we aren't picked? Doesn't that make us . . ." He fidgeted.

"Heretics?" Varriguhl suggested.

"Yes."

"All of you are here because you've been chosen by Eannis, blessed by her grace. You all know some magic, or you wouldn't be here. If you are not chosen by a dragon, you are still called to serve as members of the Church. So no, you will not be heretics, because none of you will be so foolish as to think you can just *leave*."

Anahrod scowled under her veil, gut clenched with the unhappy reminder of her own mistakes.

There was more murmuring, more whispers. At least one or two students started crying.

His gaze swept over the group once more. He seemed disappointed in what he saw. "Classes will start in three days at dawn. Your guardians are welcome to escort you to the classroom, but this will be the only time they may attend any class themselves. This is not up for discussion. Unless there is a rampant dragon in the area, they wait outside."

He paused, waiting to see if anyone would raise their hand one last time. No one did.

"Very well," Varriguhl said. "You have the next two days to unpack and acclimate yourselves. I strongly recommend you rest. Let me also stress that you don't have permission to enter the city. If you or your guardians discover you are missing some vital supply or equipment, talk to Administration. I will see you all in three days." He made a dismissing motion.

Since Anahrod and Gwydinion were in the back, they were among the first to leave. Not a moment too soon, in Anahrod's opinion.

One thing was certain: she still hated Varriguhl's guts.

⌄

Yagra'hai wasn't a city that encouraged greenery. Individual dragons might like gardens, but as a species, dragons were hard on their environments. Plants seldom survived any of the dozen different flavors of destruction that a dragon might favor.

But Varriguhl rarely granted dragons permission to enter the school grounds, giving flora a safe refuge on the campus. The gardens had become havens where plants flourished. Whether Ivarion would've tolerated such horticultural efforts was unknown: Varriguhl had spent the last century left to his own devices.

The gardens were a sculptured, controlled sort of prettiness. The grass had been clipped in layers, forming textural designs. Low hedges of fragrant simora blossoms surrounded walking paths of polished granite. Larger flowering trees of white, yellow, and pale pink sat farther back, like parents gathered together to watch their children go to school.

A piercing longing came over Anahrod, not for Crystalspire, but for the Deep, for fruit trees and flowering vines and wildlife everywhere.

"What next?" Gwydinion asked.

She hadn't planned to return through the gardens, both because of an excess of caution and because the rain made it hard to appreciate flowers. They were cutting across the garden to one of the public tunnel entrances.

"You in front of a fire"—Anahrod adjusted the boy's mantle—"with soup. Half the class will be out on the first day because they've caught a cold."

Conversely, the rain-laden air was so humid, Anahrod found it pleasant, if still far too thin. She reminded herself to look through their supplies for sharproot, and make sure Kaibren created more emergency inscriptions for Sicaryon to help with the air pressure.

She should probably ask for one for herself, too. It didn't matter that she'd been born in the Skylands—after seventeen years, her body had grown used to the Deep. She hadn't even finished acclimating to the thin air of Seven Crests before traveling to an even taller mountain.

"It's not fair!" someone yelled behind them.

Anahrod recognized the voice and sighed. Kimat came careening down a path, followed by her guard. "I was picked out personally by a dragon! I shouldn't have to go through this!"

Gwydinion gave Anahrod a look; she instantly knew that he was about to volunteer that he too had been picked by a dragon.

Anahrod shook her head at him.

"Oh, it's you." The girl stopped short of easy reach, her attention now focused on Gwydinion. She gave a passable impression of someone who hadn't expected to see Gwydinion.

Anahrod didn't believe it for a moment.

"Kimat," her guard scolded as he rushed over to hold a mantle over her head. "We don't have time for this."

"What's your name?" Kimat ignored her babysitter.

Gwydinion glanced back at Anahrod.

"Do you need permission to talk?" Kimat's tone was scathing. "Are you still a child? Is that your parent?"

He rolled his eyes. Anahrod only wished she could as well.

"I'm Gwydinion Doreyl," he said. "My father's the mayor of Crystalspire."

"Oh? Well, I'm Kimat Kelnaor, and my mother is magistrix of Grayshroud." She raised her chin, daring him to make something of it. Perhaps that's just what she wanted: for Gwydinion to say something, make some inference about Kimat's family or the criminal leanings of Grayshroud.

Some excuse for a fight.

"Nice to meet you again," Gwydinion said pleasantly, "but we must be on our way. I'm not done unpacking." To emphasize that point, he turned away.

"Hey! I'm not done talking to you!"

Anahrod wondered if she'd have to interfere. Before she decided, however, Gwydinion swiveled. "Really? I have time tomorrow. We both have the day off. Why don't you come over to my apartment at eight bells? My cook makes the most amazing chena you've ever had."

A long pause followed.

Kimat's bodyguard, Waja, said, "Are you . . . ? Are you asking Lady Kelnaor out on a date?"

Anahrod had wondered the same thing.

"Only if she says yes," Gwydinion admitted. His smile was blinding, the sun peeking out from behind rain clouds.

Kimat held up her hands. "You've checked my rings, right?"

"Late-blooming?" Gwydinion nodded. "I noticed. And a good thing, too: I haven't officially picked out my garden rings yet, but I already plan to pick flowers, so it's lucky you qualify."

Kimat began to say something, stopped, started to say something else, stopped herself again. Anahrod almost felt sorry for the poor girl.

Kimat finally settled on: "How old *are* you?"

"Fifteen."

"Fifteen," Kimat repeated. "Fifteen! I don't date fifteen-year-olds. I'm *seventeen*."

"That's not a problem: I like older women."

The other guard muffled a laugh. Personally, Anahrod was once again glad for the veil. She was really seeing the benefits of them as a clothing accessory.

This was adorable. Although by Eannis and all her scaly little children, Anahrod had never been this smooth at fifteen.

She wasn't this smooth *now*.

Kimat sputtered. "I'm not an older—! How dare—!"

Then the girl ran off, leaving her guard still grinning for a moment before he realized his ward had abandoned him. He hurried after her, yelling.

Anahrod stared at her young protégé. "Are you secretly Zavad? Be honest now. I won't judge."

This time, her brother flushed. "It made her leave, didn't it?"

"And what if she'd said yes?"

His eyes widened. "Why, I'd have asked you for your recipe for chena." He bit his lip. "You would tell me, wouldn't you? I mean, we're—you know."

We're family.

"I would," Anahrod said, "but you can't make chena in a day."

"Oh? That's a shame." Gwydinion brightened. "Good thing she doesn't know what chena really is. We could just make something else and call it that."

"She didn't say yes," Anahrod reminded him.

"She didn't say no, either," Gwydinion said. "Wouldn't it be sunshine if she still shows up tomorrow?"

"Yes. Let's invite the girl trying to get you kicked out of school into our quarters. What could go wrong?"

He grinned. "Bet you she shows up."

"You're officially spending too much time around Claw. Anyway, my mother taught me to never gamble against *Zavad himself.*"

Gwydinion just laughed.

"We should hurry back," Anahrod murmured as they walked away from where they'd run into the spoiled girl and her taciturn minder. "Find out if Ris and Sicaryon have killed each other yet."

"Or kissed." Gwydinion glanced sideways at her. "Are you going to sleep with either of them?"

"That is really none of your business."

"If I were you—"

"Gwydinion—"

He grinned. "I'm just saying, if I were you, I wouldn't sleep with one of them."

That hadn't been the editorial comment she'd expected. "You wouldn't?"

"Nope!" He shook his head. "No. I mean, how would you choose? They're both so pretty. You should sleep with *both* of them."

Anahrod stopped walking and put her hands on Gwydinion's shoulders. "Does our mother have any idea how much of a problem you're going to be the second you get your garden rings?"

Her brother shrugged. "She suspects. Kind of feel bad for Dad, though."

"And they've talked to you about proper etiquette and safety—?"

"Yes!" He rolled his eyes. "And I know I have to wait until I've earned my rings, too. Stop acting like Mom."

"Oh, no. You wanted a big sister. Now you've got one." She grabbed his arm and all but marched him over to the tunnel entrance. She suddenly felt the need to keep an eye on her little brother for reasons that had nothing to do with impending threats.

Unless the threat in question was puberty.

PART SIX

A
DRAGON,
RAMPANT

31

THE MISSION BRIEFING

"Neveranimas has quite possibly the most impenetrable vaults ever created," Ris began. She had several maps spread out on a large wooden table in the study. The map she currently referenced was an architectural elevation drawing, highlighting a tunnel system, broken up by several rectangles.

They'd cleaned up the study as best as they could, but after two days it was still a bit of a mess. At least the school had provided them with better furniture.

"It's set at the top of Mount Yagra," she continued, "right above a magma chamber. And just in case someone has the magical means of surviving a swim through that, it's also protected by layers of magical shields—all of which are powered by the volcano, so good luck hoping that the shields ever run dry." She tapped on a long rectangle. "Entrance to the vault is through a secret entrance at the back of her 'official' vault, which links through this hallway here."

Claw glanced down at a label. "Oh yes. *The Hall of Death*." She stared at Ris. "Are you fucking kidding me?"

"Sounds homey," Sicaryon said.

"No," Naeron said, looking slightly wide-eyed.

"Don't blame me. I didn't name it, but unfortunately the name is accurate." Ris tapped a fingernail on the location. "It's heavily trapped—both mundane traps kept magically active and magical traps that cannot be disabled. A human would be unlikely to make it from one side of the hall to the other without setting off the security measures. For a dragon? Impossible. The only way to deactivate the traps is a pressure plate inside the vault itself, and even that only works for a few minutes before the entire system resets. I shouldn't have to mention the traps are all extra lethal."

An uncomfortable silence fell over the table. Jaemeh scrubbed a hand over his face.

Anahrod had almost forgotten that Peralon had promised to include the dragonrider. Jaemeh looked faint.

The dragonrider turned to Anahrod. "Okay, so how are we getting into this?"

Nope. She wasn't playing this game. Anahrod was not in the mood. "Ris will explain it."

Ris gazed longingly at the drinks table for a second. "This"—she gestured again to the Hall of Death—"is nothing but a meaningless diversion to trick thieves. The actual entrance is a steam vent at the edge of Neveranimas's palace. It's a two-thousand-foot drop straight over that magma chamber I mentioned earlier—"

Anahrod's brain tried to run screaming from the room at the mention of "two-thousand-foot drop," but she had wrestled herself back under control with some difficulty. She couldn't afford to let her fears show.

But at least she knew why Peralon and Ris had thought it so important for her to get over her phobia.

Ris continued: "There's a lock embedded into the wall a thousand feet down, then another five hundred feet before a side tunnel leads directly to the vault. None of which is trapped, because it's the entrance Neveranimas actually uses."

"Except the moment anyone who isn't Neveranimas enters that steam vent, she'll know. You can't tell me she hasn't created a warning spell . . . in the last seventeen years." Anahrod didn't think Jaemeh had noticed the split second of hesitation before she added that qualifier. After all, she shouldn't be confessing ignorance to security measures she was supposed to have already encountered.

"That's not a trap," Ris pointed out. "That's an alarm."

"Eannis," Jaemeh murmured. He gave Anahrod a look of amazement. "And you broke into that?"

"Mmm," Anahrod replied.

Kaibren shook his head sadly. "In winter's waltz, a fiery show, a tale of contrasts gleaming aglow."

"You can say that again," Claw agreed.

Anahrod left the table to pour herself a glass of wine. After a second's deliberation, she poured one for Ris as well.

She was still mad at the woman, but at least Ris was explaining matters. That deserved a reward.

Anahrod silently set the glass in front of the dragonrider and returned to her own seat.

"There is a key," Ris explained. "Opens up the entire thing." She paused a beat. "We don't have it."

Jaemeh wasn't the only person who rolled their eyes.

"That's not the problem," Ris said. "We know exactly where the key is. No, the problem is who owns the key: the dragonrider Brauge."

Jaemeh exhaled sharply. "That's Zentoazax's rider."

"And thus, why it's a problem," Ris agreed.

"Mind explaining it to the non-dragonriders in the room?" Sicaryon said archly.

"Zentoazax is on the elders' council. Now, if it were anyone else, then when the dragon sensed something had happened to their rider, they'd probably fly over and investigate on their own. Which is bad," Ris said. "Any angry dragon showing up is bad. But a dragon on the council has the authority to order entire dragon flights to investigate, which means if this goes wrong, we will have the scariest dragons in the city arriving on our doorstep immediately. So yes, it's a problem."

"No, it's not," Sicaryon said. "That's not an obstacle. That's motivation."

Claw snorted.

Jaemeh, however, looked like he was seconds from storming off in a fury.

"Calm down before you rile up Tiendremos," Ris told him. "It's taken care of. The key looks like a sword. Brauge keeps it above the fireplace in her parlor. She has no idea of its real significance. Claw will infiltrate the household staff."

"Just like that?" Jaemeh scoffed.

"Oh, fuck off," Claw said before she raised her chin theatrically. "Kaibren's been teaching me. My acting skills are superlative."

"If they weren't, I wouldn't be sending you," Ris said absently.

Claw blinked at the dragonrider, shocked. Anahrod had the sense that Claw had no idea what to do with the compliment, and so had frozen in place.

Ris continued: "Anyway, one of the current household servants just quit, having come into an unexpectedly large inheritance. Besides being a fantastic inscriber, Kaibren here is also a wonderful forger. Claw will have all her papers in order. Once inside, she'll take a rubbing of the sword, which we'll use to make a duplicate. As for how we'll make the switch . . . that's the easiest part. Every week, Brauge leaves the estate to attend a book club meeting that runs concurrently to the elder council meetings."

"Sissara hosts those. I was invited once." Jaemeh shrugged. "I'm not really a reader."

"Consider soliciting another invitation," Ris told him. "We could use someone to make sure Brauge doesn't return early. We'll use that window to substitute the fake sword for the real thing. Brauge will never know. Thus, Zentoazax will never know."

"Great," Jaemeh said. "Then what?"

Ris smiled. "Then, we're going to attach ourselves via harness to Peralon, who'll fly us down into the steam vent where Neveranimas has hidden the back entrance to her vault. This will require Kaibren to create the protective inscriptions, so we don't burn to death or suffocate."

"Reassuring," Sicaryon said, sincerely.

"Once there, we'll unlock the vault and send someone down. This key unlocks two entrances. One is dragon-sized and used by Neveranimas. The second is human-sized, one-way, and used by no one. We'll bypass Neveranimas's entrance because, as Anahrod pointed out, we can't be certain she hasn't added additional security."

"And how do we know she hasn't added security to the human door?" Jaemeh asked, which was a fair question.

"Because she's too big to fit inside, she doesn't have a rider to send in her place, but most importantly, because she doesn't know it exists. If she did, she'd have destroyed it," Ris explained. "As I was saying: we'll send someone down by the human entrance. Their job will be twofold: first, to find and unlock the secret vault where the diamonds are hidden, and second, to disengage all the traps in the Hall of Death. Once that's done, the rest of us will enter by the front entrance on the mountainside and load all the shiny rocks onto Peralon. The last person out will re-engage the traps, giving themselves a one-minute window to escape. Neveranimas won't know how we entered and won't be able to tell anyone what we took."

Everyone settled back in their chairs, exhaling slowly.

"Damn, Ris," Claw said. "You know I love it when you talk sexy."

"And after?" Sicaryon asked. "What's the escape plan? She might tell no one what we stole from her, but she can still shut everything down and start running her claws through random pockets until something shiny drops out." He rubbed a finger under his lip. "And we should assume she has additional alarms. We better be able to do this in the time she takes to fly from the elders' council chambers back to her vault, or be able to guarantee we can keep her from responding if her alarms go off."

"How long would it take her to fly back?" Anahrod asked.

"Seven minutes," Ris answered, then shrugged. "Technically, just a hair under eight minutes, but let's assume she'll push herself. As for the escape plan, you'll have directions to a safe house and private berth on a cutter waiting for anyone not flying out by dragonback." She raised her hands. "So. Are we good?"

Claw started to say something, and Kaibren elbowed her.

They were not good. Yes, it seemed like Ris had spelled out the essential plan, but she hadn't mentioned a single word about the Five Locks, or the link between Neveranimas and Anahrod, or Gwydinion being in danger . . .

The woman still had secrets.

Sicaryon put his hand over Anahrod's. "We're good," he told Ris. He squeezed Anahrod's hand in a way she could interpret as easily as breathing.

Be patient. This isn't over.

TERRIBLE OMENS

Nothing happened for two weeks.

No problems happened, anyway. Gwydinion disagreed, as his date with Kimat failed to materialize, but his opinion was in the minority. Claw found employment at the Brauge estate, a rubbing of a certain sword was gained shortly thereafter, and Naeron made arrangements with a friendly blacksmith. Kaibren holed up in his room, drafting the inscriptions that would keep everyone from roasting to death. Sicaryon and Anahrod traded off guard duties escorting Gwydinion, who began classes. Jaemeh never made an appearance, but he was likely stuck at the docks playing interrogator.

Then it came time for Gwydinion's consecration ceremony, which was when everything went wrong.

It was supposed to happen like this: every day, the priests escorted a few candidates, one at a time, to the Great Cathedral, to be blessed by the high priest and dedicated to Eannis. The priests would then kill a wind shrike and use hieromancy to divine various omens about the candidate's fitness. Sadly, this was an important part of the dragonrider selection process; dragons often lingered near the cathedral for these ceremonies, hoping to spot an auspicious candidate.

The consecration ceremony was also an investiture, the first step in a candidate's entry into the priesthood should they fail to catch a dragon's eye.

Anahrod's augury had been so joyously full of prescience for her success as a dragonrider it had drawn Neveranimas's attention. Such predictions had certainly not borne edible fruit. Indeed, Anahrod suspected no priest would ever admit to having claimed such a star-blessed future for "Anahrod the Wicked."

They all agreed Anahrod shouldn't escort Gwydinion. She would be too much at risk of being spotted by Neveranimas. Far too dangerous.

All Anahrod could do was sit in the apartment, wondering if she could justify cleaning her sword a third time, when an overwhelming emotional barrage hammered at her. Terrible anger and burning fury, coming from a location she couldn't see, someplace far off in the distance. Someone had distilled a thunderstorm into a bottle, creating a seething, roiling avatar of hate. The hairs on the back of her neck prickled.

A second later, the rampant bells rang.

She knew what the sound meant. Everyone did. Anyone outside an apartment ran into the service tunnels. Everyone inside an apartment closed every door and window.

Anahrod ran outside.

The dragon's screaming was easier to hear from outside, even over the jangling alarm bells. Thankfully, the roar was distant—a dragon hadn't gone rampant right over the school. She couldn't see . . .

Anahrod ran to a teacher whose name she'd never caught. She was calmly directing people into a shelter.

"Where's the attack happening?" Anahrod demanded.

The woman scowled. "Not near here. Just get in the shelter and everything—"

"Do you know where the rampant attack started?" Anahrod resisted the urge to grab the other woman by the shoulders and shake her.

"The Great Cathedral," the woman answered irritably, "but it's a rampant dragon. They can fly, you know. It could end up anywhere. You need to get inside."

The words sank in like knives, stabbing her anytime she tried to breathe. The Great Cathedral—where Gwydinion and Sicaryon had gone.

"Where's your candidate?" the woman asked.

Anahrod stared at her in dull, numb shock.

"The Great Cathedral," she whispered.

Anahrod ran back toward the apartment, toward the entrance to the service tunnels.

⌄

If any part of Yagra'hai was conveniently designed for humans, it was by accident. Roads existed, but only for delivering cargo and supplies.

For this reason, the default response to a rampant dragon attack was to go to ground. Literally so, in either underground safety shelters or the service tunnels crazing their way beneath the city.

By law and custom, shelters were open to anyone who might need them. In Yagra'hai, as in Seven Crests, rampant shelters were always underground, always built into the mountainside. Normal doors capped the tunnels, which were seldom larger than five feet across. The idea being that if a dragon wanted to dig through a hundred feet of mountain rock to crack open a shelter, no vault door would stop them.

Since "out of sight, out of mind" was typically an effective defense against rampant dragons, this generally worked out. Assuming people reached the shelters in time. Assuming nothing happened to the tunnels.

Anahrod wasn't using the tunnels for safety, but for speed. Not having to navigate through a maze of fiefs and estates drastically reduced her travel time to the Great Cathedral.

She soon began encountering people running in the other direction. At first, they were just panicked. People who'd heard the first roars and had done the immediate smart thing. Quickly, however, she began fighting her way past survivors, the injured and dying. Which meant she knew the nature of the dragon she was dealing with before she exited the tunnels.

This rampant dragon breathed acid.

Dragons shouted in her mind, a barrage of chatter so constant and loud as to be unintelligible, like trying to pick a single voice from a screaming mob. Just like the humans, the dragons were panicked, upset, angry, and scared.

Anahrod spotted the dragon as she exited the tunnel in the rear of the Great Cathedral's western wing. The miracle would've been overlooking the dragon: it was a bright, vivid yellow edging into an equally bright lime across its back fins and claws. Shiny black stripes ran their entire length on each side, from nostril to tail. Beautiful and sleek and utterly mad.

It opened its mouth, vomiting a stream of yellow liquid at something out of sight. Clouds of toxic vapor billowed up into the sky. The air tasted sharp, stabbing the inside of Anahrod's nose.

But the dragon wasn't Anahrod's primary concern. She scanned the temple floor, searching for human bodies.

The problem—the gut-wrenching, bile-inducing problem—was that what bodies remained might not be identifiable. She forced herself to ignore that possibility.

The cathedral, like many dragon-oriented buildings, had no roof, more akin to a temple complex filled with wide, open courtyards and large pillars for dragons to perch upon. The dragon was destroying the grand entrance presidium, having already finished at the main altar.

And, oh Eannis, how the dragon had destroyed the main altar. The high priest was dead, his head and half his torso melted away. Bodies and body parts were everywhere. The body of a white dragon slumped in the center of the cathedral—possibly someone attached to the Church, because while dragons were never priests, they were often called upon for spiritual guidance. Onlooker or sage, however, the yellow dragon had ripped this one apart, giant raking claw wounds straight down its belly. The disemboweled dragon had left a steaming pile of viscera to add to the already overwhelming collection of smells.

She didn't see—

She didn't see anyone wearing the silver dragon embroidery of a candidate's tabard. No one wearing Sicaryon's dark brown leathers. No sign of his sword, which would've surely survived to some extent, even in an acid bath.

Behind her, the dragon's roar shook the ground, followed by a stronger quake as the dragon crashed into something. People screamed.

[Modelakast! Modelakast, stop this at once!]

A crack of thunder rolled over the area, followed by a telepathic voice Anahrod recognized. [Don't bother. She can't understand you. Save yourself.]

Tiendremos had arrived.

He cast a dark shadow over the cathedral complex as he flew over, and if it wasn't large enough to cover the entire site, that was only because the cathedral was so large. Storm clouds followed him like gray scuttling scrabbers.

Where would Sicaryon have taken her brother? She knew roughly what their starting position would've been—near the altar. If they'd survived—

No, they survived. They had to have survived. Where would they go? Could they be hiding behind a pillar, just as she was?

A massive boom interrupted her study of the main temple area, coinciding with a blinding flash of lightning that shattered a pillar. Her vision whited out, overwhelmed, before returning several seconds later.

Wonderful. Now she had to worry about dodging attacks from Modelakast *and* Tiendremos.

When she peeked out from behind the pillar, she saw a gargantuan twisting column of yellow and blue. She couldn't tell who was winning. Tiendremos was a larger dragon; Modelakast seemed faster—and angrier.

They were too intertwined for breath weapons, however, so she ran behind a different set of pillars. She edged closer to the altar in the cathedral's heart, searching for clues.

Then she noticed an odd detail: although the dead white dragon had been slashed to death, the acid hadn't damaged it at all. That happened sometimes— dragon lineages were odd, and a dragon born of ice and fire parents might look like one but possess immunity to both. Acid had splashed against the dragon's spine only to slide off and pool, eating away at the stone underneath. The dragon had died first, perhaps attempting to buy everyone else time to flee to safety.

Maybe Gwydinion and Sicaryon had escaped already. Maybe she'd passed them in the tunnels and hadn't realized it. She might be putting herself in danger when they were already safe.

Eannis, she wished she could talk to humans the same way she could talk to dragons or animals.

She growled at herself. If she'd been *thinking*, she would've grabbed Naeron and had him use his magic to pinpoint Gwydinion's location.

She glanced up at the fighting. Rampant dragons were much harder to deal with than their non-rampant counterparts. Modelakast didn't seem big enough to be an elder, yet she was causing Tiendremos trouble. A rampant dragon was impervious to pain and cared nothing for its own survival. Anahrod felt the rage, a terrible, blistering sun scorching the dragon's mind from the inside out.

This might be Anahrod's best and only chance.

She ran for the dead dragon.

The white dragon had died on its side, mouth ajar and tongue rolling. It was average sized, but an average-sized dragon was still monstrously large. The head on its side was taller than her, its teeth as long as her forearm.

She heard muffled coughing.

Anahrod squatted down and peered into the darkness of the dragon's mouth. "Gwydinion? Sicaryon?"

She swallowed a yelp when a hand grabbed hers and yanked her inside the dead dragon's mouth. The orifice was as unpleasant as she would've expected, but in unexpected ways: wet, yes, but also cold and smelling of blood and ice.

There were worse places to hide. Unless the dragon dumped acid directly on top of the skull, they'd avoid splashes. A dragon's skull was also the most damage-resistant part of their whole body. They'd be protected even if a dragon fell on them.

But the air was going to kill them if they stayed for much longer.

"Anah." Sicaryon's voice was a low whisper. "You're not supposed to be here."

"None of us are supposed to be here." She pulled him to her by the back of his neck, kissed him before she'd given any thought to the wisdom of doing so. "Just thank Eannis you did what I would've done—where's Gwydinion?"

"I'm here, I'm here." Her little brother stood behind Sicaryon. He shuddered in the way people do when they're trying to cry without making noise. She let go of Sicaryon to hug her brother next, but she wished she had four arms or was a dragon herself—some native creature who didn't have to let either of them go.

She winced as she felt a dragon scream. Not Modelakast. Not Tiendremos, either. The dragons were trying to put a stop to the rampage. They just hadn't managed it yet.

"The fighting's heading in the other direction," Anahrod said. "We should run for it."

"I can't, I can't—" Gwydinion was crying. "If we stay here—"

"If we stay here, we choke to death." Anahrod reached around Sicaryon and pulled her brother to his feet. "You can do this. Who didn't flinch at riding a titan drake or running from angry rock wyrms? Who body-rode underground river rapids for an hour before jumping into the Bay of Bones? Compared to that, this is nothing."

He could do this. This was just shock and too long spent with nothing to do but think about how close death lurked, all roaring screams and spitting acid.

"I'll be right behind you," Sicaryon told him.

Anahrod didn't give Gwydinion a chance to say no after that. She took his hand and started running. She heard his hitched breath behind her and ached inside. He'd be having nightmares about this for months, maybe years. So many dead. Chances were excellent that he'd been speaking to those people, smiling at them, just seconds before.

They made it to a pillar and hid there, catching their breath. Sicaryon had his hand on her stomach, and if it had been anyone else, she'd have lashed out, intolerant of what she would've interpreted as possessive, controlling behavior. She knew him well enough to know that he was just reassuring himself that she was still there, still alive.

"What now?" Sicaryon whispered to her. "Is the tunnel entrance open?"

"Yes, but we'll have to run—"

Stone pillars buckled and crashed into each other as Tiendremos bowled into the west wing of the complex. Lightning flashed over the nearby stones and arced over the acid pools. The dragon roared and launched himself to the side just in time to dodge an acid stream that hit the ground where Tiendremos had been seconds before.

"Change of plans," Anahrod said. "There's another entrance in front of the cathedral."

"They were fighting up there," Sicaryon pointed out.

"Then let's hope it's not melted." She pointed in the right direction, kept a tight hold on her brother's hand, and ran.

They had one advantage: now that other dragons were fighting, the rampant dragon wasn't hunting humans. Tiendremos was far more noticeable and significant a threat. Unfortunately, the dragons might still kill them by accident, collateral damage in the fight between giants.

Anahrod almost found herself caught under a pillar that had waited until the most inopportune moment to fall, but Sicaryon pulled her back in time. In turn,

Anahrod stopped Sicaryon from stumbling into a still-bubbling pool of acid, after he slipped on blood-slick marble floors. Gwydinion, more cautious or just luckier, suffered no near misses at all.

They reached the entrance and found the lintel melted away, along with the first few steps down, but otherwise accessible.

Sicaryon jumped first and held out his arms to catch Gwydinion. He repeated it with Anahrod and then they ran, the tunnels still shuddering around them from the fighting up above.

"What happened?" Anahrod asked Gwydinion as they hurried, now traveling with the proper flow of refugees fleeing the battle.

"I don't know," Gwydinion sniffed. "They were about to kill the shrike when a dragon screamed and just started throwing up acid everywhere. And Neveranimas—"

Anahrod stopped in the tunnel, threw Sicaryon a worried look. "Neveranimas was there?"

"She was," Gwydinion said, "but she vanished when the fighting started."

"Good survival instincts," Sicaryon said.

"You're not hurt, are you?" Anahrod asked Gwydinion. She could tell that he'd been crying. "Nothing splashed on you . . . ?"

"No, I just—" Gwydinion made a face. "I'm fine."

She doubted that.

"Surprising," Sicaryon commented. "I'm sure as fuck not fine. How often does this *happen*, Anah?"

She didn't know what to say. "It's not . . . I mean . . ."

"We run drills." Gwydinion's voice was void of all emotion.

"It's supposed to happen less often with dragonriders," Anahrod said.

"I don't think it's working!" Sicaryon's sarcasm dripped thicker than the acid upstairs. "I can't believe you people just shrug and say, 'Oh well, you know how it is. Sometimes the dragons just go berserk and kill *everyone*. What can you do?'" Bright outrage sharpened his voice to a keen edge. "How can you just accept this as *normal*?"

Anahrod glanced at Gwydinion. "Let's talk about this later."

Sicaryon raised his eyebrows. "He just had to hide in a dead dragon's mouth to stay alive. I think he already knows there's a problem."

Gwydinion said nothing.

"I am the last—!" She looked around at the people still streaming around them. Much fewer now. "I am the last person who will defend the dragons about this, Cary, but let's reach safety first. Then you can yell at me about matters out of my control."

"Dragon attacks have tripled in the last hundred years," Gwydinion said numbly. "That's what Mom says. And that nobody knows why."

Anahrod felt ill. "Something tells me the priests don't mention that in church sermons. Come on. Let's hurry back."

Gwydinion shook his head. "No, we should help. Survivors—"

"No. We're not trained for it, and we'll just make it harder for the people who are. I'm getting you back to safety. We'll join the other students at school. And then we'll—" Her voice trailed off.

She didn't know what they'd do. She just didn't know.

33

SILVER ON THE WALL

When they reached the shelter where Varriguhl had gathered the other dragon-rider candidates, they discovered the headmaster had turned the rampant attack into an opportunity to give a lecture.

This particular shelter was unusually comfortable, as if the headmaster had long since decided that if forced to remain in such a place, he'd do so in style. Cushions littered the floor, along with blankets, chairs, and niches clearly designed for naps. Unlike some shelters Anahrod had seen, entering this one did not require navigating a staircase, which made sense considering the headmaster's mobility needs.

Students were crying, holding pillows, blankets, each other.

Anahrod could hardly blame them.

The headmaster, though . . .

Anahrod forcibly reminded herself that she shouldn't draw attention to herself, that she shouldn't grab the bastard by the shoulders and demand to know what he thought he was doing.

He was still teaching class—but he was using the attack to do it.

Magic turned one entire wall in the room into a mirrorlike surface. This mirror didn't reflect the room but showed a slowly rotating view of Yagra'hai.

A giant scrying mirror, showing the rampant attack as it was happening.

Modelakast was still alive.

The dragons had made a serious effort at rectifying that. Burns from Tiendremos branched and snaked across one of Modelakast's wings, and she was bleeding freely. She just didn't seem to care.

"—one of Segramikar's clutches. Young, as these things are measured," Varriguhl said. "She did not yet have a rider but had expressed interest in this year's candidates. And this is why—" He broke off when he saw Gwydinion. "Doreyl, you're still alive."

Anahrod couldn't tell whether Varriguhl approved. The other students, though, were less ambiguous, immediately swarming him, some with questions, but most just wanting to express their relief that he was safe. Kimat was one of the latter—Anahrod was surprised at how happy the tear-streaked girl looked.

"Class, quiet down!" Varriguhl snapped. "Sit down." The headmaster wheeled himself toward Gwydinion. He gave both Anahrod and Sicaryon, officially Gwydinion's bodyguards, an approving nod. "I'm sure the young man's parents will be relieved to know their money was well spent. Are you uninjured, Doreyl?"

Gwydinion nodded. "Yes, Headmaster."

Varriguhl's eyes softened fractionally, a moment of sympathy for the boy. Then he immediately launched into: "What did the augury say?"

Gwydinion cast about the room as if he might find the right answer scribbled on the walls somewhere. He gave a minuscule headshake. "I'm sorry, Headmaster. They never got as far as the sacrifice."

"I don't know," Sicaryon muttered under his breath, "does dragon count?"

"What was that?" Varriguhl questioned sharply.

Anahrod would've hit Sicaryon if that wouldn't have made the situation worse. Instead, all she could do was glare with great intention.

Sicaryon shifted uncomfortably. He hadn't meant to be overheard. "There was uh—a dragon was killed in the temple," he explained. "Disemboweled."

The blood drained from Anahrod's face. She tightened her hand on her sword hilt until her knuckles turned white. She hadn't thought about the dragon's death that way, but now it seemed obvious.

No dragon would ever pick Gwydinion after this.

Dragons were no more immune to superstition than humans. How easy would it be to gaze at the body of a dragon, dead and gutted, in the same temple of Eannis that should've seen the sacrifice of a smaller stand-in, and think that yes, this was meant to be the augury? She couldn't imagine any dragon thinking it was a good augury, a sign of Eannis's favor. It was much more likely to be a dire warning, Eannis spelling out just how much of a threat one human could be.

Then, at some point, some enterprising soul would figure out—just as Ris had—that Gwydinion Doreyl was the brother of Anahrod the Wicked. His fate would be sealed. Gwydinion was in no danger of a dragon ever picking him to be their rider.

But if he didn't become a rider, by law he went to the Church. That would be its own death sentence, because even if he never gave them cause to declare him a heretic, they'd invent one.

Anahrod should've run with Gwydinion. With an acid dragon, no one but Naeron would be truly certain that Gwydinion hadn't died in the attack.

But she hadn't, and couldn't—the moment Gwydinion left the school, the heist team's permissions left with him.

While all these thoughts raced through her head, Varriguhl narrowed his eyes at Sicaryon. "That's an interesting accent. Where are you from?"

Sicaryon just smiled. "I've lived in Snowfell since I was a child, but my parents are immigrants from Mirorweal."

"Mirorweal? I've never heard of the place."

"I'm not surprised," Sicaryon said. "It's a long way to the north."

And also, was likely a name that Sicaryon had just invented.

Someone in the room screamed.

"Oh no," Gwydinion said.

Anahrod's eyes snapped back to the scrying mirror. She didn't see Tiendremos anymore. She wondered if he'd been injured or if he'd traded off with some other dragon. At some point in the fighting, someone's attack must have cracked open a section of ground; Modelakast breathed into the area revealed.

A human area, Anahrod realized. One of the underground human zones. She felt sick.

That feeling only intensified when another dragon came into view, flying straight for Modelakast. If the rampant dragon was young, this one was a child, barely old enough to fly on its own, barely more than a hatchling. It was the dragon equivalent of Gwydinion, and it was being incredibly reckless.

The dragon's coloring was different than Modelakast's—green—but the shiny black stripes were the same. So not just any hatchling, but one of Modelakast's own, likely convinced that they could somehow snap their mother out of her rampage.

Modelakast's head whipped around, and she screamed at her child. From the look in the dragon's eyes, she neither recognized nor held a single tender thought toward the hatchling. Dimly in the distance, Anahrod felt the dragon's anger, weaker only in that she was tiring, not calming down.

The first blast of acid caught the dragon hatchling straight on. Under most circumstances, that would've finished matters. But as this was Modelakast's child, the acid only pushed the tiny dragon backward. The child understood the threat, though, even if it didn't understand the reason. It tried to fly backward, to escape its mother's rage.

Modelakast surged forward, claws extended, teeth bared.

Anahrod wanted to scream at Varriguhl to turn it off, to stop watching. One student screamed. Anahrod could only sympathize.

The dragon hatchling flew backward, but wasn't watching where it was going—it smacked into a stone tower and fell. The mother pounced—with the size difference between them, she was as likely to swallow her child whole as to claw it to pieces.

"Don't watch," Anahrod told Gwydinion.

A flash of gold crossed between the mother and her child.

Peralon.

The tiny figure on the dragon's back had to be Ris, although Anahrod couldn't make out any greater detail.

[Not today. As the humans say, pick on someone your own size.]

Modelakast changed targets without hesitation, giving the little hatchling the opening it needed to scramble away. The students' cheers were short-lived, however, because the fighting was far from finished: Modelakast raked her claws over Peralon.

Anahrod made a noise as the claws struck true, but slid away harmlessly. A wave of magical energy spread out over Peralon's body in time with the attack, something different from the dragon's normal gold scales. It looked like someone had placed an invisible shield over the dragon's body, a fractal spiral of energy only visible in the moment of being struck.

"Interesting," Varriguhl murmured.

Modelakast leaped at Peralon, outrage building on top of outrage in reaction to her first attack's failure. She grappled with him, raising her hind legs in the same maneuver that had killed the white dragon.

This, too, slid away harmlessly.

Peralon returned the grab, allowed Modelakast to rake while he pulled her into the air. He appeared to be trying to force her out of the city, or at least out of the more populated areas. Admittedly, he could only drag her so far—neither dragon would want to stray so far that they hit the storm wall surrounding the mountaintop.

Modelakast untangled herself from Peralon enough to pull her head back and breathe, yellow liquid splashing over his body—and across his back.

"No!" Varriguhl gave Anahrod a sharp look, one familiar to any student who'd ever talked too loud in a library. She felt a hand snake around her waist as Sicaryon came up from behind, taking one of her hands so she'd have something to squeeze besides a threatening sword.

The acid fell away from Peralon. Ris was still on his back, but from this distance it was impossible to tell if the woman was fine, or injured, or dead.

Except, no. If Peralon was the one using magic, he would've protected Ris, and if Ris was doing it, she'd have included herself in the spell. Ris was fine.

[Hold on. I don't care to fight her here.]

Anahrod exhaled. Peralon wouldn't be talking to Ris like that if she was injured.

"Sunshine . . ." Gwydinion murmured. Kimat, who somehow was standing right next to him, nodded in agreement.

"That is the rider," Varriguhl said. "That is the rider's spellwork, warding their dragon with perfect synchronization. Better than any I've ever seen before." He leaned forward in his chair.

"What does a gold dragon breathe?" a student asked.

Anahrod hadn't the least idea.

"First, remember your lessons. Color may suggest elemental affinity, but it does not *predict* elemental affinity." In a much quieter and significantly more annoyed voice, Varriguhl murmured, "Also, I don't know. He's listed in very few records."

Peralon had dragged Modelakast to an abandoned estate, but that meant little if he couldn't hold her attention. He seemed singularly equipped for that, however.

He was much faster. Combined with Ris's magical wards and his own speed, Modelakast suddenly found it difficult to land any attacks at all.

"Where is everyone?" Gwydinion called out. "Tiendremos was there earlier. What happened to him?"

"Injured," Varriguhl answered. "Few wish to fight a rampant dragon." His face twisted with bitterness. "Especially not a dragon who spits acid. It's a distinctly unpleasant affinity."

"Aren't they all," Anahrod chuntered. Sicaryon pinched her waist as a reminder to stop talking.

As if he were in any position to judge, but she didn't call him on it, because he was also correct.

In some ways, Peralon had the same problem as his opponent. Modelakast was obnoxiously fast, and by playing a defensive game, Peralon wasn't landing many hits of his own. Whatever his breath weapon was, he didn't seem inclined to use it.

At some point, the acid dragon realized Peralon had a rider, and that said rider was therefore a better target. She switched from breathing acid to throwing things—boulders, walls, huge handfuls of dirt—trying to knock Ris from her harness. She must have come close, too, because Peralon veered away to interpose his own body between the rampant dragon and Ris, literally showing his underbelly.

Modelakast screamed triumphantly and launched herself at Peralon.

Except a vast ice sheet formed across Modelakast's tail, pinning it to the ground. The attack hadn't come from Peralon, who seemed just as surprised as the acid dragon.

Neveranimas had arrived.

34

THE DRAGON QUEEN

The students in the classroom cheered, like Eannis herself had just swooped down to save the day. Anahrod tasted bile and was, once again, glad for her veil.

Modelakast pulled so hard to free herself from Neveranimas's ice that she severed her own tail. She paid no attention to the self-inflicted injury, instead flying up in a bright yellow flash, intent on evading both dragons.

She was also flying back into populated areas.

With a scream of frustration, Peralon chased after her, roaring.

[Stop her! Before she reaches the city!]

[Don't give me orders, worm.]

Anahrod scowled as she heard Neveranimas's voice.

Then Neveranimas vanished.

"What just happened?" Sicaryon murmured.

Anahrod could only shake her head. She had no idea. The dragon was simply gone.

Varriguhl let out a dismissive snort. "Wait for it."

The violet dragon reappeared in midair above Modelakast. Neveranimas hovered, wings beating lazily.

"Neveranimas can teleport?" Anahrod gaped at the scrying mirror.

Shit.

"Yes," Varriguhl answered. "I'm afraid so."

Modelakast began flying strafing runs over the city, as though intent on spraying acid on as many structures as possible. More than one building seemed immune to the acid until the moment it buckled, collapsing in a screech of shearing metal and stone.

Neveranimas breathed ice again at Modelakast, which the smaller, faster dragon dodged. In response, Modelakast lunged at the regent, who vanished just before the other dragon's claws would've hit.

"That's not fair," Sicaryon murmured.

[Enough. This has become embarrassing.]

Neveranimas's next teleport left a band of violet energy in its wake, which encircled Modelakast's wings and tightened. The acid dragon plummeted as flying became impossible.

When Modelakast crashed, the violet band duplicated, splitting into a dozen identical strips of energy that bound the dragon more effectively than any chain.

Anahrod exhaled. Much as she loathed Neveranimas, she'd done it. She'd done what all the other dragons had failed to do for over an hour. She'd subdued a rampant dragon.

[Hurry!] Peralon screamed. [We need to—]

Neveranimas moved oddly, made a strange growl.

The bands contracted again, just as they had with the wings, except this time they didn't stop.

Modelakast never even screamed. She didn't have a chance to. She simply fell apart, dissected into a dozen pieces.

The ball of rage hovering at the edge of Anahrod's perceptions vanished.

For a second, no one in the shelter watching reacted. There was a single, sharp inhale from the entire room, followed by stunned silence.

Peralon swung around and snapped at Neveranimas, outright growled at her. [We could've captured her! She might have recovered!]

Neveranimas's lip curled back in a sneer. [I will not wager the lives of my people against the chance that she might have recovered.]

[We'll never know, will we?] Peralon bared his teeth. If he shifted slightly, he'd be in position to challenge her to a duel. Although he had no cause—the rules under which dragons might legally fight were specific.

This didn't qualify.

[Mind your place. You're a guest in this city. Ivarion isn't here to vouch for you anymore. One more comment like that and I'll make sure you're never allowed to return.] Neveranimas gave the gold dragon a haughty glare, a dare in her eyes.

Peralon glared back at her. Then he launched himself up into the air and flew out of view.

"Neveranimas has never taken a rider, has she?"

"No," Varriguhl answered flatly. "Never." He gave an unfriendly sideways glance at Gwydinion. "She expresses an interest from time to time." He waved a hand at the wall, and the mirror surface turned dull and then vanished.

"No." Anahrod ignored what Varriguhl had just implied, for the moment. There'd be time to scream into pillows later. "I mean, if she's never taken a rider, how has she never gone rampant? She used so much magic just now. I thought the more magic a dragon used, the higher the risk?"

Varriguhl gave her a sharp look. "You've studied this."

Leave it to Varriguhl to focus on the last thing she wanted. "One hears things."

"Yes," he said dryly. "I suppose one does. But to answer your question—" He paused. "Well." He smiled tightly. "It's an excellent question." He turned away from her then and yelled out. "The emergency is over! Everyone return to class. This does not excuse students from their lessons!"

Varriguhl's attention focused back on Anahrod. "Except for Doreyl. He's excused from classes for the day. We will reschedule his consecration later." He paused, seemed to consider some weighty matter for a moment, and then said to Gwydinion, "Did anyone see you at the consecration?" He corrected himself. "Anyone still alive, I mean."

Gwydinion nodded. "Neveranimas."

Varriguhl's eyes narrowed. "She was there? When Modelakast went rampant?"

"Yes, Headmaster, but then she—" He glanced at the wall where she scrying mirror had been. "—she vanished."

Varriguhl smiled a tight, unfriendly line at that. "She has been known to do so. I suppose I can understand why she was there. She had asked to meet with you in a preliminary interview." He pursed his lips. "I can work with this."

Gwydinion's eyes grew large at the news that Neveranimas had already singled him out. "Headmaster?"

Varriguhl refocused on him. "Hmm? What are you still doing here?"

"When—" Gwydinion swallowed. "When is the interview supposed to be?"

"I haven't the faintest clue," Varriguhl said. "Interviews aren't allowed until after consecrations, and yours will be postponed. As I do not know when the cathedral will be repaired, I cannot give you a date." He seemed rather smugly pleased by that idea. "Now go, and take your minders with you."

<hr>

They retreated to the study/headquarters after that.

She shouldn't have brought her brother inside, but she wouldn't leave him alone after what had happened.

"That was Neveranimas?" Sicaryon stabbed a finger vaguely toward the city proper.

"Yes," Anahrod said.

Sicaryon wiped a hand over his face. "She doesn't look like she should be that scary," he said. "It's the lavender color. She looks like a stuffed dragon doll you'd find in a Skylander child's bedroom."

"Probably is," Anahrod commented. "Her likeness, anyway." She felt numb. She had no idea what Gwydinion was feeling, but he'd just seen at least two dragons and dozens of humans die. No fifteen-year-old should have that burden.

Sicaryon said, "I've seen dragons swoop down and set entire valleys on fire. Dragons that spread disease. Dragons that create storms. There's that dragon who spits boiling, poisonous blood. Terrifying. But not half as terrifying as that." He threw up his hands. "And she can teleport!"

"You noticed that, too." Anahrod dragged two chairs together, sat Gwydinion down in one, herself in the other. "So much for it taking her seven minutes to fly back."

Gwydinion leaned into her shoulder. "Why hasn't she gone rampant? It's been at least a hundred years . . . nobody's willpower is that strong."

Sicaryon sighed. "Maybe she secretly worships Zavad, so he's giving her a free pass."

The three fell silent.

Anahrod raised an eyebrow at Sicaryon. "You don't believe in Eannis, so you can't believe in Zavad. Besides, if a dragon who was so powerful he could corrupt magic itself existed, he wouldn't be hiding."

Gwydinion exhaled.

Sicaryon gave a noncommittal shrug before he asked, with painfully false brightness: "Think I could persuade Varriguhl to teach me that mirror trick?"

"No."

Sicaryon made a face. "I could do so much with that spell."

"Yes, but that was a *spell*, not an inscription, and you"—Anahrod mimed punching him in the arm—"are not a dragonrider. Thus, Varriguhl will never, ever, teach you."

Sicaryon sighed.

Anahrod's thoughts floated randomly as she stared at nothing. "Think Modelakast's rider could've stopped this? If she'd had a rider, I mean. What happens when a rider swaps with their rampant dragon? Would they stay rampant? Or would it just . . . stop?"

Gwydinion lifted his head. "Riders can't . . . riders can do that?"

Anahrod nodded grimly. "Don't recommend you mention that in front of Varriguhl, but I've seen it, multiple times now. The link can go both ways, if the dragon lets it." She grimaced. "Which they usually don't."

Gwydinion blinked. "But why not? If there's a chance it could possibly stop rampancy . . . ?"

"You're talking logic and common sense," Sicaryon said. "That's not what motivates people. Or dragons."

"I guess not," Gwydinion said. "You'd have to trust your partner so much to give up control like that."

"That assumes you have a choice," Anahrod said. "Riders don't."

Gwydinion flushed and looked down at the floor.

The door to the service tunnel slammed open. Claw marched through. Her unveiled face was smudged with black soot, as if she'd forgotten her hands were dirty when she'd wiped away sweat. Kaibren and Naeron followed, all in similar states. An odor wafted in with them: smoke, blood, and the sharp tang of acid.

"We're fucked," Claw announced. "Absolutely, positively, fucked."

PART SEVEN

BEFORE THE HEIST, A HEIST

35

ONE MORE BOTTLE

The dragonriders were the last to arrive. Anahrod wasn't sure they would've shown at all if she hadn't reached out to Peralon and demanded it. Ris looked exhausted, her normal seashell delicacy threatening to crack at any moment. Anahrod bit back on the urge to wrap the woman in a blanket and make her tea.

Jaemeh was even worse: he had an arm in a sling and bandages on the right side of his face and down one leg.

"Damn, Jaemeh," Claw said. "You okay?"

He waved her off. "I'll be fine. Just some burns."

Ris noticed Gwydinion. An enormous look of relief came over the dragon-rider, suggesting that Peralon had told his rider about Anahrod's survival, but hadn't known about his. Ris pulled a chair from the table where all the maps were spread out, flipped it around, and sat on it backward. "What happened?"

"Well," Anahrod said, "I have it on good authority that we're fucked." She gestured at Claw.

Claw nodded grimly. "Blacksmith's shop melted."

Jaemeh swore and slammed his fist—the one not in a sling—on the table.

Ris grimaced. "And the blacksmith?"

"Melted," said Naeron.

"You can kiss the duplicate sword goodbye," Claw elaborated. "We're back to zero."

"It's worse than that," Sicaryon said.

Everyone paused and stared at the new guy.

"How?" Ris asked, squinting.

"Were you watching when Neveranimas killed—" Sicaryon looked at Anahrod.

"Modelakast," she said.

"Right. If you watched that fight—"

"I didn't watch it," Ris said. "I was *in* it."

"*My point,*" Sicaryon pressed, "is that Neveranimas *teleports.* How long will it take her to get from the council chambers to her vault? I'd guess seconds."

"Great," Claw said. "That's just great."

Jaemeh sighed. "So that's one and two. Let me share three."

"What do you mean?" Anahrod asked.

"Peralon just pissed off Neveranimas," Jaemeh said, throwing Ris a dirty look, "so he's gone from 'visiting dragon who can go where he likes as long as he doesn't cause trouble' to 'being watched.' Guess who shouldn't be anywhere near Neveranimas's estate, let alone flying everyone into the entry shaft?"

"Tiendremos—" Naeron began.

"Too big," Ris said, sighing. "And has an injured wing."

In Anahrod's mind's eye, a giant yawning chasm opened. A giant yawning chasm that they now had no way to safely lower themselves into. She shuddered. "All right. Is that it?"

"Nope," Claw said. "Last but not least." She tilted her head at Ris. "Want to share with the other kids in class why we can't just walk into Brauge's parlor and make the sword swap while she's off at book club?"

Ris groaned and scrubbed a hand over her face.

Anahrod rubbed her temples. "Did they cancel book club?" She dimly recalled Varriguhl saying something about dragonrider procedures after a rampant dragon attack.

"They canceled *everything*," Jaemeh said. "Sometimes a dragon going rampant will trigger other dragons. So, no parties, no absences, none of that. Every dragonrider is expected to stay at home and sing mantras or snort sky amber or do whatever is necessary to keep our dragons sane." He waved at Claw. "You're right. We're screwed. Even if we had a substitute sword, Brauge won't be leaving the house for long enough for us to steal it."

No one said anything for several long, awkward seconds.

Ris stood up. "I'm calling it for today. None of these problems are insurmountable, but we're not figuring them out tonight. Personally, I'm going to get very drunk, and I encourage you all to join me if you're that way inclined." She pointed a finger at Gwydinion. "Except you. You get juice."

Gwydinion gave her a strained smile, too out of sorts to manage the mandatory teenage protest.

Ris immediately turned to Jaemeh. "You're welcome to stay."

He looked seriously tempted for a moment, and then the dragonrider shook his head. "No," he said. "Tiendremos wouldn't . . ." He smiled tightly. "I can't stay."

"Of course," Ris said. "I understand."

Anahrod wished like hell that she didn't. She thought about saying something complimentary to pass along—he had been one of the only dragons with enough guts to fight the rampant dragon, after all—but she was very certain Tiendremos didn't give a damn what she thought about him. He couldn't be thrilled with the idea that Peralon and Neveranimas had both done what he couldn't. No, Anahrod imagined that hadn't helped his ego at all.

She was also very certain that those burns Jaemeh was sporting were specifically acid burns, because if Jaemeh had been riding on Tiendremos's back during that fight, she honestly didn't know how much of an effort the blue dragon would've made to protect him.

They all watched the dragonrider leave, and then Ris turned toward the others and said, "We do have alcohol here, right?"

They did.

"Before we start." Ris had wagged a finger at Gwydinion. "You should not come away from this with the impression that this is a suitable method of dealing with emotional pain and grief. It's terrible and unhealthy. Also: exceedingly bad for your liver."

Gwydinion had narrowed his eyes, sensing an adult inside joke. "But you're going to do it anyway."

"Oh yes," Ris said. "You're old enough by now to understand that age is no bulwark against foolishness. If you had any illusions about the dignity of your elders, you're about to be very disappointed."

And then she'd cracked open the first bottle.

Not everyone drank. Gwydinion wasn't allowed and Naeron didn't by choice. Kaibren might've under certain circumstances but chose to stay sober and quote entire stage plays to an audience comprised of Claw and Gwydinion.

Anahrod frowned as she considered the scene, and said to Ris: "I won't have a problem with him, will I?"

Kaibren's rings declared he was not interested in sex at all, flowers, leaves, or anything in between, but people lied about their rings, particularly if polite society frowned on their true preferences. The inscriptionist had always struck Anahrod as an exceptionally eccentric uncle, but she'd never been the trusting sort.

"Kaibren?" Ris had just refilled a glass of wine, which she examined critically before returning her attention to her oldest team member. "Just the opposite, really. He's an excellent guard dog against that sort of thing."

Anahrod gave her a questioning look, and Ris shrugged. "He was a dragonrider candidate himself once, you know."

Anahrod startled. She hadn't known.

"Unpicked, of course," Ris murmured. "So, he was sent to the Church and . . ." Her smile turned bitter. Anahrod's stomach tightened in response, knowing she would loathe the next words Ris spoke. "The Church is well-intentioned enough, but it's an institution that gathers children who cannot leave on pain of death, who have no recourse. They're vulnerable, and the vulnerable always attract predators."

"Is that why—" Anahrod glanced at Claw, who was well on her way to proving herself to be the happy sort of drunk instead of any other kind. The young woman was near bent over double, laughing at Kaibren's recital.

She never finished the sentence or even properly asked, but Ris seemed to understand her meaning, regardless. "Claw? Yes. It wasn't sexual, but she was being abused, mentally and physically. Kaibren put a stop to it."

Which went a long way to explaining why Claw would fight her way through flights of dragons to protect the man.

"Why do intelligent beings always take having power over another as an excuse to do their worst?" Sicaryon's rhetorical question was equal parts angry, sad, and resigned. He held up a bottle to the two women, offering to refresh their drinks.

"Yes, please." Anahrod held out her glass.

"How do you stop that?" Sicaryon asked, and this time the question did not seem rhetorical at all.

She knew it wasn't. Anahrod had spent too much time during the hottest, most miserable parts of the day hidden in a cave or up in a tree, debating such matters with Sicaryon because there was nothing else to do but sleep, fuck, or talk, and it'd been too hot for the first two.

Ris downed her glass in one long, elegant swallow, tipping her head back so the movement of her throat was a carnal shudder. Anahrod knew Sicaryon was looking. So was she.

"You don't." Ris held out her glass for Sicaryon to fill. "You can't. All you can do is make it unacceptable and inexcusable." She wasn't watching Kaibren anymore, but she wasn't watching much of anything.

Sicaryon stared at her like he was still trying to comprehend the puzzle in front of him. How someone like Ris could exist. "Even dragons?" Sicaryon murmured as he refilled her glass.

"Especially dragons," Ris agreed.

Sicaryon drained the last wine into his own glass and set the dead soldier over on the table. He turned to Anahrod. "I meant to say thank you."

She raised an eyebrow. "For what?"

He scoffed. "Saving my life. This morning, remember?"

"Did she?" Ris looked intrigued.

"You'd have saved yourself," Anahrod replied, hoping her face wasn't flushed.

She wasn't good with compliments. "You already were. You and Gwydinion both."

"That wasn't—" Sicaryon frowned. "I need to find out the name of that dragon." He said the words quietly and to himself, a mental note for something to do later.

Anahrod squinted. Which dragon—? Ah. "You mean the white one?"

"It saved our lives," Sicaryon explained. "Not just . . . not just because we used the body to hide, later. It saved us from the start. That stupid acid dragon tried to throw up right on top of us, except the white dragon blocked it." He shook his head, made a small, shocked sound. "It could've flown away. Plenty of the other dragons did. Instead, it sacrificed its own life to save a bunch of humans." He looked appalled. "And you—" He pointed a finger at Ris. "You and Peralon. You didn't have to do that either."

"No, you're wrong," Ris gently corrected. "We did."

Anahrod wanted to kiss her so badly at that moment the only thing that stopped her was the awkwardness of Sicaryon's presence.

Also, that she wanted to kiss him just as much.

"I think I'll grab another bottle of wine," Ris said. "We're going to be here a while."

———

Anahrod woke up the next day in her bed, with a hammering headache and the uncomfortable knowledge that she'd made all the bad choices she'd expected of herself. She confirmed that by raising her head enough to see that the naked, pale legs next to her in the bed were attached to a body with a shock of red hair at the other end.

Sicaryon grumbled behind her as he tightened his arm around her waist, nuzzling at her neck. He pressed up against her back, warm and solid. A little less muscular than she remembered, since the day-to-day life of an average Skylander was less demanding than a Deeper's, but not by much. His body was still a pleasurable map of smooth planes and curves.

A laugh escaped her, doing nothing to help her hangover. Who had she been kidding? This had been inevitable.

She groaned and rubbed a finger into her eye. Why make a single bad decision, she supposed, when she could make two at the same time. Much more efficient. Ris and Sicaryon both. Why not?

The previous night's memories were a pleasant blur, such that despite the hangover Anahrod fought off the temptation to do it all over again, this time sober.

If she were smart, she'd get out of bed, dress, and get the hell out. Leave Ris and Sicaryon to work out the awkward morning after.

She couldn't make herself move.

Sicaryon's hand shifted, his breathing quickening as he woke. His hand wandered up her arm, ended on her shoulder. His breath tickled the fine hairs around her ear as he whispered, "Shall we keep her?"

The spell broke.

A red flash of anger warmed her skin as she pushed away the blankets and rolled off the bed. The fast, violent movements woke Ris, who made adorable mewling noises at the injustice of being forced to wake.

Anahrod glared at Sicaryon as she grabbed her clothing. He had an anguished expression on his face: the look of a man who knew he must've messed up but didn't quite understand how. He'd misplaced his wig somewhere, so he appeared the way she'd known him most of her life: bald except for a braid of blond hair down one side.

Ris blinked again and pushed herself up on her elbows. The spill of red hair over her shoulders just barely covered her breasts, the sort of too-convenient conceit Anahrod had always assumed was an artistic device to convey nudity without offending delicate sensibilities.

"Wait," Ris said. "Are we fighting? Why are we fighting?"

"Anahrod—" Sicaryon's mouth twisted in frustration.

"No," she told him. Having this conversation while tugging on her trousers took the righteous superiority out of the situation, but a retreat followed by a slamming door also lost its drama if she were naked while doing so. "I need time. I can't just go back to—" She swallowed. "You interpret me sleeping with either of you after the day we had yesterday as anything other than—"

"No," Sicaryon said. "No lies. We both know it means something. You don't like that it means something, but that's not the same thing."

"Ah," Ris said. "That's why we're fighting. Only, could we fight at a softer volume? My head feels like a split melon."

Anahrod grabbed her breast wraps. "Fine," she said. "You want honesty?"

"Wait," Ris said. "No."

"Let start with the forty spouses."

"I told you I don't have forty spouses." Sicaryon tugged hard on his lock of hair. "I don't have any—"

Anahrod paused in the middle of adjusting her breast wraps, thought the matter over for a second. "I don't believe you," she said, and continued dressing.

"Damn it!" Sicaryon threw off what blankets they hadn't yet tossed to the floor and rolled out of bed. "I'm telling the truth. I don't—" His expression turned thoughtful. "Forty . . . ? Wait . . . just stop for a minute." He sighed. "Do you mean the Assembly?" When she didn't reply immediately, he rubbed his chin and sighed again. "Every time we add new communities, I make them elect a representative and send them to us. Maybe . . . maybe to an outsider that looks like I'm demanding brides or some such. I suppose that's possible . . ."

Anahrod blinked. "Representatives?"

Sicaryon gestured broadly. "Sure. This every-person-gets-a-vote thing is great if you're a densely packed city, but in the Deep? It's not practical. So, elective representatives, who all go to the capital and debate each other endlessly. Nothing gets done."

Her head throbbed as she tried to understand what he was saying. "I thought you were king?" she finally spat out.

"I was, yes," he agreed. "For three years. And I hated every second of it. So, I asked each village to send me a representative and I threw them a very nice feast in my largest banquet hall and told them they had three days to figure out a new government. Then I locked the door."

Ris had frozen in the middle of retrieving her shirt. "Did that work?"

"No," Sicaryon admitted. "They came out after three days and told me that the wisest people in the realm had decided I was the best person to lead them." He shrugged. "They'd decided it was a test of loyalty. So, I sent them back and told them that whatever they came up with had better work without me, because the moment they figured it out, I was gone." He chuckled darkly. "Fourth time was the charm."

"And *that* worked?" Anahrod might've squeaked a little.

It's not that she didn't think a democracy would work. Exactly the opposite. She just hadn't thought the Deepers would ever . . .

Sicaryon had just . . .

Sicaryon shrugged. "I wasn't exaggerating when I said they spend all their time arguing. But weirdly, that seems to be working. Or at least, I'll take a bunch of people shouting at each other in a big room over the endless wars and raids."

"Are you or are you not king?" Anahrod asked again.

"It's in a transitional state," he said. "Technically, I run the army. I estimate it will take five years until I can comfortably call myself nothing but a figurehead."

Anahrod sat down on the edge of the bed. "You gave up power? Why?" She'd grown up in a house obsessed with power, which was part of the reason she'd rebelled so hard the other way. And even though she'd known her father had done the same thing, this felt different. Her father hadn't had a choice. Sicaryon had.

"Did I not mention that I hated it? Because it's a lot of work. Not fun work, either. And um—" He pressed his lips together for a moment. "All that power couldn't get me what I really wanted."

She just stared.

"I'm going to kiss you," Anahrod told him. "But I want you to know that if I find out you were lying about any of this—"

"Sword to the gut," Sicaryon said. "I know the rules."

She started to kiss him.

"Isn't that sweet?" Ris's voice was darker than night, colder than winter.

Sicaryon kissed Anahrod's forehead instead and let her go. "You make a good point," he said. "We *should* talk about what happened yesterday." There was something resigned and unhappy to his expression that made Anahrod uncomfortable. Like he was preparing to do a deeply unpleasant but necessary task.

"You mean the rampant dragon?" Ris raised an eyebrow as she slid on her trousers.

"Sure. Mostly the people who died because of you."

Ris froze.

"Cary, what are you saying? She had nothing to do with that dragon going rampant."

Ris's skin flushed and her eyes widened. "How dare you. I did not—You're accusing me—"

Anahrod glanced around nervously. Some of the smaller knickknacks in the room started to vibrate.

"Why did that dragon go rampant?" Sicaryon asked.

"Why does any dragon go rampant?" Ris snapped back. "Corrupt magic. I had nothing to do with that!"

"No, that's a how. I asked why." Sicaryon's gray eyes looked sharp enough to cut. "Let's not pretend that yesterday was an accident. Yesterday was an assassination attempt."

Anahrod couldn't breathe. An assassination? But who—

Sicaryon was right. Somehow, Neveranimas had orchestrated the entire debacle. It was just too much coincidence that the only time a dragon went rampant was when Gwydinion was most vulnerable.

And Gwydinion was only in Yagra'hai at all because Ris insisted.

Anahrod saw the moment when Ris realized that, too, when she followed that trail to its logical conclusion.

The dragonrider fell to her knees.

"I—" Her eyes were glassy bright.

"Oh, I've been there," Sicaryon said, his voice both harsh and so, so gentle.

"You thought that because you didn't attack anyone this time, because you didn't personally kill everyone you saw and bathe in their blood, that your hands would be clean."

She put her face in her hands and sobbed.

"Sicaryon, I think that's enough," Anahrod said.

"No," he said, shaking his head. "She has to understand." He said to Ris, "You knew Gwydinion was bait. You knew she was after him. Well, congratulations— she took the bait."

Ris raised her head from her hands, her eyes red and tear-streaked. She glared at him hatefully.

Then her eyes glowed.

"No," Anahrod snapped. "Don't you dare, Peralon. I know you love her, and I know you don't want to see her in pain, but don't let her run."

Peralon stared at Anahrod for an interminably long second, and then Anahrod was looking at Ris's green eyes once more.

The dragonrider drew in a shuddery, phlegm-soaked breath.

"Now let's talk about how yesterday wasn't your fault," Sicaryon said.

Ris let out a disbelieving scoff. Anahrod could hardly blame her.

Sicaryon shrugged. "You don't control Neveranimas. You don't control any dragon—although Peralon may or may not disagree—but what happened yesterday was a direct consequence of decisions that you do control. You knew it was a risk. We could've waited and found another way into the city."

"No, if we lost that opportunity—"

"So maybe it would end up taking a couple of years. Aren't you over a hundred years old? How are you this impatient? You didn't want to wait; you didn't want to find someone else. You thought the risk was worth it." He paused a beat. "Was it?"

"I hate you," she whispered.

He shrugged. "I get that a lot."

All Anahrod could do was watch or . . . no. She wiped her eyes, because apparently, she was sympathy crying, and sat down next to Ris and pulled the woman into her arms. She petted her hair and let Ris sob, scowling at Sicaryon.

"I'm willing to be the villain, if I have to," he said. "I know where this road leads." He reached out and touched Ris's back. "I know the toll, and you can pay it. I know you can pay it. It's just the price will keep going up and you need to ask yourself if it's worth it, because believe me, it can get worse."

Ris wiped her eyes and tilted her head to the side to look at him. "Did you work long on that speech?"

He cleared his throat, looking more than a little surprised. "Not really?"

"Entire civilization based on flying and you try to comfort me with road metaphors. Genius."

Anahrod laughed darkly.

"It's almost like I come from a kingdom at sea level," Sicaryon grumbled. "Looks like my job is done." He grabbed his clothes and that wig off the floor. "I'll leave you ladies to finish and make my retreat."

He left.

He was still naked.

Anahrod and Ris paused, waiting. A few seconds later, they heard someone shout and then a loud cat whistle.

"The Scarsea don't have a nudity taboo?" Ris asked quietly.

"Not really, no."

Ris nodded, like that explained a few things. She started dressing herself, but her movements were slow and overly careful, like a terribly injured person trying not to reopen their wounds.

"What happens to us?" Ris asked.

Anahrod sighed. It was the very last question she wanted to answer just then.

"That depends on you," Anahrod finally said.

Ris blinked back tears, staring. "After everything I've done, if you're telling me that . . . Is this is an ultimatum . . . ?"

"No," Anahrod said, smiling sadly. "No, I've tried that. Doesn't work." She stood up from the bed and walked a pace, feeling the tension lurking in every bone and muscle. "I could go run away with Sicaryon. He'd be thrilled to take me back—" She sniffed, shook her head. "I guess I'm greedy as a dragon. I don't want to choose. And I don't claim to be a saint, Ris. I'm invested in this, too. I'm not asking you to walk away. I'm just . . . I'm asking you to trust me."

She wasn't prepared for the soft scoff that Ris made in response. "Trust," the woman murmured. "As if you're not every bit as allergic to it."

"Ris, I—" Her throat closed on her.

"Hardest thing in the world, trust." Her voice was bitter and dark. "People will tell you it's love or forgiveness or saying you're sorry, but no. None of that. It's trust."

Anahrod let her talk. She had nothing to say.

"That's why you were all by yourself in the jungle, wasn't it? You could've found a village, a holler. I bet so many people tried to recruit you," Ris whispered. "But in the jungle, you don't have to trust."

"Oh, no. You can trust the jungle," Anahrod disagreed. "You can have absolute faith that it always wants to kill you. It's simple and honest and it never judges."

Ris's eyes flicked up at the last part. Anahrod nodded slowly. "That's it. That's the real issue, isn't it? Not trust. Judgment. Knowing you've sinned and knowing that you've hurt the people you love and knowing that you will have to confess your crimes and you don't know how they'll judge you. It's easier to lie."

"It was easier," Ris corrected, "when the only person I loved was a dragon." Then she realized what she'd just said and sighed, closed her eyes, hung her head. "You're both like damn jungle vines."

Hopefully that was because they were growing on her, and not because she thought they both needed to be pruned with a sword.

Anahrod had finished dressing, or at least, as much as she felt capable of doing. Fixing her hair was out of the question. "I'm going to go . . . I'm going to go check on Gwydinion."

Ris raised her head. "Tell the others I'm calling a meeting. We have work to do."

Anahrod felt the edge of those words, sharp and prickling, but she nodded anyway.

They did indeed have work to do.

36

PROBLEM-SOLVING

"We'll have to rappel down," Ris announced.

Anahrod had pulled everyone into a meeting, just not right away. Not everyone was hung over, but everyone was in shock over what had happened, and the entire campus had all the cheer of a looted mausoleum. It was evening by the time everyone was in a state to pretend they were human.

Anahrod shuddered. Two thousand feet down, with a lake of magma at the bottom. Perhaps that had been exaggeration, fun hyperbole to stress the danger of the situation, but Anahrod knew she wouldn't be that lucky.

They were all gathered around the map table, drinks in hand, awkward in manner. At least as far as Sicaryon and Anahrod were concerned. They had yet to speak to each other a single word more than necessary after that morning.

Ris noticed the motion. "I thought you said your fear of heights wasn't a problem anymore?"

"*Probably* wasn't an issue anymore."

"In shadows cast by unseen plight, a journey fought both day and night. The dark shrike's dance of strength and pain, a tale of courage, not in vain," Kaibren recited over his cup of tea.

Claw snorted. "That means it's always going to be 'probably,' and you better damn well not let that stop you. It's not like the entire job is depending on this or anything."

"Claw," Ris admonished.

The other woman shrugged. "Not sorry. Not wrong."

Jaemeh wasn't at this meeting. He knew about it; he just hadn't shown. Peralon said Jaemeh and Tiendremos were resting from their injuries, and they were fine.

Anahrod tipped her head back to stare at the ceiling. "I'm handling it." Before Claw could make a derisive comment, she added, "What about the rest of it? Brauge, the rubbings, the sword, the timing?" She was no expert on robbery—no matter what Tiendremos believed—but she would've thought that when things went wrong, they did it in dribbles. Not this all-at-once tidal wave.

"Brauge is a problem," Ris admitted, "but one with a solution. Two things: first, she's a gregarious sort. In a few weeks, she'll be bouncing off the walls wanting to talk to someone. Second, she's a heavy drinker."

"She has a hell of a wine collection," Claw admitted.

"You're suggesting we drug her?" Anahrod asked.

"Unnoticed remains the mundane," Kaibren said.

"True," Claw said. "If her dragon's used to her drinking herself under, he won't fuss when it happens again."

"And this 'stay at home and pay attention to your dragon' thing," Anahrod said to Ris. "She can receive guests?"

"Yes. She may invite a few friends over as long as she's not throwing an orgy or anything equally indecorous." Ris chewed on her lower lip. "Ultimately, it depends on her dragon, but Zentoazax doesn't have a reputation for being jealous."

Claw brightened. "What about—"

Ris shook her head. "Prefers leaves."

Claw's gaze slid over to Sicaryon. She smiled.

Sicaryon returned that smile with the proper amount of wariness. "What am I being volunteered to do?"

"We'll discuss it later," Ris said. "As for other issues, we've re-created the rubbing, thank you Kaibren"—she tipped her head to the inscriber, who returned her bow—"and it has gone to a different smith, but—"

"But he ain't near as good as the first one," Claw said. "So don't expect the sword to hold up to close inspection. And it's going to take a month."

Anahrod grimaced. "That's cutting it close."

"Yes," Naeron agreed unhappily.

"Why?" Claw asked. "Since when are we on a deadline?"

Anahrod replied, "Since Neveranimas has asked to interview Gwydinion. The only good side to that is it can't happen until Gwydinion's consecrated, so we have until they repair the Great Cathedral."

"Is that the only church in the city?" Sicaryon asked. "And if it isn't, is there anything stopping them from using a different church for the ceremony?"

"No," Kaibren said.

Anahrod blinked. Naeron hadn't given that negative—*Kaibren* had. She supposed he was still quoting something, just in the most truncated way possible.

The meaning of that negative, though, was worse. She knew there were multiple churches in the city. She just hadn't stopped to consider the ramifications. "There's a chapel here at the school. There're others in town. Neveranimas is smart enough to think of it, which means we don't have a month. We might not have a week."

Claw set her cup down. "You're talking about it like Neveranimas's only goal is to kill that boy."

"No," Naeron said. "Not her only goal."

Claw scoffed. "Why does she give a shit? What's so important about Gwydinion Doreyl?"

Anahrod hesitated, just for a second, thinking of an unpleasant recent memory and a single, important word.

Trust.

Perhaps she didn't want to be that much of a hypocrite.

Anahrod exhaled. "He's my brother. He's showing every sign that he'll one day be able to do everything that I can do. And I can talk to dragons, remember?" She took a sip of her cup, realized she'd already drained the thing, and got up to refill it. "Had I stayed and accepted Neveranimas's bond, I wouldn't have lived long."

Ris made a face. "You think Neveranimas tried to assassinate a fifteen-year-old boy using a rampant dragon?"

"Oh sure," Claw said, apparently in agreement, "because that fucking bitch can control when and where a dragon goes rampant."

Silence.

Claw looked around the table with an expression of increasing annoyance. "Fucking hell. She can't, right?"

"It's possible," Ris finally said. "She tends to benefit from rampancies in odd ways." She added, "It changes nothing."

Anahrod blinked. "Changes nothing? Ris!"

"What does she think you can do?" Sicaryon asked Anahrod. "What does she think you can do that scares her this much?"

"I have no idea," Anahrod said. "Maybe she thinks I can take possession of a dragon the same way I can an animal—"

"You can do *what*?" Claw's mouth dropped open.

Anahrod did a quick mental recount on who knew what, and revised what she'd been about to say. "I can talk to animals, control them. I can also take possession of them, project my mind into their body. It's like what a dragon does with their rider." She realized she'd been standing at the tea tray for the last five minutes with a cup in her hand, doing absolutely nothing. She fixed that and returned to the table. "I would say it's the last power, but I have it on good authority that any dragonrider can do something similar with training."

"But only if the dragon allows it," Ris pointed out.

"That might be true for me, too," Anahrod pointed out. "Don't you think it's a little much for her to just assume? I *didn't* know I could do that when she tried to have me executed."

"What could you do?" Sicaryon asked. "What did she know you could do?"

"Talk to dragons," Anahrod said. She paused. "Talk to animals . . . calm animals, too, I suppose."

"Calm them down," Ris said slowly, enunciating the words as carefully as if cradling something small and precious. "Think. You're a highly intelligent, ambitious individual who's eliminated all obstacles to power with an undetectable, incurable poison. Then, a child appears who can effortlessly cure that poison whenever she wishes. How do you respond?"

"Control her," Sicaryon answered. "It could be handy to be the only person with the antidote."

"But if you can't do that . . ." Claw ran a finger across her throat.

"The boy." Naeron stared at Anahrod. "Same blessing?"

She nodded. "Yes."

"Oh yeah," Claw said. "He's as good as dead."

Ris glanced sideways at Kaibren. "How are the diplomacy lessons coming, again?"

"Hey, fuck you," Claw snapped. "This is no time for dancing around a titan drake and claiming it's a scale cat."

"I appreciate the bluntness, Claw," Anahrod told her.

"See!" Claw pointed with both hands.

"Fine. Speed up the sword's completion," Ris told Claw. "I understand the quality won't be as good, but it doesn't need to hold up to close inspection. Once Brauge wakes up from the drugging, she'll sense something's amiss and inform Zentoazax. We'll have to have finished the job and left Yagra'hai by then." She turned to Sicaryon. "Where's Anahrod's sword?"

"It'll be here."

"It had better be," Ris spat. "Because we have a week." She swept her arm out. "Tell me where it is. Peralon and I will go pick it up—"

Sicaryon's eyebrows rose. "You can't—"

"One week," she repeated. "Don't make me spell out the consequences if you can't."

"It's already on its way. It. Will. Be. Here."

If Anahrod needed an example of why it wasn't wise to sleep with one's team members, this whole meeting qualified.

"Claw, deal with the sword. Kaibren, I need two ways to knock out Brauge. Naeron, find climbing kit and rappelling gear for the whole crew. Cary—the *other damn sword.*" Ris snapped out orders with a precision most generals would envy. Sicaryon stared at her like she'd just started a striptease.

Anahrod didn't ask how they planned to deal with the fact that it might only take seconds for Neveranimas to return after someone triggered an alarm. She already knew the answer: there was no plan. If it happened, they were screwed.

But someone had been left out of the orders. "Wait," Anahrod said. "What am I doing?"

"You're coming with me," Ris said. "We're going flying."

FOR HIS OWN GOOD

When Anahrod returned from her flying lesson, she could barely walk. Not that she'd used her legs for any physical exertion, but because she'd tensed her muscles bowstring tight the entire flight, her body urging her to run while strapped down and immobile.

The flight itself had gone well. Ris had tried to tease but gave up when she saw Anahrod's heart wasn't it. They concentrated on making sure Anahrod wouldn't freeze at the wrong time.

Ris had pointed out that she didn't need to be cured of her phobia. She only needed enough control to keep from panicking for roughly seven minutes.

When Anahrod entered the apartment, everything was chaos. All the household staff were throwing supplies and equipment into boxes, both regular and the folding kind.

They were packing to leave.

One looked up, her expression one of simultaneous relief and guilt. She pointed at the stairs. "Master Gwydinion is in his room, miss. You should talk to him. He's in a state."

"What happened?"

The woman glanced up one more time before she returned to folding linens. "Go talk to him, please."

Anahrod ran upstairs, taking the steps three at a time. She paused in front of Gwydinion's door, halted by the sound of crying. She knocked instead of barging in. "Gwydinion? What happened? Why aren't you in class?"

A hard drum of footsteps heralded Gwydinion, a few seconds before the door flung open.

"Why aren't I in class?" He sounded incredulous. His face was streaked with tear tracks. "Why weren't you!? Where *were* you? Why weren't you waiting for me?"

"Cary—" She paused. Sicaryon had been given a job to do, hadn't he? And Ris had pulled Anahrod away. There would've been no one waiting for Gwydinion, no bodyguard even as they rushed about trying to protect him. She tasted bile.

"Go back inside." Anahrod pushed him back through the door, then followed him.

Anahrod closed the door behind them. "What happened?"

"I'm being kicked out of school!" Gwydinion shouted. "That's what happened. You and the rest of the staff are all supposed to go home, and I'm being picked up by someone from the Church!"

Anahrod's gut twisted. No . . .

"What happened?" Anahrod asked again.

"What you wanted," Gwydinion said bitterly. "That's what happened."

She scoffed. "What I wanted? No. Absolutely not."

He threw up his arms. "The headmaster caught me cheating on a test. No second chances, just . . . kicked out."

"Did you?" Anahrod asked. "Cheat on a test?"

"No!" Gwydinion screamed. "Of course I didn't. I didn't need to! They planted it on me. It wasn't even subtle." He wiped his eyes. "It's what you wanted. It's what Mother wanted. I will never get to be a dragonrider. I guess after what happened at the consecration ceremony, I already knew that. This just makes it official."

"This isn't what I wanted," Anahrod told him.

"Yes, it is," he spat. "You think I don't know the deal Ris worked out with our mother? All the help Ris could possibly want, and all she had to do was make sure that I didn't get picked. I'd be blaming her if I hadn't seen Varriguhl palm the questions. None of you wanted me to bond with a dragon, and did you think to ask me what I wanted? No!"

She sat down on the edge of his bed.

They hadn't, had they? Not once had Anahrod ever asked, just assuming he'd be far too sensible to want something so foolhardy. That like Anahrod, he was being told what he wanted, rather than being allowed to figure it out for himself.

Her little brother *wanted* to be a dragonrider.

"I'm sorry," she said.

He sniffed and wiped his nose. "Go take sorry to the marketplace and see what it buys you."

"I didn't do this. I wouldn't do this. You being kicked out ruins everything," she told him, because it was true. "They'll throw us all out, and we're not ready."

He frowned. "You can't hide? They'll—" He wrinkled his nose. "No, they'll check exit papers, won't they? And kick up a fuss if you never show up. Shit."

"You've been hanging out with Claw too much," Anahrod said.

She remembered the satisfied look on Varriguhl's face when he'd commented that Neveranimas couldn't see Gwydinion until after he was consecrated, which meant not until after the cathedral was repaired. How was Varriguhl handling the news that any old chapel would work just as well?

"Your consecration ceremony," Anahrod began. "Who else needs to have theirs done, besides you?"

Gwydinion looked up, swallowing back tears. "No one. I was last. The order was random."

"Eannis's left tit, the order was random." Anahrod stood up.

Varriguhl had saved him for last, delayed the ceremony for as long as possible. That old bastard knew exactly who Gwydinion was. He'd always known.

"Where are you going?"

"To go threaten the old man who's screwing everything up by trying to save your life."

———

Anahrod considered various ways to approach Varriguhl as she walked to his house before she performed the mental equivalent of a shrug and knocked on his door.

More like banged on his door, but she wasn't in a good mood.

At first, no one answered. She contemplated the possibility that Varriguhl wasn't home, instead making some other student's life miserable. Then the door swung open, and she was staring at Varriguhl's pinched expression.

"I should've known," he commented, before wheeling his chair around and rolling back inside. "Come inside, then. Prove yourself better than a Windsong vel keeper by closing the door behind you."

His house was lovely, a fact that annoyed her but came as no surprise given his role as the rider of the First Dragon of Yagra'hai. The absence of stairs was also expected, removed in favor of ramps and an inscribed lift. The furnishings ranged in style, more vibrant and colorful than she'd expected. The most striking feature in the room, however, was a pet firebird—a huge specimen with scintillated red and orange scales, long tail features—who groomed itself as it perched on the arm of a sofa. Despite its name, the bird was not ablaze, but its talons had left deep gouges in the sofa's wooden arm. The rest of the sofa was draped in velvet, a rich shade of red-purple.

"I want to talk about—"

"Or don't prove yourself better than a Windsong vel keeper. At least one of those would introduce themselves. They might even ask how I was doing, but I don't know that I'd want to bet on that."

She heard a noise from somewhere off to the right, something that sounded suspiciously like choked-off laughter.

"Fine," she growled. "My name is Anari. Are you having a nice day now that you've conspired to have my ward expelled on false charges?"

He regarded her in surprise. "Where have you spent the last seventeen years, Anahrod? It's done nothing for your manners." He rolled his chair over to a side table and reached for a clay pot. "Would you care for tea?"

Anahrod yanked the veil off her face. There really wasn't any point, was there? "Thank you." Habit forced the words from her. "As long as we're being so honest with each other—" She canted her neck to the side. "Kimat, you might as well come out. I know you're there."

A heavy drape moved aside as the troublesome teenager from Grayshroud revealed herself. "How did you know?" she demanded.

"I didn't. I guessed, and you confirmed it." Anahrod ignored Kimat's indignant squawk, turning back to her old teacher. "But that's not how you knew who I was."

"No," Varriguhl admitted, "but you still ball your hands into fists in the same way when you're angry but are forcing yourself to be polite."

Anahrod unclenched her fists and smoothed her palms against her thighs.

"I also don't know many guards, no matter how well paid, who will run into an active rampant zone to protect their charge. An older sister, though . . ." He paused while pouring water into the pot. She couldn't see a way to heat the water, but he was Ivarion's rider. No doubt fire magic came easily. "You know that Gwydinion's your brother, yes? I'd hate to think you just found out from me." He sounded chagrined.

"I knew," she said.

"Thank Eannis."

"How is he?" Kimat asked, sounding like she cared. "How's Gwydinion?"

"How do you think?" Anahrod said. "Feeling betrayed."

She flinched. "Tell him I'm sorry."

"No, I don't think I will."

"We had to—!" Kimat's eyes were bright.

"Kimat!" Varriguhl scolded. "That's enough."

Anahrod was feeling on the back foot, even though she didn't think she was alone in that. She sat down on the sofa next to the firebird, who promptly waddled over and shoved its head against her shoulder, demanding attention.

"Seperan likes you," Varriguhl said, then rolled his eyes. "What am I saying? Of course he does. I imagine all animals do."

"Not all," Anahrod said. "A hungry tidefisher has no friends. And I know why you're having Gwydinion expelled."

His hand froze while pulling apart a tea brick, setting the curled black strands into a strainer. "You do?"

"It's not because he cheated." Anahrod's smile was forced. "He saw you palm the test answers." She rubbed the crest on the firebird's head, eliciting a satisfied coo. "You're trying to keep him out of Neveranimas's clutches, the same way you tried with me. Which is why I'm not fighting you on it."

Varriguhl's eyes narrowed. "You're not?" He closed the teapot lid.

"You're not?" Unlike Varriguhl, Kimat sounded disappointed.

"I'm not," she repeated. "But I need two weeks."

"Impossible," Varriguhl snapped.

"Two weeks," Anahrod repeated. "You file no expulsion paperwork, nothing goes on his record, and Gwydinion and I will vanish."

"You don't have two weeks." Varriguhl wheeled over toward her. "I'm not the one who's setting the deadline here. Neveranimas wants him consecrated *tomorrow*. After that, I can delay one, maybe two days, before the interview."

"She won't be alone," Anahrod pointed out. "Interviews need interpreters. Another dragonrider, another dragon."

"And if that other dragon is a loyal lackey? Tiendremos or Aldegon?"

Anahrod froze. Would Tiendremos care?

No. No, Tiendremos would not. And Jaemeh wouldn't dare cross his dragon's will.

Varriguhl waved a hand. "It doesn't matter. Accidents happen. Especially when dragons are so very large and teenage boys are so tiny." He leaned forward in his seat. "I've arranged things with a friend in the Church. Gwydinion will be picked up and processed and his paperwork *lost*. By the time anyone realizes otherwise, your brother will be back in Crystalspire, apprenticed to a lore keeper under the wrong name." He leaned back again. "If you have another option, I'm willing to consider it, but it cannot wait two weeks. It cannot even wait one."

Anahrod closed her eyes. They couldn't do this in a day or two. Sicaryon had procrastinated retrieving the sword, thinking he couldn't be sent away if they were waiting on it. He'd had time, hadn't he? They'd had all the time they needed.

"May I ask what is so important that you'd jeopardize your brother's safety by delaying?"

She lifted her head. "You may not." She narrowed her eyes at the man, Kimat lurking nearby. "What's the relationship between you two, anyway? It can't just be the Grayshroud magistrix's daughter selling her services."

"She's my great-great-granddaughter," Varriguhl answered primly.

"Ah."

Varriguhl placed his hand against the side of the clay pot. "How did you survive your execution?"

She rubbed her neck. "Asked a flock of blood crows to catch me."

Varriguhl's eyes widened. "And that worked?"

"Sort of. Broke a lot of bones."

"But you lived." He evidently decided the tea was ready and poured out three cups. He handed two to Kimat and motioned for the girl to bring one to Anahrod.

"Yes." Anahrod murmured thanks to the girl and stared at the tea in bemused silence. It would be the sort of irony confined to stage tragedies if she reached this state only to be poisoned or drugged and turned over to Neveranimas. She sniffed the tea, detecting nothing untoward about the aroma.

She started to take a sip, then set the cup down on the table. On purpose, in part because she wanted to see their reaction. Kimat, for all her skills as a pickpocket, wasn't the best actress she'd ever met.

"What if he ran away?" she asked the headmaster.

Varriguhl paused mid-sip, swallowed. "What was that?"

"What if Gwydinion ran away? He's distraught—not even a lie—and has been given horrible news compounded with a huge mental shock. It wouldn't be difficult to believe that a teenage boy in such circumstances might run. Would *that* buy me a week?"

His eyes bored into hers. "I think . . . yes. She'll rip apart the undercity looking for him, you realize. Probably the docks, too."

"She won't find him." In some ways, this would make the heist harder, because security would be tighter . . .

She paused. No.

The weakest chain in any defense was always the people—dragon or human. Neveranimas would demand more of people who'd already spent weeks running themselves up and down cliffs. If at that point Gwydinion were to be found . . . just for a day or so . . . ?

If he went missing a second time, people would be too exhausted and sick of wild-crow chases to give matters the attention they deserved. You could silence the warning bells by making sure they never rang, or you could make them ring so often and so loud that people ignored the real alarm.

Anahrod knew what to do about Neveranimas's response time.

"You're thinking yourself very clever right now," Varriguhl commented.

"No," Anahrod responded, "just very sure about human nature. Draconic, too, I suppose." She glanced back up at the headmaster. "One week, then Gwydinion will be found. When that happens, place him under guard—for his own protection—and let Neveranimas know she can meet with him as soon as the ceremony is finished." She raised a hand. "I realize she'll want to rush things. Agree to whatever she wants. I promise Gwydinion won't make it to that meeting. Indeed, Gwydinion won't be seen in Yagra'hai again." Because if they pulled this off . . . Ris or Sicaryon both seemed like they might have sanctuaries. Gwydinion would adapt to the Deep. She had.

"You honestly think this will work?" Varriguhl seemed faintly skeptical.

"You don't know what 'this' is," Anahrod pointed out. "It won't be worse than your plans to invest him in the Church. Neveranimas wouldn't let that one fly either."

The man paused, long fingers wrapped around his cup. "Have you figured out why?"

"Why she wants us dead so badly, you mean?"

"Yes. Just so."

Anahrod looked back and forth between Kimat and her great-great-something-grandfather. She didn't know why she was trusting him now of all times, but . . .

No. She knew. Because wretched as he'd been, every action he'd ever taken made perfect sense in hindsight, from the perspective of a man trying as hard as he could to save someone's life despite themselves. Even if he had to ruin them to do it. Whatever else, he didn't want Gwydinion to die, just as he hadn't wanted her to die either.

"Eannis," Anahrod said, staring. "I'm not the first one, am I? She's killed others."

He glanced down at his tea, pressed his lips together. "Yes," he said. "Rarely often enough to seem suspicious. Around sixty years ago, I noticed children with certain blessings of Eannis never left Yagra'hai. Rampant dragons are so dangerous." He sipped his tea.

Anahrod shuddered, leaned back, and petted the firebird for a few minutes. "I'm uncertain," she admitted. "But my theory is that she thinks we can cure a rampant dragon. Not . . . not make one less likely to go rampant, the way a dragon's rider can, but stop a dragon mid-frenzy."

Varriguhl's cursing drew her attention away from the firebird. The headmaster was patting at his lap, having spilled his tea.

"Let me get you—" Kimat ran for a towel.

"Can you?" The man's voice held a desperation that Anahrod had never, ever heard before.

Of course. Ivarion.

"I don't know," she responded honestly. "I don't—" She remembered that ball of pain and hate and rage that had been Modelakast's mind. Like a condensed hurricane, so powerful that to come too close was to guarantee disaster. "I don't know that I could without destroying myself," she said. "It would be like someone who knows fire spells trying to stop a volcano from exploding."

He nodded with a bitter smile on his face. "Yes, well. Perhaps it's the potential she fears. The idea that you might one day . . . Thank you, dear." Kimat had returned with the towel. "She'll be furious if she thinks he's escaped her."

"Maybe we can do something about that, too," Anahrod said vaguely. Ris had seemed certain this heist would somehow remove Neveranimas from power. If that happened, then Gwydinion could return the following year, if he was still set on becoming a dragonrider.

It was the best she could do.

She stood up. "We have a deal, then? You never file the paperwork that says he's been expelled, and he runs away?"

The man was instantly full of bluster. "The cheating is important if—"

"He doesn't get consecrated if he's been expelled, Headmaster," Anahrod reminded him. "And no consecration means no personal interview. Neveranimas needs to think that's still happening."

"The priests are leery of performing that ceremony," Varriguhl explained. "I don't need to spell out the reason when his augury was provided by a dragon's death, do I?"

"Were the omens that inauspicious?"

He glared at her. "As long as it's just an accident, they can pretend it never happened. No priest wants to confirm those readings, though."

"That bad?"

"No, they were that good. For him, anyway."

She didn't know how she felt about that, a weird mixture of dread and pride, so she instead shoved that feeling aside. "Then don't have the consecration, just lie, and say you did. Neveranimas won't be checking to confirm your story."

"What is wrong with you?" Kimat said. "Do you actually want this to happen?"

"No, I want Neveranimas to think it's going to happen. I want her to think she's in control. Do you want Neveranimas to think she's about to lose him to some priest's cloister because you kicked him out of school? She'll kill every priest in town." She found herself frowning.

Why hadn't Neveranimas attacked the school, or rather, made a rampant dragon attack the school? Was there something special about this place beyond its headmaster and some draconic points of etiquette?

"Has a rampant dragon ever attacked the school?" she asked idly.

"Oh yes, many times." Varriguhl smirked at her. "Suspiciously often in the early days of my tenure. But this place is so riddled with underground shelters and tunnel systems we're like ants retreating into our nests. She can't kill me here. She knows it." The smile faltered somewhat. "That's why I never leave."

She contemplated what the last hundred years must have been like. Year after year of training kids to serve dragons, all the while knowing that some might be abused, but all would be dominated. Meanwhile, Neveranimas circling, picking off anyone with a chance of stopping her. She wasn't sure if she respected him for it or despised him. How many children believed their lives were ruined when in fact they'd been saved?

She retied her veil. "You have an escape plan? A way to leave the city if the situation deteriorates?"

He sniffed. "Of course."

"Good." She gave the firebird one last head scratch. "Thanks for the tea. I'll return tomorrow morning to give you the bad news about Gwydinion's reaction to recent events." She gave Kimat one last appraising look. The girl was in danger of forgetting she didn't date fifteen-year-olds. Probably for the best that the teenagers didn't have time for anything serious.

"I'll tell him you're sorry," she said, just before leaving.

38

DEPENDENCIES

Claw paced the room. The full crew was there, including Jaemeh, although he was still injured. Fresh injuries, Anahrod noted. He looked like he'd been thrown down a flight of stairs or lost a fight against a wall. When pressed for an explanation, he'd demurred, saying he healed fast and it was his own fault for being so clumsy, anyway.

Even Gwydinion was present—he had to be.

Claw faced Anahrod. "Did it occur to you to check in with us before you made a decision that jeopardized the entire plan? Did it?"

Anahrod gazed at the woman calmly. "It also occurred to me that by the time I did, the opportunity would've passed. I had to reach Varriguhl before he made the expulsion official."

"So, I'm not expelled," Gwydinion said, "but it doesn't matter, because in a week we're running away?"

"We're escaping," Anahrod said, "not running. And you're not expelled, so in a year or two, you can return. If it's safe."

"The duplicate sword won't be ready in a week!" Claw screamed. "We don't even know if his damn sword will be here." She pointed at Sicaryon.

"My sword arrives the day after tomorrow," Sicaryon responded. "And technically speaking, we don't need your sword."

"Wait," Jaemeh said. "There's more than one sword?"

"Yes," Ris stopped chewing on a nail to say. "And we need all of them."

Sicaryon was undeterred. "We'll have all of them just as soon as we steal the one from Brauge's parlor. We won't have the duplicate, but does that matter, since we're running, anyway?"

Anahrod laughed. "It helps us. We want as many alarms, alerts, and problems triggering at the same time as possible. If we can't tackle this with careful planning, let's try pure chaos instead."

Ris smiled around the thumb she was biting. She pulled her thumb free with a pop. "You just might have saved this. I should kiss you."

"Later," Anahrod said.

"Boss!" Claw was still distraught.

Anahrod understood. She really did. Claw had put a lot of work into infiltrating the Brauge household, stealing the sword rubbings, organizing the manufacturer of a counterfeit. Changing plans so none of that was necessary negated all her hard work.

Ris pointed at Kaibren. "Inscriptions and folding boxes ready?" He nodded.

Next was Naeron. "Climbing gear?"

"No," the man replied, "but in three days? Yes."

"Good enough. Am I forgetting anything?" Ris asked the group.

"Yes," Claw said. "How the fuck we're going to get Brauge to open her front door!"

"He's going to do that." Ris hooked a thumb in Sicaryon's direction, grinning.

The Scarsea king straightened. "I'm sorry. Why is she opening the door to me?"

"Because you are a sexy bastard," Ris said, "and because she's lonely. Officially you'll be—" She dramatically pondered for a moment, forefinger to chin, then turned to Kaibren. "Poet, you think?"

Kaibren nodded. "A gift's true worth is oft lost in wrapping's art."

Sicaryon stared at him, narrow-eyed. "Did you just insult me? Because I feel like you just insulted me."

"She's not going to notice you can't rhyme," Claw translated, "because she's going to be too busy staring at your ass." She made a show of tilting her head as if looking behind him, although the angle was wrong. "Which—fair."

Sicaryon scowled. "And what? I'm supposed to slip the drug into her drink?"

"No," Anahrod said. "You're distracting her. I'm slipping the drug into her drink."

He raised an eyebrow at her. "You'll be with me?"

"It can't be Kaibren, Naeron wouldn't be believable, Ris and Jaemeh are both dragonriders, no way in hell is Gwydinion going, and Claw will be recognized. So yes." She pursed her lips. "How complicated is that inscription you used to knock out everyone at the guesthouse back in Duskcloud?"

"Very," Sicaryon said, "so I can't draw it in silverpoint on the lady's chalice while she isn't looking."

"We could steam off a wine label," Gwydinion suggested. "Draw it on the inside and then glue it back in place."

Everyone paused to look at the teenager, who fidgeted. "What?"

"That would work," Anahrod said.

Sicaryon pointed. "Has he always been this terrifying—?"

"Oh yeah," Ris said, while the others all nodded in agreement.

"What do you need me to do?" Jaemeh said then.

He'd been so uncharacteristically quiet that Anahrod had almost forgotten he was there.

"Heal," Ris told him. "You have one week. Keep your ears open for any new security procedures that might cause us a problem." She paused. "The cutter's ready, isn't it?"

"It is," Jaemeh agreed. "Pier 7, berth 23. That's where we'll meet when the job's done."

"All right," Ris said. "Then let's get ready."

As everyone else filed out, Anahrod turned to Gwydinion. "You're staying in your room, understand? This whole plan falls apart if you're found early."

"I'm not a child," Gwydinion said. "I understand how important it is."

"Good," Anahrod said. "Grab some snacks from the kitchen. I'll be back later with dinner to keep you company."

Gwydinion blinked. "What? You're not staying with me now?"

"Apologies," Anahrod said, "but I need to talk to some birds."

❧

Several things happened over the next week.

Gwydinion Doreyl, traumatized from the recent rampant attack, ran away from the school. Neveranimas didn't turn out every force in the city to find the boy. In hindsight, that made sense: it would've looked too odd. Every guard had a drawing of his likeness, though, and rumors spoke of wide-net sweeps (for criminals, of course) in the undercity's poorer areas. The dragon was looking—and spending significant resources in doing so.

Good.

A courier dropped off Sicaryon's sword at the school administrative center two days later. The sword arrived in a flat wooden box wrapped in paper, neatly labeled, and stamped with the Seven Crests seal.

Ris stared at Sicaryon. "You mailed it? You *mailed* the fifth sword?"

Sicaryon shrugged. "Safest way. The delivery couriers are all screened, and it's not illegal to deliver an antique." He flipped the latches on the box and opened it. "I will remind you that this is fragile."

Anahrod reached out and touched the blade. It was a beautiful sword, gracefully curving, with beasts picked out in bas-relief on the blade. It also looked like it would break the next time someone used it to butter toast.

"I'm aware," Ris said. "All of them are, except for mine. They haven't been maintained—the magic's been eating away at it for close to a hundred years.

The first time we use these to open the lock will also be the last, because half the swords will shatter on the spot."

Sicaryon sighed. "You didn't say that when I agreed to this."

Ris smirked. "That's because you would've said no."

The look on his face suggested he would be inventing new curse words to use on Ris for the rest of the morning.

And lastly, Yagra'hai was overcome with a plague.

Not the disease kind of plague. The animal kind. Two unseasonal, large infestations gripped the city: scrabbers and blood crows.

Neither of which had been easy to arrange. Anahrod had always struggled to control animal groups, but she found she could cheat by targeting pack leaders. Neveranimas had to feel like she wasn't special, wasn't being singled out. She couldn't be the only dragon who found scrabber eggs in her vault entrance, the only one with blood crows heckling her. Once established, Anahrod found it relatively simple to gain the information she needed.

For example: Neveranimas could teleport from the elder dragon council chambers to her own estate in five seconds.

Anahrod also learned that Neveranimas had added alarms to the Five Locks Division's original work. After the third time an animal triggered the alarms, that delay turned into thirty seconds. By the seventh, Neveranimas took three minutes to respond. By the twelfth time, fifteen minutes. Then she began sending other dragons, unwilling to waste her time on nonsense.

Neveranimas would get around to updating those wards. At the very least, she'd rewrite them to exclude scrabbers and blood crows (itself a vulnerability that Anahrod could've exploited under other circumstances). In the meantime, Neveranimas was dealing with disasters of her own making: the rampant attack aftermath, the animal infestations, the heightened security, the humans and dragons both complaining.

Somewhere in all that, Neveranimas needed to find the time to kill a fifteen-year-old boy. There just weren't enough hours in the day.

Anahrod sympathized.

Technically speaking, Gwydinion was allowed anywhere in the apartments, but they all thought it was safer he stayed in his room. Everyone but Jaemeh dropped by at one point or another, aware that the boy was restless. They played cards and told stories. Kaibren taught him how to draw an inscription that functioned as a reliable compass. Sicaryon shared a few choice phrases in Sumulye.

Anahrod slept in Gwydinion's room, and neither Sicaryon nor Ris were foolish enough to suggest she alter that arrangement.

The pair also took time for a brother-sister group family project, namely brewing up a batch of sedative for Brauge.

She knew several recipes that would work, but for the sort of sleeping draught that a dragonrider wouldn't realize had affected her later, there was only one: daervi powder. Fortunately for her, Belsaor the alchemist had sent along an excessive amount of alchemy supplies.

Daervi powder was easily manufactured and undetectable when taken in alcohol. Other potions were faster but more obvious.

They made two batches, just in case they might need a spare. If everything went well, she wouldn't need them—using the inscribed wine bottle to knock out Brauge would be ideal, especially as people sometimes had odd reactions to herbal sedatives.

Five days, and then Gwydinion quietly presented himself to Headmaster Varriguhl, looking small and vulnerable and very dirty, to beg forgiveness. He was sent back to his assigned apartment with Sicaryon and Anahrod ordered to keep him under guard.

Later, a note was delivered with little fanfare.

It read: *Interview tonight in Neveranimas's office, 9th bells.*

Now they had a time for the robbery.

39

LONELY PEOPLE

"We're fine doing this at night?" Claw asked, later.

"Absolutely," Ris said. "She's doing us a favor. I'd hate to spend all this energy avoiding the attention of various dragons only to have some eight-year-old point us out and say, 'Mommy, Mommy, what are those people doing in that well?'"

Anahrod winced. She was trying not to remember that the evening would see her hanging over a long drop by a slender rope.

"Once we've taken what we need," Claw said, "we'll need to move. No way to know how long our dragonrider girl will be out."

"If she drinks from the wine bottle," Sicaryon said, "then she will be out for exactly eight hours. No more, no less, like magic. If not—" He glanced in Anahrod's direction.

"That depends," Anahrod said, "but the larger the dosage, the greater the risk of a medical complication. I recommend no more than an hour."

Ris nodded. "More than enough."

"Lucky it's the backup plan. Because . . ." Claw grinned at everyone's raised eyebrows. She reached under the table and pulled out an old, carefully polished curved sword.

"You—what—" Ris floundered for something to say.

"Worth it just to see you that speechless," Claw cackled.

"The blacksmith finished it in time?" Anahrod asked.

"No." Naeron rolled his eyes.

Anahrod gave him a grateful nod, even as Claw stuck her tongue out at Naeron for spoiling her fun.

"It's not finished. I found this in a pawnshop and had Kaibren inscribe it. Does a good job, though, don't you think?" She looked proud of herself.

"Having not seen the original sword, I can't say for sure," Sicaryon said, "but it seems impressive."

"It's an illusion," Claw said. "It'll last longer than Anahrod's drug potion, but not as long as Sicaryon's wine bottle." She shrugged. "Long enough."

"I knew I kept you around for a reason," Ris murmured.

"Night is that joy of sin, that beauty of dark thoughts, and mystery of secrets;

such that no thought that sneaks about under its cover is pure or bright or shining," Kaibren said.

Ris tilted her head. "Did you just quote a line from *Daughter of Darkness*?"

Kaibren shrugged.

Right. *Daughter of Darkness*. That play was about her, wasn't it? No wonder Claw was so pleased.

"Anyway," the Blackglass woman said when she finally stopped laughing, "what Kaibren means is that Brauge is more likely to commit a few indiscretions if it's late." Claw squinted at Anahrod. "You said the drug has to be given in wine?"

"Something alcoholic," Anahrod corrected. "Distilled spirits would be better than wine. His job"—she pointed at Sicaryon—"will be to either convince her to drink from our bottle or distract her for long enough so I can slip a dose into her glass."

"What about the rest of us?" Ris said. "Are we doing anything?" Her tone was clipped. Her smile forced.

Anahrod tilted her head. She wasn't sure if the woman was actively jealous or just so used to being at the center of every event that she didn't know what to do with herself in other situations.

Or maybe she was just worried.

"You're waiting for us at the ready site," Anahrod reminded the rest of the group. "Once we're done with Brauge's, we will meet you there."

"One change," Ris said.

Anahrod paused. "Yes?"

"Gwydinion will help us with the keys. I want you with Jaemeh in the vault."

Gwydinion said "Yes!" in the background, while Anahrod and Jaemeh both looked indignant. "Excuse me?" Anahrod said.

"You don't trust me—" Jaemeh said.

Ris pressed her lips together. "Two things." She held up the appropriate number of fingers. "First, putting Anahrod on the ground does exactly that— puts her *on the ground*. The less time she spends hanging over a lake of magma, the better she's going to be."

"Lake of what?" Gwydinion said, suddenly not whooping.

Ris ignored him. "Second, she's been there before. She'll have an easier time finding the secret entrance to the vault we really want. And we need you there to communicate with your dragon and thus warn us if anything goes wrong. It's not a matter of trust."

Anahrod raised an eyebrow at Ris, outside of Jaemeh's view. They were still playing the "don't let Tiendremos know" game. That was . . . interesting.

[Peralon, why are we changing plans?]

"Fantastic," Sicaryon said. "So, it'll be the three of us."

[We're not.]

"Uh, no," Ris said.

[Then why am I suddenly going into the vault?]

"Uh, yes," Sicaryon responded. "Not open for debate."

[Because we need something found, and we can't trust Jaemeh.]

Ris and Sicaryon stared at each other.

Anahrod waited for Peralon to give more details. She sighed. She had some suspicions about where Ris might have picked up some of her bad habits.

"All right," Ris said. "Might as well."

Anahrod's mouth quirked. Ris had given up much too easily.

[Well? Are you going to give me any more information to go off than "something"?]

[I will. Soon. Trust *me*. I promise we're not leaving you in darkness.]

"I'm fine with both of them," Jaemeh said. "More hands to carry my diamonds." He picked up a coil of rope. "Let's start setting up. Once this ball gets rolling, we won't have time to stop for supplies."

⌄

"Why did you insist on coming with us to the vault?" Anahrod asked Sicaryon later. Brauge's estate was on the other side of Yagra'hai—too far for them to walk or use the tunnels. So they rode in the back of a rented flyer, in theory safe from eavesdropping. In theory.

"I told you," Sicaryon said. "I don't trust them, especially Jaemeh." He paused. "Scratch that. I especially don't trust Tiendremos."

Anahrod studied the man. "Neither does Ris, I think. I can talk to Peralon. If Tiendremos tries to double-cross us, we'll know—although if he wanted to betray us to Neveranimas, there were better opportunities."

"Fair."

It didn't take long to arrive at Zentoazax's estate.

Most of the estate consisted of stepped terraces for raising domesticated herds for the dragons. The main house was a large, intricate mansion built in the Windsong style. Anahrod doubted it was the original construction.

"The house looks new," she commented. "I wonder who lived here before?"

"The Baojhyr family," Sicaryon answered. When she looked at him in surprise, he shrugged. "I had nothing else to do, so I researched."

"Oh."

"Funny thing," he continued, "they were part of a division called the Five Locks."

Anahrod froze. "Is that so?"

"Rampant dragon attack," Sicaryon said. "Electrocuted everyone, very tragic. Also, a funny thing, the youngest daughter of the family—presumed dead—was named Maevris. 'Ris' for short."

"Poor Ris," she murmured, but it's not like she hadn't known it was personal. Ris had told her from the start this was about revenge. "Wait. Electrocuted everyone? It was a storm dragon?"

"See, that's the other reason I didn't want you going down into the vault alone with Jaemeh."

Her gut twisted. "No."

"Yes," he said. "One of the few times when a 'rampant' dragon"—he used finger quotes—"made a full recovery. Positively miraculous. Apparently, his rider valiantly sacrificed her life to save Tiendremos. An example for every dragonrider, truly."

"And people believed that load of garbage? Fuck."

If Tiendremos had been involved with helping Neveranimas wipe out the Five Locks . . . well. No wonder Ris had been so insistent Jaemeh never be told. Because if Tiendremos knew that the robbery was being perpetrated by living descendants of the Five Locks, it wouldn't be such a stretch to guess that Neveranimas might not be the only target marked for revenge.

And Ris *was* targeting Tiendremos. Anahrod just wasn't sure exactly how she planned to do it.

He said, "While Ris is all kinds of intriguing and sexy and fantastic in bed, I can't be sure—I can't take the risk—that her need for revenge outweighs your safety."

"No, I don't think so."

He blinked at her. "What do you mean?"

"I mean that while you all were arguing it out, Peralon was talking to me. Ris and Peralon are looking for something, it's not diamonds, and they want me to find it before Jaemeh does. Ris wants someone she can trust."

Sicaryon didn't move. He studied her in the darkness of the carriage. "Are you? Someone she can trust?"

"I think I just might be, yes." Anahrod pulled a small journal from under her mantle, as well as a sharpened charcoal stick.

Sicaryon raised an eyebrow.

"I'm your assistant, remember?" She'd pulled her hair back in an unflattering style and based her clothing on what she'd seen worn by university students in Duskcloud.

Anahrod bounded from the flyer when it landed, holding out a hand for Sicaryon. He stepped down, his expression sublimely bored.

Arriving by flyer wasn't at all the same as arriving by carriage. A carriage might be ignored at the gate, but a flyer landed inside the walls, often on the roof. So even though their arrival was unexpected, servants still came immediately, offering Sicaryon and Anahrod a bowl of water to wash their hands.

"I am here to see Naryae," Sicaryon announced. "Please inform her that the poet Galav Wordsong has arrived." He sounded imperious.

Anahrod thought he was laying it on a bit thick.

The dragonrider, Brauge, arrived soon after.

She was the sort of person capable of hiking a herd animal over her shoulders and delivering it to her dragon personally, who could crush a man with her thighs, both figuratively and literally.

Next to Anahrod, Sicaryon gulped.

"Greetings!" Brauge held out her arms, grinning widely. "No one named Naryae lives here, and I have no idea who you are!" She grabbed Sicaryon's hands between her own in greeting, possibly breaking fingers in the process. "I'm Brauge. It's a pleasure. My, you have beautiful eyes, don't you? I bet you have crap night vision, though. You said you were a poet? Why don't you come inside?"

Brauge began herding Sicaryon inside before Anahrod said a word. The woman was . . . overwhelming. Anahrod mentally readjusted the dosage she'd need to use.

"What poems do you write? Is this Naryae a patron? You know, if the goddess has seen fit to drop you on my doorstep, you are honor bound to stay. Those are the rules!" Brauge threw her head back and laughed. She was louder than Overbite's roar, but only because Overbite's roar mostly fell outside the range of human hearing.

While Sicaryon looked like he'd just been stampeded by rock wyrms, Anahrod stepped forward and bowed. "Honored Rider Brauge, we apologize for the error that brought us to your estate. The pilot must've made a mistake. In apologies, we would present you with this wine from the Honey Cemor Division of Snowfell."

The woman's grin faltered. "Ah," she said. "Your gift is most appreciated. Thank you. But please, let me bring you someplace more comfortable than this hallway. I'd love to hear your master's poetry."

Anahrod looked inquiringly at Sicaryon, who nodded once in response. She could tell he was panicking, though. They hadn't brought Kaibren because they'd thought someone younger would be more successful. That was only true, however, if Brauge was more interested in the poet than in the poetry.

Anahrod glanced at the woman's rings. Leaves, available, not in a relationship. The theory had been sound.

"Very well," Anahrod said to Brauge. "After you."

Brauge never stopped talking—about what a serendipitous honor this was (whether an honor for Brauge or for "Galav Wordsong" was unclear), how long Brauge had been a rider (roughly forty years), that her family were all riders, that her dragon, Zentoazax, was the best dragon that had ever lived.

"What does your dragon hoard, Honored Rider?"

"Helmets!"

Anahrod made a hmm sound and wrote that down in her notebook.

"I assume you've already eaten," Brauge said, "but if you'd like an after-dinner amusement, I'd be happy to oblige."

Sicaryon held up his bottle. "I would like this, but I brought enough to share."

Again, the dragonrider's expression flickered. "Oh."

Something was wrong.

"My sincerest apologies." Brauge's eyes shifted from Sicaryon's face to the bottle. "But Zentoazax doesn't like it when I drink alcohol, so I've quit." A dash of resentment peeked out from behind her faux embarrassment. "Apparently, I'm not a nice drunk, and with the recent unpleasantness, he's concerned."

Anahrod stopped walking. Sicaryon did likewise.

She'd suspected Brauge might be too paranoid to drink wine brought by two uninvited strangers. Anahrod hadn't been prepared for—hadn't even given thought to—the idea that Brauge no longer drank alcohol at all.

[We have a problem,] Anahrod told Peralon. [The rider doesn't drink alcohol.]

[Really? I remember her as being a notorious lush.]

[Yes. I suspect that's why she doesn't do it anymore.]

"How embarrassing," Sicaryon said. "I had meant to present this to someone who is a great connoisseur, Honored Rider. I'd never have dreamed of bringing it to you, had I come here intentionally. What a shame; it's a rare vintage."

Anahrod had to fight not to give Sicaryon a dirty look. He knew what he was doing. It was one thing to invite the dragonrider for a drink—even to seduction—but this felt malicious and manipulative. Sordid.

The woman shuddered. "No, no. There's no embarrassment. It's just impossible. My dragon would never forgive me, you see." She then continued walking, assuming no further explanation would be necessary.

True enough. Who wouldn't understand that a dragonrider must obey every whim of their dragon, after all?

They had a problem. Anahrod cast about for a way of working around the issue. She could slip the herbal mixture she brought into something else—some sweet vinegar water, perhaps, but it was only truly tasteless in alcohol. And that was no longer an option.

Anahrod couldn't even try to slip something into food, because it was well after dinner. And they needed to hurry if they wanted to make the nine-bell window given by Neveranimas.

The manor house was majestic by candlelight, which flickered against the walls, revealing beautiful tapestries and comfortable sitting areas. The lightning flashed from the storm outside to brighten the rooms like a stage performer changing to a new scene.

Perhaps it was best Ris hadn't come along, though, because Anahrod had a nasty suspicion that they had looted half the furnishings from the previous owners. What Ris would do if she came face-to-face with a person cheerfully sitting on her murdered family's stolen furniture was anyone's guess, but Anahrod suspected it would involve blood and lots of it.

They ended up in the parlor, sitting on Brauge's stolen antique furniture, next to a cheerfully burning fireplace. The very sword they'd come to steal hung over the mantel, looking like a war trophy.

The servants brought in tea, boiled sweets, and pastries. Anahrod pretended to write while Sicaryon flirted shamelessly to avoid having to quote poetry.

In the distance, an animal cried out in distress, almost lost under the peals of thunder that shook the building foundations. It wasn't raining, per se, but Brauge's estate was close to the eyewall to ensure the sound was a constant melody in the background.

Not long after, someone in rough, rain-soaked leathers rushed in. Anahrod eyed the muddy boots and changed her mind about whether it was raining outside. The man paid no attention at all to the muck he tracked across the dragonrider's carpets while he whispered in the dragonrider's ear. Brauge's face turned ash gray.

"My apologies," the woman said, standing. "But it seems lightning hit one of the nearby fields and has caused a stampede. Please make yourself comfortable and ask the servants if you should need anything. I'll be back soon." She wagged a finger at Sicaryon. "I want to hear those poems!"

She followed the farm hand out the door, leaving the two alone.

Sicaryon and Anahrod looked at each other for a moment.

Then up to the mantel and the sword.

PART EIGHT

THE
FIVE
LOCKS
JOB

40

THE HEIST

Later, when their flyer returned, Ris, Claw, Kaibren, Jaemeh, and Gwydinion waited. Gwydinion was grinning wickedly.

"Did it work? Did you get it?" he asked before either Sicaryon or Anahrod could say a word.

Anahrod stopped. "You."

The boy smiled harder. "Wouldn't take much to make a herd panic so close to a major storm."

Ris ruffled the boy's hair. "I'm so proud of our son."

He rolled his eyes as he ducked away from her hand. "I'm not your son, you know."

"Oh, no," Ris said. "I've adopted you. It's already decided. I'll be letting your parents know later."

"A famine in the land, a feast on the table, yet the lady calls for a song," Kaibren said.

Claw barked out a laugh. "He said: You got the key, didn't you?"

Anahrod pulled Gwydinion's folding box out from under her mantle, unfolded it, and removed the stolen blade.

It looked ancient. Like something that should indeed be hung up over a mantel rather than ever being used for violence. It looked far older than the hundred years that Ris claimed, eaten away by the magic it empowered.

"That's what we need?" Jaemeh asked. He frowned. "Why do we need this, again?"

"Because it's the key," Ris explained, "to opening a very special lock." She was grinning with maniacal intensity, something in her eyes suggesting that it would be a terrible idea to be someone who might try to stop Ris at that moment. Nothing was going to stop her.

Nothing and no one.

"So . . . what happens next?" Jaemeh asked.

"The fun part," Ris said reverently. "Let's rob that bitch blind."

Kaibren made them uniforms.

Anahrod hadn't expected uniforms, but he'd used the same template for everyone, to make his job easier.

The outfits covered them fully, from gloves to a thin gauze over the eyes, all designed to keep them from baking to death. The only variation was in color.

Ris's was deep maroon, Claw's a dark gray, Kaibren's indigo, Sicaryon's dark violet, Naeron's bloodred, Gwydinion's teal, and Anahrod's green. Kaibren had put both her and Sicaryon in their skin-paint colors, although she couldn't say whether that was a sign of respect or mockery.

The steam vent was a circular pit fifty feet in diameter—easy for an average dragon to enter, verging on impossible for someone like Tiendremos.

Yagra was volcanic, as were several of Seven Crests' mountains. Legend had it that the pact between humans and dragons involved a promise of protection against the volcanoes. Anahrod believed it, since the volcanoes that dragons called their homes had a curious tendency to either not erupt or do so in only the gentlest and most well-behaved ways. She suspected artificial vents such as this one existed to release pressure, but the dragons weren't in the habit of confirming such suspicions.

Jaemeh, Kaibren, and Naeron had snuck over to Neveranimas's estate earlier in the day, hammering in pitons and leaving ready neat piles of rope under tarps. Now all they had to do was show up, uncoil it all, hook in, and drop down.

Anahrod tried not to think about the length of drop down.

She failed.

If Anahrod had been under any illusion that she'd concealed her anxiety, it broke quickly as Ris put a hand on her shoulder. "You're going to be all right?"

Anahrod nodded. "Don't even have to drop until you've already unlocked the door. It'll be fine."

"Really?"

"Do I have a choice?" she whispered back. "You're not telling me everything, are you?"

Ris glanced in Jaemeh's direction, but he was busy clipping in his ropes.

"Peralon will tell you what to do." Ris kissed the tips of Anahrod's gloved fingers.

"If you two are done flirting, can we get on with this?" Jaemeh snapped. "We're on the clock, you know."

His annoyance engendered in Anahrod a fervent desire to pull her mask off and really kiss Ris, but he also wasn't wrong. They didn't have time.

Anahrod double-checked Sicaryon's lines to make sure he'd tied them off correctly, checked her own, and waited for the others to drop.

There'd never been a Seven Crests child who didn't know how to climb a mountain, and Ris and Naeron seemed comfortable enough. Sicaryon was the most at risk, which is why Anahrod planned to spot him the whole way.

Claw and Kaibren lowered themselves first, followed by Ris, Gwydinion, and Naeron. Ris carried all five swords, although "carry" in her case meant telekinetically lifting each one in the air behind her, like some kind of beautiful dark war goddess.

"Push!" Ris cried out from below. "To your right, push!"

For a good thirty seconds, nothing happened, then Ris shouted, "It's open. Come down."

Anahrod dropped over the side.

She didn't feel warm, but that just meant Kaibren's inscriptions were doing their job. She rappelled down until she reached the lock itself.

And that was it. All she needed to do. The whole thing took so little effort that she was left reeling, not by her phobia, but purely because it should've been some sort of epic, fantastical feat or gesture.

Little victories, she supposed.

The lock was much prettier than she'd expected. Beautifully crafted, for no reason other than aesthetics. Arabesques and traceries curling outward, flower-like, surrounded the five slots in the wall—the perfect size to sheath five large talons or swords, embossed into the rock itself. The angle was such that neither a human nor a dragon could see it from above.

Ris placed a sword in each slot. The five chosen people grabbed a hilt, and all five rotated their hilts in the same direction.

A single black doorway appeared in the rock face above the lock. Anahrod didn't think it had been visible before, and suspected it wouldn't be visible to a dragon using the lock either.

That strongly implied that either Neveranimas never exited her vault this way, or the door would automatically shut behind them.

That was fine. They wouldn't be exiting this way either.

The door being so close to the top increased her fall potential. If someone cut her rope, if she should plummet . . . A wave of dizziness overcame her.

"Stop it," Jaemeh hissed at her. "Don't you dare lose your nerve."

She shook herself and continued lowering herself downward. "You know just what to say to a girl."

Below her, Sicaryon chuckled. "Yeah, a real charmer."

Jaemeh ignored them both.

The dark doorway led to a hallway and stairs, all just tall enough and wide enough for a single person to walk. Sicaryon and Anahrod both pulled out the light lockets that Kaibren had made for them, while Jaemeh surrounded a hand with electricity, the blue arcs lighting the air.

Anahrod had not given sufficient thought to how many stairs there would be. She stopped counting flights, only telling herself to be grateful they didn't have to leave this way. It was a toss-up who fared best in descending the stairs. Sicaryon and Anahrod seemed in better shape than Jaemeh, but he was better adjusted to the thinner air.

[Are you all right?] Peralon asked.

[Fine,] she thought. [Just descending the endless staircase.]

[Good. Ris was worrying.]

The light up ahead stopped bouncing off the narrow tunnel walls and diffused: they'd reached the end of the tunnel.

[We're here.]

They debouched into a marble-lined room—medium-sized for a dragon and enormous for a human. Shelves lined the room, upon which rested the dragonstones that Neveranimas officially collected. Most of them were amethysts, but a few other stones were also present, including a few oddities like marble or rainbow feldspar. On the far side of the room, a large archway led to the Hall of Death and the "official" front entrance of the vault. A pattern of intertwined star shapes framed the archway from ceiling to floor. A section along the floor deactivated the traps.

She also noted the section that reactivated the traps, closed the doors, reset the locks (except for the Five Locks' secret door, which reset automatically). Fortunately, it was high on the archway and not easily triggered.

"We're looking for the fifth—" Anahrod pointed. "Fifth bookcase on the right. There it is. We need to push it toward the archway, and that should unlock the secret vault."

"Nice," Jaemeh said.

All three of them pushed the bookcase. It moved easily, making only a faint scraping sound. The room beyond was smaller, but again, small for a dragon was not small for a human.

However, that wasn't the problem.

"Where are the fucking diamonds?" Jaemeh asked.

Anahrod stepped forward, frowning.

What lay beyond looked less like a hoard than a museum. Each piece had been meticulously organized, labeled, and displayed. Certain items were elevated on plinths or pedestals for better display.

But Jaemeh was right. No diamonds.

There were gems. One pedestal contained a bowl filled with bright uncut rocks that might've been sapphires, emeralds, and other corundum. She didn't think they were diamonds—besides being exceptionally vivid, they didn't have the right eight-sided shape. Something about these stones seemed artificial and somehow creepy, although she couldn't explain why. She put a rock back in its bowl and kept looking.

There were daggers and a wicked-looking black sword. She noted an odd, silvery rectangle that looked like a failed attempt to make a mirror, but any time she looked away, it seemed to shift. Human-style books filled another set of shelves, some crumbling, and others pristine. One book was bound in rune-covered black metal, with a screaming skull on the cover. She noticed a blood-soaked set of clothing, sized for a child.

"If I may be so bold," Sicaryon said, "what the fuck?"

[Anahrod,] Peralon whispered in her mind, [you're looking for a dragon-stone. Probably amethyst, but I can't guarantee it. It will probably be in this room. Once you find it, take possession of it and under no circumstances allow Jaemeh to have it.]

[A dragonstone? You realize that's what she hoards, don't you?]

[This one won't be just a book.]

"No kidding, what the fuck," Jaemeh agreed with great depth of feeling.

"Keep looking," Anahrod said. "We're missing something."

Right, she thought, like the fact there aren't any diamonds. She cursed Ris. Had there *ever* been any diamonds?

This was exactly the sort of thing Ris should've trusted her to know.

She kept looking. She found a mangled gold necklace sized for a dragon, set with rubies. Crowns, both dragon- and human-sized, peasant shirts, maps written on vellum, a globe with another map carefully pasted to cover it completely. She did not see a dragonstone.

Jaemeh picked up a book, flipped through the pages, and then dropped it as though it burned.

"What was that?" Sicaryon asked him.

"A hymnal to Zavad," Jaemeh answered. "I don't understand this. She's a Zavad worshiper?"

"I don't think so." Anahrod eyed a large crown, then blinked as her perception shifted and she identified it as a dragon's ring. What she had taken for rust was blood, long since dried to a powder. Now that she thought about it, almost everything in the room was damaged or defaced in some manner.

Almost everything.

"So, what's the theme?" Sicaryon asked. "Dragons always collect to a theme, right? What is this—stuff people wore when they died?" He was examining a wall covered in different styles of armor.

"Huh. I wonder what this is doing here instead of in the first room?" Jaemeh said.

Anahrod whirled around. Jaemeh stood on the other side of the room, holding a large amethyst dragonstone with both hands.

Of all the unlucky . . . "Any more of them over there?"

He shook his head. "This is the only one."

She tried to stay calm as she held out her hand. She didn't know why Peralon wanted the damn thing, but if she had to weigh her trust for Ris and Peralon against her trust for Tiendremos and Jaemeh, the winner was obvious. "May I see it? It is odd that it's the only one in this room."

"Haha!" Sicaryon shouted as he did something with a giant helmet, and a wall slid away. The room beyond glittered with gems—some cut, some uncut, some white, but others in colors of champagne, pink, red, green, or even blue.

Piles and piles of gemstones.

❯

[Peralon, we found the diamonds.]

There was a pause. [That's wonderful. Do you have the front path open? I'll tell Ris to start sending everyone down to pack the folding boxes.]

Anahrod swallowed. She knew, knew as soon as she felt the delay, that he hadn't really known if the diamonds would be there. None of Ris's floor plans had hinted at a third secret space . . .

Secret . . .

Anahrod pulled a paper book down from the shelf. She flipped it open and found neat rows of numbers and notations written down the side. Meaningless to her, but she bet someone out there would've killed to keep anyone from seeing it.

"She collects secrets!" Anahrod called out. This made perfect sense. In this room, Neveranimas had collected evidence of murders, affairs, thefts, heresy, larceny, and every shame experienced by human or dragon. Neveranimas probably kept patent recipes and inscription designs, too.

"That's great," Jaemeh said in the condescending tone of someone who didn't care and thought it silly that Anahrod did. "Now, will you please help us load these boxes?"

She gave the bookcase a longing glance, but since they didn't have time to waste, hurried over to help him dump diamonds into an open folding box. She wondered if they'd have enough boxes, despite the extras Kaibren had crafted.

Claw was right: they were about to become very rich.

Sicaryon was the first to finish, folding his box back to a smaller size and lifting it with visible effort. He laughed. "You may not want to load these up as heavy," he warned. "They don't lighten weight, do they?"

Anahrod shook her head. "No." She glanced at where Jaemeh had set down the dragonstone, but she couldn't see it.

"You've shut off all the traps, right?" Sicaryon asked.

She nodded. "Hall of Death is clear."

"Then I'll be right back with everyone else."

Jaemeh gave a distracted nod and continued shoveling diamonds.

[Peralon, Jaemeh found the stone before I did.] She could almost hear the dragon equivalent of cursing on the other side.

[But he hasn't used it yet, has he?]

[No, I don't think so. Why?]

No answer.

The others started trickling in, but Anahrod didn't want to leave Jaemeh alone, so she handed off a box to Claw and continued working. Jaemeh did the same, each working faster as a result. She still couldn't tell what Jaemeh had done with the dragonstone, though.

Because the boxes were heavy, it took longer to leave than to return. There came a point where Jaemeh and Anahrod were alone again.

"We're almost done," Anahrod said. "Just these two boxes left."

[Peralon, tell the others to stay put. We're bringing out the last two boxes.]

"Nice." Jaemeh started closing his box.

Anahrod kept her voice friendly, nonchalant. "Hey, where'd you put that dragonstone?"

"This one?" He reached behind him. He'd been sitting on the damn thing like an egg. "You wanted to look? I haven't had a chance to, yet. I forgot I had it." He rolled the stone over to Anahrod.

She picked up the stone. It looked exactly like the dragonstone that Peralon had given her, except it was an amethyst.

She wondered why Peralon had been so insistent that Jaemeh didn't see it. The warning seemed unnecessary. Jaemeh hadn't even tried.

Just before she slipped into the stone's memory space, she glanced up at Jaemeh. He stared back at her with a grim expression on his face, one of iron determination.

She realized she'd made a mistake.

This wasn't like the ride back from the *Crimson Skies*—Tiendremos didn't need her anymore. She'd served her purpose. Anahrod tried to abort the attempt, drop the stone.

But it was too late.

Her universe vanished, replaced by Neveranimas's.

WHILE SHE SLEPT

Later, Anahrod would be told that it went like this:

The team had been loading boxes for the last time when they'd heard a scream from the far side of the Hall of Death. Several tons of stone slammed down with a force that echoed, shook the floors. Not all of them understood, for several grim, drawn-out seconds, that the vault door had slammed shut.

Kaibren had understood, though. He ran *back*, likely in the hope he could somehow raise the slab again.

Meanwhile, Jaemeh was running forward, screaming, "Run! Go! Go! It's all been reset! Do you hear me? It's reset!"

One minute had seemed more than sufficient to cross a trapped hallway, but the timing had been meant to give a dragon time to traverse the area safely, not humans. Distances were correspondingly multiplied.

Some of them were lucky. Naeron and Claw had already been on the stairs; Ris had been waiting next to Peralon outside.

That had left Jaemeh, Gwydinion, Claw, and Kaibren in the Hall of Death. Jaemeh, Claw, and Gwydinion were all young, fit, and fast runners.

Kaibren was none of those things. For a few fateful seconds, he'd even been running the wrong way.

Everyone heard the crackling roar and the scream that followed as flame filled the entire space between the last two pillars where Kaibren had been fleeing a second before.

Kaibren burned in fire.

Momentum carried him out. His inscribed clothing protected him from some of the damage—was, in fact, the only reason he wasn't instantly incinerated—but the clothing's limits were overwhelmed. He was still smoldering, still steaming, as he collapsed past the raging wall of fire.

"Kaibren!" Claw had screamed.

Jaemeh caught her by the arm as she tried to run back. "We can't. There's no way that trap going off didn't alert Neveranimas! We must leave right now!"

"Fuck you!" Claw swiped at him with a knife as emphasis.

He backed away, shaking his head, washing his hands of her fate.

Claw ran to Kaibren's side, fell to her knees, sobbing. She tried to figure out what to do, where to even start.

If Kaibren said anything to her, Claw never repeated it.

"What . . . happened?" Ris's voice was raw and choked.

Jaemeh didn't stop moving. "I don't know! Anahrod must've triggered something! She yelled at me to run and I . . ." He made a choking sound.

"Where's Anahrod?" Sicaryon demanded.

"I don't know!" Jaemeh yelled. "She must be back in the vault. I don't think she made it outside."

Gwydinion started to say something, ask something, and Ris put a hand on his shoulder and squeezed. He closed his mouth.

Jaemeh's expression had twisted, like he might cry or slam his fist into the wall. Instead, the dragonrider said, "I'll meet you all at the safe house. I need to find Tiendremos." And then, for the second time, he ran, this time for the thin set of stairs leading from the main entrance back to the top of the mountain.

Ris stared after him, eyes wide and murderous, her breath coming fast from shock and rage. Her sword—the one sword that had survived the lock—floated next to her, ready to strike.

But she lowered her hand, her sword returned to her side, and she turned back to the others. "Is Kaibren—?" she asked Naeron.

The man was hunched over, one hand grabbing the other wrist. He rocked back and forth twice and then forced himself to straighten.

"No pulse," he told her.

"Claw," Ris called out, "we have to go."

If Claw heard, she gave no sign. She murmured a string of expletives under her breath.

"Claw!" Ris called out again.

"What do we—" Gwydinion sounded close to tears himself. He turned to Ris, to Sicaryon, finally to Naeron.

Naeron took the young man's hand. "We go to the docks, to the safe house."

"Lerahven!" Ris screamed, the first and only time anyone heard Ris use Claw's real name.

It worked, though. Claw raised her head. She picked up one of Kaibren's blackened hands, kissed it, and laid it across the man's chest. She stalked back to the rest of them.

"Much as I hate to agree with that asshole," Ris said, "we must leave. She's on her way."

"She" being Neveranimas.

"No," Sicaryon said. "She's not. Anahrod spent all week throwing swarms of pests against those alarms. Neveranimas won't show up right away." He sounded . . . not tired, exactly, but empty. Wiped clean of all emotion.

"But what about my sister?" Gwydinion had cried out then.

"Peralon can't—he can't reach her," Ris said with a broken voice. "We have to leave. You know she wouldn't want us to be caught." She put a hand on Sicaryon's arm.

Sicaryon shrugged her off. "No," he said. "You go. I'll wait here."

Ris stepped up to him. "No," she said. "You don't get your way this time. I have the most chance of getting her back. If I have to, I know what I can use to pay her ransom." She put her hand over his. "This one is mine."

"Ransom?" Sicaryon didn't bother to hide his confusion. "You mean the diamonds—?"

"No, that's not what Neveranimas really wants. I promise I'll get her back. And I can protect myself."

Gwydinion thought the unspoken statement to Sicaryon was obvious: *Ris could protect herself, like Sicaryon couldn't.*

Gwydinion watched them both with wide eyes. He couldn't believe how quickly everything had fallen apart. "I'm pretty sure my sister wouldn't want either of you hurt," he told them.

"That's why it should be me," Ris agreed. She stepped close to Sicaryon and stood on her tiptoes to kiss the man on the lips. "Don't get yourself killed. She wouldn't want that and I . . . I don't either."

He looked surprised, then motioned to Gwydinion. "Let's hurry to the safe house."

The last Gwydinion saw of Ris, she was climbing up Peralon, who launched himself into the air, heading back to the steam vent.

⌄

Peralon's dragonstone had held a single memory, but it had been so clear, so vivid, that more than once Anahrod had forgotten she didn't know Ivarion herself. That single dragonstone memory had left her all too fond of a dragon she'd never met.

This was different. Not bizarrely so, but the details were fuzzier along the edges, the colors not as bright or crisp. It was still a memory, though. Still a dragon's memory.

Neveranimas's memory.

But for all that, it was a remarkably bland memory. She sat at the Council of Elders summit, listening to a dragon, Modelakast, talk about the importance of church attendance and meditation practices.

Incredibly boring. Neveranimas was listening, though, because she was regent, and it was her job. But Eannis, it was dull.

Modelakast finished her speech. Notile flew up on the main pedestal and—

The memory was interrupted. Anahrod never finished it.

42

INSURANCE

By the time they reached the safe house, the team of eight was a team of four. Sicaryon and Naeron, Claw and Gwydinion—they all made it back uninjured, but certainly not whole. Gwydinion's entire body ached—there had been a human-sized path from the landing to Neveranimas's vault, but the dragon had felt no need to keep it well maintained or safe. The climb back had seemed endless.

Claw stared out at nothing, unresponsive to anything around her, while Gwydinion sat in a corner, petting Legless's head. He was trying not to think about what had just happened, what it meant. Sicaryon paced back and forth, harkening to metaphors of animals and cages, all tightly wound restless energy with no release in sight. He looked like he might turn around at any moment and run back to the vault.

"Don't tell me you lost Ris?" Jaemeh said as he shut the door behind him.

Gwydinion's jaw dropped. What was Jaemeh even doing there?

The dragonrider looked worse for wear—tired and wet from the rain outside—but also had the pleased air of someone who'd done a good day's work. He carried a knapsack slung over one shoulder and wore an additional shirt and coat over Kaibren's inscribed clothing.

Sicaryon smoothly turned on his heel to face Jaemeh. He smiled, just a touch too bright to be sincere. "Stubborn woman. She's trying to see what she can do to rescue Anahrod. But I think the better question is, why are you here? Shouldn't you be with your dragon, pretending you have no idea what's going on?"

Gwydinion told Legless to hide back in his sleeve again. He stood up and walked closer. Something was going on. Jaemeh shouldn't be there.

Jaemeh raised an eyebrow. "Excuse me? We agreed we'd meet here."

"Those of us leaving agreed to meet here," Sicaryon corrected. "But you're staying behind in Yagra'hai with Tiendremos."

"I just want to make sure everyone is safe, Cary," Jaemeh pointed out as he stepped a hair to the side. The tension in the room rose, as if they were preparing to have a duel.

Sicaryon angled around to Jaemeh's side.

The dragonrider must have noticed, some instinct whispering to let no one into his blind spots. He moved, too, one step at a time, both men smiling at each other and pretending everything was fine.

Just as Gwydinion considered taking a step back, both men sprang into action, their movements a blur.

When the movement stopped, Sicaryon's sword paused midair, arrested at the fulcrum of its swing, just a hair's breadth from Gwydinion's neck.

Jaemeh had grabbed Gwydinion, pulling the teenager into Sicaryon's path with a bright, crackling blue rope of energy looped around his neck. Gwydinion smelled ozone and burning fabric, felt the heat of that rope. It reminded him of lightning, and he was pretty sure it would kill him like lightning, too.

"Careful now," Jaemeh told Sicaryon. "This is a lethal charge I've wrapped around the boy. Something to think about if you're considering anything that might make me break my concentration."

Claw stood up, her eyes finally focusing. "You're bluffing," Claw growled.

"You know I'm not. I also think you know lightning is attracted to metal—your knives, Cary's sword. If you were to do something rash, who knows where this might jump?" He smiled. "I wouldn't want anyone to get hurt."

"Let the boy go," Sicaryon ordered.

"Maybe later." Jaemeh tilted his head in Naeron's direction. "Don't get any ideas. I'll fry your brain long before you boil the blood in mine." He smiled at Sicaryon. "That was a nice sword strike," Jaemeh said. "Don't meet many Skylanders who know how to use a sword unless they're dragonriders."

"If that was supposed to be a question, the answer is no—I'm not a dragonrider," Sicaryon said. "I just like swords."

"Then don't get any bright ideas and you'll continue to play with yours for many years to come." Jaemeh stopped the play of electricity surrounding one hand for long enough to dip his fingers into a coat pocket and pull out an embroidered blue bag, which he tossed on the table.

On closer inspection, the bag wasn't embroidered. It was inscribed.

"If everyone would put their folding box in that bag, Gwydinion would appreciate it." Jaemeh smiled. "As would I."

"You can't . . ." Gwydinion swallowed. "You can't put folding boxes inside each other, you know."

"It's not a folding box," Jaemeh said. "Don't worry about that."

"You cheating bastard—" Claw's eyes were wide with rage, her nostrils flared.

"Careful," he warned her. The lightning was back around his fingers. "Kaibren would be upset if you died less than an hour after he did, so honor his memory by not being a fool."

"Stand down, Claw," Sicaryon murmured.

"Fuck off. You're not my boss."

"Maybe you should do what he says anyway," Jaemeh said. "Cary's smart, and you're running out of friends to lose."

Gwydinion thought she might forget herself and attack the man anyway, so he decided it might be a good idea to remind Claw he was being used as a shield.

"What did you do with Anahrod?" Gwydinion demanded of Jaemeh.

"That's not important—"

"He locked her in the vault." Sicaryon's voice was soft. "He knocked her unconscious and reset the traps that killed Kaibren. That is what you did, isn't it?"

"It's not my fault the man didn't run the right way."

"You—!" Claw made a choking sound and reached for her weapons.

Naeron sighed and shook his head. A moment later, Claw slumped forward, unconscious.

"Thank you, Naeron," Sicaryon said. "We'll make it up to her later."

Gwydinion swallowed thickly, felt tears at the corners of his eyes, hoping he'd misunderstood what was going on. "Jaemeh, four of the five keys broke! If you locked her in there, she can't get herself back out."

Without the keys, the only way for Anahrod to escape the vault was if someone opened the door for her.

Only one being could: Neveranimas.

Which meant Anahrod hadn't just been left behind—she'd been murdered.

"Sorry about that." Jaemeh didn't bother to cloak himself with even the faintest veneer of sincerity. "But worry less about her and more about yourself." He let out the line of blue electricity like it was a leash. "Go pick up the bag."

Gwydinion did, surprised to discover that the bag weighed almost nothing.

"See you soon," Sicaryon promised as Jaemeh dragged the boy to the door.

Jaemeh snorted. "I doubt that."

"I wasn't talking to you." Sicaryon seemed to be trying to communicate something to Gwydinion, at least if the intensity of his stare was anything to go by. Unfortunately, Sicaryon wasn't an actual animal, despite the association with trolls, so Gwydinion didn't know what.

"If you hurt him," Sicaryon shouted, "there's no place you'll be able to hide."

Then the shack door slammed shut, and muffled anything else the Deeper king might've said. Jaemeh dragged Gwydinion by the electrified leash.

"Don't worry," he said to the boy. "I'm not a monster. As long as you don't make me hurt you, you'll be fine."

Gwydinion didn't dignify that with a reply.

Jaemeh dragged him onboard the flyer.

⌄

Anahrod woke with a pounding headache and the knowledge that something was wrong. The only light came from her inscribed necklace, fallen to the ground. Around it, a few remaining diamonds glittered, casting rainbow sparks against the walls. She felt the side of her head, winced at the knot there. Someone had hit her on the head, hard.

She was still inside the vault.

Jaemeh, however, wasn't. The dragonstone was also—

The dragonstone was on the ground right in front of her.

She picked it up. It was the same one she'd been looking at earlier. Jaemeh just hadn't taken it.

She ran outside the third vault, then outside the second, and stared at the exit. She searched for the pressure plates, for the one that opened the vault entrance.

Someone had removed one of the metal shields from the vault of secrets and tossed it over the main pressure plate. They'd then melted the edges, welding the shield to the floor. She tried jumping on the metal plate. It didn't even dent. Jaemeh hadn't just abandoned her—he'd trapped her.

[Peralon?] She reached out, unsure if the gold dragon could hear her.

For a few seconds, she feared the worst, then a faint whisper brushed against her.

[Anahrod! Are you safe?]

She laughed bitterly. [The opposite of safe. Jaemeh knocked me out, but I don't understand. He didn't take the dragonstone. Only—] She exhaled. [He must not have thought it was important?]

Even as she said the words, she knew they were wrong.

In the distance, she felt a now familiar knot of pain, hate, and rage spin up into being. Her heartbeat pounded against her throat.

[A dragon's going rampant,] she told Peralon.

He didn't answer for a long beat. [Yes, apparently so.] Again, a pause. [I'm more concerned about freeing you.]

She shook her head, stopped when her headache blazed white-hot in response. [I appreciate the sentiment. I really do, but it's not happening. Peralon . . . why is this dragonstone so damn important? What haven't you and Ris told me?] A feeling of dread threatened to overwhelm her. She looked around the first vault, the one that Neveranimas officially admitted to collecting. It was meticulously organized. Every dragonstone had a place upon rows and rows of shelves.

[It was where Neveranimas kept all the details of her most horrible crimes,]

Peralon confessed. [Details of her *and* of Tiendremos. And that's why we had to make sure he never suspected our actual goal wasn't those stupid diamonds.]

Anahrod cursed. That made sense. It would've given Ris her revenge against both dragons. And it certainly explained why Ris and Peralon had kept that detail so close to the chest—because at even the faintest hint that the true goal was evidence implicating Tiendremos, too, he'd have either fled or, worse, turned tail and gone straight to Neveranimas.

Neveranimas, who might arrive at any moment.

Anahrod pushed that anxiety from her mind. It did nothing to help her. Instead, she picked up the light locket, held it high, and studied the room. She paused as she spotted two empty places on the shelves, right next to each other.

Anahrod *had* to be holding the dragonstone that went into one of those cubbyholes. Jaemeh must have grabbed it as he'd walked past to use as a decoy.

She winced as the dragon chatter in her mind grew more intense. If she'd been above ground or near any human centers, the shelter bells would be ringing.

That first cubbyhole . . . she examined the edges of the stone opening. She saw a lot of wear and very little dust. Whatever was normally stored there was something Neveranimas used often.

Anahrod realized she was grinding her teeth.

[With all respect, Peralon, you're very mistaken. Tiendremos *does* know about that dragonstone, and it was always his target. Neither one of you cared about the damn diamonds. Tiendremos knows exactly what that dragonstone looks like and likely shared that information with Jaemeh.]

Peralon didn't answer.

[Peralon?]

[There's one problem with your theory.] The flavor of the dragon's mental "speech" turned grim and tense.

[What is it?]

[The dragon who just went rampant is Tiendremos.]

She couldn't breathe. No. Tiendremos gone rampant? That would be *apocalyptic.*

[You need to see this.]

Peralon grabbed hold of her thoughts and yanked.

Anahrod stared at chaos.

She looked out at the world through Peralon's eyes. He hadn't switched places with her, as he did with Ris: she was a passenger, an observer, and nothing more.

Hilariously, the location was familiar because she'd just seen it in one of Neveranimas's dragonstones. This was the stone plateau where the dragon elders met, one of the highest points in the city.

It was under attack.

The storm perpetually circling the city had been drawn inward, pooling in a tightening spiral stretching down to the surface like the accusing finger of an angry god. Dangerous debris and even more dangerous dragons were tossed about by the winds. Lightning crashed to the ground in lethal chains of white fire. Verbal speech would've been impossible given the thunder slamming against all ears.

Tiendremos was at the center. One of his wings was still bandaged from his injury fighting Modelakast, but he no longer seemed to feel the pain. The dragon hissed and screamed and launched itself at a nearby green dragon, raking his claws before ripping away the other dragon's throat. Tiendremos's eyes were mad, lost in berserk fury.

Tiendremos was rampant. For real, this time.

But why now?

[I think,] Peralon told her unhappily, [that this dragonstone must be more than we suspected.]

[This is how she was doing it,] Anahrod said, stunned. [This is how Neveranimas has been making dragons go rampant. Not a spell or a curse. An artifact. And Jaemeh just used it on his own dragon.]

A part of her immediately whispered: *Of course he did.*

She'd known Jaemeh wasn't happy as Tiendremos's rider. Hell, they'd all known that. How could he have been? At best, Jaemeh had been a toy doll Tiendremos had used to talk to the humans. Tiendremos had seen his rider—had always seen all his riders—as entirely expendable.

Jaemeh had seen a way out and he'd taken it.

The dragon elders seemed less reluctant to enter the fray here than they'd been with Modelakast. Perhaps because Tiendremos was one of their own, but more likely because he'd wasted no time attacking them personally.

It was terrible to see.

The dragons used claw and tooth because their breath attacks seldom discriminated friend from foe. There were exceptions: a large black dragon with indigo blue wingtips and tail breathed out some kind of black, sticky substance that it controlled at will. Tiendremos writhed whenever any of the sludge contacted him. Another dragon had breathed out a stream of sickly blue liquid, but when it missed and hit a different dragon, didn't try again.

[Wait. Where's Neveranimas? She was here, wasn't she?] Anahrod could see within Peralon's field of view.

[I thought—] The dragon craned his head, turning with impressive, dizzying speed as he scanned for the violet dragon. [She must have left. The traps—a trap was triggered before we left. It's possible she's investigating.]

Anahrod laughed. [No. She's coming back because Tiendremos just went rampant for no reason, and she knows *she* isn't responsible.] For all Tiendremos's bad qualities, he hadn't been on the verge of going rampant. For him to do so now must have set off metaphorical alarm bells of the sort that couldn't be disarmed.

Neveranimas only knew of one method for forcing rampancy, so she'd left to check on its whereabouts.

[You must escape.] Peralon's mental voice sounded frantic. Without warning, the connection to his sight vanished. She was back in the vault again.

A grinding noise echoed as the steam vent door opened. Anahrod ran back into the Vault of Secrets, but there was no time to hide what they'd done. The second and third vaults were both open, Ivarion's diamonds obviously missing. She might have delighted in Neveranimas's scream of outrage upon discovering the invasion and theft were she not trapped herself.

She barely had time to duck behind a carved block of granite before the ground shivered in a slow, steady drumbeat. She snapped shut the light locket, stuffed the whole thing into her shirt, plunged the room back into darkness.

Neveranimas had returned to her vault.

43

BREAKING THE SKY

Anahrod's only hope was that Neveranimas would leave in a rage the moment she realized. The flaw in that hope made itself terrifyingly clear just moments after the dragon entered the outer vault.

The vault was silent, so still and silent.

Slowly, sounds reemerged, like they were actors stepping onto a stage. A grinding noise as the amethyst dragonstone she'd dropped earlier continued its slow roll across the floor. The heavy, dull thud of an enormous dragon carefully making her way through the rooms. A metallic clink of impossibly large, dragon-scaled jewelry. The soft sibilance of scales rubbing against each other.

Lights flickered on, softer than a human might prefer, but just perfect for dragon senses.

[I can smell you.]

Anahrod closed her eyes. Dragon senses are not too dissimilar to a titan drake's. Hiding was impossible; Neveranimas already knew they had invaded her lair, already knew someone remained behind. Anahrod's only chance was that Neveranimas might be bluffing. She might not know for certain if any robbers remained.

Anahrod stayed still, slowed her breathing, and waited in the dark.

[How long has it been, Anahrod? Seems like it was just yesterday, but my people feel the passage of time less keenly than yours.]

Damn.

[Did Crystalspire lie about executing you?] The dragon seemed curious as much as angry.

More worrying, though, was that she recognized Anahrod's scent. That she remembered it.

Anahrod wasn't so foolish as to think the dragon would spare her. Neveranimas might keep her alive for long enough to find out what Anahrod knew, but she'd never let her live.

[This is indecorous, little beast. Have some dignity. It's not as though I won't find your partners. Do you think I'd be so foolish as to neglect to place tracking runes on everything I own? I don't care about the diamonds, but whichever one of your friends took my Rampant Stone will be found.]

Anahrod almost laughed. She'd given it a name. Wonderful.

[She's here,] Anahrod told Peralon as the heavy footsteps came closer.

[Hide,] he told her unnecessarily. [Whatever happens, stay hidden. I'm on my way.]

Anahrod appreciated the attempt, but Peralon wouldn't make it in time, and had no way to get inside the vault even if he did. If she was going to get out of this, she'd have to do it on her own.

Metal crashed as the dragon swiped a dozen pedestals and shelves out of the way, scattering her carefully curated hoard of secret knowledge.

[Show yourself!] Neveranimas demanded. [You're not a dragon, silly beast. You cannot stand against me.]

Anahrod shut her eyes, staying still. No, Anahrod was not a dragon. Not even the rider of a dragon . . .

Wait.

She'd wondered, once, if she could take possession of a dragon, regardless of bond. Anahrod already knew she could see through dragon eyes: she'd just done that with Peralon. *Could* she take control of a dragon?

Did she have anything to lose by trying?

Anahrod wanted the switch to be like what she did with Overbite, but she feared it would more closely resemble Peralon and Ris—a mutual exchange.

Anahrod had to assume that if she took control of the dragon's body, the dragon would take control of hers.

How to guarantee Neveranimas couldn't cause any mischief?

She fumbled through her coat pockets until she found the sleeping-potion bottles she'd created for Rider Brauge. It wouldn't take effect instantly—these things never did—but it might buy her enough time.

And if she was wrong, at least she'd be unconscious when Neveranimas killed her.

Anahrod uncorked the bottle and drank it all down in one gulp, wincing at the acid taste. A glass of wine would've been welcome at that moment.

Neveranimas must've heard something, or smelled something, or both. [Ha! I told you that you'll never—]

Anahrod rolled out from her hiding spot. She brushed the dust off her sleeves and tugged at her belt. She wished she'd brought her sword; not because she had any illusions about its effectiveness against a dragon but just for its familiarity.

"Heard you the first time. I can't hide from you. I'm aware. Confirm something for me: You're the one who turned Ivarion rampant, yes?" The moment she asked, Anahrod knew it was the wrong approach. Neveranimas hoarded secrets. She didn't give them away.

Neveranimas wasn't the largest dragon that Anahrod had ever seen, but she was monstrously larger than Anahrod. So large she had to lean back and brace herself against a table to see the underside of the dragon's chin. Each of those claws—

Well. Each of those claws was the size of a sword, weren't they?

Neveranimas still looked the same as she had seventeen years previously. Except now Anahrod knew better than to be awed. Afraid? Yes. But the burning contempt she felt pushed that down, made it meaningless. The only emotion she had left for this dragon was hate.

Anahrod told herself to think of Neveranimas as just a larger, winged version of Overbite. No more intimidating, no more difficult to overcome.

Neveranimas stared down at Anahrod. [It is you.]

"Yes," Anahrod said. "But more important are the dragons who helped put me inside this room. The ones working against you."

If Neveranimas collected secrets, perhaps Anahrod could buy herself time by dangling a few.

The dragon huffed out a cloud of ice vapor. [You're lying. No dragon helped you. But I would like to know how you entered my vault.]

"You helped," Anahrod said.

Neveranimas growled. Anahrod reminded herself that it might not be wise to bait the dragon into losing her temper.

"Those families you wiped out all those years ago? The ones who built this place?" She gestured. "They had another way in. And no motivation to keep such a way secret after you betrayed them." She paused. "I'm not lying about the dragons, though. Or do you not care if there's a secret cabal working against you?"

Anahrod felt the edges of Neveranimas's mind—a distant, high place, obscured by clouds and cold, dark winds. Beautiful.

Vulnerable.

Neveranimas snarled at the mention of a cabal. She was both paranoid and curious—yes, of course, she wanted to know about a clandestine plot. She wanted to know everything.

[Tell me!] the dragon demanded. [Tell me who would—] Neveranimas canted her head to the side, regarding Anahrod with a single eye. [Oh, I know who it is,] she said. [Ivarion's old lover. That annoying little gold plaything. That's who's responsible for this?]

She was right, but Anahrod would never admit it. "No." Anahrod's voice dropped scorn. "Tiendremos."

Maybe Neveranimas never considered that someone who would do anything to be their second might also do anything to surpass them. Maybe she had different reasons for thinking Tiendremos fanatically loyal. The dragon reared back, eyes wide and teeth showing as she grimaced.

Which was when Anahrod attacked.

It was much harder than taking control of Overbite. The farther down Anahrod pierced, however, the less it mattered. Under that civil and cold exterior, Neveranimas was an animal—feral, full of rage and hate and endless fear. It was like trying to grab on to a rabid, shrieking drake, one lashing out with six flailing limbs.

Neveranimas's eyes widened. She lifted a giant, clawed hand to silence Anahrod forever.

She wasn't fast enough.

Anahrod was glad she'd taken the sleeping draught. She could feel Neveranimas slip into her body, even as she took control of the dragon.

The shift was painful and euphoric, an overwhelming wrongness combined with a sensation of power. Her point of view shifted, became something much higher than she'd ever experienced with Overbite. The anger took her by surprise, a never-ending storm whirling inside her. Neveranimas felt—

She felt close to going rampant. Anahrod was forced to take a moment to collect herself, to push down that awful, cold fury.

On the ground, "Anahrod" began screaming.

Understandable, Anahrod thought as she steadied herself. Neveranimas had never tried to use human vocal cords. She was screaming for the same reason babies did. Whereas Anahrod had spent weeks rehearsing how to move and fly while wearing a dragon's skin.

Neveranimas deciphered running with commendable speed. Unfortunately, she didn't have anywhere to go, being no more capable of escaping the vault now than Anahrod had been earlier. Anahrod had concerns that the dragon might try to damage her new body, so she (carefully, oh so carefully) scooped up the struggling human form with one hand and limped to the vault entrance using the other three limbs. She brushed aside the welded shield like the improvised toy it was, pressed the pressure plate, deactivated the traps, unlocked the doors.

By the time she reached the back entrance, Neveranimas had stopped struggling. Her human body was still alive, but Neveranimas's panic had helped the sleeping potion kick in earlier.

Now Anahrod just had to figure out what to do.

If she switched back, then Neveranimas would have full control again, because the dragon's body wasn't drugged. Whereas Anahrod's body would be unconscious for hours.

She needed to incapacitate Neveranimas's body so thoroughly that it wouldn't matter when they switched back again.

Incapacitate, but preferably kill.

Anahrod climbed back out of the steam vent rather than using the front exit through the Hall of Death. She discovered on the way she could use her wings to climb with as well as her forearms, just not with the same strength or dexterity. Still, it made the trip a great deal faster than she would've thought.

Once she reached the top, she looked around for a place where she could hide her human body. She had to approach this carefully. She couldn't see Peralon, but he was approaching fast. Would she have enough time to explain herself before he attacked her? If he did attack her, would she be able to maintain control over Neveranimas's body?

She didn't think she should risk it.

"Stop!"

A tiny figure appeared in front of her, and Anahrod realized she had even more problems than she'd realized.

It was Ris.

Peralon must have left Ris behind earlier, and he wasn't answering Anahrod's calls to him. That meant that Anahrod had no way to communicate with Ris. She had no way to explain that the dragon that looked like Neveranimas was really Anahrod.

Ris jumped up on top of a boulder and held up a knapsack. It looked like it contained something hard, heavy, and round. "I have the dragonstone!" she yelled. "Just let her go, and it's yours. We'll leave and you'll never see us again."

Anahrod's mind raced furiously.

—could *Ris* have been the one who sent Tiendremos rampant?

Now that she was thinking about it, it would be a monstrously ironic and appropriate way for Tiendremos to die, wouldn't it?

"Please." Ris's voice was broken, and her eyes haunted. She spoke low enough that the only reason Anahrod could hear her was because of the superiority of dragon hearing. "Please, I'll give you anything. Just let her go."

Even if Anahrod could speak, she didn't think she would be able to. This was

Ris's revenge, her chance to get back at Neveranimas. She was just offering it up? Giving it away?

"Please," Ris begged. "What do you want?"

Anahrod-in-Neveranimas set her unconscious human body down on the ground in front of Ris, who threw so many wards on top of Anahrod's sleeping form that she was difficult to see for several seconds.

Anahrod thought the expression on Ris's face when Anahrod didn't pick up that knapsack was also adorable, cycling as it did through determination, shock, and surprise. She idly wondered if Ris might have trapped it.

Anahrod launched herself into the air.

She kept flying up.

Anahrod soared higher and higher. She didn't look down; that would come soon enough.

Flying was heaven. Her fear of heights didn't kick in, couldn't kick in—not when she was in control. Flying came easily, just as running in a human body had come easily to Neveranimas. The body knew the skill. If she never made the mistake of thinking about it too hard, the dragon body knew what to do.

Anahrod flew higher.

She flew until the sky turned from pale blue to deep indigo. So high that the air became hypoxic. So high that when she paused, Anahrod saw the entire world curve lazily underneath her. Fifty thousand feet—the point past which neither humans nor dragons ventured without magical assistance, the air too thin to support life. The height from which she'd been thrown.

This felt *just*.

She hung there for a glittering, perfect moment, perched on the lid of the sky.

She folded her wings and dove.

Anahrod had thought she'd panic. How could she not when stooping from a height? Instead, she felt a grim, cold thrill, a vicious satisfaction.

The difference between falling and jumping was as vast as the sky itself.

The hardest part wasn't the flying, but the waiting. Waiting until the last possible moment, until the jungle tree leaves were so close she could see their purple veining. Waiting until the last second before she tore her mind away from Neveranimas's body, snapped back into her own.

Anahrod hadn't been sure it would work, or if it did, that the cost wouldn't be her own life as well.

She felt the thin, wispy, cloudlike trail of herself, a lead line guiding herself back to her own body. She leaped for that thread, grabbed on with both hands, followed it back as fast and hard as she could—

And then nothing.

Nothing at all.

⌄

Anahrod stared at the cloth-wrapped ceiling above her for several seconds before her brain caught up enough to supply a location. She was in Gwydinion's room.

She sat up.

It hadn't been a dream; she still wore Kaibren's dark green inscription suit. She also had a sore throat and a headache.

Anahrod put a hand to head, felt the bruises there, and winced. She wasn't sure where those had come from, but if she had to guess—Jaemeh must have hit her to knock her out. Probably with a dragonstone.

Just as painful was the knot of rage at the edge of her consciousness, because it could only mean one thing:

They hadn't killed Tiendremos yet.

Voices nearby shouted, including one that by cadence and tone she identified as Sicaryon's. She wandered out into the main room to find her identification correct, with Sicaryon and Ris screaming at each other. Naeron leaned against a wall with his arms wrapped around his head as if to block out the sound, while Claw sat at the table with perfect posture, no expression on her face whatsoever. They all looked exhausted.

"—had just told us the fucking dragon had an artifact that would send other dragons rampant, maybe we could've done something about Jaemeh!"

"I didn't know!" Ris screamed back. "We suspected she had some method, but honestly, we thought she was casting a spell, a curse! Why would we think it was a dragonstone?"

"I think Tiendremos believed it was where she kept all her blackmail material," Anahrod offered, massaging her temples. "He might still be right. Who's to say?"

Ris's head whipped around. "Anahrod, how are you feeling—?"

"Like someone hit my head with a big, shiny rock," Anahrod said. "What time is it?"

Ris made a face. "Early morning. Very early. Dawn won't be for hours yet."

Anahrod sighed. She didn't ask if they'd been arguing since Ris returned with Anahrod's body. She knew the answer.

"Where's Gwydinion?" she asked instead. "Where's Kaibren?"

The room fell quiet.

Ris ran a hand over her face and looked pained. "Kaibren's dead and Jaemeh took Gwydinion, he took the diamonds, and we think he has the fucking dragonstone, too."

"The dragonstone? But you offered to give that back to Neveranimas," Anahrod said.

"You did what?" Sicaryon gave Ris a wide-eyed, accusative stare.

Ris sighed. "No, it's—" She sighed. "I was trying out this strategy. Very new. Very experimental. It's called *lying*. Lying out of my teeth." She glared at Sicaryon. "At least it worked."

"Oh." Anahrod seesawed a hand back and forth. "Not exactly."

Ris gave her a confused look. "What?"

"You didn't say all of that to Neveranimas," Anahrod said. "You—you said it to me. I was"—she made a linking motion with her fingers—"possessing her body, to carry mine out of the vault." She felt ridiculously embarrassed about the whole thing. "We speculated that I might be able to do this. I tried it—and it worked."

Silence.

"I don't believe you." Claw's stare at Anahrod was venomous. "What ridiculous shit is this? No, the only way you escaped without a scratch is if Neveranimas let you out, and why would she do that unless you were working with her?" She pulled a knife from her belt and leaned forward.

"Calm down, Claw," Ris told her.

"Fuck you," Claw said. "And if Naeron knocks me out again, you better make it for good, or I'm gutting him the moment I'm conscious—" She paused.

The tip of Anahrod's sword rested against Claw's throat. Under other circumstances, she might've teased Claw about letting her guard down like that, taking her eyes off the target—but these were not other circumstances.

"Calm yourself," Anahrod said. "I told you exactly what I could do. Don't say that I've been deceiving you."

"Well, I don't believe you!"

"That's your problem," Anahrod said. "I still told you the truth. Hell, you've seen me do it, Claw. I wasn't unconscious when those Scarsea soldiers were carrying my body away; I was possessing Overbite."

Claw mulled that one over for a moment. Her eyes flicked to the side, to Ris, to Sicaryon, possibly to Naeron. Anahrod couldn't see what they were doing; she didn't let her focus stray.

"She's telling the truth about the possession ability," Sicaryon said. "I've seen her do it."

Claw narrowed her eyes. "So, you had control of Neveranimas and you just, what, let her go?"

"I'm not a fool either," Anahrod sneered. "I flew her up to fifty thousand, flipped, and dove straight back down." She pulled back her sword, just enough to emphasize the confrontation was over. Anahrod glanced at Ris. "Please tell me I killed her."

Ris sighed and said nothing.

Anahrod sheathed her sword, angrily. "How could she have survived that?"

Naeron mumbled something. As the yelling had stopped, he'd removed his arms from over his head and had gone back to tapping his wrist. Honestly, Anahrod was a bit surprised that he'd stayed in the room at all.

Anahrod turned toward him. "What?"

He looked up at her with red, teary eyes. "She teleports."

Anahrod exhaled. If she'd teleported the instant she had control of her body again . . .

She'd given Neveranimas so little time to get her bearings, to recover. Half a second, if that. How had she managed such a thing?

"Valid," she acknowledged. "Jaemeh has the Rampant Stone—which Neveranimas claimed she could track—as well as the diamonds and my brother. Neveranimas isn't dead and worse, knows that I'm not dead. And now that she knows what I can do, she'll be rousing every dragon in the city to hunt me down. Did I miss anything?"

"Jaemeh also stole our flyer," Claw said, "which was our only exit plan except for Peralon—who we can't fucking use either."

"Peralon's hiding," Ris said. "At least until we figure out what we're doing. Neveranimas has a kill-on-sight order out on him."

"I didn't say he wasn't smart to hide," Claw snapped. "Just that it puts us in a bit of a tight spot, doesn't it? How the hell do we leave this damn city?"

Anahrod pursed her lips. "That, I might be able to do something about."

44

LAST REQUESTS

Normally, Varriguhl would've been in his house at that time of night, but a rampant alert was in progress. Anahrod didn't think he would shelter in place at his house, so she led the group to the closest underground shelter.

Still, she hadn't expected to find him with his students. Since the rampant alert had happened at night, the teenagers should've sheltered at their various assigned quarters. Instead, at least half the normal class had gathered in Varriguhl's preferred underground shelter. Not just students, either; caretakers and guardians had also gathered in the room. All of them were watching Varriguhl's silver mirror, even though there wasn't much to see. The gale-force winds and rain blocked most details.

"What are they doing here?" Anahrod asked without prelude as she stepped inside. She wasn't wearing her veil, but it's not like she was trying to pretend anymore.

Varriguhl didn't tell her to be quiet or take a seat. He also didn't ask where Gwydinion was. He raised an eyebrow at the group she'd brought with her—Sicaryon, Ris, Naeron, and Claw—but made no further comment.

He frowned at her question. "They've been here since the alert first went out," Varriguhl said. "They feel safer here."

She grimaced. That . . . made sense. The hardest part about hiding in the shelters was not knowing. Not knowing what was going on, where the dragon was, where the danger was. At least being in the same shelter as Varriguhl allowed them that benefit.

It's not like any of these people would be sleeping, anyway.

"I heard the notice go out," Varriguhl told her. "Be on the lookout for Anahrod Amnead, an accurate description, kill on sight, and oh, by the way, she can control dragons." He made it sound like an expected poor result on an academic test: disappointing but not a surprise.

"Not control," Anahrod corrected as the teacher wheeled over toward a desk pushed against a wall. "Possess."

Varriguhl's chair lurched to a halt.

"Possess? Truly?" Varriguhl sounded like he wasn't sure whether to be incredulous or hopeful.

"I just found out myself," Anahrod admitted. "But I can understand why Neveranimas didn't want to admit she 'allowed' a human to possess her body, so 'control' is scary enough to be a motivation."

"Eannis help me," the dragonrider murmured.

Kimat rushed over to them. "Where's Gwydinion?"

Anahrod shook her head. "With any luck, a long way away from here."

"I should hope so," Varriguhl said, "because Neveranimas is well past the point of discretion. If you've scared her this badly, she won't be content with pruning a branch from your family when she can uproot the entire tree."

Anahrod's throat dried. He was right. Neveranimas would go after every blood relative she had. She might not even bother to distinguish between maternal, paternal, and adoptive lines.

The Amnead family was a large one in Crystalspire. She didn't know how large Aiden e'Doreyl's family was, but . . . an impatient, angry dragon might well say to hell with it, and order the entire city razed, just to be sure.

A dragon roar shook the underground room.

There was a second of pause, a moment of consideration. Humans who had grown up around dragons all their lives stopped dead.

"That was nearby," Varriguhl said.

"Too close," Anahrod agreed. "That's inside the school grounds."

"Who would dare?" Varriguhl waved a hand, changing the view on the scrying glass. Images flew by, as though they were seeing through a bird's eyes. The mirror settled, focused on the draconic form digging up decades' worth of meticulous landscaping.

It was Neveranimas.

"She's tunneling in this direction," Varriguhl whispered. It still sounded like an accusation, which it was. How could Neveranimas possibly know where to find them?

Neveranimas wasn't a dragon of earthly affinity—those were rare. Her progress was slower as a result, but she'd still reach them . . . eventually.

"How can you tell?" Claw asked.

"This is my school. I can tell." Varriguhl waved a hand again, returning the mirror to its original view. He cast a concerned gaze at his students, clearly wanting to avoid any panic.

"Class!" Varriguhl called out. "There's an issue that I find I must deal with personally, so I must step away for a few minutes. I will leave Damreala in charge while I'm gone." He gave the group a stern look. "If I hear any of you have behaved inappropriately, you will regret it." He rolled his chair toward the door.

He gave Anahrod an imperious stare. "Coming?"

Anahrod, Ris, Sicaryon, Claw, and Naeron followed him. Belatedly, Anahrod noticed Kimat was also trailing behind them.

"Either Neveranimas has finally decided to come after me," Varriguhl explained in remarkably dry tones, "or she's pursuing one of you. Regardless, our priority must be to swiftly distance ourselves from the children." He stopped the chair for a moment and looked over his shoulder. "Kimat, don't think I didn't notice you. Go back to the shelter."

"Make me," she snapped, and instead of retreating moved up to his chair and began pushing him forward.

"We don't have time to argue," Anahrod pointed out as they hurried down the tunnel. "My suspicion is that she's tracking us. Does anyone have anything from the vault with them? Something you picked up? A diamond, a piece of jewelry, *anything*? She claimed she could track all of it."

"What vault?" Varriguhl's lip curled. "Anahrod, what have you done?"

"I'll explain later," Anahrod snapped, fully intending to do no such thing.

Anahrod continued focusing on the others. Claw, she thought. Claw was an excellent candidate for someone who might've kept a trackable souvenir.

But it was Sicaryon who pulled a folding box from his coat, held it out with both hands. "I had stashed a box before Jaemeh showed up, so he never stole it."

She couldn't even be mad at him. This had been the whole point of the robbery, after all. It hardly counted as trickery when he was just the only person who'd managed to keep his share.

"All right." She took the box from Sicaryon and immediately regretted it. She'd forgotten how heavy the damn things were. Part of a dragon's hoard of diamonds. "We're leaving, now. Headmaster, you said you had an escape plan. We need it. Everyone else will go with you, while I take this into the tunnels and lead—"

The protests were immediate. Kimat pushed Varriguhl ahead a few strides before she realized they had all stopped walking.

"You will do no such thing," Ris snapped. "Give that to me. Peralon and I will—"

Varriguhl whistled, stopping everyone. "Much as it amuses to hear you debate which of you will nobly sacrifice yourselves, we've little time and my 'escape plan' is a one-person inscribed lift that leads to a dock platform underneath the storm zone. Parked at that dock is a flyer—also for one person." He gave Anahrod an irritated scowl. "You never asked what my escape plan *was*, you silly child. Whatever yours is to be, you'll need something else if you intend to take more than a single person."

Sicaryon eyed the headmaster. "You're not planning to use that flyer yourself?"

Varriguhl tipped back his head and stared imperiously. "I shall not be needing it. I'd planned to have Kimat use it, but if I have your word that you'll escort her safely from the city, I'd allow another access."

"No," Kimat said, "I'm not leaving."

"You'll do as you're told," the man said crisply.

"Change of plans then," Sicaryon said, "I'll take the folding box and use his one-person flyer. That should draw that bitch away from everyone else." He said to Anahrod, "I'll head to the Deep. If Jaemeh and Gwydinion go there, I'll find them."

Anahrod squinted. "Why would Jaemeh and Gwydinion go to the Deep?"

Both Sicaryon's eyebrows rose, as if he was surprised he had to explain. "You're going to back to Seven Crests, right? To warn your family?"

Anahrod nodded. She had to.

"If Jaemeh and Gwydinion go there, you'll find them." He pointed his chin in Naeron's direction. "But if I were someone who could control animals, and I were also a precocious, manipulative little brat"—he ignored the choked-off laughter from Ris with great dignity—"then I'd convince my kidnapper that he should take me someplace with a lot of animals. You know, like the Deep."

Anahrod let out a single, sharp huff of breath, the closest thing to laughter she could manage just then. Yes, outside of convincing Jaemeh to turn himself over to Mayor Aiden e'Doreyl, a retreat to the Deep made sense. Her brother might not be an expert on jungle survival, but he knew more than Jaemeh. He was smart enough to use it to his advantage.

"Do you know how to pilot a flyer?" Claw demanded of Sicaryon.

"How do you think I move back and forth between the Deep and Seven Crests so quickly?" Sicaryon replied, but his gaze was still locked with Anahrod's.

"Sicaryon, that's suicide," Ris said in a wretched tone. "Neveranimas will catch you, and you'll have no defenses."

Sicaryon gave her a one-sided smile. "Careful, Ris. People might think you care."

"You asshole," she spat. "I'm calling Peralon out of hiding," she announced. "We'll distract her so everyone can make a run for it."

Varriguhl sighed. "Silly children. We don't have time for this."

Ris scowled. "Excuse you, I'm almost as old as you!"

"Only chronologically," the schoolteacher said mildly. "In any event, this is my school. I will deal with this." He pulled a medallion from his neck and handed it to Sicaryon. "That will allow you to operate the lift. Follow the south hallway until you reach the four-way intersection, take a right, then follow the hallway to the end. It's the only door."

Sicaryon took the medallion and then turned to Anahrod.

There was no guarantee he'd draw Neveranimas's attention. Just the opposite: recovering Ivarion's diamonds wouldn't be the violet dragon's highest priority.

Anahrod set the folding box in his hands. "Don't die," she told him.

"So far, so good." For a second, he looked like he might try to kiss her, but he stepped back, winked in a way that might have been meant for Anahrod, Ris, or both, and sprinted down the hall.

"The rest of you," Varriguhl said, "follow the hallway. You should find yourselves in familiar territory, considering the service tunnels you've been abusing since your arrival. I can't sneak you out of the city, but I can at least sneak you out of the school. Perhaps you can commandeer a cutter or liner and make an escape that way."

Anahrod laughed in spite of herself, in spite of the danger. "Did you just advocate *piracy*?"

He smiled sadly at her. "You always were a quick one, Miss Amnead." Just as she was about to turn away, he caught her wrist. "Promise me one thing."

Anahrod glanced down at her wrist, then at him. "If I can."

"Promise me, on your word, that you'll try to wake Ivarion."

She hated the way her throat closed up, the stinging in her nostrils. "I already told you—"

"That you'll *try*," he emphasized. "That's all I can ask. Promise me you'll make the attempt." His manner was as it had ever been—elegant, dignified, arrogant—but now desperate.

And resigned.

"You think Neveranimas is going to kill you," Anahrod said.

"I don't 'think' it," the headmaster corrected. "She's been looking for any excuse for the better part of a century. Even if she's chasing you, she won't let this opportunity slip by." He gave her a grim, hard smile. "I do plan to make her fight for it, however. I am the First Rider. That still means something."

Anahrod had no idea what to say.

"Go," he said, now irritated. "I'm not your beloved mentor and I'm not doing this to provide you with some object lesson on heroism. I'm doing this because you are the only person who has a chance of stopping that bitch. Run!"

Anahrod did.

Behind her, Varriguhl turned his wheelchair toward the sound of digging.

⮜

She hadn't caught up to the others when the evacuation bells rang. Not the "take shelter" bells, but "get out." Anahrod hoped people listened. In theory, people had already retreated to the shelters, and Varriguhl had lured Neveranimas away from his students. In theory, the children wouldn't be anywhere near the dragon.

But not if she kept digging up the tunnels.

A giant noise stopped everyone, so loud they heard it even down in the tunnels. The noise wasn't as recognizable as a dragon's roar, but it was still common enough to be identified.

Collapsing buildings.

They ran until they reached a familiar spot, then made the turn that led to the undercity. A few minutes later, Kimat clutched at a pendant, screamed, "No!" and turned around to run back.

Naeron blocked her way.

Claw didn't say a word. She just scooped the girl up and swung her up over a shoulder.

"No, let me go! He's in trouble!" Kimat squirmed a free hand toward her belt.

Claw took the knife away before the girl could unsheathe it and handed the weapon to Anahrod.

"I'm sorry," Ris told Kimat. "I really am."

"Bitch! Let me go! He needs me . . ." Kimat gave her pendant one last despairing look, eyes wide with disbelief, and then stopped struggling against Claw. The reason couldn't have been clearer: she'd stopped fighting because there wasn't any point.

Anahrod's throat clenched, rubbed raw and tender by her own feelings. She'd hated that man for so long.

Unjustly, it seemed.

Claw turned back to the others, steadying the girl with an arm around her legs. "So, what now? The docks? We're really stealing a flyer?" She squinted. "It's not that I'm against it, mind you. Just there's only four of us—"

Kimat muttered something and Claw snapped, "No, you don't count." She continued, "There's only four of us and cutter crews are what? A couple dozen? More? If we killed everyone, that would be one thing, but we'd need them alive and we have to sleep sometime."

Ris sighed. "We may not have a choice."

"Repair yard," Naeron suggested.

Ris pursed her lips. "That's not a bad idea. We might steal a smaller flyer, one that doesn't have a crew yet."

"Do any of us know how to fly?" Anahrod asked.

Kimat mumbled something that sounded suspiciously like "I do!"

Sure. Varriguhl would've taught her to use his flyer—but there was a wide chasm between the mountaintops of "single-person flyer" and "twelve-person cutter."

Anahrod paused. The runaway storm of hate that had been lurking at the edge of her consciousness disappeared. It felt very much like a storm spending itself out, leaving behind devastation and wispy, faint clouds.

"Tiendremos just died," Anahrod said.

Ris shuddered. She had an indecipherable expression on her face, something like pleasure, but also loss, grief, and anger. She closed her eyes, visibly clenching her jaw.

Anahrod took her hand. "Come on," Anahrod suggested gently. "We'll see what our options are, and then we'll worry about how we get it off the ground." She dug her veil out of a pocket. Neveranimas was circulating her description, after all. "And put Kimat down, Claw. She's a smart girl. She knows her best chance is sticking with us."

"Fuck you," Kimat mumbled as Claw set her back on her feet. "I want my knife back."

"It's nice to want things, isn't it?" Claw said.

"Let's hurry," Anahrod told them.

45

WHY BIRDS FLOCK

The storm wall surrounding the city had mostly retreated to its normal gyre once it was no longer under Tiendremos's influence, which meant that at least it had stopped raining by the time they came up from the underground near the docks.

Unfortunately, it also gave them all a distressingly clear view of the sky.

Every dragon in Yagra'hai must've been circling, calling out to each other. She heard them the same way she might've heard a waterfall or an avalanche or a riot—a dull roar in the distance. She understood why Ris hadn't insisted that Peralon could rescue them: it was impossible. The best he could do was keep his head down until he could make a break for it. She didn't see any flyers leaving either, but that was a mountain she hadn't reached yet.

"These pieces of junk look like they can barely fly," Claw complained. "And don't try to tell me that they'll look better by daylight, because you know that they'll look worse."

Sadly, Anahrod had to agree. That was the problem with looking at the repair yard: most of the flyers needed *repairs*.

At least none of the flyers seemed to have suffered a great deal of storm damage. That made sense though: if there was one city where she'd expect everyone to have excellent protections against inclement weather, it was Yagra'hai.

"Pity that whaling cutter's too large," Kimat said. "That one's in great shape."

Anahrod nodded absently as she continued looking, then blinked. "Where?" She located Kimat and followed the girl's stare to the cutter.

"Good job, Kimat," Anahrod said as she stared at the smooth, flowing form of the *Crimson Skies*. "I think you've just found our way out."

⌄

Anahrod found Captain Bederigha at the third drinking house she tried. Under normal circumstances, everyone would be in bed, but nothing about the night had been normal. Once the rampant alert had been called off, Bederigha had taken his crew to a tavern, where they'd taken over one of the back rooms.

They were pretty clearly intending to drink until the sun rose.

Anahrod sympathized, but if she had anything to say about it, their evening was going to go a different way.

She waited by the door while Ris swayed forward with those hips and that waist and a smile that was utterly wasted on Bederigha but still made a healthy chunk of the crew pause from whatever they were doing.

The captain smiled at Ris in a bemused way when she reached his table. He looked tired, but probably everyone in Yagra'hai was tired just then. "I am so sorry to disappoint you, miss, but—"

Ris set a bag on the table, open at the top so scales spilled out when it tipped over. "Might we speak with you in private?"

The captain snagged the drawstring with his hook and pulled the bag in his direction. "This buys you a few minutes of my time, yes." He leaned around her and yelled out, "All right, crew! Go get yourselves some drinks at the bar! Thrasion, Valagh, you two stand watch at the door. Grexam, you stay with me." He eyed Anahrod's group with an assessing gaze. He raised an eyebrow at Kimat's age, passed over Claw and Naeron, and then stopped dead at Anahrod. He frowned at Anahrod's waist.

More specifically, he frowned at Anahrod's sword. It was a thoughtful frown, like he was trying to place why the sword seemed familiar.

Naeron shut the door and plastered one of Kaibren's silencing inscriptions on the inside panel. Anahrod's throat clenched. That was likely one of the last ones the man had ever made . . .

No, she refused to think about it.

Claw cruised around the tables, inspecting everyone's cards. After a tiny hesitation, Kimat joined her.

Anahrod removed her veil. "Captain—"

Bederigha pushed back from his chair and stood. "No!" he told her like he was scolding a pet. "No, no, no. Absolutely not. Do you have any idea how many people are looking for you right now?"

"All of them, I think," Anahrod answered. "That's why I need your help."

The captain hadn't called for Grexam to do anything, hadn't called for his men to return. The smallest ember of hope flared in her chest.

"You got my cutter half-destroyed last time," Bederigha argued.

"I also made sure they fixed it," she pointed out.

"Made sure they fixed it? Ha!" Bederigha spat. "Have you ever tried to part a dragon with so much as a single scale? I'm arguing with them over every bolt, every weld! You'd think I was stealing from their hoards. I'm going to leave here owing those bastards money!"

Ris smiled, smooth as cream, as she leaned her hip against the table. It was not the hip where she wore her sword. "Would you like to fix that?"

The cutter captain started to retort, then stopped, blinked, and took a good, hard look at her. "You're a dragonrider."

"Yes, I am," she admitted.

He pointed at Anahrod and raised an eyebrow, as if to say: *How do you explain that then?*

Ris shrugged. "She's really good in bed."

Grexam coughed over a laugh while Anahrod smiled ruefully.

Bederigha squinted and took a moment to study the ceiling. He scratched the side of his cheek with his hook. Then he said to Ris: "Why aren't you riding your dragon? You're not running, are you?" He frowned. "Is that even possible?"

"No," Ris replied. "It isn't. Let's say the only dragon more unpopular than mine right now is Zavad himself."

The captain scoffed. "I don't know about that. I think that dragon that just went rampant is pretty unpopular."

"And pretty dead," Anahrod agreed.

Bederigha grunted in acknowledgment. He squinted at Ris. "Your dragon. He's not a fire dragon, is he?"

"No." Ris looked thoughtful. "Why?"

"A dock fire would be just what we need," Bederigha said. "What you want is for every captain in this city to get it into their head that it's not safe to stay here and they need to leave, now. The only reason it didn't happen earlier was because the storm made it too dangerous." He snorted. "Two dragons rampant in a week, one of them an elder. It wouldn't take much."

"Do you need the docks on fire or is it enough if they start collapsing?" Ris asked.

Anahrod gave her an odd look. Acid, then? Was Peralon's breath weapon acid?

"Collapsing is better, honestly, if you can do it slow enough that people have plenty of time to get out. Fires have a bad habit of escaping their leash." Bederigha nodded to himself, patted his coat as though making sure something valuable was still where he'd left it. "And what exactly are you offering for me jeopardizing my crew and my cutter and having us potentially cross paths with angry dragons?" He moved the scales on the table about with his hook. "This ain't going to cut it."

Fortunately, Anahrod had thought this part through. "No tariffs on sky amber for the next full cycle in Crystalspire."

The captain squinted at her, then scowled. "You can't promise me that."

"I can," Anahrod said. "The current mayor of Crystalspire is my father." Anahrod shrugged. "And my mother is his wife, Belsaor, and you know what they say about *her*."

"The dragon lady of Crystalspire," he mused. "She does have a reputation. There's a drinking song about her making the rounds."

Anahrod didn't want to know. "My point is, I can make good on the offer." Her mother wouldn't be happy about the agreement, but Anahrod would make damn certain she honored it.

He scratched his cheek with the edge of the hook, looking thoughtful. "Funny, though, I thought that woman only had one daughter—" Captain Bederigha gave Anahrod a knowing glance.

She felt her gut twist. "You've figured it out." He knew who she was, knew that she was "Anahrod the Wicked." Damn it all.

"Yeah, I figured it out," he agreed.

The room fell silent, and Anahrod felt a horrible sense of dread. She didn't want—

If this was ruined because of those stupid stories . . .

Captain Bederigha sucked on his teeth. "You throw in your casserole recipe, and we have a deal." When Grexam made a surprised sound, the smaller, rounder man said, "Oh, you didn't try it, darling. I'm doing humanity a favor by ensuring it's recorded for posterity." When Anahrod stared at him in surprise, he grinned. "I've seen you at your worst, girl. And at your best. And in neither one of those cases were you sacrificing any babies. I'll take my chances."

He took a long drink and said, "All right, Red. You have your dragon do whatever shenanigans it needs to do to start the docks crumbling. Probably want to wait until dawn, though. Best if people can see where they're running. When the other flyers start stampeding, we'll sneak out in the other direction."

Anahrod cocked her head. "The other direction" made little sense. There was no "other direction." The only clear path out of Yagra'hai was up.

"Captain—" Grexam's voice was full of warning.

Bederigha grinned into his cider. "Always wanted to try a hurricane slingshot."

"Captain, no!"

"Hurricane . . ." Ris stared at him with wide eyes. "You're going to take us *through the storm wall?*"

He shrugged. "You gotta admit, no one will look that way."

"That's because it's insanity." Ris laughed. "You're a madman!" She clearly meant it as the highest of all possible compliments.

Anahrod said, "You have a deal, Captain."

Grexam released a tired sigh.

"Great." Captain Bederigha set down his drink on the table with a happy thump. "Now put your damn mask on, woman. Do you have any idea how much money they're offering for you? My crew's only human. Let's not give them an excuse to make bad decisions."

That was a fair point. Ris was giving Grexam a suspicious look, but Anahrod would allay her concerns later. Grexam was no fool. No tariffs for five years was a lot more money than what Yagra'hai was offering for her capture or death.

The deal done, the captain made his own arrangements, and Anahrod and her four companions headed for the whaling cutter to wait for the dawn.

Escaping from the city was so anticlimactic as to be dull. Anahrod never saw what Peralon did; for all his bright, reflective coloration, he still sabotaged the docks without being noticed.

Anahrod felt an odd ringing in her ears, but it quickly vanished.

The repair yard sat next to the docks, close enough to give the whole crew a ringside seat to the show. The first symptoms were easily overlooked, but eventually a creaking groan grew too loud to be ignored. People began running and shouting, in the manner of all emergencies. Most tried to save their cargo, to hold tight to profits and livelihoods.

Anahrod felt bad, but she reminded herself the city would have to pay for repairs and compensate for the loss of goods. These people wouldn't be beggared by this.

Probably.

Then some captain let greed override sense and spent too long reloading cargo. They were still doing so when the entire section of the pier gave way and collapsed with a creaking, splintering crash.

It reminded Anahrod of the sound falling trees made in a flood.

The sky-amber-inscribed hull wouldn't allow the cloud cutter to fall, but the wind grabbed at its wings. The cutter spun lazily in the air before flipping upside down like a wheelbarrow. Luckily, transports weren't open at the top, but she hated to imagine the crew slamming against the walls, then the ceiling, then the walls again.

It did the trick, though.

At first, it seemed like the various flyers just meant to pull anchor and relocate closer to wharfside. As the pier's giant pylons crumbled, however, the flyers all seemed to reach the same conclusion: the smart thing to do was leave Yagra'hai. With or without permission.

It was chaos and mayhem. Some dragons were happy to see the whiny, always-complaining humans stop distracting them from more important problems. Others were the opposite, understanding how easy it might be for at least one of their problems to escape in the panic. Still other dragons urged calm, considering future relationships with Seven Crests.

During all this, the *Crimson Skies* cut ties and surged straight at the churning gray-green wall of storm cloud surrounding the city.

Anahrod found a tie-off point and hooked herself in. Everyone else, seeing this, followed in kind.

"This is going to be bad, isn't it?" Kimat's voice was small.

"Oh yeah," Claw told her. "But it's okay. We'll get through this." The scarred woman hadn't been more than five feet away from Kimat since she'd tossed the girl over her shoulder back in the tunnels. At some point, Claw had exchanged the role of jailer for that of a big sister. Maybe Claw had latched on to the girl—as a fellow resident of Grayshroud, as a distraction from her grief, as both.

If Kimat didn't watch herself, she'd find herself apprenticed to a stone-cold killer. Anahrod quietly laughed: Kimat would almost certainly see that as an encouragement rather than caution.

Anahrod's mind was wandering, and she came back to herself as she felt delicate fingers interlock with hers, looked over to see Ris's green eyes staring into hers.

"Are you going to be all right?" Ris whispered. She had hooked herself close enough to Anahrod to make reaching out no effort at all. Anahrod pulled Ris closer, setting her hand against the back of the other woman's neck.

"I have survived worse," Anahrod admitted, which wasn't even a lie. The cutter wouldn't fall, couldn't fall. It might be flung about at ridiculous speeds or even smashed against the mountainside in a downdraft—

No. Best not to think of that.

"What about you?"

Confusion flickered over Ris's expression. "You mean Kaibren? I'm upset—"

"I mean Tiendremos," Anahrod corrected. "You never saw him die."

Her eyes widened. Anahrod cursed herself, because Ris looked like she'd just been stabbed. Utterly gutted, and perhaps more than a little mortified that someone had noticed. "Oh. Yes, well . . ."

She fell into silence.

Anahrod thought that was it, that the dragonrider had nothing more to say on the matter, but she was wrong.

"I was just a child," Ris whispered. "I couldn't have been more than five years old. I didn't understand why this was happening, why the dragons who were our friends were attacking us. I'll never forget Tiendremos breathing lightning out over the house while a storm raged around him. My mother told me to run, so I did. I ran and then I stole aboard a cutter to get out of the city." She made a breathy sound that only technically qualified as laughter. "The cutter had already left the city when they found me."

"Oh, Ris." Anahrod squeezed her hand. She wanted to think that they'd found an adorable moppet of a stowaway and had done the right thing, but she already knew that wasn't how this story ended.

Ris sniffed and swallowed thickly. "I thought they'd be mad. I didn't think—" She made a face. "The bastards sold me."

"To the Valekings?" Anahrod said.

Ris's gaze flicked to Anahrod's, eyes narrowed and searching.

"I was eavesdropping when you talked to Sicaryon about it," Anahrod confessed.

Ris huffed. "I see. I guess I don't have to explain that, then." Her gaze focused on something sharp and unpleasant, very far away. "Eventually I tried to run away and ended up—" She refocused her green eyes on Anahrod. "I stumbled onto Peralon's lair and woke him. Not a thing I recommend doing, but if you absolutely must, make sure you're the reincarnation of their previous rider. Much happier outcome that way."

Anahrod frowned. "Wait, you—" She blinked. "Peralon thinks you're the reincarnation of Senros?"

Ris just stared, her lips flat.

Anahrod cleared her throat. "Peralon mentioned Senros to Ivarion in that dragonstone memory he gave me."

"Ah. Yes. He thinks I'm Senros." She shrugged. "I can't say whether he's right or wrong. I don't remember any past lives. All I know is that he's wonderful in this one."

"Did he share any sunny stories about Cynakris?" Anahrod asked the dragonrider. The cutter lurched unexpectedly, and a noise intruded on their quiet conversation—howling wind, muffled by the hull. Anahrod felt a weight pressing her back against the wall.

"Cynakris?" Ris narrowed her eyes, but the fact she was taking the question as an accusation was a kind of confession. "King Cynakris never existed, you know, just like Zavad never existed. They're just stories."

Anahrod picked up Ris's other hand, kissed her fingers. "I know the power of stories, and I know how stories shift and morph. The Anahrod they talk about in plays and books is nothing like me, and I'm betting that's true, too, for whoever inspired the stories about Zavad. Maybe the original dragon didn't hoard gold at all. Maybe they meant to say he *was* gold."

Ris stared at her for a moment in shock, then leaned her head against Anahrod's. "You silly, wonderful woman," she said. "No one will ever believe you."

"Good," Anahrod whispered back. "I should start my own hoard of secrets."

"The other dragons never forgave him for saving humanity," Ris whispered, although it seemed less like whispering against the rising volume of background noise. "They never forgave him for refusing to allow us to be exterminated or enslaved. So they made him the villain, because they could. And now no dragons are left alive who remember otherwise."

Anahrod blinked away the stinging in her eyes. "We're still in chains," she told the woman. "They just call it something else. There's always going to be another Neveranimas, another Tiendremos, because there's nobody to stop them. They've taught us to accept our own enslavement as an act of faith, force us to send them our children. They always, always are ultimately the ones in charge. It can't keep going on like this, Ris. It can't."

Ris put her hands on either side of Anahrod's, cradling her face. "You have no idea how pure and beautiful and good you are, do you?"

"Ris—"

"That's why I became a dragonrider, you know." Ris laughed. "Okay, part of why. I mean, you've met Peralon. He's amazing. But I also want to change things, because there are only a few paths forward from here. What Sicaryon wants is—" Ris shook her head. "Sure, it'll free humanity eventually, but he'll have to burn the sky and flood the mountains with blood to do it. He'll end up killing, maybe not all dragons, but so many of them they will never trust us again. We will push and push and drive them to the harsher, wilder corners of the world until finally it will be like they were never here. They will be . . . stories. Nothing but stories. All the wrong parts of them mangled and warped and repeated forever."

Anahrod knew tears were rolling down her face and didn't care. "Not just dragon blood."

"No," Ris agreed. "It would mean war with the Skylands, too, and maybe that's not a war he'll win—"

"Oh, he would," Anahrod said.

"But even if he doesn't," Ris insisted, "the damage will be done there, too. The trolls of the Deep will stop being stories and become threats, and if the Deep doesn't conquer the Skylands, the reverse will happen. We both know it." She curled her fingers around Anahrod's. "The only way this ends differently is from the inside. Dragons and dragonriders who refuse to treat each other as anything but equals, refuse to let the rest of humanity be treated as nothing but thralls."

"And how in all the heavens do you plan to pull that off?"

Ris stared into Anahrod's eyes sadly. "I have no idea. Revenge was easier, even if I didn't get to see Tiendremos gutted like a rabid vel hound the way he deserved."

"Who knows," Anahrod said as she tipped the other woman's face toward hers, "maybe we can still swing something with Neveranimas."

Ris smiled. "You sure know how to sweet-talk a girl."

Anahrod kissed her as the *Crimson Skies* shook in earnest. From the other side of the hold, either Kimat or Claw or both made "Ew!" sounds in their general direction.

She ignored them.

46

RETURN TO CRYSTALSPIRE

The *Crimson Skies* rattled, occasionally dropping with gut-churning swiftness as the winds tossed it about. The cutter couldn't fly a straight line from the safe, placid eye of the hurricane. Instead, they flew in an increasingly violent, frenzied arc, an arrow pushed astray after being loosed at the target.

Anahrod couldn't judge the speed, but it seemed tremendous. For several hours she had little recourse but to grab the bolt handles, stay clipped in, and distract herself with the taste of Ris's lips.

Kimat became violently sick at one point, but she was hardly the only person on board with that problem. Even those not prone to airsickness succumbed to nausea in such turbulence.

The whole cutter seemed to sigh in relief when the cloud cover broke and the rains lightened from waterfalls to showers. The extraordinary velocity of Captain Bederigha's "slingshot" slowed to something easier to tolerate. The crew busied themselves with damage assessment while Kimat left to wash her mouth and change her clothes.

Ris and Anahrod were repeatedly told to find a room.

Anahrod would've gladly done so if rooms had been available, but as Captain Bederigha had once pointed out to Jaemeh, the *Crimson Skies* was not a passenger liner. Rooms were either already occupied or filled with equipment and supplies. Anahrod and Ris were, like the crew itself, relegated to the main hold.

Anahrod might've contemplated retreating to the pantry if having sex on top of food stores didn't violate every rule of safe cooking practices. But it did and she wouldn't, so they stayed in the hold. Anahrod made rude finger gestures at anyone who had a problem with kissing.

Most of them didn't have a problem with it, but they wanted to tease.

"You're nervous," Ris told her at one point.

"We're flying back to Crystalspire where my last, angry words to my mother were a promise that I'd keep the child she *really* loves safe. I'm going to have to tell her I didn't even do that." Anahrod scoffed. "What's to be nervous about?"

Ris caressed her face. "You're also coming back with the means to track him down and people skilled enough to rescue him."

"Don't forget the news that they're going to have to evacuate the entire city because Neveranimas is going to order Crystalspire burned to the foundations—because of me."

Ris opened her mouth to say something and then closed it again. "Hmm."

"Right. So again, what's to be nervous about?"

Ris sighed. "I'd offer to let them all come to Viridhaven, but we can't take in that many people. Crystalspire's easily twice the size."

Anahrod stared at her. Sicaryon used to joke that her sword—which used to be his family sword—was made in Viridhaven, but she'd always assumed . . .

"You're serious."

Green eyes met hers. "Of course I am."

"I thought—" She blinked. "Even if Viridhaven ever existed, wasn't it destroyed when the Cauldron blew . . . ?"

"We moved," Ris explained simply.

"Right," Anahrod said. "You moved to the Deep?"

Ris pressed her face against Anahrod's neck and nodded. "Long before I was born, but yes. They moved to the Deep. The dragons have no idea where Viridhaven's located. It's stayed hidden and secure for centuries. We could hide there."

"Hiding isn't the answer," Anahrod whispered, feeling an ugly finality steal over her. Varriguhl hadn't been wrong—she might be the only one who could stop Neveranimas. And she needed to be stopped—not placated, not driven off, not fooled.

If she didn't kill Neveranimas, the dragon would come for her, her family, Crystalspire, and finally Seven Crests. And it seemed unlikely she would stop there.

Maybe it always would've come to this.

"What do you have in mind?" Ris asked her.

Anahrod didn't answer. She didn't have an answer.

Instead, she gave the redhead a saucy grin and eyed the eye bolts, the rings, all the various places designed to tie off ropes spread out around the hold, and indeed around the cutter. "You know, I think I screwed up," Anahrod said.

Ris tilted her head. "How do you mean?"

"I shouldn't have just let you clip in during that ride through the storm," Anahrod murmured. "You should've been tied down. Thoroughly lashed to the wall, so you could only writhe against your restraints."

The pupils of Ris's eyes grew large. "With all these people here watching?"

"Probably for the best that we keep you clothed, because the ropes they use on these whaling cutters are coarse, harsh things. Where I'd have to tie you . . ."

She leaned in, whispering. "With every bounce, every jump, the ropes would've tugged and yanked, rubbed against your breasts, between your legs. If you were nude . . . the burns would've been torture."

Ris closed her eyes, breathing fast.

"I'd keep your clothes on," Anahrod continued, "just suspend you from the ceiling with enough slack that you'd really feel the tugs and pulls, the vibrations from the turbulence. You'd be helpless, only able to writhe and squirm and beg. Oh, you'd have begged."

Ris dragged her bottom lip through her teeth. "Begging for you to untie me?"

"No." Anahrod moved her back against the wall, leaned her head against Ris's shoulder. They didn't look like they were doing anything more than recovering from the storm. "Not begging for that kind of release, anyway," Anahrod whispered in Ris's ear. "The ropes wouldn't be enough, you see. They wouldn't press hard enough, tight enough, they wouldn't rub in the right places. After an hour, you'd be begging me to shove anything—anything at all—inside you. A dagger hilt, a belaying pin, my fingers, my tongue. You'd be screaming for it."

Ris shivered, her eyes heavy-lidded as they both watched other people come and go through the room. Other than Anahrod's head on Ris's shoulder, they weren't even touching.

"Everyone would know, you realize," Anahrod whispered matter-of-factly. "The clothing wouldn't fool them. You'd be panting for it, screaming, and everyone could tell. Some of the crew might even take pity on you and offer to fuck you, but I'd tell them no. I'd tell them you're mine and I'm the only one allowed to touch you. Then to make sure they really understood, I'd cut away your pants until the only thing covering your pussy was scratchy, knotted rope and I'd shove my fingers—"

Ris bit down on her lip hard, grabbed at a ring as if her life might be at risk if she let go, and shuddered. She was trying with all her might not to betray how her muscles were clenching, the way she wanted to arch her back, to scream.

"Shhh," Anahrod whispered. "I've got you. Don't worry now. I've got you." She gently pried the other woman's fingers from the bar, interlaced them with her own. She stroked the other woman's hand.

Ris exhaled in one long stream and didn't move for a minute.

"I think you might be the cruelest woman I've ever known," Ris told her finally.

Anahrod just smiled. "And you love that about me."

"And I do," she sighed happily. "So much."

"Let you in on a secret," Anahrod said.

Ris raised her head. "Oh?"

"You know how Sicaryon has roses on his garden rings?"

Ris frowned. "I noticed that, although it didn't really match his behavior in bed—" She stopped. "Wait. Was he *lying?*"

Anahrod laughed. "I can't say for certain—tastes change—but . . . the Sicaryon I knew was much more of a fan of following orders in bed than giving them."

"Oh, what a brat." She gave Anahrod a faux serious look. "Someone needs to train him better."

Anahrod sighed. "So I'm realizing." She pushed herself away from the wall. "I'm hungry. Do you want me to bring you back something?"

"Yes, please." Ris raised an eyebrow. "Anahrod."

"Yes?"

Ris's expression turned serious, and her eyes lost their flirtatious sparkle. "Don't think I didn't notice how you didn't answer my question and changed the subject. I loved it, mind you, but I still noticed."

Anahrod still didn't have an answer to that, or rather, she didn't have an answer that she dared speak out loud. Technically, Ris hadn't repeated her question, so Anahrod chose not to acknowledge it.

Some things hadn't changed since when she met this frustrating, intoxicating, glorious woman. Anahrod still wished they'd been born under different stars. Rather than stealing diamonds, Anahrod wished they'd been better about stealing time with each other. She wished she'd been less of a proud, stubborn fool, that she'd let herself enjoy what few moments she'd been given. It ultimately would've changed nothing, but it would've been nice to die with better memories than a drunken three-way and a few words whispered in the hold of a leviathan harvester.

Ris should've been worshiped—she deserved that, damn it—and Anahrod had been too busy telling herself that admitting her feelings meant surrender to bother entering the church.

She left to see if she could beg something from the galley without waiting until mealtime.

Because humans could make smart decisions, they rarely spoke of how modern flyers—flush with the latest inscriptions, built to the latest standards—traveled faster than most dragons flew. It was only after too much wine, lounging in a drinking house that dragonriders never visited, that they might lower their guard enough to brag about speed records.

It isn't because cutters are faster. Rather, dragons have to stop to rest, to sleep, to eat. Whereas a flyer only stops when it reaches its destination.

Combined with the violent but effective head start they'd gained from the hurricane, it wasn't such a surprise when the *Crimson Skies* arrived at Crystal-spire before any dragons flying there from Yagra'hai.

With one exception. Apparently, Peralon flew so fast he still made it to Crystal-spire before the *Crimson Skies*.

Once they disembarked, they took a carriage to the dragon landing yard where Peralon waited. Ris ran over and pressed herself full body against the dragon's head. She then ignored everyone else in favor of scratching the dragon's cheek while crooning softly.

"Why are we here, again?" Claw asked as they watched Ris's reunion with her dragon.

Anahrod sighed. "We're waiting for my mother's spies to report to her."

"Oh," Kimat said. "That makes sense."

Eventually, two carriages pulled up, one of them the familiar, gaudy official mayoral carriage. That carriage door opened, revealing Belsaor Doreyl, who looked like a queen who'd forgotten to wear her crown.

She dressed like it, too—as though Belsaor suspected that at any moment some palace revolt would force her to flee Seven Crests with only the wealth she carried on her person. Anahrod wondered if the ostentatious display of wealth had worked for or against her mother's political aspirations. In Crystalspire? It was just as likely to be taken as proof of Eannis's favor.

Belsaor walked forward. Her gaze swept over the group, noted who was present and who was absent. Her eyes finally landed on Anahrod and stayed there. Her expression was as cold as the highest mountaintops, twice as sharp, and every bit as dangerous. Anahrod was so surprised to find herself unslapped that for several seconds she could only return the woman's stare.

There was no sense delaying the worst, was there?

"The other dragonrider who was involved in this, Jaemeh, has murdered his dragon and kidnapped Gwydinion," Anahrod explained without prelude. "Jaemeh's fled with him, and we plan to track down Gwydinion the same way they originally found me."

Belsaor digested that news with a sour expression. Finally, she said, "Why are you here, then, and not doing that?"

"Because Neveranimas knows who I am and that I'm alive," Anahrod said, "and we discovered that the whole reason she wanted me dead—the reason she still wants me dead—is because of my blessing. Because I can calm animals. And since Gwydinion has the same blessing, and she knows the two of us are siblings—"

"She'll come here to kill the whole family," Belsaor finished for her.

"You might be underestimating just how little she cares about humans," Ris said as she walked back from greeting Peralon. "Don't assume Neveranimas will content herself with the Doreyl family when she can instead wipe out the entire city."

"Since Gwydinion's a lot harder to find than a city right now," Anahrod said, "we came here first."

Belsaor looked like she had just swallowed raw fruit. "Given the magnitude of the two options, there's no reason to think she wouldn't do them both at the same time. She knows how to delegate." She walked up to Anahrod and rested a hand against her daughter's face.

It was strange indeed to realize the woman had to look up to do it.

"Do you need anything?" Belsaor asked her. "Food, supplies, weapons. Anything?"

Naeron pushed forward. "A map."

The woman turned to him. "A map of what?"

"The south," he told her. "Aerial map of land from mountains here south to coast, from Yagra'hai to east of Seven Crests." He paused. "Include the Bay of Bones."

"The Bay of Bones will be accurate in location since it's a common navigational reference point, but don't expect any great fidelity to the shape of the coastline. It changes too often, no one goes there, and thus no one cares if the cartography isn't faithful."

Ris visibly stopped herself from responding.

"Close is fine," Naeron replied.

"Food might be a good idea," Anahrod said. "We ate on the cutter that brought us here, but we don't have our own stores." She smiled at her mother. "Oh yes, and the cost for hiring a whaling cutter to sneak us out of Yagra'hai when every dragon in the city wanted to kill us is an exemption from all sky amber tariffs for the next five years."

Belsaor opened her mouth and then shut it again with a sharp, angry click. "Fine."

Anahrod raised an eyebrow. She'd expected more of a fight on that one.

Belsaor stood there for a second, glaring at Anahrod with her glittering, sharp eyes. Her gaze was judgmental and appraising.

"Take that off," her mother demanded, pointing to the veil.

"Do you think that's a good idea?" A rhetorical question: it was a terrible idea. Anahrod had zero doubt that it would be a political disaster for her biological father if word spread that not only was Anahrod the Wicked back but had been given aid and succor by her parents.

"I don't care," Belsaor announced. "I want to see you."

Anahrod hated the way her stomach clenched, the way she felt like she was about to be graded and found wanting. Told to straighten up, neaten her clothes, put a comb through her hair . . .

She pulled off the veil.

Her mother stared at her with an expression that Anahrod had no idea how to interpret. She didn't think she'd ever seen it before on her mother's face. She had no basis for comparison. Her mother's mouth twisted strangely . . .

Oh. She was smiling.

"My little girl," Belsaor whispered. "My baby. I don't know how you managed to survive all these years. I didn't even let myself dare dream you might still be alive. This might be the only chance I have, so I have to tell you"—her mother stepped closer and wrapped her arms around Anahrod—"I am so proud of you."

After a panicked second of confusion, Anahrod realized that her mother was crying.

So was she.

Belsaor pulled back, hands still on Anahrod's arms. Tears were still falling down her cheeks, sparkling in the light. Anahrod nearly laughed, even though it would've been inappropriate, because her mother was a beautiful crier.

Of course she was.

"That bastard never told me," her mother said, "not until you were already . . . already gone. I didn't know. You have to believe I didn't know."

"I believe you," Anahrod said. She did. She couldn't imagine her mother lowering herself to tears and a public scene for anything less than the actual truth. Not when those tears, that scene, would cost her so much.

"Your brother let nothing stop him from bringing you back to us," Belsaor said. "Now it's your turn. I know you'll succeed, because what has ever stopped you?"

Anahrod laughed and reached out, mirroring her mother's hands on her arms. "Okay, that's enough. I can only handle so much sincerity before I go into shock and then I'll be useless to everyone."

"I fear that allergy comes from my side of the family." Her mother took a step back. "I'll have supplies delivered immediately, along with a map. Don't worry about us. We have an evacuation plan for just such circumstances. We'll start right away."

Anahrod exhaled. She'd feared her mother wouldn't take the danger seriously, that she'd accuse Anahrod of exaggeration. To have her word accepted immediately meant more than anything her mother might have said about being proud.

It meant her mother *trusted* her.

Anahrod swallowed thickly. "Thank you."

Belsaor sniffed. "When this is all over, return to us. You'll spend time with your father, understand? And you'll bring your girlfriend for dinner." She gestured in Ris's direction.

Anahrod gaped. "How could you know—?"

"Your brother said you two couldn't keep your eyes off each other the entire trip back from the Deep," her mother said primly. "I'm expected to believe you left it at flirting? Please. I have eyes." She swept away from her daughter, back toward the carriage.

Ris watched the woman go, then turned to Anahrod. "Did your mother just say I'm sexy?"

"Yes, I believe she did," Anahrod said, "and we will never speak of this again."

Ris's laughter followed her all the way back to the Deep.

PART NINE

WHAT GWYDINION SAW

A CHANGE IN PLANS

"How are you planning to escape?" Gwydinion sullenly asked as Jaemeh steered the cutter. "You can't use the eye. They'll see you."

Jaemeh gave him an annoyed look. "Did you forget I rode a storm dragon? We'll leave through the storm wall, and it'll be the smoothest flight you've ever experienced."

Gwydinion crossed his arms over his chest to cover for checking on Legless's position. "No one in Seven Crests will help you. Not after what you've done."

"You're an annoying little boy, has anyone told you that?" Jaemeh snapped. The dragonrider was grimacing, a thin sheen of sweat at his hairline.

"Are you injured?" Gwydinion hoped he wasn't: Gwydinion knew how to fly a cutter, but not through a hurricane.

Jaemeh didn't answer as he steered the flyer. He took care to make sure they stayed at roughly ten thousand feet above the mountain slope, which Gwydinion thought was interesting. When the winds began to batter the craft, Jaemeh closed his eyes. He seemed to be casting a spell, one that took considerable effort and energy.

The man was vulnerable and yet Gwydinion didn't dare do anything. Unfair.

"Don't get any ideas," Jaemeh said when he opened his eyes. "You're convenient. You're not essential."

"I haven't tried to escape," Gwydinion protested. "And being concerned about our destination isn't unreasonable."

Jaemeh ground his teeth together and bent over, hand to his stomach. He breathed shallowly through his mouth.

"You're not doing well," Gwydinion said. "Really, are you hurt?"

"No . . . but *he* is." Jaemeh laughed. "Sure, now he shares himself."

"Tiendremos?" Gwydinion couldn't help but feel a horrible fascination.

"Yeah." Jaemeh showed all his teeth. He wasn't smiling. "He's putting up a fight. Always knew he was a tough bastard."

"He hurt you, didn't he?" Gwydinion's voice was small.

Jaemeh snapped out of the daze that had threatened to take over. "How did that work out for him?"

Gwydinion had no answer for that. All he could think about was Tiendre-mos being rampant. Neveranimas wasn't a fool. The moment she noticed, she'd check on her hoard, and then she'd find Anahrod.

And then his sister would be dead.

Gwydinion felt his throat close, his eyes sting. He couldn't believe . . .

He wiped his eyes, and then his nose.

Neither of them spoke for some time after that. They couldn't have talked if they'd wanted to, given the noise of the storm. Jaemeh's magic had softened the turbulence, but lightning strobed, thunder hammered, and wind howled.

It was hours before they'd passed through the storm, the churning clouds scattering to reveal a star-pricked sky. Then Jaemeh cried out, stifling a scream between clenched teeth. After the noise tapered off, he slumped against the flyer seat, each muscle slowly unwinding from a rigid, locked position.

Jaemeh started laughing and didn't stop.

Gwydinion knew what it meant: Tiendremos had died.

He shuddered and wondered how many people had died this time.

"You can't be that upset about a dead dragon," Jaemeh told him. "He was a bastard."

"I don't care about him," Gwydinion replied sullenly. Gwydinion allowed himself time to feel sorry for himself. To wonder if Ris would rescue him.

She couldn't, could she? Maybe if Anahrod had been alive, they'd have been able to find him using Naeron. But now? They'd have to return to his mother. Except he had a terrible feeling that Ris and Peralon were about to have their own problems.

Gwydinion was on his own.

"Look, once we get to a safe place, I'll let you go," Jaemeh reassured him. "I just needed you to make sure that Ris didn't pull anything. You see that, right?"

Gwydinion saw, all right. "And then what?"

Jaemeh looked away. "Don't worry about that."

Gwydinion didn't move, didn't react.

Jaemeh didn't have a plan. The dragonrider had been angry and desperate and when this impossible chance had dropped into his lap, he'd grabbed it with both hands, but it'd all been improvised. He had no idea what he was doing.

Gwydinion would've felt sorry for Jaemeh, if he hadn't killed Anahrod. That changed matters.

It would change matters for Sicaryon, too.

Sicaryon would return to the Deep, and he'd be angry. That's what Sicaryon had been trying to tell him. Jaemeh didn't have a clue, either, since Gwydinion was pretty sure Jaemeh didn't realize "Cary" and "Sicaryon" were the same person. Jaemeh knew he had enemies in Seven Crests and Yagra'hai. He didn't know he had them in the Deep, too.

Gwydinion reached into his coat and pulled out a handkerchief. In doing so, he dropped a folded piece of paper and bent over to retrieve it.

Jaemeh beat him to it.

"What's this?" the former dragonrider asked as he unfolded one of Anahrod's wanted posters.

"Nothing," Gwydinion said too quickly.

Jaemeh examined it curiously. He could only read the parts written in Haudan, but that was enough.

"Can I have that back, please?" Gwydinion asked.

Jaemeh instead showed the page to him. "The person guaranteeing this reward . . . Sicaryon. Who's he, again?"

"He's a self-proclaimed king," Gwydinion said. "Down in the Deep. He hates dragons and he wanted Anahrod to work for him. That's how Ris found her—because Sicaryon had spread these wanted posters everywhere. Ris must have told you."

"I think I remember her mentioning this." Jaemeh studied the page again. "Hates dragons, you say?"

"Dragons killed his parents." It sounded like a good, easily understandable motive for hating dragons. He'd claim he'd misheard if it became important later. "But I don't know how to find him."

Jaemeh paused. "I didn't ask if you did."

Gwydinion widened his eyes. "Oh. Right. That's good. We ran into some of his soldiers when we were down there and they'd trained rock wyrms to fight for them. It was scary."

"I imagine." Jaemeh folded the poster and tucked it into a pocket.

Gwydinion studied the dragonrider—or rather, the former dragonrider. Jaemeh was more shaken than he pretended, with trembling fingers and an uncontrolled tic below one eye. The excitement, the fear, the shock of what he'd done had him wound tight, but the tension was draining.

"How did you do it?" he asked.

Jaemeh blinked at him.

"How did you kill Tiendremos?"

Jaemeh gave him a hard stare, such that Gwydinion wondered if he'd pushed his luck too far. Then Jaemeh fished through his sack and pulled out a large grayish-brown stone—a sphere of rainbow feldspar, meticulously polished, which caught the light with flashes of red, orange, and green. "This is Neveranimas's alternative to having a dragonrider. She calls it the Rampant Stone, because . . . I don't know. She likes to call a door a door, I guess. She dumps all her anger, all her emotions, into this thing, and when it can't hold anymore, she empties it out into some convenient dragon. Who goes rampant."

"And you used it on Tiendremos."

The man scowled. "Don't give me that look. You'd have done it too if you'd suffered even a quarter of the shit that bastard did to me. He—" Jaemeh shuddered. "He deserved it," the man whispered.

But Anahrod hadn't. Kaibren hadn't. Gwydinion didn't say the words out loud.

Jaemeh scratched his cheek. "I'm going to land us on an unpopulated mountain. Get some sleep. I'll figure out where we're headed next in the morning." The man paused and added. "Do I need to mention that if you try to escape, I'll kill you? Because we can discuss it if you think it'll help you make smart choices."

Gwydinion raised his chin. "No, you don't need to mention that."

"Good. That makes this easier."

Gwydinion went into the back area. Ris (no, it would've been Jaemeh, wouldn't it?) had provided them with a small but well-appointed cutter. Given the general assumption that most of the crew would've used it, it did not surprise him to see hammocks slung across the main cabin, with a further set of cots on the floor. Everyone had their own sleeping area. Practically luxurious.

Less nice, now that he shared the cabin with Jaemeh alone.

Gwydinion searched the cabinets. He discovered bottles of flavored vinegar water and a variety of foods. Several days' worth if the full crew had been on board, easily weeks for the two of them. A small galley could be used for cooking.

Gwydinion didn't feel hungry, but his body was too busy tying itself into stress knots to communicate basic information like "you should eat something." He pulled out a bottle of pickled vegetables and some bohr grains and tried cooking himself dinner. He wouldn't claim to be a good cook, but he could make something edible.

It's not like he'd be able to taste it, anyway.

Gwydinion didn't make enough for Jaemeh, but Jaemeh never asked for any. He probably wasn't hungry either.

Afterward, Gwydinion cleaned up after himself, straightened the area, and picked a hammock. He lay in it for a long time, stared up at the ceiling, and thought about what he'd need to do next if he wanted to get out of this alive.

Jaemeh nudged Gwydinion awake.

"This Sicaryon fellow. Think you could find him?" Jaemeh asked without prelude.

Gwydinion rubbed his eyes. "I'm sorry?"

Jaemeh scowled. "The fucking troll king! The one who put out this reward for Anahrod." He shook the parchment at Gwydinion. "Do you know how to find him?"

Gwydinion swallowed. "Well, I—"

"The truth," Jaemeh said.

"Maybe," Gwydinion admitted. "He burned down a swamp. It has to be visible from the air. But . . . we don't even speak their language."

"We don't have to." Jaemeh waved the wanted poster again. "Half of this is written in Haudan—they speak ours."

Gwydinion gulped. "The swamp was east of the Bay of Bones."

"Fine," Jaemeh said. "Come help me look."

Gwydinion did so. He even managed it without smiling.

48

DRAGONRIDER IN GREEN

"Eannis," Jaemeh muttered. "How can they stand living like this?"

Gwydinion gave the former dragonrider a look. "They" could only be Deepers, and Gwydinion and Jaemeh had yet to find any. The green jungle canopy spread out under them, a soft, nubby pile resembling lichen from a distance.

The air thickened noticeably as they descended—that was likely what Jaemeh was complaining about.

Gwydinion agreed: it was unpleasant. He hadn't been able to stop whining about it the first time: it had felt like breathing through a wet towel even with Kaibren's inscribed clothes. This time was more bearable since Kaibren had improved his design, but . . .

He needed to stop thinking about Kaibren.

"I don't think they have a choice," Gwydinion said.

"No, I suppose not. Poor bastards. There's no way I could ever live down here," Jaemeh said.

"Anahrod says you get used to it." He paused. "Said, I mean."

Jaemeh's mouth twisted, but he ignored the slip.

A dark shape caught Gwydinion's attention. He pointed. "There! That has to be it!"

"That's what you said the last three times, kid," Jaemeh muttered, but steered the flyer in that direction.

Gwydinion was certain that this was the area where their group had been forced underground. Unfortunately, he'd forgotten an important point: the targrove trees were resistant to the fires that spread easily through the area. So, while the trees were blackened and stripped of leaves, they were otherwise strong and healthy.

They didn't have a clear place to land.

"Do you think we could tie the flyer off to a tree and climb down?" Gwydinion asked.

There had to be an air dock in the Scarsea lands for Sicaryon, but Gwydinion had no idea where he'd find it. He would've had to pretend ignorance even if he had known.

"I guess I didn't think this one through," Jaemeh admitted. "If we're careful to pull up near a larger tree—"

An enormous boom, like a thunderclap, split the air. A second later, the entire flyer bucked violently, slamming Gwydinion against the side. Jaemeh fought to hang on to the steering controls. A loud whistling sound screamed behind them.

The blood drained from Gwydinion's face as he looked over his shoulder, at the back of the flyer.

Because there was no back. The aft section of the flyer was *gone.*

"What the hell—?" Jaemeh glanced back and began swearing. "Someone's casting spells at us."

"Land!" Gwydinion shouted.

Not that they had a choice. The flyer didn't have enough structural integrity to keep them airborne.

"I don't—" Jaemeh abandoned his protest and instead jumped out of the gaping hole.

Gwydinion swore. Jaemeh hadn't even pretended he gave a damn about what happened to Gwydinion, had he?

Gwydinion activated the bracelets on his wingsuit and jumped.

He dodged around the gigantic trees, coasting down low enough to roll into a landing. He felt bruised, but otherwise uninjured.

Definitely a win.

Gwydinion paused as he heard the flyer crash through the trees. Somewhere ahead in the targrove swamp, he thought.

He made a point of remembering that for later—Jaemeh had abandoned all the folding boxes full of diamonds when he'd abandoned the flyer.

He also didn't see any sign of Jaemeh, however, which was more worrisome. Gwydinion wasn't such an optimist as to think the man dead—he assumed dragonriders learned spells to slow their falls.

Animals moved nearby, but it wasn't easy to distinguish type. Hopefully he'd sense any dangerous predators in time to do something.

If he was being honest, he hoped the Scarsea captured him. They'd keep him safe.

Then he heard a strange, crackling, buzzing sound. He couldn't identify it at first, and then paled when he did: electricity.

"No!" He started running toward the lightning. "No, Jaemeh, stop attacking! Stop attacking them!"

The foliage gave way unexpectedly. Gwydinion saw Jaemeh, three Scarsea warriors, and three rock wyrms. Two rock wyrms, technically, because the third had collapsed on the ground, dead.

"We surrender!" Gwydinion yelled in Sumulye. "We have food!"

A Scarsea spotted him, leveled a spear, and said something too fast for him to decipher.

"I don't speak Sumulye," Gwydinion told the warrior, keeping his hands raised. "We surrender. We have food."

The man gestured at Jaemeh and asked a question. Gwydinion had a pretty good hunch that if he understood Sumulye, it would've translated as something like: *Oh yeah? Then why is this asshole still trying to fight us?*

"Jaemeh!" Gwydinion yelled. "If you kill these people, we won't get to see the king because we'll be dead!"

More noise came from the nearby foliage. This time Gwydinion identified the animals: more rock wyrms.

They were being surrounded.

"They can try to kill me, but I won't make it easy." Jaemeh lifted his hand, again crackling with hot-blue energy.

"No!" Gwydinion told him. "Sicaryon won't forgive you if you kill his people. Surrender!"

Jaemeh threw him an annoyed look, but he lowered his hand. The timing was perfect, because a few seconds later more harnessed rock wyrms sprang from the bushes, along with more purple-painted Scarsea soldiers. None of them looked friendly. In fact, they looked less friendly than the group already pointing weapons at them.

"We surrender!" Gwydinion called out. "We have food!"

Jaemeh scowled. "I thought you said you don't speak the language?"

"I don't," Gwydinion protested. "I learned how to say a few phrases."

"Please tell me you haven't been asking for directions to the bathroom."

"Nope," Gwydinion said. "I've been telling them we surrender, and that they don't have to kill us because we brought our own food, so we won't be a drain on their resources." The boy shrugged. "More or less."

One of the Scarsea started yelling an interrogative at Jaemeh.

"Tell her 'I don't speak Sumulye,'" Gwydinion suggested. "It means you don't speak their language."

Jaemeh dutifully repeated the phrase. He tried, anyway.

The Scarsea started laughing.

Jaemeh scowled and turned red. He wasn't used to being laughed at. "What did I just say to them?" he demanded.

"How should I know?" Gwydinion said. "But their language is tonal, so it definitely wasn't what I said."

"Kid, I swear I'm going to kick your ass so hard—"

Gwydinion turned to the guards and said, very carefully, "My blood sister is Anahrod, whose sword-brother is Sicaryon. I call on you to deliver me to the brother of my sister."

The jungle was never quiet, but the Scarsea all stopped yelling or talking or whatever they'd been doing to stare at Gwydinion. Someone asked a question; Gwydinion repeated the phrase, and prayed he'd got it right. It would really suck to find out he'd just threatened to assassinate the king or called his mother ugly or something.

The Scarsea fell to talking among themselves, with someone periodically pointing at Gwydinion. At no point did the archers ever look away.

"What the hell did you just say to them?" Jaemeh looked around at the people.

"I . . . uh . . . I think I told them I'm Anahrod's brother and I want to see King Sicaryon? At least, I hope that's what I said. That also officially exhausts all the phrases I know."

"That one sure seems to have caught their attention."

A Scarsea led a rock wyrm to Gwydinion. The warrior then bent down next to it and cupped his hands into a U shape.

"What's . . . what's he doing?" Gwydinion asked.

"Looks like he's offering to help you up into the saddle." Jaemeh snorted. "Whatever you said must've worked."

"Right. Okay, yeah. Sunshine." Gwydinion let the man help him up and didn't protest when the same man settled into the saddle behind him. It's not like Gwydinion knew how to ride a rock wyrm.

A different Scarsea warrior pointed at Jaemeh, and then gestured forward with what was clearly an "after you" meaning.

Jaemeh raised an eyebrow. "What, I don't get a ride?"

A warrior stepped in behind Jaemeh and shoved him forward.

"Stupid trolls—"

"Don't fight!" Gwydinion ordered. "Just go along with it. We'll get it all sorted out once we reach King Sicaryon's court. I'm sure someone there speaks Haudan."

Jaemeh grumbled as he started walking. The former dragonrider seemed to be regretting all his life choices, which made Gwydinion smile.

At least on the inside.

As they traveled, just how many Deepers lurked nearby soon became obvious. Lots of rock wyrms, too, now identifiable as tame by their harnesses and decorative hide paint.

Jaemeh glanced uneasily at all the soldiers around them. He called out, "Would they really have killed us if we didn't have our own food?"

"I don't know," Gwydinion said. "Might be one of those cultural things that's just polite now, when it used to be a matter of life and death? Anahrod—"

He stopped talking.

When they arrived at their destination, Gwydinion didn't realize at first. He stared at their captors (or escorts or whatever they were) with obvious confusion when everyone stopped, so the rider sitting behind him took pity on him. He grabbed the back of Gwydinion's coat and pulled until the boy's head tilted up.

Even then, it took Gwydinion a moment. What he noticed first was not the evidence of his eyes, but the noise and the smell, which didn't fit his previous experiences in the Deep. Instead of the wet, clean smells of humus and vegetation, he smelled woodsmoke and cooking food, the scent of human habitation.

Gwydinion's brain finished interpreting what his eyes saw: this was a village. It was just a village that had been strung up among the trees rather than sitting on the forest floor.

Calling it a village was unfair, he decided. This was a large settlement, even if he couldn't judge the full scale. For all he knew, it stretched a hundred miles in every direction—the trees blocked his view.

"Zavad's balls," Jaemeh said. "They're using inscriptions."

They were indeed. The inscribed lights were the easiest to spot, but Gwydinion also saw inscribed platforms being used to transfer people and goods from the jungle floor to the village level and back again.

Gwydinion stared. Inscriptions had been carved into the trees themselves. And while using inscriptions on living beings was frowned upon because of shortened life expectancy, the damage might be negligible if the living being was massive enough.

These trees qualified.

"Hey, cut that out!" Jaemeh snapped as a guard pushed him forward. Gwydinion's kidnapper looked on the verge of doing something rash, with spell, sword, or both.

"They can't understand you," Gwydinion reminded him.

"Really? I hadn't figured that out yet." Jaemeh scowled. "I have no idea why I thought this was a good idea."

Because just like Tiendremos, you're not as smart as you think you are. Gwydinion knew better than to say it out loud.

Soldiers escorted them farther into the complex. Each time they were handed off to new soldiers the old ones would point at Gwydinion. After which their manner changed to something polite, even deferential—but only in their treatment of Gwydinion.

This only had to happen twice before Gwydinion wished he knew enough Sumulye to tell them to cut it out, because Jaemeh was becoming suspicious.

"Why are all these trolls treating you like some long-lost prince?" Jaemeh snapped.

"I don't know," he answered truthfully. This seemed a bit much.

The soldiers escorted them across several bridges from tree to tree. The buildings were made from wood with clever, elegant construction techniques.

Gwydinion knew Sicaryon, of course, but that had been back in the Skylands, with Sicaryon doing his best to blend with Skylander culture and customs. These people seemed inhuman, which Gwydinion was pretty sure couldn't possibly be true.

None of the structures—not one—had any areas open to the sky. Everything was roofed, covered, barred. Because even if the larger predators of the Deep couldn't reach them in the trees, plenty of threats still could: blood crows, night flyers, all sorts of horrible insects.

Gwydinion also started seeing Deepers who weren't wearing body paint, or rather, were only wearing body paint artfully, rather than as a survival necessity. This was likely only possible because the interiors were so much cooler—almost certainly the result of inscriptions.

Eannis, he thought. It was little wonder the Scarsea had been rampaging over every other tribe, village, and holler in the Deep. Sicaryon probably hadn't even needed to use violence, just show how people in his new country could live.

Without their camouflage, Gwydinion noticed other differences, strange enough to make him wonder if there might be some truth to the idea that Deepers were a different race. The Deepers came in every shade and color, from pale to darker than any Skylander. He saw a lot of unnatural hair colors—bright blues and vivid greens, fiery reds and strong purples. If they were back in Seven Crests, he'd have assumed someone had invented some new dye formula. Here, though? He didn't know. Maybe he was being prejudiced, automatically assuming that anything good in the Deep had been stolen from the Skylands.

He reminded himself how often it was the reverse.

Another point of weirdness was how no one—not a single person yet encountered—had body hair. Eyebrows, yes. Hair on their head, yes. But he hadn't spotted a single beard or hairy chest, not even the stubble that Jaemeh sported after a night without shaving. Everyone's skin was perfectly smooth. The more Gwydinion looked, the less human that skin seemed.

A sharp voice broke his contemplation.

While he'd taken the time to examine those around him, the Scarsea led them to a large floating courtyard supported by four enormous trees. A man waited for them.

He wasn't Scarsea. His decorations were different—green instead of purple. His head was smooth except for a circle of hair at the top, which had been grown long and braided in the same frizzy ropes that Anahrod had sported when they first found her in the Deep. He wore what Gwydinion had initially assumed was a robe. When he moved, however, the robe was revealed to be nothing but ribbons sewn together at strategic points. In theory, the ribbons hid nothing, but in practice they never gaped enough to show anything interesting.

Still, he seemed very . . . fit.

"Cool breezes to you who come into our house." His Haudan was thickly accented, but he had a pleasant voice—all dark and velvety—that more than made up for it. "Follow in my footsteps." The man turned and entered the large double doors behind him.

Did he mean literally put his feet in the spots where—no. Gwydinion was overthinking it. He ran to catch up with Jaemeh, who had strode after the man without hesitation.

The room was large, although not by dragon standards. What looked like a wide, shallow firepit rested in the center, but he suspected it was something else. It didn't look like it'd ever held a fire, nor like it should, given the wooden construction and general temperature. Inscribed lights had been placed in a spiral leading up the pitched ceiling toward the apex. Artwork decorated the chamber—all different in color and style.

Then Gwydinion made the connection. Each piece of art likely represented a different culture or people, now absorbed into the Scarsea.

The impression of many peoples and many cultures was further emphasized by all the different styles of the people gathered.

The crowd parted as the guards brought Gwydinion and Jaemeh forward, revealing what had been previously hidden: a throne.

It was a large chair, anyway; wooden, and beautifully carved. Someone had set it on a dais, though—Gwydinion suspected that made it a throne. The dais wasn't so high that a person sitting in the chair would be visible over the height of the assembled people. That's why Gwydinion didn't realize that the chair wasn't empty until everyone moved out of the way.

The man on the throne wasn't wearing much, although that was true for everyone except Gwydinion and Jaemeh. What he did wear, however, was unusual even by Scarsea standards.

He wore a short jacket that was wrapped around his arms and left his chest bare. Blood crow feathers had been sewn into the fabric in a convincing imitation of artificial wings. Gemstones caught the light along his arms. The conceit had been continued with the man's hands, where he wore elaborate gauntlets that formed sharp metal talons at the end of every finger. The talons extended a good two inches and looked wickedly sharp.

Claw would be so jealous, he thought.

His body was . . . Gwydinion swallowed. Musculature aside, strips of the man's pale skin caught the light with iridescent flashes, like it was something other than human skin, something . . .

Scaled. It had to be body paint, and if that wasn't the truth then Gwydinion was just going to ignore it, because he had more important things to worry about.

The man wore a golden mask, made to look like a blood crow skull. Then the man raised his head from his chest and Gwydinion realized it was a helmet, but the man had been bending his head so far forward only the top of his helmet was initially in view. He wore little else: a loincloth and sandals, although both were embroidered and jeweled.

This had to be Sicaryon's stand-in, someone who took his place, so no one ever knew if the king was really at home or not. Gwydinion thought it clever, even if he wasn't sure how to take advantage of it.

The ribboned man who'd escorted them crouched next to the throne and spoke with the "king" for a moment. Then he stood and called out, "Gwydinion, brother of Anahrod, you are welcome here. You may take of our food and our protection." The man turned to Jaemeh. "But who are you who comes to us, and what do you offer?"

Jaemeh rubbed his face and stepped forward. He looked tired, physically and spiritually. "My name is Jaemeh. And I'm here to request asylum. As for what I can offer—" He glanced at Gwydinion and scowled.

Jaemeh had meant to offer him, Gwydinion realized. He'd probably figured that if the king had offered a reward for Anahrod's capture, he'd also give one for Anahrod's brother, who could be used as bait.

Except he'd misunderstood their relationship, and "King Sicaryon" had removed the option by claiming Gwydinion as his own before Jaemeh could even speak.

Jaemeh reached into his knapsack and removed the Rampant Stone. "I offer a way to cause dragons to go rampant, crazed. They won't dare attack you if they know you can do this."

The ribboned man acted as translator, whispering to the king again. When he straightened, the translator said, "A rampant dragon destroys everything in its path, Skylander. Forcing such a state on a dragon who is already attacking does us no favors. If that item works as you say, it is not a deterrent nor a defense. It is a tool for sowing terror, and nothing else."

Jaemeh sighed. "Then have your people take it up to the Skylands and use it on the dragons there. Then make your demands."

The ribbon man looked disgusted. He didn't even check with the faux king before replying: "You are a Skylander, yourself. You would unleash this evil on your own people? Have you no—" He quieted as the king reached out and touched a claw against the other man's arm.

Jaemeh ground his teeth together. "If you don't want to use it yourself, then ransom it back to them. I just need . . ." He shook his head. "I just need food, safety, and a place to hide out for a while. What do you need from me? A vow of loyalty?"

The king started laughing.

Gwydinion's head snapped up. He knew that laugh. He'd been mistaken: this wasn't a stand-in at all.

The king raised his head fully, revealing Sicaryon's features. His eyes glittered like the sky peeking through storm clouds.

"Oh, Jaemeh," the king of the Scarsea chided fondly. "A vow of loyalty from you, a man who murdered his own dragon and betrayed his team, means less than nothing. If you want to offer me something, let's start with the rest of the diamonds."

49

THE TROLL KING

Jaemeh stared in shock. Gwydinion even sympathized a little: he'd have been in shock too if he hadn't already known Sicaryon's true identity. As it was, Gwydinion felt elation and no small amount of glee.

"You?" Jaemeh spat. "Cary? You're Sicaryon? The troll king?"

"Let me guess," Sicaryon said as he stood. "You expected me to be green."

Jaemeh grabbed for Gwydinion, intent on retaking his hostage.

This time, Gwydinion was ready. He'd slowly inched away from the dragon-rider. By the time Sicaryon revealed himself, Gwydinion was outside Jaemeh's reach.

Gwydinion dove under the legs of the nearby courtiers.

Those same courtiers stepped forward, hands raised at Jaemeh. Magical energies surged around their fingers. Jaemeh halted, eyeing the sorcerers warily. He held his sword in one hand while crackling electricity encased the other.

"It's a pity you couldn't have shown more loyalty." Sicaryon stepped off the dais.

"Don't talk to me about loyalty," Jaemeh snapped. "I saw what's on that damn stone. Ris was going to let Tiendremos and me burn."

"No," Sicaryon corrected. "Just Tiendremos."

Jaemeh squinted. "What did you say?"

"Her revenge was against Tiendremos, not you," Sicaryon explained in much the same way one would to a child. "You weren't Tiendremos's rider when he murdered her family. She wanted him dead, yes, but you? You would've been free and rich. If only you'd trusted us."

Jaemeh hesitated. "I don't believe you."

"I don't care." Sicaryon drew his sword. "Here's how this will go. You have two choices: fall to your knees and receive a quick death. Or fight me, knowing that if you win, I'll let you walk away, as is the custom of my people. If you use any magic, though, you're in a room full of sorcerers. The Assembly will not grant you a quick death."

Sicaryon smiled. "So, which shall it be?"

The sunken area wasn't a firepit, but a fighting pit.

Gwydinion felt anxious about the outcome. For all that Sicaryon had crowned himself king, that didn't mean he was an unbeatable duelist, whereas Jaemeh had accepted the fight offer with an unsettling confidence.

A man stepped forward and presented Sicaryon his sword.

This was no Skylander style, and certainly nothing like the swords used to unlock Neveranimas's vault. The sword was single-edged, three feet long, and thin at the hilt, but it widened until it ended with a sharp, ragged angle akin to a saw blade. Like Anahrod's sword, the metal mimicked flowing water with a pattern of rippling light and dark metals. Unlike hers, though, this had a wooden hilt shaped like an open-mouthed dragon's head, with a tuft of blood crow feathers erupting from the lower jaw. It was a giant blade—heavy and capable of felling trees as easily as people.

Sicaryon used it one-handed.

Jaemeh used the kind of sword that used to be popular in Seven Crests, and still was among dragonriders: a long, straight, two-sided blade with an ornate metal basket to guard his hand. It was a fast sword designed for slicing.

Gwydinion's mouth dropped open in shock as Jaemeh said, "Keep an eye on this, would you?" and tossed him the Rampant Stone.

Although, who else could Jaemeh ask to hold it? Jaemeh risked the chance Gwydinion might give the stone to the Scarsea, but it was less risk than if he handed it over directly.

The two men circled each other. Jaemeh eyed the large blade. "You might be overcompensating for something." He lunged.

Sicaryon batted the broadsword aside. "We'll see, won't we?" Suddenly his sword didn't move lazily at all, as he flicked the sword upward, sliced toward Jaemeh's hand.

He missed as Jaemeh leaped backward; Sicaryon smiled and returned to his idle circling.

Jaemeh repeated the maneuver.

He was testing Sicaryon, trying to determine how quickly his opponent could move that sword. Sicaryon allowed this with the amused tolerance of a training instructor.

The second time, Sicaryon's response changed. He sliced an upward arc that transformed into a powerful horizontal swing. Had Jaemeh been slower, he wouldn't have blocked in time.

Jaemeh wasn't slower, though. Sicaryon frowned at the man and set his other hand on the dragon hilt's lower jaw, transforming it into a two-handed weapon.

Sicaryon lunged forward, brought his blade straight down from overhead—a fast, intimidating maneuver.

Again, Jaemeh jumped backward, sneering.

Gwydinion studied the fight. Jaemeh wouldn't block if he could dodge; it wasn't prudence, but fear.

Sicaryon continued moving, using Jaemeh's backward leap to give himself the room he needed to raise the sword again. This time, he stepped in and reversed his swing. If Sicaryon had connected, the fight would've been over; Jaemeh would've lost either his life or his hand.

Jaemeh counterattacked poorly, allowing Sicaryon to knock the Skylander's blade out of alignment. Only Jaemeh's speed allowed him to dodge in time.

Jaemeh was too fast, faster than he should've been. He was still cheating, still using magic, just doing so in a more subtle manner than lightning bolts.

The Scarsea king pressed forward, moving his sword in an elaborate figure eight. He had no more trouble wielding the sword than Gwydinion would've had with a stick.

Jaemeh lunged forward, stabbed his blade into Sicaryon's arm. The feathered jacket made it impossible to judge the severity of the wound but couldn't conceal the blood splattering across the floor.

Jaemeh might've said something then, might have made a witty comment, but Sicaryon didn't give him the chance. Instead of giving any visible acknowledgment of the injury, Sicaryon tried to smash his sword down on Jaemeh's. The former dragonrider leaped out of the way. The two circled each other once more.

The smart thing for Jaemeh to do was drag it out, let loss of blood weaken his opponent. Sicaryon was already slowing, making foolish mistakes. He switched feet, bringing his left foot forward instead of his right. With his two-handed grip, he'd just shackled himself.

Jaemeh noticed and smirked. Sicaryon brought his sword up for another one of those high overhand passes, this time tilted to the left. Jaemeh easily avoided the blow as he stepped to the side. As he did, he swept out with his sword and sliced a line of red across Sicaryon's leg. The wound looked shallow, but Sicaryon hissed and pulled his leg back, while Jaemeh pressed forward.

Sicaryon had yet to pull up his blade from the failed overhand swipe. He did so then, knocking Jaemeh's sword away, while his own continued in a smooth, tight arc to come down on Jaemeh's outstretched sword arm . . .

Jaemeh pulled his blade up in time, his movement a blur, but the ragged, saw-like teeth of Sicaryon's sword still ripped their way across Jaemeh's arm. Jaemeh cursed, but instead of pushing the other man away, he pulled a dagger from his belt and tried to stab Sicaryon's arm. At first it seemed like he'd succeed—Sicaryon's sword wasn't aligned to block—but the Scarsea parried with his hilt instead.

Both men backed away from each other.

"You've never played true your whole life, have you?" Sicaryon said as they circled each other.

"I've survived." Jaemeh now held a broadsword in one hand and a dagger in the other.

Sicaryon's expression turned contemptuous as he shifted the grip on his sword. "Not for much longer."

Jaemeh attacked first, feinting with the dagger while he aimed at Sicaryon's undefended legs. Sicaryon brought his blade down. He feinted and used the time to release a catch on his hilt. He pulled apart the hilt's dragon jaws, leaving him with a sword in one hand and a knife in the other.

But he didn't stop moving his sword. Sicaryon brought the blade down hard on Jaemeh's sword, slamming it down into the wood floor, which he followed by stomping his leg down on the flat of the blade, snapping it.

Sicaryon embedded the knife in Jaemeh's throat.

Jaemeh looked surprised as he dropped to the ground. A few seconds later, he was dead.

Sicaryon stared at the body as he panted for air. He motioned for someone to take and presumably clean his weapons.

"What a fucking waste," the man muttered. "Never found out what he did with the diamonds."

⌄

The crowd was still cheering when drums began to sound. Sicaryon tensed while his expression turned terrifyingly grim. People ran—not fleeing as much as finding their posts. The king yelled out commands in Sumulye.

Then he marched over to Gwydinion. "It's good to see you." Sicaryon's tone was jarringly amiable. "He didn't hurt you, did he?"

"No, he—"

"Your sister's alive," Sicaryon said.

Gwydinion gaped. "What? But I thought he locked her inside—"

"She's never been that easy to kill. She went to Crystalspire to warn your parents." The Scarsea king didn't have blood dripping down his jacket anymore, but Gwydinion still thought he should have someone look at his arm soon.

"This way." Sicaryon started rushing him through the palace corridors.

"Dragons have been spotted approaching the city. Honestly, you have my apology. I shouldn't have indulged myself with Jaemeh."

"It's fine. The whole reason I tricked him into coming here was so you could kill him."

"Considerate of you."

"You're welcome." Gwydinion was less sure how he should feel now that he knew Anahrod lived, but Jaemeh had tried to kill her, so . . .

Never mind. Gwydinion felt no guilt at all.

Sicaryon pulled Gwydinion into a wide, treeless courtyard. A broad wooden platform encircled the space, although a thick railing and fine gauze net still blocked access to the open sky.

"How did you get back so quickly from Yagra'hai?" Gwydinion asked.

"A fast flyer," Sicaryon answered. "Although just between us, the only reason I beat you here was because my people shot your flyer from the sky with thunder lances and forced you to travel here the slow way. I only made it back a few hours ago."

"Wow." Gwydinion wanted to know what a thunder lance was, but also didn't want Sicaryon to become so annoyed at all the questions he refused to answer the important ones. Such as: "Where are we going?"

"We aren't going anywhere. Anahrod would raise me from the dead and then kill me again if I let anything happen to you, so you'll be evacuating to safety, and I shall be defending my people."

"But—Sicaryon, wait!" Gwydinion called as the man continued to march him across the walkway. Animals made noises nearby. "Why are the dragons attacking here?"

Sicaryon glanced at the knapsack in Gwydinion's hands. "I imagine because Her Scaliness wants her paperweight back. Anahrod says that Neveranimas can track its location. For a while we thought Neveranimas could track all of it—the diamonds, too—but she's shown no interest in chasing me." He scowled as he stopped at a large, thick metal box, and flipped open the lid. He pulled out a fat satchel. "The dragons arrived faster than I expected. They'll get around to Crystalspire eventually, but you have a little time."

"But what about you?"

For just a second, hopelessness lurked in Sicaryon's eyes. "We would've been ready to fight off a full dragon attack in five years. Had it all figured out." He paused and stared out at nothing. "Pity we don't have five years."

Gwydinion grimaced, his tongue thick and dry and trying to choke off all the air.

"Hurry." Sicaryon grabbed the knapsack from Gwydinion's hands and traded it for the satchel. "That's a scout kit. It has a week's food if you're careful. The kennels are on the ground level. The rock wyrms will take you, but if you think you can manage it, Anahrod's titan drake is there—"

"Overbite! Overbite's here? She lived?"

Sicaryon made a face. "She named it Overbite? Gods, your whole family sucks at naming things. Yes, she's harnessed and ready, but don't take her unless you're certain you can manage it. Whichever mount you choose, head west until you hit the coastline. That'll be the Bay of Bones. Keep it on your left as you travel and head north. Keep going. Viridhaven is at the bay's apex. That's Ris and Peralon's city. Throw their names around the same way you did with Anahrod's here and you'll be fine."

"Do you—" Gwydinion bit his lip. "Is there anything you want me to tell my sister?"

Sicaryon's face froze—not a lack of emotions but an attempt to keep overwhelming feelings at bay. His mouth twisted and he seemed unable to speak. "Tell her—" He pulled off the gold helmet and set it on the box lid. His hair was a mess. "Tell my sword-sister that I love her," he said. "I love her and I really . . . I would've given it all up for her." Then he laughed. "I guess I am, aren't I?"

A tear slid down Gwydinion's cheek; he wiped it aside.

In a small voice, he asked, "Could I . . . get a hug, maybe?"

Sicaryon huffed out a laugh. He looked around; people hurried about, but they were all focused on their tasks. Only rarely did anyone do a double take as if to say, *Hey, is that the king over there?*

"Just this once." Sicaryon laughed darkly.

Gwydinion put his arms around the king, giving him a good, long hug. Lingering was important, because Legless needed enough time to move into position.

"Ow! Lihi!" Sicaryon swore and leaped from Gwydinion, dropping the knapsack containing the Rampant Stone. He gave a horrified stare to where Legless had just bitten his arm. "What—? You bit me! You little brat! Why?"

Gwydinion let Legless curl around his neck. He'd been a good boy.

"Technically Legless bit you? But I know what you meant. I apologize, because I'm sure this won't help your ability to trust others." Gwydinion picked up the knapsack. "You said you have an antidote for this venom, so I hope you weren't just trying to impress Anahrod. Anyway, you should be fine if you hurry." He threw the knapsack strap over his chest cross-body and turned to climb down the ladder.

"Gwydinion, what do you think you're doing?" The man grimaced in pain as he held his arm.

Gwydinion glanced up. "If the dragons are tracking this stupid rock, it makes no sense to keep it where all the innocent people are, does it? I'm leading the dragons away."

"You little fool, they'll find you and kill you!" Sicaryon lunged at him—or tried to—and half collapsed against the railing.

Gwydinion sucked in his breath. "You should find a healer right away. Anahrod will be so mad if I accidentally kill you."

Sicaryon grimaced. "I cannot believe I let a boy . . . Hey, brat?"

"Yeah?"

"Good luck," he said. "Now get out before someone notices you poisoned the king."

Gwydinion climbed down quickly.

50

RUNNING FOR THE BONES

"Hey girl, remember me?" Gwydinion walked toward the titan drake slowly.

As promised, she was harnessed and ready. Her injured leg had fully healed, and she wasn't caged, but why would she go anywhere else? The Scarsea were pampering her like she was a visiting goddess.

Overbite still missed Anahrod, though. The gargantuan titan drake associated his smells with hers: she was friendlier to him as a result.

He had to fight to remain standing when she nudged him.

"I'll take that as a yes," he said, laughing.

Then her head snapped up to the sky. Overbite whimpered and slinked backward under the canopy shade. A second later, loud booms rang out—the same noises he'd heard when the Scarsea had destroyed Jaemeh's flyer with thunder lances.

He didn't know what the range on those weapons was, but if they were firing, the dragons were too close. More explosions sounded, thunderclaps rattling against each other like gods playing drums.

He had no more time to spend on renewing his friendship with Overbite—he just had to hope that the idea that he was encouraging her to run away from the dragons was enough motivation. Right now, he didn't care so much about direction as long as it was "away."

He clipped himself to the harness as she ran. Her speed was soon so fast he ducked to protect his eyes from the wind.

Gwydinion had never experienced Overbite running flat out on all six legs. He hadn't imagined how fast she could move—maybe not faster than Peralon, but certainly more than most dragons. He lay flat against the titan drake's back and shielded himself with the leather satchel.

Thunder lances echoed behind him, the sound mixed with the roaring of dragons.

Gwydinion wondered how quickly Neveranimas would realize her quarry had fled. He was of two minds about it—the faster she did, the fewer lives would be lost, but the longer it took, the more time he had to escape.

After a few minutes, Overbite slowed her pace. Still fast, but titan drakes in the wild likely didn't need to maintain such speeds for longer than it took to fasten their teeth around dinner's throat. Unfortunately, this meant it wasn't a case of "if" the dragons would catch up to them, but "when."

Gwydinion studied the Rampant Stone swinging full and heavy from the tied-off knapsack. In theory, he could send the first dragon they encountered rampant. It still might attack them, but Gwydinion thought it likely that a wing mate would suffer before the rampant dragon ripped its way through the canopy to him. Still risky, though.

Gwydinion pursed his lips, and then reached for the stone. It's not like his attention was required for anything more than literally hanging around.

Perhaps Neveranimas had a few useful secrets to learn.

⌄

Neveranimas landed on the caldera's edge. A shudder ran down her scales. Under the best of circumstances, she wasn't a fan of fire or heat, and this place burned heavy with both.

This wasn't just any caldera either, but the Cauldron; so named because the open pool of boiling lava reminded humans of a cooking pot. The dragon name for the mountain was Prugukuzhanuak—even most dragons had taken to using the human name instead.

The mountain had once been the tallest in the region, possibly the tallest in the world. These days it was a truncated stratovolcano that had been bubbling away since before Neveranimas's birth.

Legends claimed that the volcano's eruption had wiped out the first human city, Viridhaven. She liked the story, even if the volcano had done a much poorer job of wiping out humanity itself.

She was not there, however, to reminisce on happy events. Neveranimas was there because of Ivarion.

"So, this is your bower, pathetic worm." There was no danger that the enormous red dragon might take offense; he was incapable of hearing anything at all.

Ivarion curled up on a spit of land emerging from the lake, his tail half submerged into the molten rock. He seemed to be sleeping.

Neveranimas knew better.

She understood the why, but the how remained a mystery. Ivarion had responded to his rampancy in a manner both confusing and intriguing. She double-checked her heat defenses before landing on top of the red dragon. It wasn't dignified—at least not for Ivarion—but he should've thought of that when he took a nap in the middle of an active volcano.

If only she could kill him and be done with it. Unfortunately, whether through extreme cleverness or stupidity, he'd taken a rider mere days before going rampant. Thus Vari-whatever would know the instant his dragon died. Everyone would make a fuss, and since she couldn't teleport all the way from the Cauldron to Yagra'hai, an alibi would be problematic.

She couldn't just kill the rider either—he never left his damn school.

So here she was, hoping to discover what Ivarion had done.

She focused on the magic skeins wrapped around him, tying him to the rock, cradling him like a hatchling in the shell. He lived—worse, he'd continue to live. Even dragons who slept for years either woke or starved, but Ivarion had tied his life to the volcano itself. As long as the volcano burned, so would he— indefinitely. As the volcano sustained him, in exchange, it took his fury.

In a short time—perhaps only a few years—Ivarion would wake, fully cured of his rampancy.

She reared onto her hind legs, narrowed her eyes, tried to tear the enchantment into shreds. Ivarion had a fire affinity, but not an earth affinity—he wasn't a "volcanic" dragon as slang described them. In theory, if she reinforced the natural boundaries, reminded both volcano and sleeping dragon of their proper places, the spell would crumble.

It did not. His enchantment defied her.

Neveranimas bared her teeth and growled. She refused to contemplate the idea that this overgrown scale kite could defeat her at magic.

But maybe . . .

Neveranimas opened the front of her pectoral necklace and removed the tiny rainbow feldspar stone into which she'd poured so much effort.

She felt an extraordinary sense of satisfaction as she used the Rampant Stone on Ivarion—satisfaction that transformed to fury when nothing happened. The magic pulling his anger into the ground shielded him from further corruption. He was simultaneously rampant and immune to rampancy.

She roared her rage. He was worse than a soft-hearted fool; he was a softhearted fool with the power to enforce it. She'd never thought him interested in magic—hadn't the previous First Dragon picked him as her successor because he was "untainted in spirit"? What did that mean for a dragon if not someone who refused magic? And yet he created this . . . this . . .

The spellwork was elegant.

She hated him so much.

Neveranimas flew to the caldera's inside ledge and paced, ignoring the resulting hissing steam. She'd never found a problem she couldn't solve, never encountered an obstacle she couldn't overcome, by trickery or magic or both. She wouldn't be bested by a fool whose primary qualification for authority had been a supreme lack of ambition.

Neveranimas paused. She couldn't remove the spell, but might it be possible for her to add to it? Let the volcano sustain him, let him give the volcano his rage. But what if the volcano gave that rampant fury right back to Ivarion again? The spell allowed him to take from the mountain—indeed, required it. If she changed the spell to mingle anger with life-giving energy, he had no way to reject the "gift." To do so would be to kill himself.

She sighed in pleasure as the spell took, as the binding changed, as the enchantment shifted from healing to a prison from which he'd never awaken.

She ran her tongue over her fangs as she studied him. Now that she'd solved the major problem, she could concentrate on prevention. This had all happened because the little snake had stolen one of her dragonstones, which, given his nature, could only mean that he'd suspected her.

It wasn't theft if it could be defined as "confiscating evidence."

She shuddered to think what might've happened had Ivarion found the Rampant Stone, but fortunately, he hadn't, and since she soul-marked all her dragonstones, she'd been able to track the one he had taken.

She needed a better vault. Something more secure. The humans were good at making those, weren't they? At least they were good for something.

Neveranimas left to plan and scheme once more.

51

CHILDREN OF EANNIS

Gwydinion gasped as he opened his own eyes.

Neveranimas was . . . she was . . .

She was rampant. Continuously, perpetually rampant.

He suspected Peralon would give all his claws to see the memory that Gwydinion had just experienced. Perhaps if Gwydinion knew more about magic, he could use that knowledge to help Ivarion, but alas, he'd only dimly followed what Neveranimas had done.

No, that memory would've been helpful for Peralon, and anything but that for Gwydinion.

But . . . was there more than one memory?

There had to be.

There had to be a way to control the order in which he experienced the memories, but he had no idea how. Perhaps he had to know what memory to look for in the first place. Since he had no idea what was on the stone, the result was effectively random.

He also didn't know how the memories worked. Did he experience them in real time? That would be catastrophic if he stumbled upon a memory lasting days.

Gwydinion glanced up. The jungle canopy was so thick he wasn't even sure what time of day it was. He thought nightfall was approaching.

Overbite could see in the dark; he had no plans of stopping.

Gwydinion needed to figure out a way to throw Neveranimas off his scent, or this ride would end horribly. In her memory, Neveranimas had mentioned that all her important possessions were "soul-marked." What did that mean? It had to be the method she was using to track the Rampant Stone, but he'd never heard the term before.

Souls weren't the province of humans, except in terms of damnation or repentance. Soul magic was the domain of dragons seeking Ascension, trying to purify themselves in the manner of Eannis.

Gwydinion fished around in the scout satchel until he found rations and water. After, he settled back down with the stone. He paused for long enough to reassure Overbite that she was still the best girl ever (which was an unarguable fact) and turned her in a different direction, perpendicular to his original path but still pointed away from the Scarsea settlement.

He concentrated on the stone again, this time focusing as hard as he could on the term "soul-marked."

⌄

When Neveranimas was young, her father Senuvarus summoned her to his cave.

She'd been confused and a little afraid. Senuvarus was an ancient and hoary dragon who rarely expressed interest in his spawn. When he did, he demanded the most exemplary of his children—the strongest, the fastest, the most powerful.

As Neveranimas was none of these, she rarely saw her sire.

Admittedly, Senuvarus wasn't a social dragon, nor well-liked. He was old and mean and anyone who crossed him regretted it. She admired and feared him in equal proportion.

She fought not to tremble when she arrived to discover they were alone.

"I didn't invite any others," Senuvarus explained. Burning sky amber thickened the air with long streams of smoke. The flowing forms echoed her father's body, himself a long, sinuous stream of silver flowing over his hoard: silver coins, silver jewelry, silver goblets, silver plates. Much of it had gone black from tarnish, also like Senuvarus.

Especially his heart, dragons liked to whisper when they were very, very sure he couldn't hear.

This was another mark of pride—her father was so ancient he hoarded a singular metal. Her eldest hatch mate Kaipholumon had already claimed hoard right when Senuvarus died, but Senuvarus had shown no inclination for doing so, despite his age. Dragons whispered Senuvarus was on the verge of Ascending, but that was just a more polite way of saying everyone wanted him to hurry and die already.

Her sire stared at her, and stared, and stared some more, until finally she crawled forward and asked, "Sire, why have you called me?"

"Have you decided your hoard yet?" Senuvarus asked, which might have been the answer as well as the question.

"Not yet," Neveranimas admitted. Others had looked at her oddly when she'd asked if one could collect magic.

Apparently not.

"Good," he rumbled. "I've been watching you."

He laughed at her when she reared back in wariness. It was not as cruel a laugh as she might've expected. "You're the only one of my children who takes after me, you know."

She tilted her head at this. Neveranimas didn't resemble Senuvarus. Silver striped her scales in places, yes, but she'd taken after her mother, Ashanorak, a dragon of glaciers and the dry, snapping cold of winter. Neveranimas was more violet than white, but the affinity had bred true.

Seeing him so close, too, she was reminded of how *small* he was. She had never reconciled how such a towering presence could be confined to such a petite body.

Senuvarus waved his tail dismissively. "Not in appearance. I care not what color shines off your scales. The others are all like their mothers—bold and proud, strong and fierce." He gazed at her with bottomless eyes. "You are the only one who inherited my love of knowledge, my contempt for weakness, and the intelligence to hide both."

Neveranimas stilled her neck frills, uneasy. Was this a test? A trap? A passion for knowledge was no bad thing, but a passion for magical knowledge was viewed with suspicion. Most dragons thought it better to push such tasks to a rider, but that was irredeemably lazy. They were dragons.

Magic was their birthright.

Her father's chuckle caused a small avalanche of coins to slide down the hill of silver. He'd been adding the coins for centuries, collecting them from wherever and whenever humans made them. He liked humans for that. It was perhaps the only thing he liked them for.

Neveranimas tried to be respectful. She settled on being afraid. "Why are you telling me this, sire?"

He grinned, closed-lipped and showing no teeth. "Because I want you to carry on my work when I'm dead. You're the only one of my spawn who can."

"When you're dead? You're not sick." She lashed her tail in frustration.

He ignored her complaint. "You will collect secrets. You will tell the others you collect something else. Something innocuous. Gradaziza just died recently—say you're taking dragonstones."

Neveranimas froze mid-lash. She lowered her head and stared at him in a posture of questioning. Her ire at being ordered to do such a thing warred with her intrigue. "Why would I collect something you cannot taste or touch? Something you cannot admire?"

"Because I shall tell you a good one," her father whispered, "and it's the most precious thing I own."

She waited.

He lifted his head from his silver pillow of ore and coin. "Eannis was not a goddess, and we are not her children. Do note the past tense, because that was not a mistake."

She canted her head to the side. "You don't believe in Eannis?"

"I believe a being named Eannis existed. She was responsible for what we are." He grinned at her hiss of confusion. "She was not our progenitor, not our ancestor, nor did she create us whole cloth as she created the universe. My parents were not dragons. They weren't even intelligent. They were nothing but animals—sky shrikes, bred large for the purpose of incubating the first true dragons." His eyes flickered with dissatisfaction at some ancient memory. "Or rather, she attempted to create true dragons. Dragons who were like herself. And in that, she failed."

Absurd. That was absurd. Surely he was going rampant. And yet—

If so, he was being very serene about it.

"Why?" In her stunned shock, it was the only question she could form. "Why would she do that?"

"Why indeed," her father said. "Eannis was a being of such power that—well. 'God' is as close a word as any. Yet she did not make this world, or any world. She did not create magic." He frowned. "She did poison our ability to use it, though."

"No, that was Zavad."

He laughed again. "No, it wasn't. I don't know why she did it. She wasn't in the habit of explaining herself to test subjects." He gave his daughter a vicious smile. "And yet somehow it was our fault when we didn't meet her standards, when we couldn't provide her companionship, when she was still *lonely*. So she left. Perhaps she continues her experiments on some other world even now, warping the native races into a parody of her own in an ongoing quest for companionship, even though she will never allow her creations to be her equals. You can be loved and feared by those who blindly worship you, but it is not the same as the love of friends."

She thought about what he was saying, or rather she tried, coming, as it was, from the other side of a vast chasm of shock. "Does one need friends?" she finally asked.

"I never did," Senuvarus admitted. "Perhaps Eannis's real problem was she told herself that she wanted peers, but secretly was terrified she might succeed."

"This can't be true . . ." Neveranimas murmured.

Senuvarus laughed cruelly. "It wouldn't need to be a secret if it was a lie. Let me tell you, child: the best secrets are never lies. Secrets are truths that hide in darkness, while lies are boldest in the sunlight."

"Are there"—she looked up at her father—"are there any others like you? First—first created?"

"A few," he said. "The last time I encountered one of my test siblings, she spent so much time whining about how much better everything would be if Eannis were still here that I ripped out her throat just to shut her up." He sighed. "It made me sad, so I stopped looking."

He stretched, raking his claws against the granite stone of the cave floor. "I will teach you everything she taught me. I will teach you the Names and the Laws and how to use them to craft sympathies and apathies. I will teach you how to move yourself in space-time and how to use soul-marks to hunt and hide. I will teach you how to see the magic, and how to make it yours."

He sighed then, resigned, tired. "You will find it's not enough, not nearly enough. She gave us more questions than answers, because 'she wanted us to discover the truth for ourselves.'" His voice took on a mocking quality.

Neveranimas blinked. "Discover—but we're not doing that! We're not discovering anything! We're not looking for answers!"

Senuvarus gave her a lazy, half-lidded smile. "No. We're not. It's not just a test of intelligence, but of bravery and will. None of what she taught me, what I will teach you, grants you immunity to the corruptive effect of magic on our bodies." He paused. "Maybe it was supposed to be motivation."

"Why," she finally asked, "are you willing to teach me this? I might go rampant and kill you."

"I have survived this long by being careful. You seem careful, too. Perhaps you'll be the one to decipher Ascension. I no longer think I will, and I have grown tired of trying. So no, I don't think you'll go rampant on me, not in time, anyway."

She was stunned into silence.

She said yes. Of course she said yes.

He did exactly as promised. He taught her everything he knew. It took shockingly little time, considering, but he'd warned her that Eannis had wanted them to figure these things out for themselves.

A week after he finished, Senuvarus turned rampant in the middle of a council meeting. He killed three other dragons before they finished him.

Neveranimas began hoarding secrets.

Hoarding secrets, and unlocking the mysteries of the universe.

52

HOW TO LOSE A DRAGON

When he woke that time, Gwydinion realized he'd been making a mistake. Or rather, he'd been making an assumption.

He set aside what he'd learned about Eannis. It was too big, too vast. Every time he tried to look at the fullness of it, he felt sick.

No, he'd assumed the dragonstone had two functions: as a magical artifact to drive dragons rampant, and as a diary.

Both assumptions were *almost* correct.

The stone's ability to induce rampancy was a side effect. She'd created the stone to better understand and explore the boundaries of magic. The stone funneled her excess magical "poison" into other dragons, which allowed her to stay functional enough to continue her research.

More importantly, the dragonstone was her grimoire.

Which meant that Gwydinion knew what he had to do to hide himself. It was all there in the dragonstone. He just had to learn it.

Gwydinion tried not to think about how long Neveranimas had taken to learn the skill. Years wouldn't have surprised him. He didn't have years. He had hours.

More realistically, he had minutes.

On his fifth attempt, he figured it out.

The problem was a translation error. Anytime Gwydinion entered the stone, he understood everything from Neveranimas's perspective, but when he left again, his brain supplied him with translations of concepts that didn't have an equivalent in any human tongue.

So it was with "soul-mark," a concept that had nothing to do with souls, or with marking them. A "soul-mark" (he needed to find a better name at some point) was a way of fooling, well, the entire universe.

Every object in the universe had a "true name" (also a label whose meaning translated poorly) which represented them. The true name *was* them, fundamentally. So if one knew the true name (it was more like a sigil or glyph, really) for Gwydinion Doreyl, one might perform all sorts of magic and be certain it would only affect Gwydinion Doreyl.

Well and good, but the universe could be tricked. Labels could be switched, misfiled. A spell cast at Gwydinion Doreyl might fail, not from error, but because the universe thought a particular chair was *also* Gwydinion Doreyl, giving the spell a fifty-fifty chance of hitting the wrong target.

Yes, it was possible to make the universe think a door was a jar.

Combined with magical sympathies, this was devastating. He already knew that sympathy could track an item or person: that's exactly what Naeron had done when he'd used Gwydinion's blood relationship to Anahrod to track her. But if you could fake the sympathy (by switching the "label") then it didn't matter that the objects carried no actual connection.

One might "mislabel" an item into something that you possessed in some fashion, tell the universe to locate it—as well as anything else out there with the same label, existentially speaking—and the universe would point you right to it.

Neveranimas was too smart to use herself as the "original." It worked both ways, after all. If the universe thought this dragonstone was Neveranimas, then someone could use it to divine her location and affect her magically.

Gwydinion mentally repeated what he'd just said to himself, but slower.

It was dark. Jungle noise filled the air, and the wind streamed by him as he lay on Overbite's back. He was sure he'd have been eaten by wild animals already, if not for her.

It occurred to him it didn't matter what Neveranimas had used as her "primary" for tracking.

All that mattered was that she *had to have it with her.*

Gwydinion could use the Rampant Stone to track Neveranimas, too.

He needed to be smart about this. Gwydinion pulled his inscribed light locket out of his shirt. He didn't open it, not yet. Then he riffled through the satchel by touch until he located a neatly folded bundle of leaves. Gwydinion then huddled under his shirt, trying to keep any stray light from escaping.

If he ever compiled a list of his most bizarre experiences, the top spot would undoubtedly go to the time he was bound to a galloping titan drake, with his shirt covering his face, desperately trying to convince the universe that a jungle leaf was actually a dragonstone. He thought it was hilariously ironic that the only thing that made it possible—the dragonstone—was the same reason he was in this mess in the first place.

Once he was convinced he'd managed it (it was impossible to explain the itchy weird vibrating feeling behind his eyeballs) Gwydinion repeated it with a second jungle leaf.

Then he changed the Rampant Stone to something *else*. This was harder, because it turned out the object fought you if someone with a really strong will (a dragon wizard, for instance) had already messed with it. Fortunately, possession was nine-tenths of magical law, and since he was touching the object, his will won out. The universe became convinced that the Rampant Stone was a piece of chena.

He was working with what he had.

At that point, Gwydinion settled down to track Neveranimas using a jungle leaf.

At first, Gwydinion thought he'd made a mistake, that the leaf was just pointing out the location of the nearest tree of the same type.

Except Overbite still cantered along at a fast clip, while the "tree" was gaining on them.

His heartbeat sped up to riotous levels and his hands turned clammy. The magic had worked perfectly; he was detecting Neveranimas.

It's just that she was only a few hundred yards behind him, closing in fast.

———

Gwydinion didn't know how long Neveranimas had been back there, trailing him from above the tree canopy. Overbite hadn't sensed her, but she could hide herself using magic.

An ice dragon was not the best suited for punching through Deep jungle canopy. Neveranimas could do it, but it would be loud and violent and would allow Gwydinion a chance to escape.

Whereas, if she waited for Gwydinion to cross a break in the canopy, because of river or meadow or just an unfortunate lightning strike from the last storm, Neveranimas could leisurely snatch him up with no trouble at all.

And since dragons saw in the dark and humans didn't, she had a better idea of when that would happen than he did.

He reached out for a night flyer. He found an entire flock of them, but one was all he needed. He held up the jungle leaf and asked for a favor. The little raptor plucked the leaf out of his hand and flew off with it.

He threw the second leaf away since he didn't have enough time to call some other animal. That left one fake dragonstone lying on the jungle floor and a second fake dragonstone flying away.

And him, on a titan drake, carrying a strangely large piece of chena.

[Turn here, Overbite.] He had no idea where he was going, but he'd given up his only means of tracking Neveranimas, so, "away from where the fake dragonstones were" seemed the wisest course.

A horrible sound echoed behind him. Snapping branches, breaking wood, entire trees being overturned and uprooted. Through it all, a strange cracking, creaking sound roared, one so foreign to the Deep that it took Gwydinion a moment to place it.

His father had taken him to the northern mountains once, to a glacier. This sounded like the thawing line of ice, terrible and loud as it broke away and tumbled to the bottom. He felt the chill behind him.

Neveranimas had clawed her way down to one of the fake stone copies, freezing and destroying trees as she went.

[There's a dragon behind us,] Gwydinion told Overbite.

She didn't need to be told to run.

⌄

By the time Overbite slowed down to a walk, too tired by that point to travel faster, Gwydinion still heard the calls of panicking animals, but no sign of a dragon.

That was scant comfort, given that Neveranimas wouldn't give him any warning.

He wished he'd been able to memorize the dragonstone's tracking signature, but he wasn't good enough for something like that.

Gwydinion thought he had done a great job under the circumstances. Varriguhl would give him top marks.

Or Varriguhl would give him top marks if everything he'd done that night hadn't been heretical and illegal.

It didn't seem fair. Humans were in a better position to figure out this stuff than dragons. No rampancy.

Maybe that was because the dragons didn't want them doing it.

He was tired, though. Bone-achingly, sleep-for-a-week tired. He didn't know whether the magic had drained him or it was the stress and strain of a week of extraordinary, ugly close calls with death and dragons. Possibly a combination.

He let Overbite lie down for a few hours. He didn't dare sleep himself, but he also didn't know if he'd have a choice. Pinching himself didn't seem to be cutting it anymore.

He just possibly fell asleep. He couldn't be certain. All he knew was that he'd closed his eyes, and when he opened them again, Overbite was lumbering to her feet in a daylit jungle.

As a dragon hadn't eaten him, he took the win and kept going.

He used one of the remaining leaves to sketch out the inscription pattern Kaibren had taught him—the one that let him know which direction was north.

That done, he turned Overbite to the west and told her to move until she hit cliffs and water.

PART TEN

A
BOILING
CAULDRON

HOW TO DESTROY A SECRET

Anahrod thought she knew what it was like to fly with Peralon—hell, to fly *as* Peralon. But she'd never experienced Peralon in a hurry before.

She had thought nothing could fly that fast.

Anahrod suspected it was only possible because Ris was using her magic to protect them. Even then, it would take hours to reach the Deep and she worried that they'd arrive too late.

[I'd go faster,] Peralon confided, [but it is difficult to breathe. Not to mention what happens if we fly faster than sound travels.]

Anahrod blinked. "What happens if you fly faster than sound travels?" She knew sound took time to move. Anyone who'd ever listened to an echo shouted from a mountain understood that. But she'd given little thought to what that *meant*.

"It's your own personal thunderclap," Ris said. "Not in a good way."

"What are we talking about?" Claw asked.

"Something we're not going to do," Anahrod answered.

Claw gave her a narrowed-eyed look, nodded, and returned to napping. Naeron still slept and would likely continue until their destination. They only had a few hours until sunrise. It came early in the Deep, with no mountains to block the way. She should take the opportunity while she could.

Anahrod couldn't. Somewhere out there, Gwydinion wasn't sleeping either. When they'd first started flying, Naeron had collected a small bit of blood from Anahrod's arm and used it on the map Belsaor had given them.

Now there were three stained areas on the map. Crystalspire had the largest concentration, including two larger blots that represented her biological parents. The second mark was herself, moving across the map in time with Peralon's flight.

Then there was that last mark, her brother Gwydinion, moving erratically but fast.

"Where's he going?" Anahrod muttered as she watched the stain. "It's random."

She'd held on to the hope that Sicaryon had already rescued her brother, but the fact that Gwydinion's mark was still moving at this hour in the morning was not a good sign.

[There are dragons circling ahead,] Peralon informed them. [I would guess Gwydinion's avoiding capture, although I'm unsure how he's traveled so quickly.]

"He might not be by himself," Anahrod murmured. "Will this tell us if he's on the ground or in the air?" She gave Naeron's parchment a dubious look.

"Not until we're closer," Ris said. "At least we know he's not in a flyer anymore. If he was, the dragons would've caught him by now."

That was not as comforting a thought as Anahrod would've liked.

Was it possible that the dragons had already captured him? Her mind threw horrible scenarios at her, suggesting that Gwydinion didn't need to be alive to show up on the map. What if it was tracking his blood in a dragon's stomach?

Anahrod made herself stop, reminded herself that if the dragons had recovered the Rampant Stone, they wouldn't still be circling the jungle like they were blood crows circling a dying yengkal.

She watched as the mark changed direction again, this time heading west. The blot traveled in a nearly a straight line. If he kept going that direction, he'd hit the Bay of Bones . . .

"If he stops once he reaches the bay, we know he's not on a dragon. And if he is . . ."

If the dragons had him, Anahrod had no idea what they'd do. "We can avoid the dragons ourselves, right?"

[Easily. They're flying so far up that we'll be impossible to see if we fly low.] He added, [The situation will change come dawn.]

The morning sun would hit Peralon's scales like a beacon, which would make stealth just a tad inconvenient.

"Any sign of Neveranimas among the circling flock?"

The moon was full, although she logically knew it was already waning, starting the five-day cycle over again. The sky was brighter for it, the world full of gray. Occasionally, the silhouette of a dragon crossed over the moon, but nothing she could identify as Neveranimas.

[I don't see her,] Peralon grumbled with concern. [I don't see her anywhere.]

Anahrod reached out to eavesdrop on every dragon she could find, but none of them were Neveranimas.

"They're waiting for orders," Anahrod said. "That's why they're just circling."

"Lovely," Ris said. "Just what I needed to hear. But where is Neveranimas?"

Anahrod put a hand to her mouth to stop the laughter from bubbling forth. "She can't tell them, can she? She must keep it a secret. She must lie and say I can control dragons—"

"To be fair, you sort of can—" Ris said.

"She can order them to attack places, people. What she can't do—what she constitutionally cannot do—is give away her secrets. She can't tell the other dragons about the Rampant Stone, or what it does, or why she needs it back. She can't risk the possibility that she'll have a dozen dragons with her when she recovers the stone or that they might wonder why she cares so much about a book."

[Ah yes, I see what you mean. I wonder how many times she might have made her life easier by explaining all she knew. But that would mean destroying a secret.]

Anahrod sighed. "She's somewhere out here, grazing the treetops just like we are, hunting my little brother."

54

HELLO, GOODBYE

They had yet to locate Neveranimas, although they found signs of her presence: an enormous gaping hole in the jungle canopy. The sky was still too dark to see fine details, but the general outline of devastation was visible enough. They flew close enough to feel the chill and smell the unmistakable scent of ice.

"Somebody's a cranky baby." Claw snickered, awake again and, like Anahrod, straining to make out details.

"No," Naeron said. When all three women looked back, he added: "An asshole."

Anahrod smiled. Yes, Neveranimas was an asshole. She thought Claw's description was appropriate, too, however: the destruction they'd witnessed was as much a tantrum as an attack.

As they flew closer to Gwydinion's expected location, Anahrod felt increasingly nauseated. If anything had happened . . . she couldn't stand it . . .

She pushed down her anxiety, her fears, and started reaching out to the jungle animals. Who was out there, who was awake. Perhaps she might find one to act as her eyes, letting her see Gwydinion.

The sun had just peeked over the horizon when she spotted Overbite.

Ris responded to Anahrod's gasp so quickly there was no doubt she, too, had been harboring anxieties about all the ways matters might go wrong.

Anahrod shook her head. "It's fine. I'm fine." She hid her grin—it seemed rude to be too happy in front of Claw just then—and said, "It's Overbite. Gwydinion's riding Overbite. He's fine."

[You can talk to him?] Peralon sounded surprised indeed.

"No, I just . . . Overbite would smell if Gwydinion were injured or sick." She inhaled deeply with relief. "I told her not to panic. She was about to scent you."

"So now we just have to figure out how to reach Gwydinion without destroying acres of land and alerting every dragon in a thousand miles," Claw said wryly. "Any ideas?"

"The bay," Naeron said. "Tide's out."

"I wonder if Gwydinion knows it's there," Ris mused.

"He's about to find out the hard way, isn't he?" Claw said.

"It's probably why he's been heading west," Anahrod told them. "I doubt he just wanted the sun at his back." She prepared to grab control of Overbite if she had to. The titan drake wouldn't run off a cliff under normal circumstances, but when a creature weighs twenty tons, momentum is a factor.

Peralon cleared the tree line, soaring out over the bay. With the tide out, it resembled a canyon more than any kind of ocean inlet. That canyon was several hundred feet deep, much of it still shadowed in darkness. What they could see of the bottom was a wet and muddy mass of browns and purples. The purple streaks were the poisonous tendrils of tidefishers, placidly drying out as they waited for the tide to slam back in and deliver the unwary or unlucky into their hungry arms. Interspersed among the mud and tendrils were white sticks of driftwood—or what one might be forgiven for mistaking as such. Anahrod knew better: they were the titular bones of the bay. A few columns of rock broke the "canyon" up—narrower at the base than at the top—which supported desperate, clinging trees and shrubs.

Large animal corpses remained from the last tidal push. They lent the charming smell of rotting meat to the bay's salt, ozone, and petrichor odor. Flocks of noisy seabirds fought over choice bits of flesh the tidefishers hadn't finished.

Somewhere along this line of cliffs, the waterfall they'd used to escape Sicaryon plummeted into the bay. Months removed from the event itself, she still shivered to think how matters might have gone if Naeron had been mistaken about the tides.

The Bay of Bones only saw calm four times a day—at the two high tides and the two low tides. At all other hours, it was an unholy monster grinding up anyone caught in its pull. When the tide returned, it did so with frightening speed, the water pushed up by the narrowing inlet into a giant wave.

"He should be visible in a minute," Anahrod said to Peralon. Anahrod fought to keep Overbite from panicking, because she knew well what dragons meant. She forced Overbite to a halt twenty feet from the edge, as the titan drake broke the cover of trees.

"Hey, kid," Claw shouted. "Do you need a ride?"

"Claw!" Gwydinion stopped struggling with Overbite's harness. He unclipped himself before sliding down Overbite's side. "Anahrod! Anahrod, you're alive!"

Anahrod smiled. She was pleased with that outcome, too. "I am. Let's hurry. We'll throw a rope down for you." She tried not to think about leaving Overbite behind again.

"No!" Gwydinion called back. "You come down! We need to talk! It's important!"

Ris laughed, perhaps just a touch more sharp than normal. It had been a long, long couple of days and everyone's tempers had thinned. "Gwydinion, we don't have time—"

"I know how to fix Ivarion!" he shouted.

⟡

They dropped ropes from Peralon's side and shimmied down to the cliff face. That done, the gold dragon positioned himself on the nearest rocky pillar like a guard hound. At least this angle made it much less likely a dragon would spot him unless they flew over the bay itself.

Anahrod hugged her brother, swung him around. Legless fussed, so she calmed him while she set her brother back down again, picking up his hands. "I am so glad to see you. Sicaryon didn't find you? He said . . ."

"No," Gwydinion assured her. "He found me. He's the one who gave me Overbite." He reached into his knapsack and pulled out a familiar rainbow feld-spar ball. "And I have this."

Anahrod scowled. "He let you go into the jungle all by yourself with the stone that Neveranimas is tracking? Oh, I'm going to hurt—"

"I wouldn't say that he *let* me," Gwydinion corrected. "He thought he was going to go out in a blaze of glory heroically defending his people. He gave me a very heartfelt speech about how much he loved you, too—"

Anahrod let out a long, suffering sigh. "Just tell me that fool is still alive."

"He should be. He said he had the antidote."

Anahrod's head snapped back up. "Gwydinion!"

He wrinkled his nose at her, which she refused to acknowledge was cute as hell. He already knew. "I didn't think it made any sense for him to keep the stone and have the dragons swarming all over Liokuhn—"

Anahrod let out a laugh. "Is that what he's calling the seat of his kingdom?"

"Pretty sure, yes. I heard his soldiers talking." He looked extremely curious, leaning forward. "Why? What does it mean?"

"'The city,'" Anahrod answered, shaking her head. "And he thinks I can't name things?"

Claw made a dismissive sound. Anahrod didn't need to see her to know the woman was rolling her eyes.

"Anyway, it made more sense for me to take the stone and lead the dragons away than try to fight them when Sicaryon said they weren't ready."

"Wow," Claw said, "so besides being shit at naming things, being suicidally heroic runs in the family, too? Good to know."

Anahrod nearly made a comment about how they'd inherited it from their father, but that wasn't the point.

"Anyway, I'm not done saying stuff." Gwydinion stopped smiling and pulled his hands away from Anahrod's. He turned to Claw and said, "Jaemeh's dead. Sicaryon killed him."

Claw looked down, ran a thumb along one of her scars absently. "Oh." She raised her head. "Was it fast?"

"He stabbed him in the neck?"

Claw squinted. She seemed to be trying to imagine the scene in her head. Then she snorted. "Good enough."

Gwydinion gave her a sharp nod, as if to say, *Now that's done*. He then turned back to Anahrod and Ris, with Naeron likely included, mostly because of where he stood. "As for this." He held up the feldspar Rampant Stone. "I've removed what Neveranimas was using to track it, so she can't find us."

Anahrod tilted her head. "I'm sorry? You did what?"

"It's hard to explain," he said. "I, uh . . . it was metaphysically mislabeled? And it still is, but now it's metaphysically mislabeled as something different. I tried to send Neveranimas on a wild-bird chase—literally—but she's probably figured out that night flyers haven't somehow developed the ability to carry around ten-pound rocks." He shrugged.

Anahrod huffed. She had a hard time believing that Varriguhl had changed his curriculum *this* much in seventeen years. "What I should've asked is, *how* did you learn how to do this?"

"Oh." He hoisted the stone again. "It's all in here. There really wasn't anything to do while I was riding around on Overbite for hours and hours, so I figured, why not look through the dragonstone? Maybe I'd find something interesting." He laughed. "I'd tell Neveranimas not to leave the instructions on how to remove magical tracking on the very thing she wants to magically track, but Mom always says you should never correct an enemy when they're making a mistake."

Ris's eyes turned gold. **"I suspect she couldn't imagine someone else being able to use those instructions. Especially not a human."** Peralon-as-Ris raised a hand. **"Would you mind returning to the part about curing Ivarion?"**

"Gotta be honest, kid," Claw said, shaking her head. "You're doing an even better impersonation of a hyper vel puppy than normal."

Gwydinion stuck out his tongue at her before turning to Peralon-as-Ris. "Sure. Neveranimas described how she sent Ivarion rampant, what he did in response, and how she twisted that into something a lot nastier. But there's a loophole." He raised a finger. "We need Varriguhl." He added, "You know, honestly, I think he could've cured Ivarion years ago, but he was trapped at the school, you know? He's going to be so mad at himself when he realizes."

"No, he won't, kid," Claw said flatly. "He's dead."

Gwydinion stared at Claw in shock.

Anahrod didn't think Gwydinion had been fond of Varriguhl, but he hadn't hated the teacher like she had. It didn't really matter, though. Gwydinion had known the man, seen him recently, and wasn't cynical enough about death to take it lightly.

"Neveranimas killed him," Anahrod told him. "He died to make sure we could escape."

Gwydinion swallowed thickly. "That was nice of him." He seemed to pull himself up, quickly wiped his eyes. "If that's the case, you'll have to do it, then."

She waited a beat for him to answer, and when he didn't, gently asked, "Do what?"

He reddened, embarrassed that he'd left out the actual explanation. To be fair, he looked tired, which made sense if he'd forgone sleep in favor of perusing the stone. "Ivarion had this idea—a clever idea. That's not just my opinion, by the way. Neveranimas thinks so too and oh, is she mad about it." He cleared his throat. "Anyway, that's why he took a nap in the Cauldron as soon as he started to go rampant."

"Of course! A nap!" Claw hit her forehead with a palm. "Why did no dragon ever think of sleeping before?"

Peralon-in-Ris started coughing.

"Do you mind?" Gwydinion said peevishly. "I'm not done."

Claw faux-bowed in his direction.

"Thank you." Gwydinion straightened his rather worse-for-wear coat. "Ivarion used magic—he was already going rampant, so why not?—to link himself to the volcano. He would sleep and slowly feed all his corrupt rampancy to the mountain, while the mountain kept him alive. When he woke up, he'd be good as new. I think that's pretty sunshine."

"Go on," Anahrod urged.

"So Neveranimas found him and changed the spell. Now, the mountain keeps him alive, sure, but he sends the volcano his corruption, and the volcano sends it all back—with interest. He can't ever heal or wake."

Peralon-as-Ris growled. **"I see. And what did you think Varriguhl could do?"**

"Break the cycle," Gwydinion answered without hesitation. "Dragonriders can cure their dragon's corruption, right? So Varriguhl—"

Peralon returned control back to Ris. "No," she told him. "I'm sorry, but dragonriders can't cure a dragon who's already rampant. I try my hardest to keep

Peralon's levels from rising so high that he'll ever *become* rampant, but that's not the same." She shrugged. "Most dragonriders don't even do that well. Peralon and I have some theories about why that is, but they don't apply to Anahrod, both because Ivarion's not conscious and she's not his rider."

Gwydinion looked deeply disappointed for a moment—so did Peralon, but in a more dignified, draconic fashion—and pressed his lips tightly together. Then Gwydinion pointed a finger at Ris. "See, that's where you're wrong. Anahrod *is* his rider—kind of. She's every dragon's rider if you think about it."

Anahrod raised her eyebrows and stared. That was . . . that was a very bold claim. And not at all—

She frowned.

Gwydinion waved his hands. "Whether Varriguhl could cure Ivarion's corruption doesn't matter. Anahrod calms animals; she does it all the time."

"A dragon is *not* the same—"

"No, he has a point," Anahrod said. "In theory, I can only trade bodies with animals, too, but I did it with Neveranimas, didn't I? But there's still a difference between calming a dragon and calming a rampant dragon."

"That's fine," Gwydinion reassured her. "Because you don't need to 'fix' Ivarion. He's been trying to fix himself for a hundred years, but the spell won't let him wake up until he's below a certain level of corruption, and right now, that will never happen. Except if someone came around and eliminated that corruption—"

"I already told you—"

Her brother sighed. "Apologies, I misspoke. I meant to say, if someone came around and took all the corruption in Ivarion and shoved it into this stupid rock"—he held up the Rampant Stone—"he won't be feeding corruption into the mountain anymore, so the mountain won't send corruption back, and then he won't technically be rampant, which will end the spell and He. Will. Wake. Up."

No one spoke. All was silent save for the rustling of the wind through trees and Overbite whining, still unhappy about this "don't run from the dragon" idea.

"That might work," Ris finally said.

"Would be kind of funny if—" Claw's face went through a complicated series of contortions.

"Claw?"

"They conquered land, and sea, and heavens high, invented gods and fates with fervent pride, yet in their boundless quest for endless light, they lauded deeds that birthed an endless night." Claw laughed bitterly. "That's what Kaibren would've said. And then I would've translated that as saying it would be ironic if we used the same thing that turned Ivarion rampant to cure him—" She blinked repeatedly, her eyes too wet.

"Excuse me." Claw walked to the cliffside, hugging her arms with hunched shoulders.

No one said anything.

"Claw!" Ris started to walk over; Anahrod caught her arm.

"Give her space," she told the dragonrider. "She just lost Kaibren."

"She's standing too close to the edge," Ris said unhappily.

Anahrod pondered that. She turned her head over her shoulder and yelled out, "Claw, mind keeping an eye on the jungle line for me? I've got Overbite so hexed out to keep her from reacting to Peralon that anything could come out of the tree line and she wouldn't say a word."

For a second, Claw didn't respond. Then she made a rude gesture and said, "Fuck off, Jungle. I don't take orders from you."

Claw stomped away from the cliff and took up a new position, leaning against a fallen tree trunk. If that let her watch the jungle's edge, it was just coincidence.

Anahrod looked at Ris. "Better?"

The other woman took her hand and squeezed it, which Anahrod assumed meant "yes."

"So, we're doing this, right?" Gwydinion asked.

Ris straightened. "Yes, we are. Or I guess, Peralon and Anahrod are. The rest of us are going home to wait this out."

Gwydinion looked dismayed. Anahrod didn't have so strong a reaction, but she could admit to being confused.

"Do you really think going back to Seven Crests—"

Ris shook her head at Anahrod. "Not your home. My home. And I must be there because while Naeron and Claw both have citizenship, they don't have the authority to bring in strangers. Your brother's coming along because Overbite's the only available transportation that can get us there in hours instead of days, and someone has to keep Overbite from eating the rest of us." She gave Anahrod a tight smile. "I told you my home is protected. The dragons don't know it exists. They won't be able to find it. I say we leave those scaled cattle flying around with their claws up their asses, waiting for their leader to herd them into the next pen. I'll make sure your brother gets his beauty sleep and when you come back with Ivarion, we'll all go fly back to Yagra'hai together."

"She'll fight," Anahrod said. "You know she won't go down without a fight."

Ris shrugged. "You say that like it's not a point of merit. Anyway, as you are *almost Ivarion's dragonrider*, I'm sure you'll have no trouble at all healing him."

Anahrod didn't think Ris was going to let her brother's comment go for a long, long time.

"Just to be clear here," Anahrod said, "when you say home, what you mean is—"

"Viridhaven," Ris answered, as though that should be the most obvious thing in the whole world.

"Right. Viridhaven," Anahrod agreed. She stared off into the distance for a moment, shook herself, and then leaned over and kissed Ris's cheek. It was a very chaste kiss, right up until Ris grabbed her and turned it into something much less so.

"Come back in one piece," Ris ordered.

"It's been my main ambition all my life," Anahrod replied.

Peralon and Anahrod watched the others load themselves up onto Overbite. Her brother waved enthusiastically, Naeron raised a hand and gave her a solemn nod, Ris blew her a kiss, and Claw's farewell used a single finger. Anahrod knew how fast Overbite moved, and it was still a shock to see how quickly they vanished out of sight.

She turned back to the dragon, who'd pushed some trees aside to accomplish something close enough to a landing for her to clamber up his side.

"I assume you know the way to the Cauldron?" Anahrod asked.

[I do, indeed.]

55

THE GREEN LADY

Anahrod thought she could be forgiven for assuming Viridhaven was nothing more than fable and myth.

The Cauldron, though?

She's always known that the mountain itself was a real place. People pilgrimaged there. Judging by the shrines stretched from base camp to summit, the only reason Ivarion wasn't officially a saint was because the Church was still debating how to canonize someone still technically alive.

It must've been a beautiful mountain once. Now the Cauldron was a squat thing, shorter than any surrounding mountains. It was as though Eannis had scooped up half the mountain, leaving behind a shallow bowl that steamed and hissed and never saw snow. The volcanic heat turned the mountain into a lady who never entertained visitors without a verdant coat of vegetation. Its slopes were full of life that normally existed much closer to sea level.

Although perhaps the Cauldron wasn't a lady, given her fondness for green. More like a troll.

Anahrod attached her mask so she wouldn't suffocate in the toxic fumes. Peralon flew a circle around the bubbling heart of the Cauldron, searching for a place to land.

Anahrod felt Ivarion before she saw him.

She felt his rampancy from the moment Peralon approached: a howling, writhing inferno, unmitigated and ruinous. His sympathy and affinity with a volcano seemed appropriate; he was as destructive and as unstoppable.

Ivarion seemed petite at first, but that was just a trick of perspective. He was a massive dragon, curled up like a hatchling resting in the shadow of its mother.

He was beautiful, but Anahrod didn't know—really, could never know—how much her perceptions were influenced by her repeated dip into Peralon's memories. *He* certainly thought Ivarion was the most beautiful dragon to ever exist.

[What do you need from me?] Peralon asked.

[Just set me down,] she said back to him. [The clothing Kaibren made should protect me from the heat here. I need to be closer.]

She had no idea if she could confirm Gwydinion's theory, but if he was right about the corruption, all she needed to do was pull the taint from Ivarion into the Rampant Stone. Ivarion would do the rest.

She unfastened her mantle, folded it, and laid it on top of a low boulder. She sat down on the blanket and concentrated on the dragon.

The caldera wasn't silent. Peralon's scales rasped against each other with a soft hissing noise. Lava burbled. Pebbles bounced down the sides of the caldera as scree shifted.

Quiet enough. As quiet as anything ever was. The scent of sulfur was more distracting.

She reached out to Ivarion.

It felt like shouting down into the caldera, an echoing clatter of noises that clashed against each other and amplified into cacophony. Little wonder Varriguhl hadn't been able to reach his dragon. Ivarion's mind was buried so deeply inside that echoing crevasse, she had no idea how anyone could extend a metaphorical hand to help him climb up. Loops of energy, corruption, and hate flowed around the vast, ugly abyss of tainted magic before entering the mountain and bubbling up again, more powerful than before.

She started with the obvious and tried to shunt the corruption into the Rampant Stone.

It didn't work. At all.

A magical shield protected Ivarion and the mountain both. They were joined, one. No one could add or remove corrupting energies. Neveranimas had created a near-infinite, self-sustaining curse. The only way to change the flow of energy at this point would be from inside the system—and anyone inside the system was trapped.

If this were a proper fable, the evil witch would've left a way to free the cursed prince. True love or some such. Alas, Neveranimas hadn't been so considerate.

[Peralon,] Anahrod said, [how does Ris keep you free from corruption? How exactly?]

He didn't answer right away. Then Peralon said, [It's the bond itself, I think. The taint naturally tapers off or disappears entirely.]

[It was the same in her earlier lives, too?]

He raised his head. [She told you?]

[Yes, but I need an answer.] She continued staring at the sleeping dragon, brows knitted with frustration.

[Yes, it was so then as well.]

She scowled. It made no sense. Plenty of dragons had riders and were perfectly capable of falling into rampancy. What were Peralon and Ris doing that others weren't?

The answer smacked her full force, so immediate and obvious that she put her hand to her mouth and groaned.

They switched places.

Not a one-sided assault like Tiendremos and Jaemeh, not a hateful thirty minutes or so like she and Neveranimas had done. Peralon and Ris switched places for hours and hours. She went flying; he read books. He could take control of her body to talk to humans while she used his body to keep them safe.

Varriguhl had once commented that they had perfect synchronization. Of course they did. They had perfect trust. They were the dream that candidates longed for when they went to Yagra'hai, that hope of a partner who both completed and understood them that bubbled so warmly in bright eyes before reality ruthlessly smeared it underfoot.

But what did that mean for Ivarion?

She sighed. That's what Gwydinion had meant when he said Varriguhl could fix this. Even if no corruption could be added or subtracted from outside the system, a bonded dragonrider was a kind of secret entrance. The bond was an exchange of souls—or at least, a tiny part of their souls. Enough to allow a dragonrider to push out the poison.

That was wonderful. That was fantastic. There was just one small, tiny, troubling matter that merited consideration.

As Peralon himself had pointed out, Anahrod wasn't Ivarion's rider. She didn't think being "kind of" his rider was going to count for much here either—it would have to be a full bond. She and Neveranimas had switched places, but that had been an attack, a hijacking. Anahrod had done what she needed to do to survive, but that didn't mean she was proud of it.

Neveranimas couldn't have initiated such a switch herself. Similarly, Tiendremos and Jaemeh had been a bonded pair in the eyes of the world, but Jaemeh had been forced every time.

All of which brought her back to the unshakable fact that Ivarion wasn't conscious enough to agree to such a bond, even if she . . .

If she would agree . . .

She scowled. Funny how the same pride, the same stubborn insistence on freedom, no matter the cost, continued to be her best and worst qualities.

[Anahrod?] Peralon's voice was a gentle nudge.

She straightened.

[You can't find a way, can you?] She hated how understanding he sounded. How he was only upset because he'd let himself hope.

[I'm not done yet,] she told him. [I am the most stubborn creature—human or dragon—that you have ever met, and for once in my life that is going to work to my favor.]

There had to be a way.

If only there was a way to trick the curse into letting her inside.

She stood and turned to face Peralon. [Do you remember what my brother was going on about back at the Bay of Bones? Something about fooling Never-animas's tracking spells by metaphysical mislabeling? Did you understand what he was talking about?]

[I believe so, yes. It's the same method that I had planned to use on the Rampant Stone when we originally stole it—to keep Neveranimas from tracking it.]

She nodded. [Wonderful.] She paused. [What does that mean?]

[Tracking spells operate on principles similar to what Naeron used to find you, or to find your brother. Establish sympathy between multiple objects and as long as you have one of those objects in your possession, you can find and affect the others.]

Anahrod blinked. [Are you telling me that Naeron can hurt me through one of my family members? Just because we're related?]

[There is a reason the dragons made a good-faith effort to eliminate anyone with such a magic talent.]

She exhaled. Never mind, that was a distraction. [Right. Back to sympathy. Can I create sympathy between, say, myself and the Cauldron?]

He chuffed. [That is highly unlikely. This is typically where the "metaphysical mislabeling" comes into play—forcing sympathy where none otherwise exists. But I do not think it will work here.]

She frowned. [Why not?]

[Because such methods aren't robust. They don't hold up under significant strain. What your brother did was mild, attempting to fool a sympathy already based on a distortion. But one reason a rampant dragon is so devastating is because the corruption that takes over them is ultimately magical. It is a lake full of water bursting out from a fractured dam. Rampancy has force and momentum. I doubt such "mislabeling" would hold up for more than a few seconds.]

She straightened. [Only need a few seconds. Can you do this?]

[Yes . . .] He sounded reluctant.

[Then "metaphorically mislabel" me with the mountain,] Anahrod said. [I'm as hard-headed as a mountain. Just ask my mother.]

[Are you certain? I don't know what this will do to you.]

She waved away the concern. [Only one way to find out.]

Ivarion's mind was buried deep. On a metaphysical (metaphorical?) level where he existed in a perpetual loop linking himself to a mountain through winding ribbons of corrupted magic and power, he was trapped inside the mountain.

The easiest way for her to find him would be if Anahrod was the mountain itself.

[Ready?] Peralon asked.

[Ready,] she replied.

For the barest second, she didn't think it had worked. She thought that this too had failed, that Neveranimas was clever enough to counter this as well.

Then her world turned into fire.

56

VIRIDHAVEN

"I need you to close your eyes," Ris told Gwydinion.

"Excuse me?"

They'd run along the bay's edge for several hours by that point. It hadn't been a comfortable ride: arguably Overbite never was, just big and intimidating and thus safer than other methods. Gwydinion had put away his improvised, inscribed compass, because Ris said she didn't need it to find Viridhaven, but he'd yet to see any sign of the city. They were about to run smack into the Drav Mountains at the apex of the bay's inlet.

"Close your eyes," she repeated. "Don't look up or the illusion will catch you."

An illusion . . .

"Oh," Gwydinion said. "I see. Or, I don't." He fumbled, put his hands over his eyes. Without looking at Ris, he said, "What about Overbite? Will she be affected?"

"No," Ris said. "It doesn't work on animals."

"That's sunshine." He'd have to tell his mother about that when they returned; she'd never been able to resist learning new techniques.

Gwydinion nodded to acknowledge he'd heard Ris. He wanted to look up and see where they were going, but . . .

Illusions. He got the idea.

A few moments later, the ground beneath Overbite's feet tilted; she now ran at a steep downward tilt. He kept his eyes down, fighting the temptation to raise his head.

Claw tapped him on the shoulder. "Open your eyes, kid. We're here."

Gwydinion looked up and gasped.

Someone had taken a Skyland city and inverted it, so that instead of houses built up along the sides of a mountain, they were instead built down into an enormous bowl carved into solid rock. Long, elegant towers had been built in circles radiating from the center of the bowl, joined to each other and to the sides of the depression by fragile bridges lined with flower boxes. There was sound, too—the murmur of people chatting, wafts of music, the laughter of children, birds singing, vel hounds baying. He didn't understand the scale at first, and then he felt lightheaded.

Viridhaven was as large as Crystalspire.

Sunlight streamed through gaps between a lattice of flowering vines overhead. It was hardly camouflage—Gwydinion couldn't understand how dragons wouldn't be able to see it from the air.

Then he remembered Ris's comment about illusions.

"How many sorcerers does it take to cloak an entire city?" Gwydinion asked.

"None." Ris pointed up at the vines. "Those are all inscribed, and yes, it took a long time." She grinned. "Lucky for us, the only dragon old enough to remember we're down here is on our side." Ris tapped Gwydinion on the shoulder. "Let's dismount here so you can send Overbite back into the jungle. She's too large to stay inside the city."

"Right . . . right." Gwydinion told Overbite to head back into the jungle and go find herself some food. He stepped back as the titan drake turned around with shocking dexterity and galloped away.

Apparently, she was hungry.

"This way," Ris said, indicating a side road. "We'll drop Naeron off with his family and then I need to fill the captains in on the plan—"

"Plan?" Claw scoffed. "Can it really be called a plan when it amounts to 'Hey, let's hide while someone goes to wake Daddy up and tell him Mother's being mean?'"

Ris stopped in the middle of the road. She turned around, and Gwydinion saw she had that look on her face. The one that meant she was not to be pushed. He'd figured that look out quickly.

And if Claw ever had, she didn't care.

"I would like you to remember," Ris said with all the sweetness of an exquisite poison, "that we have *one* dragon. One. Neveranimas has hundreds. Thousands, should she feel ambitious, but for our discussion, let's assume hundreds." She put thumb and forefinger together. "We are hiding because that is the smart thing to do when you are this outnumbered."

Claw made a face. "Fine. I get it. Thank you for the lecture, strategy mom."

Ris took a deep breath and then exhaled. She tilted her head and gave Claw a fake smile. "We are this outnumbered *only* until we manage to 'wake Daddy.' At which point, we will be the ones with hundreds of dragons, and she will be the one outnumbered."

Claw sighed, but she gave the other woman a nod.

As Ris walked away, bells rang in an overlapping chime.

Gwydinion didn't know what that meant, but from the way everyone else froze, it wasn't good.

"No." Naeron spat the word like a curse.

"It's a flyover," Claw said, but she didn't sound convincing. "How could they track us?" She gave Gwydinion an unfriendly look, and the question sounded less rhetorical than accusative.

Gwydinion protested. "If Neveranimas was still tracking me, she'd have snatched me up before you arrived. Why would she wait?"

"That wasn't the 'flyover' alarm," Ris snapped. "That was the 'dragons are on the ground' alarm. Dragons, as in plural." She turned to Naeron. "Go get your family to a shelter." To Claw, she said, "Find the captains and let them know what they're dealing with. Make sure no one else tries to play this off as a false alarm."

Claw ran across the nearest bridge to one of the central towers, Naeron, into a doorway. Or rather, into a tunnel.

The moment the bells started, people on the street retreated into buildings. Not everyone: perhaps one in ten moved across the bridges to the central towers.

"Hurry," Ris said, grabbing Gwydinion by the arm. "Let's get you to safety."

Gwydinion tried to wiggle out of her grip. "You have illusions covering every inch of this place. How much danger—"

A furious, deafening roar clashed against the hard stone buildings of the city. Earth and stone rained down from several hundred feet away. Gwydinion looked up in time to see a dragon rabidly beating its wings to forestall plummeting downward. The dragon was a bright cerulean blue, with an opalescent stomach and bright, hot-red hands, feet, and frills.

Not hands, though. Just the one hand, because the dragon had unknowingly grabbed at one of the inscribed vines, which had cleanly severed the dragon's wrist. The vine was now blood-covered and missing the niceties of its previous floral cloak.

The illusion was broken. The dragon stared down into the city.

"Dayevedies." Ris spat out the name in recognition. "He's a fire dragon. Run—!"

The dragon pulled back, inhaled, and breathed.

IN THE DARKNESS

An earth dragon might have warned Anahrod of the danger, but neither Never-animas nor Peralon were earth dragons. Perhaps more importantly, neither were foolish enough, desperate enough to try what she just had. The problem was not that the Cauldron was a volcano, or rather, the problem was not that volcanoes were creations of fire and stone.

The problem was this: active volcanoes were *children*.

Any active volcano was a budding child, still tied to their mother's magma-hot apron strings, still sucking at her teats. Volcanoes were fed by the pressures and geological movements that had borne them and they were still joined with their parent.

To become one with the Cauldron was to become one with the *world*.

Anahrod's problem was diving too deep. Those few seconds were a lifetime's temptation. At first, she wondered if this was what it was like to be a dragon, her affinity tied to the earth and all the fires beneath it, but it was more. She perched on the edge of being joined to something that never judged, never lied, was never hateful, or ambitious, or cruel. The world only ever told the truth, with endless, infinite patience.

But if the world was never cruel, it was also never kind. It showed no compassion, couldn't forgive, and held no capacity to love. Its truth was as hard and unyielding as one might expect of stone.

She dragged herself back after a few seconds that lasted years. She dragged herself back and remembered that her name was Anahrod. She dragged herself back, and then threw herself forward again, this time into the inky black chasm of Ivarion's mind.

She made it just in time.

❯

Ivarion appeared much the same as his sleeping form in the Cauldron, but he was smaller, younger. At first, she thought he slept there, too, until he opened his red eyes.

[Ivarion?] She stepped forward.

Nothing surrounded them. Just blackness, everywhere, except for Ivarion, except for her. Space didn't matter here. Likely, neither did time.

[Is that who I am?] He sounded faintly puzzled.

[It is. My name is Anahrod, and I'm here to free you.]

He narrowed his eyes, more in confusion than anger. [From what?]

She stared at him. [Don't you know that you're trapped? You've been asleep for a hundred years.] Anahrod found it difficult to summon up the proper feeling, but she made her best effort.

A hundred years wasn't that long to a dragon—or a mountain.

[That sounds bad.] He was just being polite.

[Problem is, for me to do that—] She took a deep breath. Why was she doing this again? Oh yes, to free Seven Crests, countless people, and the Deep from Neveranimas. To try to change things, this time from the inside—

The dragon gave her a strange look as she laughed. Anahrod wasn't sure how to explain that the universe seemed done with subtlety.

She cleared her throat. [For me to help you, I would have to become your bonded rider.]

[Oh,] Ivarion said.

There was a silence, and then he asked, [Don't I have one of those?]

[You remember? That's a good sign. Yes, you did. Do you remember his name?]

He gazed at her sadly. [I haven't the slightest idea.]

Ivarion had only been bonded to his rider for a few days before Neveranimas had struck. Perhaps he truly didn't remember. [It was Varriguhl,] she told him. [Although that was a hundred years ago. He's dead now.] She'd get into specifics later.

[And you want to take his place?] Ivarion suddenly looked distrustful. [Why? You don't know me. We might hate each other.]

Anahrod raised her arms in faux surrender. [I know! Believe me, I know. I have the same concerns. But if I can't wake you up, terrible things are going to happen by the claws of a dragon who's only in charge because she's kept you asleep. People I love might die.] She paused. [Already have died. And people you love might die, too. So, I must trust that you—that you won't mind how imperfect I am. And I'll try my hardest to do the same for you.] She swallowed, suddenly full of nerves and dread. [If I had a different option, believe me, I would offer it. I won't force you to accept though—]

[*Could* you force me?] Ivarion sounded intrigued by the idea.

Slowly, Anahrod nodded. [Probably. Yes. I have a lot of power over dragons. But I don't want to be the person who would only ever use that power to my benefit, at the expense of everyone else.]

If this were anywhere else, she'd roll her eyes before Claw had the chance, accuse herself of being unforgivably trite and lying to everyone, herself most of all.

She didn't think she could lie there. There was still enough of the mountain to this place to forbid it. Or maybe that was just a result of being in Ivarion's mind.

Anahrod tried to smile. [So, what do you say?]

58

SIEGING DRAGONS

Dayevedies still swept his head from side to side, bathing entire streets in swaths of white-hot fire.

Something happened. Gwydinion felt the heat of the attack, heard screams, but he'd only just reached the tunnel mouth when the dragon made a choking sound and the attack stopped. Gwydinion turned back.

"No." Ris refused to release his arm. "The shelters. Now."

Gwydinion decided to save his questions for later.

He'd seen shelters before. Why, he'd seen one just a few weeks before in Yagra'hai, when Modelakast had gone rampant. But long before they reached this one, he knew these weren't the same.

The tunnels were wider than he was used to (although still too narrow for a dragon's head). Rather than ending in a room, the passageway changed direction every hundred feet, each shift marked by a giant inscribed door.

At each door, a resident of Viridhaven waited. Their eyes widened in surprise when they saw how few people were behind Gwydinion and Ris.

Ris didn't slow down. A few seconds after they passed each checkpoint, a loud boom echoed down the passage as the previous door was closed.

After three such doors, Ris pulled them into a narrow side passage so cleverly concealed that Gwydinion would've walked right past it.

Once in the new passage, Ris started running.

By the time they arrived at a large room, Gwydinion was so turned around that he had no idea where they were, except that it was "somewhere underground."

The room wasn't a shelter in the sense he knew it. A circular pool filled with rippling dark liquid dominated one end of the room, reminding him of Varriguhl's scrying mirrors. A bright line of white light seared its way across the surface, followed by a curiously flat image of an explosion. All around the pool, people gathered to watch, only to call out orders to messengers.

Gwydinion paused. "This is a command center." No one paid attention to him.

"What are we dealing with?" Ris asked as she crossed to the pool.

A white-haired man raised his head from concentrating on the dark waters. "What are you doing—?" He gestured angrily. "Where's Peralon?"

"Busy. Report."

He made a frustrated noise. "It's not great, obviously. Mioghal, Incivulia, Jaezerinoth, Ilguavon, and Segrimakar. Dayevedies retreated: bleeding too badly from the severed limb. But he burned the whole damn net before he left, so that line of defense is gone. We won't get that lucky again."

"No Zentoazax?" Ris asked.

"Not so far. No sign of Notile, either." The man inhaled. "Let's hope it stays that way."

"Where's Neveranimas?" Gwydinion asked as he pushed forward. "Shouldn't she be here, too?"

Both Ris and the man stopped and glanced at Gwydinion; the man with annoyance, Ris with chagrin.

"What he said," Ris repeated. "Where's Neveranimas?"

"Not here," he told her. "We haven't spotted her."

The ground shook.

Gwydinion frowned. Why wouldn't Neveranimas be here? The dragons couldn't have followed the Rampant Stone—it wasn't here. It had never been here. So, what had given them away?

The ground shook again. Gwydinion scanned the pool to see a tower in the center of the city crack and topple, a horrible slow collapse as giant blocks of stone fell away and connecting bridges unraveled.

"Eannis, I hope Claw's okay," Gwydinion whispered. He hated he couldn't do anything but watch.

The ground shook a third time, this time so hard that people stumbled, and chips of stone fell from the ceiling.

Ris inhaled sharply. "None of the dragons you named should cause this. Jaezerinoth and Segrimakar both breathe poison gas for fuck's sake. Finyan, I need a view up above the bowl!"

The woman she shouted as she spread her hands. "They've taken out all the watch stones. What am I supposed to do?"

"What are we looking for?" Gwydinion said.

"There has to be another dragon—"

Gwydinion tugged on Ris's sleeve. "No, I mean, what does the dragon look like?"

Ris hesitated. "A pitch-black dragon or a white one with gold and brown accents."

"Okay." Gwydinion made no promises, because he didn't know if this would work. It was proving a banner day for him to learn magical skills under pressure.

He wished Anahrod were here. This would've been so easy for her.

59

STRATEGIC RETREATS

[Anahrod.]

[Anahrod!] Peralon's voice was all but a shout, pulling her from Ivarion's mind.

She opened her eyes. Anahrod was still sitting on folded blanket on a boulder, still staring at a still-sleeping Ivarion.

Meanwhile, Peralon sounded panicked.

[What's wrong?]

[We must've overlooked something. The dragons are attacking Viridhaven.]

Anahrod's heartbeat jumped. She thought he said it was impossible . . .

Obviously not.

Anahrod glanced back at Ivarion. She couldn't see any sign of change, any sign that he might wake this side of the next century. Anahrod needed more time. And time wasn't something she had in any supply, large or small.

[Go to them,] she told Peralon. [I'll stay here and wake up Ivarion, then join you.]

He gave Ivarion a hopeless look. [Can you? Wake him?]

[Just go.]

Peralon wanted to argue. He would be abandoning her, leaving Anahrod alone with nothing but her own abilities, the dragonstone, and a dragon who might never wake again. But Ris was down there. Gwydinion was down there. What choice did they have?

If Peralon had to choose between letting Neveranimas have the entire world and protecting his rider, Anahrod knew which way he'd pick. He'd send Neveranimas some gems from his personal hoard as a good-luck gift, if he had to.

Peralon needed Anahrod's assurance that he wasn't abandoning her.

She gave it to him. [I'll be fine. I should have Ivarion up in just a few minutes. Go. We'll catch up later.]

[Thank you.] Peralon took to the skies and turned into a gold streak fading into the distance.

A sharp cracking sound echoed in the sky.

Anahrod turned back to Ivarion. Or she started to. Because when she did, something shimmered from off to the side. Something violet and silver.

Seventeen years of survival instincts kicked in. Anahrod rolled to the side just as a dragon claw crashed into the ground where she'd stood. The blow smashed the boulder upon which she'd been sitting to pieces.

[Honestly,] Neveranimas said, [I thought he'd never leave.]

60

AFFINITIES

Ris gestured toward the command staff, toward Gwydinion. As soon as the veils of energy fell into place, Gwydinion recognized them as Ris's trademark wards.

Inside, it was quiet.

The ground shook more often now, and more violently. A glass orb on the far side of the room that had some unknown significance lit up. Gwydinion couldn't hear what anyone said, but he saw people rushing to the orb and then shouting panicked orders. Whatever had happened wasn't good.

Should he try to find Overbite? Convince her to come back? But no . . . she was rightfully terrified of dragons. He didn't think his polite suggestions would be nearly enough to convince the titan drake to do something that suicidal.

He just needed to find an animal who let him see through their eyes.

Later, he opened his eyes unhappily and gasped, "I can't. It's not working."

"Have you done this before?"

His face twisted. "Yeah."

"Then it's nerves, and you absolutely can." Ris crouched down next to him. "I have never seen anyone figure out how to block tracking spells in a single night of studying. But you did. You can do this."

He gave her a lopsided smile. "Just believe in myself?"

She ruffled his hair. "You get the idea. And think how impressed Kimat will be."

Gwydinion cleared his throat. He hadn't even asked about Kimat . . . "Is she okay?"

"I'm sure she's been better, but we left her with your mother, so she'll be fine."

Gwydinion inhaled deeply. If she wanted to distract him from worrying about this by having him worry about something else instead, she was doing a fantastic job. "Right. Just believe in myself."

He was good with birds. Best with birds, really, although Legless had come easily enough, probably because he was just a baby. The night flyers would all be tucked in for the night, but blood crows were everywhere, and there were also those seabirds he'd seen flying over the bay. Any of those would work. He searched.

After a few minutes, he opened his eyes again. "There's a white dragon perched at the edge of the Bay of Bones," he told Ris, "looking this way. Does that help?"

Ris looked sick. "That's Zentoazax. He's nearly indestructible. And given enough time, he can cause earthquakes." To underline that statement, the chamber shuddered.

Gwydinion straightened. "Wait. Zentoazax? That's Brauge's dragon! You don't think she's with him, do you?" It was an ugly thought, because it meant Brauge was helping Zentoazax kill a lot of people.

Ris pointed a finger at him. "Distract him by attacking her. That's evil. I like it. Think you can handle it?"

"What? But I—" He inhaled. "I mean to say, sure, I can arrange something." It still wouldn't be anything more than birds, but birds could be very annoying.

Seeing that the situation seemed in hand, Ris began to leave again, sword drawn.

"Wait," Gwydinion stood, horror clutching at his throat. She'd had that with her the whole time, hadn't she? It wouldn't have meant anything to him before, but now that he understood how sympathy worked . . .

"Ris, your sword."

She glanced down at it. "What about—"

She froze, and what little color had ever been in her face washed away completely. A second later Ris shook herself, mouth pressed in an angry line. "It's too late to do anything now," she murmured, and then continued running.

One more time, the room shook . . . and this time, it didn't stop. He couldn't claim any sort of steady feet with the floor shifting the way it was, but he tried. "What's going on?"

The white-haired man looked positively sick as he pointed at the pool. "We found Notile."

Gwydinion crossed over to stare down into the water, or whatever it was. In the reflection, he saw what the man meant.

Notile was a sleek, beautiful deep black dragon with indigo accents. She was breathing out a painfully bright white fire that simply melted whatever it touched—including stone. She was using it with horrifying abandon on the city itself. Rock glowed red-hot, softened and collapsed, turning every building into a boiling mass of molten rock.

She showed no sign of stopping, either. Everyone hiding in the shelters would be trapped inside until Zentoazax dropped the roof on their heads or the air ran out.

Ris must have left to do something about her.

Gwydinion felt sick, too, and more than a little like crying. There was no way Ris could stop that dragon. How could she even begin?

He ground his teeth together and sat back down. If Ris was going to do something about Notile, the least he could do was make sure Brauge had a terrible day as well.

A FEW CLEVER TRICKS

Anahrod wasn't a fool: she tried possessing Neveranimas again. It was the very first thing she did after she finished rolling to the side.

It just didn't work.

The dragon felt the mental intrusion and smiled. [You caught me unaware before. I won't make that mistake again.]

The dragon circled, steam rising as her cold feet contacted hot stone. Neveranimas gave no sign that the clash of temperatures bothered her.

Of course she isn't worried, Anahrod thought. She doesn't think I can do a thing to her.

"Wonderful," Anahrod said. "You're so clever. But it doesn't change the fact that people know what you can do now."

[People?] Neveranimas's telepathic voice was mocking. [You mean humans like the Deepers, like the citizens of Crystalspire? Those "people"? It won't matter what they think. I created the Rampant Stone. I can destroy it and create a new one later on. How hard do you think it will be to convince the dragon elders that this was a plot, a conspiracy, between Crystalspire and the Deep? Best to wipe clean the entire infection, they'll agree.]

Anahrod shuddered. She could see it all too easily. The peoples of the Deep had always been disposable—trolls, demons, monsters—and if Crystalspire was viewed as less so, Seven Crests had six other cities, did they not? An object lesson or two would go a long way to keep the humans in line.

"You ordered the dragons to attack Viridhaven as a distraction, didn't you?"

[Is that what that settlement is called? Now that's just begging for trouble, isn't it? But yes, I did. Your friends took something with them when they left my vault. Something they've kept. One of those keys you used to break into my vault.]

Anahrod cursed. *Ris's sword.* Ris had told everyone to brush the debris from the shattered keys down into the magma lake, but someone might have missed a fragment, or a shard landed on a rock outcropping not hot enough to melt it . . . whatever the mistake, Neveranimas had taken advantage of it.

Which meant that the moment Neveranimas stopped being able to track the Rampant Stone, she turned to tracking Ris instead. The dragonrider had unwittingly led the dragons directly to their hidden city.

[Peralon's weakness has always been an excessive fondness for you little creatures. I knew he'd try to protect them.]

"I'm impressed," Anahrod said. "But how did you track the Rampant Stone here? I was told someone had made that impossible."

Anahrod was trying to buy time. She hoped Neveranimas would be eager to finally talk to someone about her life's work. What a genius she was. How no one could stop her.

The usual garbage.

All the while Anahrod sorted through her options, which looked increasingly grim short of Eannis herself showing up and saving the day. Which didn't seem terribly likely.

She was going to be cutting this very close.

[Is that what happened? But no, I wasn't tracking the Stone. I just knew at least one of your people would come here. I'd hoped it would be you, and I was right.]

Anahrod glanced back at Ivarion. She was too close. Way too close.

Anahrod had one trick up her sleeve, though. It was odd enough and strange enough that she didn't think Neveranimas would think of defending against it.

Just as Ris hadn't, when Anahrod had used it against her.

Anahrod rarely mirrored animals. It took so much energy; it stood a high chance of hurting whoever she used as the power source—the animal or herself. But here? With an active volcano and a dragon she wanted to hurt?

Anahrod had all the energy she could ever need.

Anahrod had been quiet for too long. Long enough for Neveranimas to realize that perhaps she shouldn't just stand there and brag. [Time for you to—]

Anahrod flew at her.

Or rather, a dragon-shaped ball of golden energy flew at Neveranimas, mouth open in a silent scream and claws extended to rake and rend. Anahrod herself was a tiny dot in the middle of all that, almost impossible to see past the glowing web of dragon-shaped magic.

Neveranimas was so surprised that Anahrod landed two good claw wounds and a bite along the dragon's neck.

Then Neveranimas vanished.

Too late, Anahrod remembered the dragon's ability to teleport. An ability that she would use to reposition herself in a fight for her best advantage. Fortunately for Anahrod, she had no intention of continuing the fight.

Funny enough, her goal had also been a kind of repositioning for advantage.

She dropped the mirroring and fell down behind some boulders big enough to provide at least a little cover.

At the same time, Neveranimas appeared over the lava lake. She opened her mouth to breathe in Anahrod's general direction.

Anahrod closed her eyes. For a second, she felt nothing.

Then she opened Ivarion's eyes . . .

. . . and Ivarion opened hers.

62

FRIENDLY NEIGHBORS

Brauge was not having a terrible day.

Gwydinion was trying as hard as possible, but he needed to control an entire flock, not one bird at a time. He was a mild annoyance, not anything so worrisome as to make Zentoazax call off the attack or shift targets. He just wasn't skilled enough, good enough. He was trying so hard.

Ris was counting on him, and he was failing her.

He was still trying when he saw something slam into Zentoazax. Gwydinion wasn't sure what it was, just that it had been traveling fast, it was loud, and it left a trail of smoke behind it. He followed the trail back to a group of purple-skinned humans loading large metal balls into equally large metal tubes.

Whatever those things were, they were knocking Zentoazax around like nobody's business. Suddenly he didn't know where Brauge was, but Zentoazax roared, because someone had hurt his rider or hurt him. Either way, the earthquakes stopped.

"Sicaryon's here!" Gwydinion screamed. "He brought his army!"

The white-haired man gave him a deeply concerned look. "Sicaryon the conqueror?"

"He's on our side," Gwydinion said.

The man all but called him a liar with that glare.

"He's attacking the dragons," Gwydinion pointed out.

"Glad somebody is," the man muttered as he walked away.

Despite that one, brief window of happiness, Sicaryon's people were trying not to engage any of the dragons directly. Instead, they were setting up, firing those—whatever they were, thunder lances?—then running before setting up again somewhere else. He saw a few of Sicaryon's sorcerers, too, but it was obvious that they were avoiding a straight-up fight.

Probably because they'd lose.

Gwydinion felt helpless, and he hated it with all his being. Time had no meaning. He stood there for what might have been seconds or what might have been hours, watching that black dragon melt what had been without doubt the most beautiful city that Gwydinion had ever seen.

Then the door opened. Claw walked inside. She was coughing like she'd breathed in something unpleasant, but otherwise seemed unharmed.

"Naeron—?" he asked.

"Made it to a shelter with his family," Claw told him decisively.

Part of him knew she had no way to be certain, but he believed her, anyway.

"Ris went to stop Notile," he told Claw.

Claw's face went blank. One of the nearby captains noticed, must have understood what it meant. He moved to stop her.

"No, let me go!" she screamed at the man.

"Claw, don't!" Gwydinion pleaded. "Ris wouldn't want you to go running after her."

"Ris isn't my fucking mother," Claw screamed.

"No, but she's still family." Gwydinion understood. He really did. And it didn't change how utterly helpless he felt.

Claw stared at him like he'd just pulled one of her daggers out and stabbed her with it. "You're a proper son of a bitch, you know that?"

"Ah," he said sagely. "So, you have met my mom."

Claw started laughing. Or possibly crying. Or both. It was really kind of difficult to tell.

"There she is!" someone yelled out.

Gwydinion craned his neck to see where everyone was pointing. He didn't want to watch, but . . .

But he *had* to see.

He only spotted Ris when Notile reared back in pain, because Ris had sent her sword directly into one of the black dragon's eyes. Gwydinion put a hand to his mouth though, at what happened next.

Notile noticed Ris.

The dragon swung her neck around and breathed in the new direction. A gasp went out around the room. It seemed like every person watching was holding their breath, because it was clearly obvious that the dragon fire was parting to each side of Ris without touching her, diverted by the shields that Ris was so good at creating. But the ground to either side of Ris was glowing red-hot, and Gwydinion didn't know if she could protect herself from the ground literally melting under her feet.

"How long can she keep that up?" someone asked.

A good question.

Then the ground shook again.

Gwydinion frowned. "That wasn't Zentoazax—"

This had felt different from the previous trembling. Softer, or . . . no. Finer. Almost a vibration, rather than a shudder or shake.

"Zavad—" someone near the pool cried out.

"What now?" the white-haired man said.

"No," a woman said, her voice triumphant. "Peralon's back!"

Gwydinion's happiness was short-lived.

Claw raised her head and said, "By himself? There's too many out there . . ."

Gwydinion's throat clenched. She was right. It's not like Peralon was even a large dragon, and while he was undeniably skilled . . .

Peralon flew into view, hovering behind Notile. Gwydinion had no idea if he said something to the other dragon. He suspected not, because she didn't turn, didn't shift her attention the way Gwydinion would've expected her to if she'd had any idea that someone who wasn't an ally had just arrived. No, she'd likely heard the wingbeats and assumed that meant an ally. Another dragon come to help her kill a heretic.

Peralon opened his mouth.

Gwydinion didn't see the gold dragon's breath weapon. He saw nothing at all. Peralon might as well have been serenading Notile as attacking her. At least that was his first impression.

Peralon was the source of those silky fine vibrations.

Before Notile could turn around, a wave of . . . something . . . passed through her. Gwydinion would have thought it was sound, but he couldn't hear anything. Maybe it was like a lot of dragon sounds, and outside the range of human hearing.

But whatever it was, as it touched Notile, she shuddered, vibrated . . .

Shattered.

Disintegrated.

Notile turned to dust, all in a matter of seconds.

The energy slanted harmlessly across Ris's ward and faded, leaving the dragonrider unharmed.

A few seconds later, the walls vibrated again as the force of Peralon's breath reached them.

Gwydinion could only stare with his mouth dropped open. Dragon fights were usually long, protracted affairs unless there was a major discrepancy in power levels, or someone got in a really lucky shot. Yeah, he had attacked her from behind, but to just disintegrate her?

Most people in the room looked just as surprised as he did. So surprised that Gwydinion knew none of them had realized what Peralon could do.

A dark red dragon with ugly puce slashes along its flanks plowed into Peralon. Peralon tumbled into a section of melted stone and screamed—less from the heat, Gwydinion thought, than because of the other dragon's talons.

"Are none of the defense towers working?" Claw demanded.

"If they were, don't you think we'd be using them?" someone snapped.

The red dragon breathed something dark and liquid at Peralon, but it never reached him. The liquid hovered in midair, a giant floating red blob of—

Gwydinion leaned forward. "Is that blood?"

"Yes," someone answered. "Incivulia spits boiling blood." They added: "Poisonous, of course."

Claw giggled, more than a little hysterically. "Blood? Nobody told me it was Naeron's birthday."

Gwydinion suspected she was right, but if he was, Naeron wasn't foolish enough to reveal himself.

A sword flew at the blood dragon's mouth, slashing at the soft tissues. Incivulia reared back, shrieking. The sword in question swung back around as Ris ran off the roof of a building and jumped, landing on Peralon's back.

Peralon breathed again, the time disintegrating the remains of a fallen block of stone smashed during the fighting. It seemed too intentional a miss to have been anything but a warning shot. The gold dragon stared intently at the larger red one.

Peralon was trying to parlay.

"What's he saying?" Gwydinion asked one of the scrying-pool people. They gave him a faintly incredulous look and Gwydinion sighed.

Yes, fine. That was a stupid question.

Gwydinion wished he could hear dragons, but that didn't seem to be a talent he was in danger of spontaneously developing.

Matters weren't looking good for Peralon, though. Whatever the two dragons were saying to each other, more elder dragons were showing up on the scene, taking up positions around the lip of the bowl. They all looked hurt, some seriously.

None of them looked like they wanted to talk.

63

FIRE VS. ICE

Anahrod was an enormous red dragon.

Also, she was rampant.

Her initial response to that was identical to how most dragons reacted to going rampant: she attacked the first living creature she saw: Neveranimas.

The violet dragon's expression shifted with surprise and just as quickly distorted into a mask of resentment and hate. None of which mattered much, because Neveranimas's resentment and rage couldn't possibly overtake Anahrod's own.

The two dragons screamed at each other and attacked.

The inside of a volcano wasn't an ideal location to fight a fire dragon. Maybe Neveranimas expected Ivarion, and by extension Anahrod, would be weakened by his hundred-year nap, but if so, she hadn't truly understood what she'd done. Anahrod breathed an inferno at Neveranimas, only to growl in frustration as the other dragon teleported to safety.

Something tickled at the back of Anahrod's mind as she snarled and snapped. She was forgetting something important.

She didn't concern herself with it at first—nothing mattered but rage—but that feeling persisted. A quiet, nagging feeling like someone was whispering to her too softly to hear, so she wanted to yell at everyone to be quiet.

It was a whisper, or something like it.

[Anahrod.] The voice was soft and warm, like a hearth fire after spending all day out in the cold. [I need you to purge the corruption. Can you do that for me?]

Anahrod was hardly winning the fight against Neveranimas. She was fighting too wildly, without intelligence or direction, and Neveranimas was someone who had a great deal of both. Anahrod had to—

She needed to—

She breathed at Neveranimas, mostly to buy her room and time. Anahrod thought about giving her anger back to the mountain, but she felt another reminder scratching at her mind.

A glint of something polished and reflective caught her attention. A rainbow flash.

Anahrod dashed to the side, avoiding some magical spell or another. She didn't bother picking up the stone—she just stepped on it, and with it touching the underside of her claw, let all her anger boil over, steam, and pour into the stone. The taint fell from her like an ugly burning tar that had lingered inside her blood, something that had brought anger with it.

With the loss of that corruption came clarity, and intelligence.

Unfortunately, that came a second after Neveranimas had sunk her teeth into Anahrod-as-Ivarion's side. She screamed.

[Anahrod! Switch back.]

She felt him push at her, and she didn't fight it. There was very little chance that she was better at fighting dragons than Ivarion was.

Anahrod gasped and sat up in her normal human form. She was still behind that boulder, although now she was also bleeding from ice shrapnel.

Meanwhile, Ivarion had gotten in a few good hits, but Neveranimas was a tough opponent. She wasn't physically tough, no, but that magic skill . . . the teleportation was a problem.

Ivarion had moved away from his previous position; Anahrod noticed the Rampant Stone, miraculously not smashed.

Which gave her an idea.

Neveranimas wasn't an inherently powerful dragon. She was a magically adept dragon—a smart dragon. If she lost that intelligence, she'd be in serious trouble. Neveranimas couldn't afford to go rampant—it cost her what was otherwise her greatest advantage.

Anahrod bounced down the caldera slope, running toward the stone. She couldn't just pick up the stone and start using it, either. The moment she did, Neveranimas would abandon her fight with Ivarion and go after her like squashing a bug . . .

Unless she had to go through Ivarion to reach her.

[Ivarion!] Anahrod shouted. [Get over here. I need to climb on your back!]

[I suppose it would be easier to keep you safe that way . . .] The dragon sounded equal parts amused and tired.

Then he vanished with a thunderclap of displaced air.

Anahrod was so startled that she almost missed her opportunity. When Ivarion reappeared, he sagged, as though the spell had taken too much energy out of him. He rolled to his side, so that for a few, short seconds, his ancient, worn metal harness hung suspended a few dozen feet away from Anahrod.

[You can teleport? You never mentioned you could teleport!]

[It is something I figured out while sleeping.] He sounded distinctly bemused by the idea.

She ran and jumped, holding on for dear life as Ivarion leaped into the air again. She rushed to belt herself in, never more necessary than at that moment.

[Just give up, you fool,] Neveranimas hissed. [I'll make your death quick.]

Instead of responding with words, Ivarion breathed at Neveranimas. Unfortunately, the other dragon summoned a shield around her body that shunted the fire harmlessly to each side. It splashed down and filled the caldera with such heat that Anahrod was glad she wasn't still down there. Weirdly, Anahrod barely felt the heat now. Maybe because she was on Ivarion's back, and not down there next to the boiling lava. Or possibly because she was Ivarion's rider. She wasn't sure. It was worth investigating . . . later.

[You said my previous rider died. How did it happen?] Ivarion asked as if he weren't in the middle of a battle to the death with his former second-in-command.

[Do you really think this is the time?] Anahrod thought back. [We're busy!] She swung to one side as a wild spell missed Ivarion but came dangerously close to hitting her instead. She felt the dragon growl in response to her spike of fear.

[I'm sorry, I assumed you would know.]

[I do! I just—] She sighed. [She killed him. Neveranimas killed him yesterday morning.]

He had no response to that, but Anahrod felt his fury, and could only look wide-eyed as he reached into the molten lake of stone with his front arms, pulling them back still dripping with lava. Neveranimas screamed as a blow connected with her, claws that were now sharp *and* covered in burning-hot lava.

Anahrod took a deep breath and concentrated on surviving long enough to use the Rampant Stone.

[Be ready,] Anahrod said. [She's about to lose her mind over this.]

Ivarion didn't answer, not in mental speech anyway, but she felt a sense of warmth and vicious satisfaction. Anahrod focused her attention on the stone, on unleashing everything that Anahrod had just dumped into the rock back out again—this time into Neveranimas.

The violet dragon screamed.

This wasn't a sound of pain, anguish, sorrow, but a pure and awful kind of hate. The violet dragon's eyes twisted with madness—the same sort of madness Anahrod had seen in the eyes of Modelakast and Tiendremos, the same sort of madness that must have shone in her own stare. It was madness in every meaning and left no room for any thought more coherent than "destroy everything."

Neveranimas leaped at Ivarion; the two dragons tumbled, all the while snapping, biting, and clawing each other. Anahrod needed both hands; rather than take the time to safely stow the dragonstone, she simply let the damn thing drop. With any luck, it would either shatter on the rocks below or fall into the lava.

Either way was fine with her. The universe was better off without that evil in it.

Anahrod held on with all her might, because while her own harness was new, all of Ivarion's equipment was a century old, and had been exposed to the elements the entire time. She'd be very surprised if any of it was more dependable than rust.

She curled in on herself when Neveranimas breathed back, too close, but the ice melted away harmlessly before it could hurt her.

Ivarion sank his teeth into Neveranimas's throat.

This part Anahrod could help with. She mirrored Neveranimas again, letting the golden image rest right on top of Ivarion's like a dragon-sized second skin. While Neveranimas clawed at Ivarion's jaws and tried to loosen his hold, Anahrod raked gouges into the other dragon's chest, so that violet-blue blood flew as the two dragons whirled in the air.

Ivarion jerked his head, and a hard, ugly cracking sound came from Neveranimas's neck.

The dragon queen of Yagra'hai stopped struggling.

He opened his mouth and Neveranimas fell, hitting the inside of the caldera. She bounced once and was still.

Ivarion landed, gingerly and in the manner of someone injured.

Anahrod resisted the temptation to fall asleep on the dragon's back, an idea that had never seemed so comfortable as at that moment. This was not the time.

[I'm sorry to say this isn't over,] she told him.

[No,] Ivarion responded. He still sounded remarkably angry, although Anahrod could tell—sense, really—that none of that anger was rampancy, and none of it was directed at her. [It's not.]

64

THE LAST STAND

A thunderclap echoed as another dragon appeared, high in the air above the city. Under other circumstances, Gwydinion might have wanted to whimper about it, because this was without doubt the largest dragon that Gwydinion had ever seen. Undoubtedly a fire dragon, red with areas of yellow and orange and eyes that glowed like the molten heart of a volcano.

"Who the hell is that?" Claw asked. Several people asked that question, or some other more polite variation of it, at the same time.

"That's Ivarion!" Gwydinion called out.

The dragon flew down to the rim of the city bowl, scattering the nearby dragons who bowed down or slinked to the side to keep out of the larger dragon's way.

There was someone on the dragon's back. Claw leaned forward and then cackled. "No," she said, "that's not just Ivarion. That's Ivarion and *Anahrod*."

There was a moment of stunned silence.

Gwydinion ran for the door. A whole lot of people followed him.

❯

Anahrod grinned as she slid down the harness rope from Ivarion's side. The rope didn't actually break, but it was a close thing.

[I'll be right here when you're done playing,] she told Ivarion, and felt him laugh in response.

The red dragon launched himself back into the air. Since he was very large, all motion in Viridhaven stopped. Debris and dust were hurled through the air by the beating of his wings. Quite a few people, peeking out from the rubble, immediately ducked back down again, but no one tried to attack him.

Anahrod had assumed that Ris had already told them that this dragon, like Peralon, was on their side.

"Now that is a lot of pissed-off lizards," she told Ris, just before she kissed her. The kiss was made interesting by virtue of the fact that Ris giggled hysterically at the time, but they managed.

"Is everyone all right?" If she sounded worried, it's only because she was, desperately so.

"Everyone's fine," Ris said, although she didn't quite hide a flinch.

"Everyone I know is fine," Anahrod corrected.

"Yes," Ris agreed. "But the whole city is designed to survive dragon attacks. Believe it or not, it looks worse than it is. That is not to say that there were no casualties."

Anahrod picked up Ris's hand and kissed it, then tilted her face up toward the sky and the jungle above. She could hear Ivarion responding to the joyous greetings of his fellow dragons.

[I am back through the Grace of Eannis, pausing in my contemplations. And yet how troubled I am to arrive here and see all of you, friends old and new—]

"Eannis," Anahrod muttered, half in disbelief. "He's giving a speech." She corrected herself. "No. I'm wrong. It's a sermon." She felt momentarily dizzy.

Ris's eyes widened. "Ivarion's . . . religious?" She blinked at Anahrod rapidly, looking like she couldn't decide whether to laugh or be completely horrified.

Anahrod couldn't seem to stop herself from smiling. How embarrassing. "No," she said, trying to stop giggling. "Not in the least. But they don't know that. I believe I shall call him Saint Ivarion from now on. All the time, yes."

"Anahrod!" That was Gwydinion's voice.

She scanned the stepped streets of the city until she spotted him, waving to catch her attention. It was growing louder with each minute as people tried to find their loved ones.

She ran to Gwydinion, who was sticking close to Claw and Naeron, and she hugged him, picked him up, and spun him around while he sputtered protests.

"You did it, didn't you?" he asked, grinning. "You found Ivarion, and you woke him?"

Anahrod nodded. "I did. Just like you said."

He tucked his head and gazed up at her mischievously. "Is he your dragon now?"

She searched his face. Anahrod had been so afraid that he would be jealous, upset with her for getting what he couldn't. She couldn't see a single trace of that emotion on his face, just happiness. Happiness for her.

"He is, yes." She looked him in the eyes. "You're not upset?"

Her little brother shrugged. "Ask me again in seventeen years, I guess. You had dibs."

She laughed and ruffled his hair and leaned over and kissed his head while he ducked away and protested. She was so happy she felt like she might burst.

She wanted to do so many things she hardly knew where to start, but Ris tugged on her sleeve and pointed her attention to where people were trying to move rubble and put out fires.

She spent the rest of the day helping where she could, which ended up being a lot of finding animals while Ivarion shamed dragons into helping move rubble. And when he wasn't doing that, she spotted Ivarion perched on the lip of Viridhaven's bowl, nuzzling Peralon's neck and practically vibrating with happiness.

Toward evening, Gwydinion found her again and, extremely excited, dragged her over to an outdoor fire, where she was delighted to find Ris.

And Sicaryon.

"Have you been here all day?" she asked as she slid into place next to him, curled up under his arm.

He was looking very violet, but it had never been an awful color on him, and considering he wasn't wearing much else, she'd never complain. If she ended up with some mud paint on her clothes, she didn't care. They were already filthy by that point.

"I have," he agreed. "We came to help with the dragons, and you know, since I was already here, I thought I might see if I could meet with any of the city leaders and talk trade deals."

"Oh, you have grown up," Anahrod told him.

He grinned. "Funny story, though. Everyone keeps pointing me toward this redhead."

Ris immediately protested, "I'm not in charge. I'm more of an adviser, or a—"

"Figurehead?" Sicaryon suggested gleefully.

"Yes," Ris said. "Exactly. A figurehead."

Anahrod bit her lip. She didn't know whether to laugh or . . .

"So, if I wanted to discuss reparations with the leader of Viridhaven because—" She paused and glanced skyward. "Oh, this hurts to say. Because I'm the First Rider of Yagra'hai, and several Yagra'hai dragons are guilty of a completely unprovoked attack on your city, would I talk to—?"

"It could be me," Ris said. "Could be others, too. There's some flexibility."

"It's strange to end up as a head of government," Sicaryon commented airily. "Becoming a dragonrider. I suppose no weirder than being born into it." He grinned. "By that token, if I wanted to negotiate some sort of treaty with Yagra'hai—"

Anahrod nodded slowly. "Ivarion, but you could start with me."

"Sounds like intense negotiations ahead of us," Sicaryon agreed.

Ris started laughing and tucked her head against Anahrod's arm. "Could take hours."

"Days," Anahrod corrected.

"Weeks, even months," Sicaryon said.

Anahrod met their smiles with her own. She wasn't a fool. They wouldn't find what they were about to do easy, by any means. Groups on every side would fight them, from ambition or greed or misguided fanaticism. Different cultures, different peoples, different races, and no guarantees at all.

She couldn't wait to get started.

EPILOGUE

Pilgrimages to the Cauldron trailed off considerably after "Saint" Ivarion was no longer there to gaze upon. A few shrines endured, but the heat and caustic fumes were making fast work of those structures. Soon, nothing would remain.

Thus, there were no visitors at all when a small one-person flyer landed at the lip of the caldera. A man exited, who wore shirt and trousers, boots, masked hood, and gloves, all fashioned from the same dark teal fabric. The clothing looked somewhat the worse for wear and stretched tightly enough across him to leave the impression that he had either accidentally shrunk his clothes by washing them at the wrong temperature, or had borrowed the clothes of a slightly younger, smaller man.

Still, none of his skin was exposed to the often-toxic air of the volcano.

He stopped for a moment to gaze at the impressive view before him.

It was a view thankfully bereft of rotting dragon corpses, because of the efforts of the gold dragon Peralon, who'd arrived one morning a few weeks after the First Dragon's awakening and left again a short time later with a very satisfied air about him.

Nothing was ever found of Neveranimas's body after that, but as one of the few people to have ever witnessed Peralon disintegrating his foes, Gwydinion couldn't say he was surprised.

He whistled cheerfully as he picked his way across the steaming ground, avoiding any pockets of bubbling lava. What he was doing was a little risky.

Wildly ill-advised, as his mother would say, but when he'd asked his sister about the best time to visit, she'd told him she had a hunch the volcano would be quiet today.

She'd somehow developed a certain knack for predicting these sorts of things.

That said, Gwydinion thought she might have had a different attitude if she'd known why he was there.

Gwydinion pulled a piece of chena from his pocket, raised it to his mouth to take a bite, and then remembered he was still wearing a mask. He sighed and promised to save that for later. Instead, he walked around for a bit more, then squatted down next to an area where the rocks had stacked against each other as they were thrown about.

He pulled several rocks off the stack, until he'd uncovered a perfectly smooth sphere of rainbow feldspar.

"Aren't you a big piece of chena?" Gwydinion said happily as he picked up the Rampant Stone and tucked it into his knapsack.

He thought it was only fair that he should have the stone. It was an evening of the scales, a small righting of wrongs after what the violet dragon had stolen from him. Neveranimas had once been told she couldn't hoard magic, but in the end, Gwydinion thought she'd managed it, to the detriment of all. She died with a wealth of magical spells, inventions, and discoveries tucked away in a vault that, in all likelihood, might not be opened again for years, assuming his sister and certain dragon friends of hers felt up to that challenge. No one would ever know what she might have shared with the world. No one would know what secrets she had discovered.

Except for this.

Gwydinion would have to be ever-so-careful—there wasn't a guild in Seven Crests that wouldn't commit murder to keep some of these techniques from coming to light—but he intended to make certain that Neveranimas ultimately failed in keeping her secrets.

Most especially the magical ones.

In his heart, he knew it was the only way there would ever be real peace between humans and dragons. Dragons would always be what dragons are—beautiful and strong and all but gods.

But humanity? With magic, who knew what humanity might be capable of achieving?

He meant to find out.

ACKNOWLEDGMENTS

First and always, I want to thank my husband, Mike, who is always there to be my emotional support human, my rubber duck, and my personal enforcer of number twelve on the list of Rules for Evil Overlords. After that, my eternal thanks go to my agent, Chris Lotts, whose faith has meant the world to me. I'd also like to thank the fastest editors in the universe, Devi Pillai and Stephanie Stein, who are both glorious, as well as my copyeditor, Christina MacDonald, for putting up with my many grammatical "quirks" with good humor and grace. Michael Rogers also did a fabulous job on the cover art, and he deserves (and has) my appreciation. I'm also very much indebted to Scarlett Gale, who originally came up with the terms "late-sprouting" and "late-blooming" and kindly allowed me to use them for this book.

Special thanks go to my beta readers (especially Ceciley, who really went above and beyond to give me feedback) and to my dear friend Jeremiah, who patiently created 3D models for me so I could make sure the dragon proportions were correct. I also want to thank Alex, Emily, Freya, Macey, Ruoxi, and Tasha, who were lights for me during some very dark days indeed.

Lastly, here's to Anne McCaffrey and George R. R. Martin, without whom this book wouldn't exist.

ABOUT THE AUTHOR

Mike Lyons

Twice-nominated Astounding Award finalist JENN LYONS lives in Atlanta, Georgia, with her husband, her cats, and a nearly infinite number of opinions on anything from Sumerian mythology to the correct way to make a martini. After spending thirty years working as a graphic artist, art director, and video game producer (in that order), Lyons now spends her days writing fantasy. She traces her geek roots back to playing first edition Dungeons & Dragons in grade school—a passion she's continued as an adult—as well as pursuing whatever craft or skill she's obsessed with this week: pyrography, beadwork, stenography, furniture upholstery, etc. Her five-book epic fantasy series, A Chorus of Dragons, begins with *The Ruin of Kings*.

www.jennlyons.com